A Road to Damascus

A Road to Damascus

Meedo Taha

Interlink Books

An imprint of Interlink Publishing Group, Inc.
Northampton, Massachusetts

Fic

First American edition published in 2018 by

INTERLINK BOOKS
An imprint of Interlink Publishing Group, Inc.
46 Crosby Street, Northampton, Massachusetts 01060
www.interlinkbooks.com

Copyright © Tamyras Editions Sarl, 2016
American edition copyright © Interlink Publishing, 2018
Published by arrangement with Tamyras Editions SARL
Cover Illustration & Design by Lloyd Jouret
Book Design by Lloyd Jouret

Library of Congress Cataloging-in-Publication Data available

ISBN 978-1-62371-992-0

Printed and bound in the United States of America

To request our complete 48-page full-color catalog, please call us toll free at 1-800-238-LINK, visit our website at www.interlinkbooks.com, or send us an e-mail: info@interlinkbooks.com

For Mona.

"There are two kinds of criminals:
those that get caught and the rest of us."

—Anonymous

1
Day Suspended

My eyes are off the road for only a second. No, I'm lying—for two, maybe three seconds. That's all, three seconds! I glance into the messenger bag on the seat next to me and realize my recorder isn't there. Just a glance! And before looking down, I inspect the predawn road ahead: murky, yes, but still empty.

As I look back up—I promise, not more than three seconds later—the nasty shriek of metal on metal fractures the delicate silence and ricochets across the hillside. The Volvo doesn't even shudder when I bring it to a screeching stop. My forehead bashes into the steering wheel, my neck jolts back, and I catch a glimpse of a passengerless bicycle skidding off into the street. My mind races with apocalyptic theories of phantom riders when, suddenly, a mass crashes onto my windshield. It tumbles off the hood with a sickening *thud* as it falls to the ground, out of sight.

Through the spiderweb now etched into the glass, I watch the bicycle's front wheel skid into the side of the hill. Detached from its metal skeleton, it rolls and, like a spinning top coming to a halt, topples to the ground.

I must have forgotten to breathe.

A silence falls over the road and I remember to inhale. My mind, spurned by the lack of oxygen, kicks into motion and I feel myself jerk the handbrake into place. I push the door open and a dreadful chill seeps into my chest as I wrench my suspended consciousness back into my body, still stiff with fear. I begin toward the front of the car, mind filled with grim expectation.

But before I can take two steps, the cyclist's smiling face sprouts out from behind the car's hood. He stands and nonchalantly brushes the dust off his shoulders, as if the entire ordeal was just a minor inconvenience. I pause.

Perhaps it's still midnight and I'm asleep at my desk back home, stuck in a bizarre dream.

The cyclist starts toward his bike. "Wait, you're limping!" I yell through my reverie.

He barely glances back. "I'm fine," he says cheerfully. "It's how I walk."

My hands fall to my side as the man drops to the ground near the site of the accident and grasps at the gravel like he's lost a contact lens. His brown blazer shifts to reveal a tuft of blood-soaked cotton, muddied by the moist gravel. A nasty gash rips through his cheek. His hair is matted with dirt and what could be blood. He's anything but fine.

The words "hospital" and "help" cross my mind, but by the time I settle on a coherent question, he's already reassembled the wheel.

Who rides a bicycle in Beirut anyway? The twisted metal looks only a tad better than its young rider, with its rear wheel dented and its basket bashed. When he gets on, it loses balance and slams against the retaining wall again, but he quickly adjusts to its misshapen dynamics, brings it in line with the road, and pedals away.

"See you later, Professor!" he says, waving a bruised arm behind him.

Then he yells out my name.

Like he knows me. Like he's always known me. By the time I can say "Wait! Do I know you?" his rickety silhouette has disappeared into the smog.

The Volvo's engine purrs in the background, oblivious to the absurd incident it had perpetrated. My open messenger bag grins back at me, its zipper a string of teeth.

No time to lose.

Handbrake released, gear in first, then second, the Volvo begins a tentative crawl up the hillside. Instead of a right turn toward my intended destination, a quick decision and a left swerve take me back along the curve of the hilltop and into the parking spot I vacated less than an hour ago.

See you later, Professor!

The words crawl under my skin. I rub my palms together, but the unsettling feeling remains.

I grab the messenger bag and make my way back up the stairs, two at a time, to the safety of my third-floor apartment.

◆

Dawn seeps into the room and I feel its warmth on my exposed ankles. The city outside remains in deep slumber, but I'm wide awake. And late.

One, two, three, and part. Repeat. One, two, three, and part. The comb rakes through my hair with an audible scratch—not loud enough to wake the girl in the bed behind the door, but deafening to my ears.

I'm late, but it's still early for her. I shiver prematurely at the thought of the cold outside. A storm is brewing. I can feel it. Even at this hour, the world has too much space, too much horizon, too many buildings and, as the bike and its reckless rider have made pointedly clear, at least one too many people.

I yearn to stay inside, if only a moment longer.

But my watch reminds me not to push my luck.

Nancy says that photographers call this time of day "magic hour," though it only lasts forty minutes. It's the time when the sun has started to light the sky, but it's not yet dawn. For me, it's the time I can see without being seen.

See you later, Professor!

He saw me. He knew me, whoever he was. I comb through the thought, pushing it deeper into my skull. Must not think. Must not be seen again. Fresh start. I pull my glasses down the bridge of my nose and tug at my lower eyelids. First left, then right. Not too long ago, Nancy observed that the whites of the eyes grow duller as men pass thirty. Since then, it's become part of my morning ritual to check mine. So far, so good.

I check the messenger bag at my feet. Is everything there? Obviously not. Why else would I be back here? I'm feeling off today. I don't like feeling off. Collecting my wits, I slide back into my bedroom, careful not to wake her up.

See you later, Professor! Where did he come from? One moment he wasn't there, and the next, he was.

I squint into the dim light of the bedroom. The movement of her chest tells me she's still asleep. Her clothes and underwear are scattered around the bed, and her foot sticks out from under the covers. I pull the patterned covers over her and tuck in her toes away from the cold.

The recorder is where it's been since midnight, hidden amongst the thicket of shrub and tree samples on my desk. I grab it and slip back out of the bedroom. With a quick glance toward the mirror, I adjust my glasses and tie. Now I can go. Messenger bag in tow, I step into the chill of dawn for the second time that day.

The wind is harsh, but I lift my face toward it, embracing the sharpness of the morning. The gravel now feels softer under my feet. My windshield is muddier and my Volvo a darker shade of brown.

The car's silhouette is perfectly camouflaged against the bleak fall backdrop. Inside it, I'm back in my element. I turn on the ignition and, while the engine revs up, reach for my messenger bag.

I speak into the recorder as I look up. "Day 1. Shit."

Daylight kisses the Achrafieh skyline. I'm late. Very, very late. That damn bicycle. "Watch where you're going asshole!" I should've yelled out of the window before driving off. Too late for that.

I scan the road ahead and then, through the rearview mirror, the road behind. Double-check, quadruple-check. No time for more delays. To the left there's the retaining wall, but then to the right through the passenger side window, I realize what must have happened earlier.

A scraggly urban staircase cuts through the lower hillside, connecting my part of Achrafieh to the lower side of town called Geitawi. The Old District, as many call it, sits atop the newly minted nightlife area. The cyclist probably carried his bicycle up those steps from there, which is why I didn't see him.

But for the moment, I need to forget that.

I hit Record and continue. "Day 1: November 16th, 5:13 a.m. En route to Damascus Road." I rev up the Volvo and make my way up the hillside.

◆

"The field is wetter than yesterday," I say into the recorder. "Skies clear, but clouds blur the horizon." I lock my car and, as I make my way toward the site, a drop of water lands on my glasses. The

15

road leading up here has been empty. I've made good time, but as I wipe my glasses on my jacket, I still feel off.

"I doubt these details will survive the technical edit of this paper," I dictate absently, "but I've found in the past that my own moods affect the outcome of my studies. I don't have a scientific basis for this premise, but I generally find greater responsiveness in my subjects when I myself am in a less discombobulated predisposition. I mean, in a less troubled mood."

That's why I've replaced the customary field notebook with a recorder. I had started using it for my memoir, but as the line between life and work blurred on me, the recorder has taken over and is now all I use. The sound of my voice brings me comfort, so this will be our—me and my—scientifically incorrect little secret.

I've arrived at my spot, marked by a sharp turn in the highway. The day is tentative, but dawn will soon be here, along the main artery that connects Lebanon and Syria, before anywhere else. I raise the recorder to my lips.

"Unlike many of its siblings in the Rosid subclass, the *Acacia tortilis* seems to thrive under a wide variety of conditions. If it receives adequate rainfall and has access to a few key minerals, it doesn't mind us leaving it alone. But this particular group has seen better days. It must be sibling rivalry; the trees are in competition for the resources available to them. This is unlike the Acacia, generally one of the more collaborative Rosids. Why have I singled out the *Acacia tortilis* among seventy thousand other Rosids? Well, why might one person choose another among nine billion? When someone finds an answer to this second question, I'll answer the first. Until then, the only reason I need to give is: because."

Pausing the recorder, I pull out yesterday's newspaper from the messenger bag. I spread it across the ground before me and lay the bag on top. There's no point in scuffing up the leather, even for such a groundbreaking research paper.

I bend down and fold up the hems of my pants, careful not to crease them too much. I kneel on the edge of the newspaper and peer at the shrub in front of me.

I hit Record. "The thorns appear to be browning out, probably due to last week's heat wave. It's all relative and this species is affected by even the smallest fluctuations in climate, especially—"

A flash of light tears through the sky, interrupting my train of thought. Then, thunder.

I set down my tape recorder to reach back under the collar of my jacket and pull up my hood. "I knew something was off today," I say, holding the device closer to my mouth. "The forecast said wet night, dry morning. It's not the first time they've been wrong. But this is unexpected." The first drops of rain speckle the newspaper, forming small puddles that warp yesterday's news into carnival mirror patterns. The Acacia leaves bend under the pressure of the water and I take a moment to appreciate the beauty of the flower swaying with the rain.

"Rain. Should make a move soon. Final notes of the day: I expect our subject to exhibit healthier shades of green over the next few days, provided it's treated to a fair amount of rainfall. I'm confident that my discovery of the plant in this part of the world is not a freak occurrence. However, why this particular growth here seems so unhealthy remains a mystery. The slope of the highway drains toward this particular spot and the soil is quite fertile. Yet the Acacias here have deteriorated rapidly over the past week. Their last hope is this rain."

The end of my monologue is garnished by another strike of lightning, followed by one of Beirut's trademark flash storms.

I must move fast.

As scientific innovation plateaus, botanists are starved for new discoveries. What was once an amicable academic community is now a race for breakthrough. Your friends will quite literally trample your work to get at the next big grant. It'll be dawn soon, and if I'm spotted skulking in the middle of nowhere, it'll raise too many questions. I can't risk the taxonomists learning about it or the focus of my career will be out in the open—fair game for all those rabid hounds to snatch at.

I reach for my messenger bag, allowing myself the briefest of moments to mourn its soggy leather exterior. I pull out rubber gloves and my spade. Very carefully, I draw a circle in the mud around the Acacia.

"Two-foot spread for this size subject," I say into the recorder. I dig in, first gently, then with more force. The moist soil gives way quite easily and, in a few short moments, the spade grazes the roots of the tree. With a sharp tug, the tree is loosened from the ground. I spread out a translucent plastic sheet inside the messenger bag, brush off the excess soil weighing down the roots, and place my sample inside. It tucks neatly into the cavity I've prepared, and I wrap the plastic around its thin sapling bark.

"Acacia collected," I say, barely able to think with the downpour pounding my scalp.

In the distance, a bus appears on Damascus Road. The unsettling feeling of this morning falls over me. I lift the metal frame of my glasses from my eyes and run a hand over my face. My fingers press my eyes closed, but unease still finds its way into my chest.

From that distance, I must appear like a speck of dust in the barren field. The thought fills me with emptiness as I'm engulfed in the Beirut storm.

◆

I'm not sure if I closed my eyes for an eternity or an instant. I pull my hands away and the glasses plop onto the ridge of my nose. During that time, the sun has broken through the clouds, striking the wet highway with a merciless glare, filling me with dread.

The bus is much closer now. Its tires screech. Something isn't right.

From where I stand, it looks like a visual echo, swerving in my direction then bouncing back and skidding farther away. It does another S-curve across the width of the highway, and then careens closer again. How could the vehicle have lost its balance so completely? It's not going fast. The road is wet, but at this speed it shouldn't matter. Even a punctured tire would still allow the driver enough control to stop. Reason eludes me as the bus crashes into a billboard on the roadside and comes to a lopsided stop. Steam puffs out of its belly, engulfing it in a milky haze.

Less than a dozen meters away, I throw the spade into my bag and sling it over my shoulder. I have no idea what to do. A thought gnaws at my mind—perhaps what one might call "scientific curiosity."

Nancy warned me yesterday that the first shower of the season is the most dangerous. "The roads are like soap," she said. I could feel the gears in my mind working.

Roads are like soap + Driver loses control = Accident. Or, Visibility is bad + Driver falls asleep = Mistake.

I need to know which it is: an error of nature or an error of man?

With my recorder safely in my jacket pocket, I make toward the highway. As I draw closer to the accident site, I can tell that

19

there's more to the collision than just the driver's loss of control. Smoke billows from the front of the bus and I hear smothered whimpers come from inside. Whether they're mechanical or human, the rain makes it impossible to surmise.

My pace quickens. I'm caught in slow motion, complete with the stretched-out, low-pitched rumble that would accompany it on a TV Movie of the Week, "I. Am. Come-*ing*!"

The street is empty except for the bus. Sunlight streams through the clouds, the only trace of the daybreak. This must be the first bus of the morning, barely ten minutes into its journey from Beirut to Damascus. I'm close enough to discern its outlines through the thickening shroud of steam. It rests on three wheels, sunken into a ditch on the side of the street. The billboard above it reads, "Beirut Night LIFE!" as if urging drivers to U-turn back into the city to party.

I kneel by the front tire and years of training color my downward gaze.

No puncture, just skid marks.

I pull off my hood and straighten myself, scanning the line of windows, now almost eye-level as the bus settles further into the ditch. There must be people onboard already; the driver, of course and by this time, at least five or six passengers.

Steam has leaked into the cabin and it's hard to see inside. Mud lines one of the windows. Strange. I reach out and realize it's on the inside of the glass. That can't be right. How could mud have gotten into—I freeze mid-thought.

That's not mud. It's blood, appearing dark only in the shroud of mist inside the bus. As I lean in for a closer look, a palm splays flat against the glass. It fumbles, as if the owner of the hand is trying to regain his footing. Suddenly, the hand pushes toward me, draining to white against the transparent surface. I instinctively press my own palm against it.

I race around the back of the bus onto the road. The only way in is from the front right, where the wheel is almost half a meter off the ground. I rest my bag under it, take a deep breath and climb on.

My eyes take a few seconds to adjust to the dim interior. Even then, it's hard to see through the thick air. I lift my hood back on and cup my palm over my mouth. Before I can take a step, a faint moan fills the space. I see the driver lying slumped over his steering wheel with an eerie finality. He could almost be snoozing on the job. But his torso is drenched in blood. Lots of it. All over the dashboard. Too much blood for a minor accident like the one I saw. It pools in his lap, dripping down the side of his thigh. Stomach wound, it looks like.

Whatever it was almost eviscerated him. He's—the word sends a chill through me—dead.

Plants die on me now and again. I mourn for a few days, then move on to the next sample. This is my first encounter with a dead human, and my system isn't quite sure how to handle it.

I trudge forward through the rainwater splish splash against my ankles. The steam thickens around me and I can barely see my hand in front of me. How could the inside of the bus be this wet? I hear the moan again come from somewhere in the back, deeper inside the barrel of the bus. I slice my palm through the opaque air, but it makes no difference in the haze.

A second body materializes into view. A woman, maybe around thirty, is twisted in a grotesque fetal position on one of the seats. Blood is everywhere. The steam takes some of the edge off the sight, but my throat constricts into a stranglehold.

The liquid at my feet is too heavy to be rainwater. It's pools of red—lots of it—all over the floor. The moan rises and I squeeze my way deeper into the bus, tripping over another body, this one with its chest wide open. I move forward and immediately

21

reel back—my shoes have come into contact with the hand of a young man at the foot of another seat, dead. An iron taste spreads through my mouth, bitter and bile-like. That's three bodies now, all barely silhouettes.

But the moan from the back belongs to someone alive. I make my way toward it, passing more fallen bodies: four, then five.

I get to the rear of the bus and find a hefty man with a thick mustache, dark suit and seemingly healthy demeanor until just a few minutes ago. An elegant black briefcase dangles from his lifeless fingers. The voice isn't his. Then I turn to his right and find the source, bloody and trembling.

"Where is she?" he says, scratching at the window. I slide my arm under his and pull his limp body to his feet. He weighs close to nothing. I inhale and pull his arm across my shoulders, drag him to the front of the bus, and step off. I sit him down on the ground and his head plops against the elevated front wheel. I wipe the grime off his cheek and tilt his face back, allowing the rain to wash off the excess blood.

Then, I recognize him. It's the young man—the one with the bicycle and the silly walk.

His blazer's gone and his elbow is visible through a rip in his white shirt, drenched in crimson.

See you later, Professor! I wonder if he does see me, but his face is empty.

"Look at me," I say, but the thunder muffles my voice. I grip his shirt, caked with blood, sweat and mud and shake him out of his stupor. My knuckles scrape against his torn flesh, but his face shows no pain. What now seems like a lifetime ago, my Volvo spared his life. But death has finally caught up with him.

If he recognizes me, it doesn't register through his delirium. But then something flashes across his eyes.

"Where is she?" he says, barely a murmur.

"She's gone," I say, smoothing his hair away from his eyes. "It's just you and me."

"The cat."

"Your cat's fine. I'll take care of you. You'll be fine too," I lie.

"Feed the cat."

He exhales, then silence.

2
Definitely Possible

On the morning of November 16th, Tony awoke from a bad dream.

He slammed a fist over the blaring alarm clock so violently that both it and the framed photograph beside it crashed to the floor. He sat up and swung his legs off the bed. He scratched his naked chest and looked down. Neatly framed by his feet, the alarm clock read 4:58 a.m. He jumped out of bed, grabbed the cell phone lying perilously close to the edge of the nightstand, and dialed a number from memory.

He was already late.

◆

Less than ten minutes later, Tony was dressed in black jeans, a light blazer and a crisp white shirt. In the bedroom, a pile of clothes spilled out of the open closet onto the floor. He had made a mess picking out his outfit, but had no time to tidy up.

He strode toward the kitchen, but allowed himself a moment to stop by the sleek leather couch, where his cat was curled up in sleep. He stroked its head, before pushing the old wooden door open into the kitchen.

Tony took out a saucer from the cabinet above the granite

counters and opened the fridge. It was dark, so he flicked on the thermostat and the light came on. He pulled out a carton of milk and poured a generous helping for the cat. In a familiar daze, he returned the carton and kicked the refrigerator door closed.

He grabbed a pack of cigarettes from the side of an ashtray overflowing with half-smoked stubs, and carried the milk into the living room, setting it at the foot of the sofa. His mind was elsewhere. It was a big day and he was already unhinged by it all.

He slid the cigarette pack in his pocket and looked toward the window. It was still dark outside. He had a few extra minutes to kill.

Tony grabbed the remote off the table and flicked on the TV. A pack of lions mutely chased after a gazelle on the Discovery Channel. He gazed at the bulging muscles on one of the lions, allowing himself a brief moment to admire their ferocity. A faint chirping outside signaled the start of dawn, stirring Tony back into action.

A large white telescope stood at the base of the window, propped up on a complicated-looking tripod. Tony peered through the lens and reached for his black leather-bound notebook off the pile of video games next to him. He pulled out the fountain pen sandwiched between the worn pages, wetting the tip with his tongue. He pursed his lips at the telescope and, after a moment's thought, scribbled a few notes in a scrawl that could rival a doctor's.

He finished his sentence with a flick of the pen and clapped the book shut. He looked back at the telescope and a worried crease settled between his eyes.

◆

Tony hurtled down the stairs, through a curtain of laundry and other hanging fabrics, to his bicycle parked in front of the aged apartment building. The worn, olive green Peugeot was a beauty, but maybe just to Tony. He adjusted the tilted straw basket tied to the back and unlocked the chain before settling comfortably on the seat.

With one hand balancing expertly on the handlebar, he took to the street, pulling the pack of cigarettes from his pocket. He poked into the box and came up empty. He tossed it on the side of the road. At the foot of the Geitawi staircase, the grocery shutter was still closed, but the grocer was already there, sorting through twelve-packs of Pepsi.

"*Marhaba*," said Tony. "Not open yet?"

"No," the grocer replied, looking up with emerald green eyes. "Did you want anything?" He lifted a cage and hooked it to a steel chain dangling from the canopy.

The parrot, which Tony had affectionately come to know as Faris, croaked.

"Some cigarettes—"

"Sure, sure. Got a minute?"

Tony glanced at his watch. "Yeah. But just a minute."

"*Manyak! Manyak!*" sang Faris. Tony chuckled. "Fucker" was an Arabic swearword he was all too familiar with.

"Stop it *wla*," said the grocer.

He pulled out a ring with a dozen keys and began going through each one. "Hold on. My wife says you never know when you'll need a key. Nothing worse than doors you can't open, she says."

Still on his bike, Tony started, "Listen, I—"

"Here it is." The grocer tried the key he chose on the lock, but it wouldn't open. "Damn, no wait, it's this one."

"Know what? Never mind."

"Nonsense. A man needs his smokes. Here, this is the one."

The grocer tried three more keys before he found the correct one. Tony glanced at his watch impatiently.

When the store was finally open, the grocer stepped in as the parrot teased, "*Sharmouta! Sharmouta!*" Whore!

"Shut up, Faris!" yelled the grocer from inside. "No more out of you!"

Tony just laughed and rattled the cage. "*Wahdak wla.* Back at you."

The grocer reached for the shelf, opened a carton and handed Tony a pack. "*Sharrif.* There you go. One pound fifty." Fifteen hundred Lebanese lira, or one US dollar. So cheap.

Tony handed him two thousand. "*Shukran,*" he yelled over his shoulder as he pedaled away. Behind him, Faris was still screeching.

"*Sharmouta! Sharmouta!*"

◆

Tony dismounted at the foot of the Geitawi staircase and heaved the bike into his arms. He climbed the steps quickly, only stopping once to secure his grip.

He plopped it on the gravel at the top of the lower hillside, got on and pedaled his bike up the slope.

Some meters ahead, a brown Volvo drove along the retaining wall, leaving him and his bike just enough space to skirt past it. Suddenly, the car skidded to the right—it couldn't have been more than a few inches—and clipped the bicycle's rear wheel.

Before he could adjust his balance, Tony was already off the bike. His mind couldn't keep up with the speed of the accident. He felt two painful blows, as if someone was beating him with a spiked baseball bat. Then, he was on the gravel.

Not today, he thought, pain shooting through his arm. With heightened senses that only appear when one is suspended between life and death, he pictured the road ahead and his absurd journey that ended before it even began. The thought only lasted an instant—death had already passed him by when he got up, elbow torn and bloody, but otherwise unharmed. His previous anxiety overcame him again, and he quickly pieced together his broken bicycle into a pathetic, but still functional, alternative.

Then he recognized the person behind the wheel.

"Wait, you're limping!" the driver said. Tony couldn't be bothered to stop. He looked over his shoulder and said, "No, I'm fine. It's how I walk."

With no time to ponder the intense irony of the situation, he got on his bike and pedaled on, ignoring the pleas behind him. He wobbled forward, then, owing the man at least the courtesy of reassurance, he called back over his shoulder.

"See you later, Professor!"

Then, just for good measure, or maybe for fun, he yelled out the professor's name.

Ignoring the colossal effect of the abrupt familiarity on the stuffy scholar staring straight at him, Tony threw his weight backwards to compensate for the compromised rear wheel, and sped up the road past upper Achrafieh. He pedaled with revived purpose and precision, heedful of the moist gravel. He could not afford to lose more time with another fall.

By the time he got to the top, the professor was a distant memory. More pressing thoughts pounded his skull now, throwing his eyes every which way. He was already running late and his blazer was ripped. This was not the day for it.

He got to the top of the hill in record time and paused to catch his breath before pedaling on.

He passed Beit el Kataeb, a political party's once-bustling base of operations, now relegated to a war relic, and Roadster, the American-themed diner with an appropriate "There goes my heart!" slogan. He crossed the street toward Leil Nhar, a popular pseudo-Lebanese restaurant, and smiled at a couple of mini-skirted, fully made up girls eating *manakeesh* outside, no doubt after a long night of heavy partying. By the time he got to the parking of ABC Mall, he had worked up quite a sweat.

He stopped again, lit a cigarette, took a puff, then tossed it and cut through the covered parking lot. He biked up the car ramp and exited to the top part of the mall, but not before pausing a third time to check the new leather manbags on display through the closed shutters of Milord boutique.

Slipping out of his blazer and wrapping it around his arm, he bounced out of ABC across the street to Sassine Square. There, he made a right and biked the entire length of the sidewalk parallel to Istiklal Street, passing several modern office buildings and one or two coffee shops.

With Baydoun Mosque to his right and Nazareth School to his left, Tony reached a fork in the road and veered to one side, following the boulevard past the mouth of Monot Street.

He almost slammed into another overzealous car. A voice from inside it yelled, "Watch where you're going asshole!" Pushing his weight into the pedals, he crossed over to the edge of the Basta Tahta district, diagonally from the Jewish Cemetery.

His breath tickled his nose as Tony eased his way under a street sign. Finally, on Damascus Road, he got off his bicycle and chained it to the post.

◆

Relieved, Tony exhaled. He'd made it. He passed two old buses parked outside the makeshift terminal booth. There was only one woman ahead of him in the line, but she was taking her sweet time to get her ticket. He tapped his foot as he waited.

A bespectacled middle-aged man peered at him through the grill of the ticket booth. "I'll be right with you," he said, then, to the woman, "Yes, Madam. It stops at Anjar. And here's your change."

The lady collected her ticket and change, flashed Tony an apologetic smile and headed out. "Good morning," he said, as he approached the booth, setting his blazer down on the counter. "Single return to Damascus."

The teller looked up inquisitively from behind his glasses. "Damascus? As I was telling the lady, you should've bought it yesterday. There's a form to fill out."

Tony noticed a hint of a southern accent in the man's speech. "It's kind of a surprise trip," he said with a drawl. "Can't you help me out? You know, relative to relative."

The teller beamed back. "You know what? I'll make an exception. Here."

He slid over the clipboard and Tony scribbled his name. The teller took it back and handed him a ticket.

"Okay, here you go. You better hurry." Tony paid, grabbed his ticket and ran out.

He got on the first bus in front of the station. It was packed with people. "Damascus, right?"

The driver looked up from a clipboard and wordlessly pointed his chewed pen at the other bus on the side of the street. Tony got off the bus and crossed the street before noticing the lightness of his arm. He cursed. He'd left his blazer back at the station. He stumbled back toward the station and, as he dashed through the doorway, he heard a loud engine growl. He turned back and watched his bus ease out.

"No, no, shit, shit, shit, shit." He ran after it. "Wait!" he called out. "Goddamn it, wait!" The bus slowed down to a stop.

The door creaked open and Tony heard the driver call "*Yalla!*"

He climbed onto the bus, made his way to the very back and took a seat next to a heavy-set man. Outside his window, the early morning sun was blocked by gray clouds.

With a puff of black smoke and the first roar of thunder, the bus toward Damascus began its journey.

3
Thesis

I pull out a plastic pot from a cupboard above the kitchen sink and set the Acacia sapling on the counter next to it. I remove the bloodstained jacket from under my arm and toss it into the washing machine. With the jacket in there solo, I slam the door shut. Detergent. Color bleach. It was getting old anyway. More detergent. Switch to warm cycle. The jacket spins to life, pink soapsuds forming around it.

As I shuffle back to the living room, I find the apartment door open. Sloppy. I toss my keys on the shelf Nancy put up for me and switch on the light. The house is tidier than it was this morning; she decided to straighten things up instead of heading to her place to change. Nice of her, but I can immediately tell that it had just gotten a quick once-over; the coffee table sits askew and the muted TV screen rattles.

We're nine months into the relationship, but it's been only three since she graduated and the news that a certain professor and student were "hooking up" spread across the Lebanese University of Science and Technology (LUST) campus. Now, she treats my apartment as an extension of her own.

Too many thoughts compete for my attention, but most pressing is the empty sofa, remote poking out from between its cushions, inviting me for a morning nap. If I give in I'll be done for the day—but no, I can't rest in an apartment so superficially tidy, so sublimely messy. First things first: I switch off the TV and lay the remote perpendicular to the edge of the table, which I then align with the sofa. I head to the bedroom and tug on the lamp chain—it flickers to life, throwing yellow light on my desk—and toss my messenger bag on the chair. Then I make my way back to the kitchen. Unable to leave it alone, I collect the pot, cradle the Acacia under my arm, and walk back to my bedroom. I push aside my last batch of samples, now dried and pressed for posterity. The Acacia sapling now occupies the vacated spot in the center of my desk. I start peeling off my water-soaked clothes, making sure to remove the tape recorder from my shirt pocket and slide it into my desk drawer.

I hurry to the bathroom as I trip out of my pants and check the clump of linen in my arms. No blood, only water. Piece by piece, I toss them into the hamper.

Moments later, in the privacy of the shower, I speak the young man's words. Not his final delirious ramblings, but the words he spoke to me minutes, hours, *eons*, earlier.

"See you later, Professor."

Exactly three and a half minutes later, I turn the faucet off, step out and dry myself with a towel. In the bedroom, I slip into a fresh pair of boxer shorts from the adjacent dresser and then pick up the pot and head to the kitchen, where I turn my attention to the Acacia. I size it up and reach below the sink for a garbage bag and a half-empty bag of soil, which I pour into the pot and then carefully plant the Acacia. The washing machine growls behind me, tossing the lonesome jacket every which way.

Keeping my mind on the Acacia, I stroke the sapling's branches, spray them with some water and wipe their thorns with a terry cloth. They remain browned and withered. I scoop the ones that fall off the counter into the garbage bag, which

I discard in the waste bin. Planted Acacia in tow, I make my way back into the bedroom. I reach under my desk, pull up my plastic toolbox and lay it in the center. As I pop the latch open, the box folds out its stepped compartments. From the middle I pull out a pair of pruning shears and snip off an unhealthy branch, which drops to the desk with a tap. Snip, another branch, then another, and another. There. That should do it. I scrape them off the desk onto my palm and toss them in the wastebasket below. Setting down my shears, I pull out a roll of gauze and some masking tape and wrap the Acacia's exposed branch stub. I pull a popsicle stick out of a bundle bound with a green rubber band and stick it deep into the pot.

I bind the gauze to the bark of the Acacia with scotch tape. "Hush now," I say to the plant. I take a step back, admiring its cleanly bandaged branch.

"We'll have you as good as new."

◆

Adjusting the potted Acacia under my arm, I lock my Volvo and cut across the empty LUST parking lot. Classes started five minutes ago. Five more, and my students start walking out. I trot under the bridged hallway connecting the School of Applied Sciences to the School of Botany and, as I swing the lobby door open, I catch a glimpse of a veiled figure running in the opposite direction toward the school cafeteria.

"Wait!" I say, releasing the door and running after the figure, Acacia bobbing against my armpit. She either doesn't hear me or simply ignores me, so I increase my pace and catch up with her a few meters from the cafeteria.

"Nadine!" I lay a hand on her shoulder, careful not to startle her, but she jumps backwards, wide-eyed, anyway. She turns, and her face relaxes. But just for an instant.

"Professor," says Nadine. "I… I can't find my friend." Instead of her lilting Syrian accent, she fires at me with a salvo of consonants.

"Everyone's already in class. She must be there too."

"No, my friend doesn't go to school here. Something's happened, everyone's scared."

"What is it?"

"I don't know. They say it's bad. No one knows. I have to find my friend. Sorry," she says, moving toward the door at the end of the hallway.

I put a hand out to stop her. "Listen, I need you to come over tomorrow afternoon—the apartment's a mess."

"Okay, okay," she murmurs absently. "I'm really sorry. I have to go." She runs ahead, slams her forearms into the cafeteria door, and disappears inside.

I frown at her retreating figure. Nadine was a previous student and is now my part-time housemaid. I've only ever seen her within the confines of the university, or otherwise in her ratty cleaning clothes in my apartment. It never occurred to me that she had friends.

I turn back toward the School of Botany. Three more minutes and my morning class will be unsalvageable.

◆

"To review," I say to the class as I walk in with my Acacia, "what is a tree?"

I turn to the whiteboard and write "GENUS" in green. I can feel the disappointed stares of my students on my back. Under it, I write "SPECIES" and link the two with a vertical line.

"A big stick with leaves on top," says a voice from the middle of the room. The students laugh. I look toward the speaker, slouched with his arms crossed and a smug look on his face. I smile at him.

"You're absolutely right." I see his confidence flicker slightly. "But that kind of answer leads to further questions. Is it just one stick, or many sticks? Look at our flag. The cedar has many trunks, which would technically make it a shrub. But to call the cedar 'a shrub' would be tantamount to high treason! And does the stick have to be made of wood? Say yes, and you disqualify the banana tree, whose trunk is made of stalks of leaves, like a cabbage. So, is a tree a big stick with leaves on top? Why, or why not?"

I rip out the cardboard cover of a notebook sitting on my desk, crumple it, and lay it on the table.

"Growing—or should I say *becoming*—a tree is not an easy thing. Life is not a state of being, but a process of becoming." I point to the cardboard. "This is the first form of life on earth: simple, monocellular, like one big ball." The ball opens slightly. "But let this sit for some time, and you'll find the cardboard has propped itself fully open, into a more complex form. This is evolution, which literally means 'unfolding.'"

The students watch the ball intently, but it remains still for now. Freshmen always enjoy visual aids, but perhaps I should have chosen one a bit less like watching paint dry. I continue. "Darwin defined evolution as 'descent with modification,' and it took centuries of descending and generations upon generations of modification to evolve earth's first life, to its first plants, to the creature you see before you." I indicate the Acacia sapling, hunched in the pot, hardly a glowing specimen of life.

"So," I say, resting one hand on the Acacia thorns and another on the word "Rosid" printed on the whiteboard since last week. "Genus and species. Which is the set and which is the subset?"

No answer.

Right, my body language is confusing. I correct my gestures, clamping an invisible box with my right hand above my head and another invisible box at chest level.

"Which box goes inside which?"

Still nothing.

My hands fall to my sides. "Come on everyone. Your final exam's next week. Naming is the first thing we covered. Someone here must have an answer."

I scan the five students in the front row and five pairs of eager eyes look back at me. These students know the answer, as tomorrow's leading botanists should, but I know they're waiting for the tough questions.

"Someone in the back?" I ask, standing on my tiptoes.

To my surprise, a tentative hand rises above the thirty heads in front of it. The floor of Classroom 2B is flat, not like the big lecture hall reserved for classes of fifty or more students, so I can only see the hand and not the arm or body attached to it.

"The species. That's the smaller box?" A girl's rising intonation tells me she's not quite sure—the kids in the back never are—so I encourage her with a small nod. With slightly more confidence, she adds, "And the genus is the big box."

"That's correct," I say, smiling. "And what's the best way to remember that?"

Janette, a front-rower, shoots her hand up. "Well," she says, resting her elbow on her desk and cupping her freckled face into her palm. "The genus is the religion and the species is the sect. Say I'm Christian, that's my genus. And my species is Maronite."

The class breaks into laughter. Good, that loosens them up. I laugh too. "Nice one," I say. "That's a good way to explain it in Lebanese."

I turn back to the whiteboard. I write "janette," small J, under

SPECIES. "But rather than religions and sects, we dendrologists prefer the first name, last name analogy." I write "Awwad" under GENUS.

"First name Janette. Last name Awwad. So, you're the janette species of the Awwad genus. Notice the genus is always capitalized. So this here would be?" I say, indicating the sapling again.

Without raising her hand, species *Awwad janette* speaks out, "*Acacia tortilis*. Capital A small T."

"Good," I say. "The common form of a tree as a big stick with leaves on top is a 'conclusion' which many lineages somewhat independently arrived at. There's something about nature that makes 'treeness' a viable response to the challenges of irrigation, aeration and solarization: the needs for water, air and sun have resulted in the treeness of trees. But look deeper and you'll find that the word 'tree' is an umbrella term encompassing a wide variety of species that have as many similarities as they do differences. This one here happens to be the *Acacia tortilis* variation." "Hey, didn't they rename this tree recently?" The voice comes from the back. That's generally where the smart-asses cower, loud and invisible.

More students seem alert now, so I grab my chance to elaborate. "You guys have read Shakespeare, right?"

Some students nod. Several continue to stare at me listlessly. "Juliet asked 'What's in a name?' As botanists we can safely answer 'Not much at all.' Local names are useful to those who understand their roots. They reflect what the individual means to the people who named them and know them. However, they're much less informative to outsiders. When you know someone individually, their name even becomes a generic limitation to the far more intimate knowledge you have of them."

I pick out a couple of students whose names I remember.

"Mazen is Mazen and Sarah is Sarah," I say. "How could their names serve as more than a simple label? In Arabic, they can't. But it's not like that in all languages. Some Native American tribes give a child a temporary name at birth, and then ritualistically bestow upon them their permanent name at puberty. The name they're given says something about their personality, their achievements, or their lineage."

"So why don't we all name our children Flaming Arrow or Baby Elephant?" asks Sarah.

"Because that's limiting too," I say. "The more specific a name, the more its owner is bound by its meaning. It's not that some naming conventions are superior to others. Like language itself, names just serve different purposes. Take those self-important academics that roam our hallways, the taxonomists. They dedicate their lives to labeling and classification, but all they do is express what each in their own way feels is important."

To my delight, several students glance toward the classroom door.

"Same as our parliament," I continue. "Muslims are one class, Christians another. Not social classes, mind you, but classes in the botanical sense. Preliminary groups. Then within those we have subclasses: Shiites, Sunnis, Maronites, Orthodox Greek and Russian, Catholics, Druze, et cetera. Classification is simply a matter of convenience, but if convenience is all we're interested in, then we can each slice up the world any way we choose, as we do come voting season."

I pause for dramatic effect as waves of groans and chuckles ripple through the room. "Labeling, however, is only the first step," I continue. "To some that makes all the difference, to others not so much. It's the same with plants. Therefore, classification requires another step beyond mere naming. Sure, it's about putting labels on individuals. But more than that, it's about identifying relationships between them. So beyond simply naming it, how do we identify a species? There are three ways."

A student from the front row raises their hand and, with the rising intonation characteristic of a first-year, says, "DNA?"

"Sure," I say. "That's one method taxonomists love: DNA imaging, where a sample is compared with a preexisting standard. What else?"

Janette raises her hand and says, "We can rely on botanical keying to identify common elements among different species."

"Right," I say. "We work through a flow chart using a process of inclusion and elimination based on common characteristics. Taxonomists enjoy that too. But there's a catch here. Can anyone tell us what it is?"

Janette already knows the answer and takes my question as her cue to continue. "Yes," she says. "Suppose I wanted to work out whether human beings were more closely related to pigs or to lizards. If I count the number of toes, then I'd conclude that we are closer to lizards than pigs because we both have five toes, whereas pigs have hooves."

"Exactly," I say. "But of course, we know that pigs and people are both classified as mammals. Even the DNA tells us that. So we can clearly see that the two methods that taxonomists favor could be in direct contradiction. So, we need a third method, which taxonomists never use. Can anyone venture a guess as to what that is?"

The room falls silent. I throw a glance at Janette, but she doesn't say anything.

I answer my own question. "The third method is common sense. We simply know. It's the most unconscious and the most subjective, yet also the most common method, known both scientifically and colloquially as 'recognition.' We look at someone and, rather than refer to DNA like image-makers or to diagnostic features like key-makers, we simply know. We take into account mannerisms of speech, quirks in appearance, and other idiosyncrasies that make the subjects who they are, and we recognize them. Nothing could be simpler and more beautiful. Yes, I realize a lot of this sounds like mumbo jumbo. And you're right. It does, even to me. But the point is we base a lot of our science on observing behavior. In this case, reproduction. How a plant procreates, and whether or not its offspring are fertile, tell us a lot about who that plant is."

I roll down our plastic taxonomy chart in front of the whiteboard and with the green marker I connect the Acacia to its closest sibling in the Rosid subclass. I set down the marker and take a step back to survey the chart. It's a work of intricate beauty.

I tap the pot of the Acacia sitting on my desk. "I collected this guy earlier today. A very rare sample from Beirut, just a few miles from here."

Cradling the pot, I take a few steps toward the center of the room to give the students a better look. Some lean forward; most stay slumped in their seats.

"Sir?" that same voice says, now from behind me. I keep telling them to call me by my first name and just speak up, that this isn't high school anymore. "If the *Acacia tortilis* is so resilient," Janette proceeds after getting my attention, "then why is it so rare here?"

"That's what I've been trying to find out," I say. "And with that—"

The door to the classroom flies open. It's one of my third-year students. "Sir," he says. "They're calling us to the Common Room. Right now."

With a scattering of excited murmurs, my students flee the classroom. I look back at my chart and whiteboard—twenty-five minutes of drawing gone to waste. Maybe it'll still be here tomorrow. I leave the class and close the door behind me.

◆

We're among the last to arrive into the Common Room. All the seats have been filled and Chairman Ramala is flitting around to get the students to settle down. She's wearing a red dress suit today, with matching lipstick—too loud for an academic, especially at the School of Agriculture. We prefer earth tones.

The air conditioning here is still running full blast from the summertime, and without the bloodstained jacket I left spinning in my washing machine back home, I feel chilly. Such a crowd crammed into such a space should warm it up, make it all nice and cozy. I rub my goosebumped arms and grimace.

I plant myself at the back of the room and lean against the wall for some warmth, and after the students quiet down, Ramala begins to speak. "We've decided to suspend all classes," she says, enunciating every letter even more than she normally does. "As some of you may have heard, there was an… accident."

She gestures to the office boy, Garo, who wheels in a Goldstar TV that looks like it could easily belong in my grandparents' living room. While all other departments at our university have already instated the more progressive position of Administrative Assistant, we've retained the archaic position of "Office Boy." He switches the TV on and half the room jumps at the explosion of static. Fumbling with the remote, he lowers the volume and flips through empty channels.

"Now I don't want you to be alarmed," Ramala says. "But what's happened is tragic. And," she hesitates, "will alter Lebanon permanently."

I suddenly realize that she is talking about the bus. The one covered in smoke, mud and blood. But seven people dying on a bus won't alter Lebanon "permanently." In this mad nation of ours, that's a bit of an overstatement.

I feel my palms go clammy. Garo has finally found a channel where an anchorwoman speaks silently into a microphone from the left side of a split screen. She's wearing turquoise and, like always, she's fully made up. A gruff male studio reporter fills the right side of the screen, appearing sepia-toned next to the vibrant woman on the other side of the split. The two speak mutely for a few moments; our office boy is clearly unfamiliar with prewar television technology. Ramala's eyes remain fixed on the anchorwoman and I allow myself a little grin as Garo finally finds the button on the archaic remote control, bringing the volume to an audible level.

"Well, at this point I can't answer that," says the anchorwoman with her hand pressed to her ear. "But we can say for sure that Former Head of Parliament Doreid Fattal has been pronounced dead on arrival at the American University of Beirut Medical Center."

With that, a loud murmur fills the room, followed by a "Shush" from one of the students. Still, the commotion continues with an assortment of shrieks, mutterings and other reactions one would expect from a panicked populace.

I remember the well-dressed man in the dark suit, slumped over in the back seat of the bus, hand clenched around a briefcase handle. In my mind's eye he grows more familiar. I share in the surprise, but don't partake in the shockwave that spreads across the room. I just listen in silence.

"This was the first public bus to travel from Beirut to Damascus in sixteen months," continues the anchorwoman. "Yesterday's ceasefire had prompted the Ministry of Transportation to take an ill-advised leap of faith in the peace process. It allowed a public bus to travel between our two capitals, only for it to be ambushed less than fifteen minutes into its journey. There were seven other passengers on board, plus the driver." She pauses, then adds, "They had no idea that journey would be their last."

Spare us the poetry.

"So Katia," the studio reporter says, "seven people, including Mr. Fattal, are confirmed dead?" It was barely a question.

"Yes," says Anchorwoman Katia, nodding into her microphone. "That appears to be the case. Mr. Fattal was in the back of the bus, alone. The big question is why such a prominent and controversial figure in our political landscape, one who had as many enemies as he did supporters, would choose such a," she pauses again, this time not for effect but in search of the right word, "popular form of transportation."

The gruff reporter picks up on his colleague's faltering confidence. "Yes, Katia," he says. "It's indeed unlikely that in our charged political landscape, a politician would choose to ride a public bus. Any thoughts on what his destination was?"

I imagine he starches his shirts with them still on.

"The bus was bound for Damascus, with a couple of preliminary stops on the way," says TV Katia. "To cross the border into Syria, all passengers must carry either a passport or an ID card, so identification of the victims is expected to be swift."

She dodged the question. Well done.

"The army has been on the scene since this morning," she continues, "and has been instructed not to make any names public until this evening." Releasing her ear and addressing the camera directly she adds, "Dear viewers, if you believe you might know anyone on board, please call the number listed below."

None of the students move—it seems no one here knew anyone on board. Thank heaven for small mercies. This ordeal will be over soon. Now if only my back would stop sweating. Searching for a window of opportunity through which to tactfully make my exit, I scan the room again and notice Nancy leaning against the left wall, wearing the same green top as last night. She was never one to mind the prosaic walk of shame. But today, she seems troubled. Her brow is furrowed, her mouth twisted into a deep grimace. I throw her a smile, but it doesn't register.

TV Katia continues, now reading from a notepad. "Besides the victims on board, there's one who apparently survived long enough to crawl outside, a young man in his late twenties, who was found leaning against the side of the bus. Everyone was shot to death with an automatic weapon, the make of which is yet to be determined."

She shakes her head and I realize that perhaps she might not be one hundred percent cardboard cutout after all. Ninety percent tops. But as she starts to look somewhat appealing, she's wiped off the screen by the studio reporter's half. "And there you have it," he says, even more gruff with his wide frame now filling the entire screen. "We'll be with you today, all day, bringing you the news as it becomes available." He follows this awkward turn of phrase Lebanese newscasters hold dear to their hearts with an ad-lib. "This Black Monday is a mark of shame on the history of our country," he says. "Condolences to the families of the victims, to the Fattal family, and to Lebanon."

Chairman Ramala gestures to Garo and, as an orchestral montage of looped shots of Damascus Road flickers across its bulbous tube, he jumps up and mutes the TV. The music is instantly replaced with the rumpus of a hundred students and I turn to leave, but from across the room Ramala's shrill voice cuts through the hubbub.

"Professor, a word?" she says, and skirts toward me through the mob of students before I can pretend I didn't see her.

"How's it going?" she asks as students file past us through the doorway.

"Well, you know," I say, fidgeting for an appropriate form of commiseration over the news that has just transpired. "I'm distressed, of course."

"Not you, Professor. Your article. Where are we with that?"

What does she mean? There is no "we." There's me, right here in this mess away from the desk, and then somewhere at a remote distance, there's her at the delivery end. "It's coming along," I say. "I've collected some subjects and I'm running tests."

"Healthy samples of *Acacia tortilis*? I thought they're extinct in this country."

Did I say healthy? Dying samples would be more accurate. "I have my methods," I say with colossal wariness.

"Well, then. Let's put your methods to work," she says. "This in no way gets you off the hook."

What hook? It's my research and I do it for myself and for the Acacia. But I just toss her a smile, which she must take as hauteur because her reptilian eyes slant into a glower. She grips my elbow and slides me into the hallway, barely out of earshot of the students leaving the common room. What's the use? They can still see their hapless teacher ensnared in her bully-hold.

"Listen, Professor," she continues. "You might not think so, but I'm on *your* side. For *your* sake I've ignored every academic policy there is. I turned a blind eye to *your*," she glances around theatrically, "indiscretions, dating students and whatnot." Your, your, your—her timbre grows more emphatic with each iteration.

47

"Leave my private life out of it," I say, my mind still on an article that could not possibly survive the impending death of its subject.

"What private life? You're a professor. You have no private life, not with your students."

"Former student," I correct her. "Singular, just the one."

Why does she insist on bringing Nancy into what is, or should be, an academic debriefing? Or is it some other form of questioning that she thinks she's conducting right here and now, in this shoddy hallway at the most inopportune, and might I add tragic, time possible?

"And you commandeer classroom 2B," she continues undeterred, "our newest and biggest lab, as your own private playpen. God knows I've pulled every string to let that one pass with the other faculty, all crammed into cubbyhole lecture rooms." She leans in and my nose sniffles with her ammoniac perfume. "Look, Professor," she says. "I believe in your 'methods,' as you call them. But they better start bearing fruit soon."

Garo tries to scurry past her, but she grabs the sleeve of his shirt and tugs him toward her. "Good morning, *Istez*," he says to me, completely missing the time of day and Ramala's glare in the process. He's the only one here who calls me "*Istez*," and I much prefer it to "Sir."

"Suspend all classes for the day. For tomorrow too," she says to Garo. "And post a bulletin. All final exams proceed this weekend as scheduled." No "please," no "thank you." He nods silently, and walks out.

I take my chance to edge a word in. "Believe? You believe in my methods?" I say with a huff. "How can you find room for belief in a school of science and technology?"

"Listen, Professor," she says, her last word barely a hiss. First she wants me to look, now to listen. I can already smell her too, so what next? Touch me, Professor? "The taxonomists are here to set us straight, to dot the T's and cross the I's." I don't correct her; she has a hard time with idioms. Instead, I allow her breathless rant to continue uninterrupted. "Don't think for a second that those hounds will spare you. They're out for blood, and I'll lead the pack if it comes to that. And when they're done mauling you, I'll take my own juicy bite out of your bleeding carcass. If things go bad, they'll be bad for you alone. I've spent too many years of my life to—"

"I get it," I say, finally cutting her off. "You'll have my results by next week."

"Not next week, Professor," says Ramala. "This week. Sunday. You have seven days, tick, tick. Publish or perish." She practically sings that tired cliché as she wags a finger across my eyes like a metronome. Then she pirouettes on her high heel and walks off.

◆

I absently stir the mashed potatoes on my plate. My appetite is shot. After a couple of spoonsful I decide the food is too buttery. The cook probably used up a full day's quota of perishable ingredients, as most of the students are long gone for the next two days. Butter doesn't go well with iron; the bile clogs my throat, unabated since this morning. The dining hall is so deathly quiet that I can hear the mashed potatoes squish as I rake my fork through them like a miniature Zen garden.

"Room for one more, Professor?"

I throw Nancy my best smile (the one she says brings out my left dimple), but she misses it as she reaches for a chair. By the time she's snuggled at a right angle from me, her mood has already brightened up a lux. You have to admire the efficiency

49

of her mood swings.

"So, shitty thing, huh?" she says to me.

"Shitty, yes. You alright?"

"Yeah," she says, exhaling so sharply that it forms ridges across my mound of mashed potatoes. "I just can't believe he's dead, you know?"

"He?"

"Doreid Fattal. His scholarship put my brother through high school. They're saying no one on that bus survived. No witness either, but they found traces of the weapon there on the bus. It's one of those Russian rifles they used during the War. You know, a Ka-shilna-kov."

"A Kalashnikov," I correct her, probably smiling a little because she pinches my shoulder. She doesn't like to be wrong, even when it's cute.

"Hey, don't make fun of me, fuckwad!" she says, but then straightens herself and reassumes a demeanor more suited to the macabre sparseness of the dead cafeteria. She plucks a baked carrot off my plate and takes a bite, then twirls the stump between her fingers. "Well anyway, I'm off to my mushrooms."

"See you tonight?"

"Nah, I'm gonna work on my endnotes. Chapter Two's due for the panel review next week." She gets up. "But tomorrow I'm enlisting your literary skills, okay?" she says with a faux-intellectual lilt.

"Literary skills? For a master's thesis?"

"Why not? I see you all the time writing in that little diary of yours," she gestures toward the messenger bag at the foot of the table, "and talking to your tape recorder. I'd like to add some spice to my work too."

"It's not a diary," I say. "It's a memoir. I just record and transcribe. No spice. And how's that different from your

Bluetooth phone thing?"

"I need my Bluetooth phone thing to do hands-free work in the field. And usually there's someone on the other end." She laughs then says, "But you, you literally talk to yourself."

"Hey, what can I say?" I offer, admitting defeat. "We have a lot to learn from each other, Me and I."

"Yeah well, tonight it's just you, yourself, and Miss Acacia. Your Flower of Jerusalem. The Christ Thorn." She sways her arms in a dance as she waxes poetic about my Acacia research, now seven days my capricious mistress. She glances down and adds, "Seems you two did some mud-wrestling this morning." She's right. My messenger bag and heels remain muddy from this morning's misadventures.

I hang my head to hide my embarrassment; if I weren't so off today, I wouldn't be caught dead in a pair of scuffed up shoes, but she teases on anyway. "Tonight, be a gentleman and cook her dinner, alright?" She eats the rest of the carrot and grins. "And one day I'll make you confess where you've been running off to every morning."

"Ha. Ha. We'll just order Chinese," I say—not my best joke, but at least it helps me dodge her bait for more info.

Still grinning, she swings her bag over her shoulder, and then cooing over it she says, "And thanks for covering up my tippy toes this morning, sweet Professor."

By the time I word a savvy retort, she's already halfway across the deserted cafeteria.

◆

Nightfall. Quick shower. Brief siesta. Time for work.

The lamp at my desk spreads its glow across the room, spilling into the adjacent darkness. I'm in my cocoon, hanging my hopes on an Acacia branch, where caterpillars blossom into butterflies, and my thoughts into words on paper. I tug further at the branch, as far as it'll go, to the tipping point right before it snaps off, then release. It springs back. There's some life in it yet.

I make a note and open the drawer. From behind the tape recorder, I pull out my shearing pliers and a tube of ointment. This morning, I could only administer first aid before I rushed to class, but now I can apply the initial phase of treatment. Snip, snip, snip, a few twigs here, some thorns there. The process normally takes me a few minutes, but it stretches over a deliberate hour as the Acacia acquires a pruned, green habit. Green, young. Green, vivacious. Green, alive.

Green, helpless.

My pen glides along the pages of my memoir, filling line after line with my progress. Nancy's right—I do see myself as a poet, every tree a sonnet, every branch a verse, every leaf a beat. "In the discipline of Botany, Dendrology is perhaps the most delicate branch"—I savor the innuendo—"in reverence for the oldest and most massive life forms on the planet. A tree is a tree is a tree, people might think. Far from it. A tree needs constant care: light, water, nutrients from the soil, all of which, even if left unchecked, nature would happily provide. However, when we intervene, when we becloud its sun with our smog, blacken its rivers with our bile, besmirch its earth with our dross, Mother Nature bows her head in defeat."

I cross the T, discard the refuse in the bin under the desk, then pull the cap off the tube of ointment. I squeeze a drop of gel the size of a pinhead on my index finger and rub it into the knots of the main branches where they connect with the bark. Then one by one I cradle the Acacia's young extremities and wipe the excess gel into their tips. The wood glistens in the orange lamplight. From the second drawer I pull out a bottle and spray not directly on, but around the branches. I set the bottle down and rotate the pot, as the hanging mist dances in the lamplight and alights onto the tree, like a haze of perfume wrapping itself around a naked female body. I jot down a few more lines of notes and set my pen down to the side of my glasses.

Crossing the inky living room, I flip on the kitchen light and it flickers into a cold, dank, sickly tinge. The washing machine clicks open and my bundled jacket falls into my arms. I plop the dank garment onto the kitchen table, then I whip it into shape, inspecting it for traces of this morning's incident.

The sleeves are fine, though the cuffs are muddied with years of baked soil. The collar is fine, the pockets too. I turn it inside out and inspect the lining, first sleeves then back. A patch of coagulated red crinkles the inseam of the torso, painting the jacket's stitching red.

How could it have gotten inside? It didn't soak through the outer surface of the jacket, which was clean. It must be from when I cradled the young man. His blood had gotten inside the jacket.

I move to the sink and sprinkle some detergent on it. Then, under the running water, I scrape the fabric against itself, first lightly then more vigorously until some of the stitching comes undone. The blood clings to it, now a very conspicuous shade of pink-red. Dejected, I crumple and throw it back into the washing machine for another rinse. I crank the switch to the extra-hot cycle and the machine growls angrily. Leaving the light on, I close the door behind me, but rather than mute the sound, it muffles it into an intolerable rumble.

The sound echoes across the empty walls of my apartment. A slit of fluorescent light bleeds through the cracks of the door and, for the first time since this morning, I feel troubled.

4

Telephone Calls

"You'll find it at your doorstep," he said. "And Tony, don't call until Friday."

Doreid Fattal hit the red cancel button on his cell phone once, then again to shut it off, and leaned back into the sofa. Lama, never too old to snuggle by her father's side, curled her hand around the back of his neck.

"You're awake," he said. "What time's your flight?"

"Four o'clock."

Doreid set his mobile phone on the glass coffee table and lifted the wireless handset to his mouth as his heart sank. "Majid, I need you here."

A familiar loneliness spread through his chest to his shoulder blades. As the time he had with his daughter dwindled, he reflected on the decision he and his wife made two years ago to send her to France to study. What did that say about a man who invested his most productive years in the service of improving education in this country? About a man who day after day went on TV to reassure his people, in meticulously crafted promises, of the rosiness of Lebanon's future?

Yet again, he consoled himself. "Planting seeds, that's what I'm doing. Until they blossom through the surface, this land will appear barren."

Majid appeared in the doorway. "Sir?" he said.

Lama straightened to a more formal posture befitting a nineteen-year-old future member of parliament. Her father beckoned Majid forward and said, "Prepare your car. You're to drive Lama to the airport in an hour." Then to Lama he added, "Would you mind leaving your keys? I have an errand next week and will need to borrow your car."

"Of course not, Father," said Lama. She reached into her purse and placed the oversized bunch of keys, complete with a pink troll key chain and a bronze Eiffel Tower, on the table. Doreid buried his hand under the armrest by his side and pulled out a ribboned gold box. "Afterwards, deliver this to Nabatieh," he said, handing it to Majid, who timidly collected it and eyed the box curiously.

"To anyone in particular?"

"To Yaqub Jaber."

"Message, sir?"

"It's inside."

"Very well," said Majid. Cradling the box like it was made of solid gold, he disappeared through the door as Lama promptly brought her forehead back to Doreid's chest.

"What's this errand?" she said.

"Just personal business, my dear."

"Future congresswoman Lama Fattal must know," she teased. "Your personal business is my personal business."

"Lama, sweetheart. We have no congress in this country. What we do have is a parliament. And, God willing, when you're a member, you'll learn what to make your business and what not to. You don't have to do everything yourself, you know. You must delegate."

"But you're not delegating this errand."

"I'm afraid not. But I'm asking that you leave this matter to me. This thread's remained loose for many years, from before I had anyone to delegate to. And as such, I must tie it myself."

"Should I be worried?"

"No. I'd never let you worry. Ever. I'd die for my baby Lammoush."

She lifted her head and looked into his eyes. "Father," she said. "I want you to live for your baby Lammoush."

As he closed his eyes against her forehead, the sadness returned. It was time to close out the past, decided Doreid Fattal, once and for all.

◆

He peeked through the narrow slit in the basket as the city flashed by. His whiskers swept back in the muggy breeze, and his nose twitched with the first warnings of a summer cold.

At least his paw felt much better. He was well cared for and felt grateful to the young man behind him, whose warmth radiated through the straw basket and whose words floated back to him like a lullaby. Even in anger, his voice was kind. This was a good man; of that, he was well aware.

But Tarboush was aware of much more; most crucial of all was his ability to adapt. He was a Turkish Angora, blind and deaf on one side, which meant that for him, half the world was a shadow. To compensate, his sighted-hearing side had evolved its powers of peripheral sensation to such an extent that it compensated—perhaps even overcompensated—for his blind-deaf side.

Signs of this extreme adaptation were evident on his body: his seeing eye so deeply encroached into the territory of his blind eye, that to other cats, he appeared squinty, shifty, sly. So even with his sickly body, competitors stayed out of his way—a happy accident of his disability.

He was the only cat the young man ever knew, so perhaps his owner thought all cats functioned this way. In fact Tarboush often wondered whether—besides the clearly physical aspects of his disability such as the squint and the fact that he had no tolerance for milk—the young man was even aware of his pet's special condition. But when they were together on the bike, his owner's vigorous pedaling fused the two of them together. What the cat lacked in audiovisual stimuli, the bike and its rider made up for in bumping over potholes, lashing through the wind, and bashing against the side mirrors of cars.

The bicycle bounced along and Tarboush felt his weight being thrown forward as they climbed the steep hillside. They were close now. Since moving to Beirut, the bicycle had become an extension of his senses, much as the young man was an extension of his emotions. The three of them formed a whole that adapted to the chaotic world much more than the individual parts ever could.

"*Manyak, Manyak!*" squawked the parrot from the cage as they rode past it.

If only he could curse back, but all he could muster was a hiss, to which the bird retorted with a shriek. Tarboush had enough and turned away.

Selective hearing was another one of his special gifts. He only turned his hearing ear toward the sounds he liked: the lilt of the man's voice, the uneven crunch of his feet, and his music. That last one somehow tied it all together so that Tarboush's experience of the world was like a variation on a theme, an improvisation of a familiar melody, order snatched from the jaws of chaos.

"Yes, fine," said the young man's voice. "Where did you leave it? Okay." His voice was sharp, but then after a shrill beep, it softened and said, "How are we doing in there? Look! We're home!"

Before the bicycle came to a complete stop, the young man jumped off and pulled it into the shade. Clank, squeak, switch went the lock and then the basket lid opened as he felt the man's warm arms tuck under his own and lift him out. He purred against the man's moist cheek as he was carried through the hanging clothes to the open space behind.

"Bu Joseph?" said the man. His musky scent made Tarboush's nose twitch into a sneeze.

"There, there," said the man called Bu Joseph. He stroked Tarboush's head, and then he looked up and added, "How'd it go?"

"Good as new," the young man said, stroking Tarboush's paw. "Thought it would never heal."

"Told you," said Bu Joseph. "Best vet in all of Achrafieh. My wife went there all the time." He let out a loud laugh, then added, "You know, when we had the dog."

"I have a letter?"

"Yes," said Bu Joseph, clearing his throat with a deafening hawk. "Slid it under your door."

Tarboush felt nauseous as he bobbed up and down the stairs. He meowed, jumped out of his owner's arms, and ran up ahead of him. The spicy smell of burning wood sticks from next door told him they had arrived on the young man's floor, and he patiently waited on the doormat as the man caught up and opened the door with a clang of keys.

Scampering through the doorway and into the apartment, he made his way to his favorite corner behind the big sound and picture box, curling his tail around him as he lay on the carpet. He watched his owner walk in, close the door behind him, and look down at something in his hand.

"Meow?" said Tarboush, pitter-pattering toward him. The man crouched down but instead of food he showed him a shiny card with his face on it. "Look at this," he said, pointing at the face. "It's official! From now on you can call me Tony."

Then he disappeared into the other room and returned with a saucer of water. Yes, that's the stuff. Tarboush buried his face in it and lap-lap-lapped the yummy clear liquid. The young man went over to the window and pressed his eye into the long white looking device, as he blindly beeped his palm-sized speaking device.

◆

Nadine squeezed her sister's hand. "What're you up to for the rest of the day?"

"Dunno," said Nissrine, squeezing her sister's hand back. "I'll just walk around. Discover the city."

The hand squeeze was something they did since they were kids, one more way of saying "I love you," though they never had a shortage of ways.

"On foot?" Nadine asked. "You must be boiling under that thing."

"It's not that bad. A dark abaya like this allows you to wear very little under it."

Now that they were both grown women, Nadine felt less like the baby sister she once was. With their small age difference, she had a lot in common with Nissrine, like she was her shadow self, just a few years later. Walking next to her, she almost felt that literally. Her sister was clad in black from head to toe. Her own veil was scandalous in comparison, even showing her bangs at the front. But when the sun hit both women, it cast the same silhouette on the ground.

They stood like that in front of the building, and then Nissrine asked, "How about you? Will you see him today?"

Nadine looked up to the Professor's apartment on the third floor then back at her sister. "No, I don't think he's home."

"I meant the boy."

"Oh, him. Maybe, if I finish early."

Nissrine took hold of her sister's hand again. "Listen, Nadine. Boys are dangerous."

"It's not like that. We're just friends."

"Even so. They have many faces, but only show you one. The one they want you to see."

Nadine let go of her sister's hand.

"Don't worry," she said and planted a kiss on her sister's cheek. "I'll see you tonight, okay?"

She skipped into the building, then the elevator, and when she was sure the doors were shut and the elevator in motion, she checked herself in its mirror. She pulled out a tube of lipstick and painted her lips. That's all she needed. Her big eyes already looked like they were drawn on with eyeliner. Even the mole at the corner of her lips was perfectly placed, like it was applied there. As the elevator hit the third floor, she pulled off her veil and tucked it into her bag. She opened the door and stepped into the hallway a new woman, in a new role.

At the doorstep, she leaned down and peeled up the corner of the mat. There the key lay in its usual spot. She picked it up, careful not to ruin her nails, unlocked the door and stepped in. Nadine made her way into the kitchen, set her bag on the counter and reached into the cupboard under the sink. She wrapped the apron around her waist and set to work. She scrubbed the kitchen walls, the sink, the inside and outside of the fridge, the bathroom, scrubbed the sink again, the tiles with a toothbrush, dusted the living room, made the bed, vacuumed everything.

And then finally, her favorite part. She checked the instructions on the desk and used the bottled formula the Professor had left behind to water the plant. According to the card, this specimen was a *Tulipus incus*. "There, there," she said as she wiped the excess droplets off its leaves. She had grown to love these plants as he did. Every week or two, he brought a new one. If one wanted to, one could chronicle his routine through observing his plants. She went to the living room and plopped herself on the couch by the window, staring blankly at the switched-off TV.

Then right on cue, her phone rang.

5
"Feed the Cat."

I lift my head from my memoir and peel off the page stuck to my cheek. Sleep had crept up on me unnoticed, devoured the sickly night, and belched out an obnoxious glare. As I wipe the drowsiness from my eyes, I draw the curtains across the two windows by the bed, leaving the one by the desk open an inch, and slide the Acacia pot into the slit of hard sunlight. By my elbow, the desk lamp prostrates dimly to the all-powerful Helios.

The shears and moisturizer go back into the bottom drawer and I pull the recorder from the top one, laying it atop my memoir.

I hit Record. "Day 2: Tuesday, November 17th, noon," I say, then clear my throat. "Acacia treated. Now it's wait and see." Rewinding the tape to the beginning, I press play, then pop the recorder in my pajama shirt pocket and adjust the Acacia in its pot. Over the years, I've learned to keep my aversion for my own voice under control. Me and I actually don't get along as well as I'd like Nancy to think.

"Day 1   Shit," says the recorder. The Volvo interrupts me with a clomp as it shifts into gear. There's a pause and then, "Day 1: November 16th, 5:13 a.m. En route to Damascus Road." The recording stutters then resumes minutes later when I'm on

Damascus Road itself.

Tape playing from my pocket, I move to the kitchen, textured with a softer, more pleasant daylight. The clothes are dry, and instead of last night's rumbling machine, thunder rolls on the tape—not as loud in playback, but my anxiety rises just the same, mirroring my dread from yesterday. I fast-forward. "Something off... They've been wrong..." Ambient sounds of my morning fieldwork continue to play on the tape: a squish here, a splat there, the occasional car and chirping birds fill the soundtrack.

From the washing machine, I pick up the jacket by the sleeves and carry it back to the bedroom, spreading it out on the bed. The extra-hot cycle left it only slightly damp, and the fabric doesn't need ironing. I'm thankful for that, a pail of relief in my well of anxiety.

As I open my closet, the bus screeches through the speakers. Of course! I left the recorder running! Then I hear my own muddy dash, squishing through the field, and then slushing across gravel. Now I'm at the bus itself. On tape it plays in tragic real time. None of the slow motion from yesterday.

In a matter of seconds, I'm on the bus. Now the man, "Where is she?" Again and again. That fruitless, blind, inane search for the beloved cat. Then my voice, "She's gone. It's just you and me."

"The cat," he says.

"Your cat's fine. I'll take care of you. You'll be fine too."

"Feed the cat."

I play it back, "Feed the cat."

◆

I clutch the phone between my chin and collarbone. How

my students spend hours on this contraption in this state of contortion, I cannot fathom. I feel as awkward as my idiomatic phrasing, which I make a mental note to share with Nancy. "Yes, Nadine. I know it's terrible, quite terrible," is all I can reciprocate about the news that has shaken the country. I step out of the elevator and cross the lobby of my building. When I walk and talk, am I pushing my ability to multitask? Either that, or the strain in both my jaw and ankles is rheumatoid arthritis brought on by three-point-five decades and a wet autumn. I prefer the first hypothesis.

"Anyway—" she cuts me off with incessant chatter. "Yes, yes I know, but you've heard school's off today too, right?" I jerk the phone from my ear. She sounds even worse than yesterday, but I don't ask about her lost friend—no time for small talk. "Look, I've stepped out for a bit, so the house is nice and quiet. You can study for your finals there." I push the lobby door open with the cell phone as Nadine pierces through the earpiece at an even higher octave. "Yes right now, the key's in the usual spot. Make yourself at home and make everything neat." I look both ways and cross the street.

The cell phone goes into my shirt pocket and I wrap my jacket around my chest. It's dry now; I just have to imagine the stain's not there until it goes to the dry cleaner's. They'll know what to do. They handle stains like that all the time. They're the stain experts. I make my way along the sidewalk to the top of the urban staircase.

I double-check my footing on the crooked steps and start my descent. The upper side of Achrafieh, a residential part of Beirut, remains quite preserved. Sure, the main streets have fallen victim to the wrecking ball and the viral spread of the Downtown project, but little pockets have remained as they were thirty, even forty, years ago. My building is in one of those, dating back to the late sixties. Except for the elevator replaced by a modern Otis a few years ago, the edifice enjoys its venerable age and all the charm and inconvenience that come with that.

I continue down the stairs and pass a corner grocery store, but then double back and peek inside. It's business as usual, except that a suspended TV screen is set to Future TV news rather than Rotana music channel, much more the staple of local grocery stores. I cross under a Marlboro-sponsored tarp and walk in. A silver parrot eyes me through the bars of its suspended cage and three ashen men stand fixated on the TV.

"*Marhaba*! Hello!" I yell out to the one behind the counter. "Skinny, darkish, twenty-year-old man. Rides an olive-green bike. Does he live around here?"

The TV glistens in the grocer's unwavering emerald eyes as he throws his arm over his shoulder. "Three buildings down that way," he says catatonically. Neither of the other men budge, but as I leave he adds, "I sold him a pack of Luckies yesterday, bright and early," he says. Then he gestures vaguely toward the TV. "Didn't see him today. With this news, who wants to leave the house, *eh*? Even for a smoke."

"Thanks," I say, followed by a useless, "What a shame." I slip out of the store as the parrot, utterly unprovoked, croaks "*Akrout*! Bastard!" after me.

I pass two buildings and go into the third, marked by a distinctive recessed entryway with damp laundry hanging from the ceiling and framing a narrower passage. Past an open staircase leading to the apartments above, I slip under another layer of laundry and through a makeshift passageway of shirts, pants, and assorted undergarments to a medium-sized courtyard. Looking around, I notice a doorway with an incandescent light shining through. Five pairs of plastic slippers of various sizes line the entrance. From the inside, TV commercials come through muffled and monotonous. I rap at the half-open metal and glass door a couple of times and when no one answers, I yell, "*Marhaba!*"

"*Aywa!* Coming!" a voice yells back. "One minute." A man resembling a healthy turnip pops his head out from the opening and studies me through a pair of eyes buried within mounds of rosy flesh, then opens the door and steps into the largest pair of slippers.

He's wearing a pair of winter pajama bottoms, and maybe his son's jogging suit top because it's two sizes too small and lettered "Batistoota" broadly across the chest. He flashes me a smile showing a full set of white teeth, but lines around his dark blue eyes betray his real age. The teeth must be the fruits of his life savings, or maybe a pension from a previous job.

"Good morning," I say. "I'm looking for one of your tenants. Actually, the pet of one of your tenants."

"Pet? What pet?" he asks, his smile instantly disappearing. As I form a mental picture of the man on the bike, a shadow crosses the man's face. I suppose animals are forbidden, but how else could I have introduced myself? The biker clearly knew much about me, but on him, I have nothing beyond the fact that he died on Damascus Road and a guess that he lived in this building. I shouldn't mention the first certainty, only the second possibility.

"He, the tenant, is," I'm careful to stick with the present tense as I fall back on the description I rehearsed, "a skinny, darkish, twenty-year-old man." None of this registers. "Rides an olive-green bike," I add encouragingly.

"Oh! Tony," he says with his first reluctant smile. "Haven't seen him since last weekend… Deputy Doreid. When we heard the news, my wife Imm Joseph screamed so loud I had to close the doors and windows."

All I get from his barrage is the word "Tony." Finally, a name. *See you later... Tony*! I grin to myself. I'll learn all there is (was) to know about this Tony, or my name isn't—but no, I must stop myself before my face betrays my inward triumph.

Bu Joseph continues. I tune out his ramblings as I think. If his wife is "Imm Joseph," mother of Joseph, then I can assume he's "Bu," father of, Joseph. His Achrafieh accent is too dense to cut through, so I can barely concentrate on his words. I spot a golden chain around his neck with a hanging yellow cross, turquoise bead and an orange and silver Harley Davidson logo. The assortment bounces against his Adam's apple as he goes on and on. "...I tell you she almost fainted. God rest their souls, Deputy Doreid and those poor people. All of them. A crying shame, it is."

"God rest their souls," I agree reluctantly. "So, Tony, he lives here, right?"

"Yeah. I keep my nose out of people's business," he says. "But him, I run into Tony all the time. Buys me cigarettes," which could either mean they were best friends or they barely knew each other. It's not what you say, but how you say it.

He continues. "But he's a solemn fellow. Are you a friend? Didn't know he had any. I've never seen anyone visit. The eighty-two-year-old widow on the fourth floor gets more company. Good for him, though. Good for him."

His voice trails off, but before Bu Joseph slips into another melancholic soliloquy, I press on, phrasing my sentences carefully; this may be the only chance. "He lived—*lives* with a cat, right? I should check on her."

"A cat? Oh yes, of course. Lovely creature, but—"

"Yes. A cat," I say. I wipe my mouth to mitigate an oncoming outburst. "Listen. You must let me into Tony's apartment."

"Let *you* in?" he asks with a touch of offense. "I don't have keys to the apartments," he says. "Nobody's. And not his."

"What floor is he on?"

"The fifth. That one, up there to the left of the metal grille."

I follow the line of his pointing finger to a pair of kitchen balconies, separated by a pattern of iron rods tipped with spearheads. I point at the other balcony to the right. "And who lives there?"

Bu Joseph's grimace instantly morphs into a sparkling white grin.

◆

Bu Joseph rings the doorbell five times before a shriek almost punctures the wooden door. I hear music coming from inside the apartment. "Alright, alright, coming! Mary, mother of God, can't you wait?" The door swings open, revealing a handsome woman of about forty-five. Her face is only half made up and, from the looks of it, it was done without a mirror.

"Oh," she says to Bu Joseph as she tugs her abaya across her bosom. His face remains frozen in the same grin, making him appear either charmed or constipated.

"Why, hello," she says to me, tilting her head. She pulls out a freshly manicured hand and her top falls open revealing a cavernous cleavage. As I shake her fingertips, Bu Joseph finds his voice.

"Madame Bogosian?" he says. "This mister here's a pal of your neighbor Tony."

Pal? Sure, why not? I nod, but he pauses for a reaction from her, which he doesn't get. Her fingers remain wrapped around my hand, her eyes locked on mine. He continues, "He wants to see the cat."

"That poor thing was meowing all night," she says, inspecting

Bu Joseph from the corner of her eye. "And where were you?"

"At home, Madam. You could've dropped by."

"The last time I dropped by, your crazy wife tried to kill me. She was smacking a carpet and before I knew it, the slipper came flying right out of her hand and whacked me right there." She taps the side of her head.

"Ah, she—"

"And you know," she says touching her cheeks, one redder than the other, "I can't go out without my face on!" Then, nodding down to my sweaty palm still clasped in hers, she adds, "Please, please come in." She pulls me in with surprising strength. Eyes glued onto the entire maneuver, Bu Joseph mutters something and shuts the door behind us.

If I had woken up in this apartment, I'd have thought myself at a Bazaar in Calcutta, except for Fairuz's voice filling the space, "*Habsi int, int habsi.* You're my prison, my prison is you." Brightly colored textiles cover the walls, cascading down into puddles of color on the floor. I cross the room, careful not to trip over the tables scattered around, all covered with bronze and wooden knickknacks.

In the corner stands a dusty TV set to National Geographic Travel and on it a docked green iPod plays my least favorite Fairuz song. Madame Bogosian approaches it and lowers the volume as her own voice takes over, "*Wintalli bikrahu, willi bhibbu int.* And you are the one I hate, and the one I adore." She swirls around, her abaya following a second later, and clasps her hands together.

"So! Tea, jasmine, thyme?" she says. "Or, an Almaza beer, perhaps?"

From the entrance miles away, "Just the cat for now if you don't mind," says Bu Joseph. Her spine stiffens and her tattooed eyebrows contort into a frown. She assumes an air of

70

professionalism, like a soldier receiving an order. "Yes. Please, follow me."

She leads us to the next room and I'm instantly transported across the Indian Ocean, back to a drab Achrafieh kitchen, complete with a rusty fridge and sky-blue ceramic tiles. She nods toward the balcony and Bu Joseph slips in between us, brushing against her and missing me by a hair. He takes command and heaves the sliding glass door open. I catch Madame Bogosian eyeing his already-sweaty forearms as the door comes to a screeching halt. We step onto the balcony and she instantly lets out a mousy sneeze. As the two overgrown school kids share a giggle, I notice the balcony is filthy.

"I never come out here in the autumn," she apologizes. "I have a pollen allergy."

"As a matter of fact, me too," I say, already feeling my nose twitch. "You say the cat meowed all night?"

"Yes, yes! My God, I tell you I could hear the weeping through the walls." She notices the silence and adds, "Oh no. You don't think…"

She turns to Bu Joseph, who lays his palm on her shoulder. "There, there," he consoles halfheartedly. "Mr. Tony wouldn't leave the cat without food."

"I know," she says, looking at me with doleful eyes. "He loves that cat. He's not much of a talker, but that cat, I swear he tells it bedtime stories. They even got into a fight yesterday morning! Dunno where on earth he's run off to, leaving that poor thing starving all by itself."

"Do you know Tony well?" I ask.

"I'm an Achrafieh girl, born and bred. I don't really understand their language. And he mostly kept to himself."

"Their language? You mean Arabic?"

"No, no, of course not," she says, flustered. "I mean, you

71

know, that Saida dialect." She could mean any of the myriad accents of not only Saida, but also Nabatieh, Sour, and other towns that dot the mountains of South Lebanon. Meanwhile, Bu Joseph is too busy ogling her to confirm or correct her statement.

"And you know what else?" she adds, her voice dropping to a whisper. "I think he was an H-O-M-O. Back in April, I think, when he first moved in, I invited him over many times for tea. You know, I tried to be all, umm, neigh-bor-ly like." She twirls her hair around her finger as she sings her words like Fairuz lyrics. "And he shut me out every single time. He's a strange one, even for one of those people."

"What people?"

"You know, those people. The H-O-M—"

"Yeah, I get it," I say, my patience at the end of its tether.

"They're all supposed to be neat and tidy, no? Well, I popped over to his house once, to borrow some eggs, and had me a little peeksy inside. The place's a pigsty."

I inspect the balcony railing and metal partition separating Madame Bogosian's balcony from Tony's. "Anyway," I say, "I should check on the cat."

"Yes, go!" she says, snapping into a dramatic falsetto. "Go save the cat!"

I shake the railing to make sure it's sturdy, then pivot one leg over it and the other. I'm now standing on the outside of the balcony, gripping the handrail. I inch my way across, trying not to be impaled by the spokes sticking out from the iron grille. One of the spearheads snags my jacket and despite Madame Bogosian's shriek, which almost causes me to hurtle down, I twist myself loose, swing myself over to the other side and land right into a tray of kitty litter.

"Shit."

"What?" she cries back.

"Nothing," I say with a grumble as I shake the stones off my shoes. I lean down and pinch my pants to shake them off. While down there I sniff and, thankfully, the litter smells clean.

Along the Achrafieh hillside, the sky has turned a burgundy red, laced with orange clouds and speckled with glowing yellow windows. Crooked rooftops jut into it and a web of power lines, some taut, some sagging under the weight of many years, slices through.

◆

"Can you see the cat in there?"

"Hold on, I'm checking," I yell back to the asymmetrically mascaraed eyes squinting through the metal partition. I turn around and tug the handle of the sliding glass door, and it glides open without a sound. Before entering, I check the soles of my shoes and find that some stones have lodged themselves between their rubber ridges. I slide them off, take a deep breath, and step over the aluminum threshold into the late Tony's home.

As my eyes adjust to the dark, the kitchen fades into view— an almost exact mirror image of Madame Bogosian's, down to the blue ceramic tiles, turned neutral gray by late afternoon light. Even the bulbous General Electric fridge propped a few centimeters off the floor could be a replica of the one next door, as could the breakfast table in the corner. The one difference, however, is that this room displays nothing to indicate that its occupant has just left, or that it was ever occupied. There are no dishes in the sink or anywhere around it, no towels or tablecloths, no utensils.

The only signs of life are an ashtray filled to the brim with cigarette butts and a dull sound that calls to mind a whale in heat. Even with no other stimuli, my unimpeded senses cannot identify its source. Maybe it's the faucet; I turn the nozzle until it lets out a burst of water, but when I close it again, the sound persists. I tilt my ear toward the sound. It's coming from my left, where a small and defective-looking fridge stands. My shoes squeak on the dirty, tiled floor and the sound grows louder.

I hear a faint scratching from inside and I'm hit with a realization. I leap toward the fridge and pull the door open. Suddenly, a large ball of fur obscures my vision. Then, all I see is the carious inside of the fridge. The stained shelves are scattered with a few petrified cloves of garlic and a molding stick of butter.

The thermostat box dangles from a frayed wire, slapping sporadically against the fridge door. I twist it loose and the sound stops.

A foul smell reaches my nose and I look down to the source. I'm standing in a murky white puddle, congealed at the edges. It's hard to differentiate it from the white of the tiles, so I lean forward as I follow it across the kitchen to the legs of a wooden chair, up the breakfast table, to a carton of milk lying on its side. It's at least two days old, judging from the smell. I see a trail of droplets leading away from the source. Paw prints.

I follow the milky footsteps out the room. "Kitty," I say, entering the living room. "Heeeere kitty, kitty."

Besides the paw prints, the apartment is exceptionally tidy—not at all the "pigsty" Madame Bogosian described. On a fat TV in the corner, a program on fireflies plays silently, bathing the room in a flickery blue light. By the main entrance, the paw prints snake past a little geek corner with a stack of video games on a stool, Street Fighter, Legend of Zelda, Mortal Kombat. On the floor next to it sits a neat pile of hardcover books on astronomy, topped with a Nintendo console attached to some cables running along the wall to the TV in the corner. By the window stands a tripod carrying an amateur white telescope.

The path of prints swerves around a white leather sofa draped with a beige bath towel, the TV light dancing across it like a shadow play. At the foot of the sofa is an empty saucer, around which the path abruptly curves into the bedroom. Here the paw prints become fainter, so I get down on all fours for a closer look, crawling around the neatly made bed, and on the way I slam head first into a floor-to-ceiling pile of records. Several clatter onto my back and bounce to the floor.

I let out a string of swears and pick up the fallen records. Eric Dolphy's *Out to Lunch*, a few Minguses, and many different versions of *Kind of Blue*, originals, bootlegs, and outtakes. Beyond the turntable on a low stool by the stack, the room is sparsely furnished. It was clearly only used for some sleeping, some reading, and lots of listening. Besides the pile of clothes on the floor, everything is in immaculate order.

Crawling along the bed I hunch down and crane my face under it, stifling a sneeze from the cloud of dust that emerges. "Kitty?" I say, sniffing. "Where are you, silly kitty?" There's nothing under the bed except a pair of socks and a long metallic case. My hand brushes against a small pile of objects, which clatter to the floor noisily. I pick up the smallest one and hold it against the dim light of the window; it's a battery—the thin, flat kind you'd find in an old-fashioned calculator.

I set it down on a bedside table, next to a retro-style alarm clock that reads 4:36 a.m. Its red alarm hand points to 5 o'clock.

I set it on the side table, next to the only other object there, a framed picture of a man standing behind a woman in a wheelchair. It's Tony, a few years younger, hair in a buzz cut, face sunken into an oversized white collar, making his head look like it's hovering a few inches over his body. His slight physique is dwarfed by a hunting rifle, which he props up with one hand. A pattern of broad lines runs down the length of his shirt chest and sleeve, rolled up at the wrist, his other hand on the woman's shoulder. She has a rugged face, thick eyebrows, and a smile that lets one forget there was ever misery in the world. I glance from the woman to Tony; the resemblance is uncanny.

The bronze frame is engraved with intricate Aztec patterns, at odds with the modern bedframe. The corner of the glass is cracked and when I pick up a shard off the floor and press it into the gap, it fits perfectly.

"Meow?"

The cry came from behind me. "Kitty cat?" I get off my knees and follow its source back to the living room. "Kitty, kitty, kitty." In the corner, I lean behind the TV and a white cat gazes at me from inside a single wool slipper.

"Meow," she cries, her eyes glistening in the blue TV light. They are asymmetrical: one blue, one hazel, though it might be a trick of the mixed light that dapples her white fur with a sundry of hues.

"There you are," I say, cradling her in the small of my arm and crossing through the kitchen onto the balcony. "Look who I found," I say, congratulating myself as I pass the cat over the railing to a sniffly Madame Bogosian on the other side. "Don't cry. She's fine."

"No, no, it's just allergies," she says. "Why hello there unsy wunsy shnookums. Yes, yes, you're staying with me now, how about that?"

"Listen!" I say. "She's purring."

"She? Who's she?" says Madame Bogosian. "The cat's a he. His name's Tarboush."

I shake my head. Tony asked, "Where is *she*?" I turn to Bu Joseph but he's busy stroking the cat's head with one hand and Madame's shoulder with the other. "Okay, I'm climbing back," I say, swinging my leg again over the railing.

"And what do you think you're doing?" asks Madame.

"Returning?" I say, suddenly feeling like I need her permission again to step onto her balcony.

"And his food?" she says, her single drawn eyebrow arching up as if caught in a fishhook. Bu Joseph, enjoying his game of house with woman and cat, grunts his support.

Back in Tony's kitchen I flip on the light and close the fridge, sealing the broken thermostat into its icy coffin. Then I go on a hunt for cat food.

Fridge top: box of stale cereal. Table: just the spilled milk. Glass cabinet: ceramic plates. Drawers: utensils.

Lifting myself, I step back into the living room again and on my way notice a massive oak armoire to my left, just outside the bedroom, hiding in plain sight.

Some light spills onto it from the kitchen, revealing a key protruding from the handle. I unlock it, reach into the bedroom doorway and flip the switch to throw some more light in. Looking inside I realize that, like my apartment this morning, Tony's place is only tidy on the surface. No orderly person could possibly live with such a mess, even locked up in an armoire. I see a solitary pink cardboard box amidst a nightmare of half-used toiletries on the bottom shelf.

"Tony, you rascal," I say to no one. "You have a lady friend after all." The pack of Kotex tampons is labeled "12," but only has four inside. I toss it back and shift my attention to the shelf above, which carries a jumble of cables, bicycle locks, some magazines, and a wooden tray filled with broken remotes. I move to the next shelf and find dozens of Meow Mix cans. The labels catch some light from the bedroom. "Let's see. Salmon, Beef in Gravy, Chicken & Liver. Ugh, garbage. Tarboush, what would you like to eat? Aha! There, Ami Cat Vegan Mix." Setting down the first can onto the empty top shelf, I file through the others for something a little more suitable, stowing the rejects on the upper shelf with the Beef in Gravy.

I find cans of white fish, liver, crab meat, and other mysterious labels, which I either pack under my arm or toss back into the cupboard, depending on my own taste. I shuffle a few empty cans out of the way and grimace at the stickiness. Then, I see something in the back of the cupboards, hidden behind a bag of cat litter. Among the boxes stands a well-worn leather journal fastened shut with a rubber band.

Sliding the fastener off, the journal pops open and several papers stuffed between its pages fan out, some tagged with Post-it notes, others lined to the edges with a neat cursive, several inscribed with figures, equations, dates, and geometric diagrams I recognize as star constellations. Another page contains a sketch of a sylphlike white cat looking over its shoulder—perhaps a younger Tarboush, and another page, a sketch of the apartment itself. I find more astronomical diagrams and sketches, some quotes from Shakespeare, and some aborted attempts at poetry. One is entitled Pluto, and bemoans its fall from grace as a planet. It laments being abandoned by its father the sun and its siblings in the solar system. Another is about iron in the core of a star causing it to collapse into itself and die in a massive supernova. There's also a name that repeats on several pages near the diagrams, "Maurice."

As I flip through the notebook, a yellow piece of paper falls out. I pick it up and read the same neat handwriting, "November 16th, 12:05 a.m.: Come, he hath hid himself among these trees, to be consorted with the humorous night."

The note ends there. It's from *Romeo and Juliet*, but it doesn't make any sense, not with the date and time. This is no poetry. It's prose, real life—it's me, at my desk, behind the tree samples, working through the night, the "humorous" night, which in

Shakespeare is not funny, but humid, dank, moist. Last night. I look up as bile crawls up my esophagus, flooding my mouth with a caustic iron taste. It's beyond all reason.

Clutching the note, I take a few steps toward the polished white telescope. Its lens catches the last hint of violet sunlight, and its shaft strobes with the electric blue TV light. Gripping the tripod, I check its pan and tilt levers; they're locked firmly in position and it doesn't budge.

Flipping my glasses onto my forehead, I squeeze my eye into the viewfinder and squint, rotating its diopter until the image comes into sharp focus: a single yellow bedroom window, and within it the stark silhouette of a thorny sapling.

I pull away in horror. "My Acacia," I say aloud. Over my shoulder, on the bedroom side table, a young Tony and his jovial mother smile back at me.

◆

It's already pushing seven o'clock when I throw my keychain on the shelf and cross through my entrance hall. The TV is on and the back of Nadine's head is silhouetted against the evening news. "Hey," I say.

She turns to me from over the sofa and smiles glumly through a tear-stained but otherwise flawless face, framed by a modest blue scarf. "I didn't think you'd mind," she says, indicating the TV. "Couldn't study."

"I don't mind," I say. "A TV break, why not?"

Her face brightens a shade. I'm always clumsy around her, always overcompensating, but gladly she never seems to mind it. I amble around the couch and sit down at the other end, as far from her as I can. Her handbag and a yellow folder form a barricade between us, creating a comfortable—and appropriate—

buffer zone. "The house is done," she says. "I was just taking a break." Her Syrian accent is much thicker than usual—it must be the emotions.

"Looks good," I say as we both turn to the TV.

"So, Minister," TV Katia asks. "How can you be sure none of the victims carried out the attack? Your preliminary investigation rules out murder-suicide."

"True. Murder, yes. Suicide, no," the mustachioed, newly appointed Minister of the Interior says with an air of decisiveness. "Two chicken farmers were first on the scene, just after five thirty in the morning. They grabbed a motorcycle cop who radioed it in and I immediately dispatched the entire Achrafieh squadron. I arrived at the scene no later than 6:00 a.m. We allowed no one on the bus until we canvassed the area. Once on board, we found a large number of Kalashnikov bullet-casings around the victims."

Nadine shifts beside me. I keep my eyes on the TV.

"So unless someone had two-meter long arms," he continues, "and shot themselves in the head—almost impossible with a rifle, mind you—then it's safe to assume that the assassin was not one of the victims and that he somehow discarded the weapon and fled the scene."

"I see," says Katia. "And none of the victims were shot in the head?"

"All the collateral victims were shot in the torso, and—perhaps at the very end—the driver was stabbed, we believe with the Kalashnikov's bayonet, no doubt to wipe him out as a witness."

The Minister's digressive, stop-and-go manner of speech starts to irk me, but then Nadine says, "Collateral?" and my concern falls back on her as a fresh stream of tears runs down her face. I hand her a tissue, which she picks out of my hand with her fingertips, carefully avoiding my outstretched palm.

The Minister continues. "The only exception is," he pauses to formulate his words, "Deputy Doreid Fattal, who was shot clean between the eyes."

There's a long pause during which the Minister adjusts his posture, as if shifting a load from one shoulder to the other. Katia resumes her line of questioning. "And our reports indicate there are no survivors," she says. "Did you confirm that none of the passengers escaped?"

"The roster lists the driver plus six passengers. That accounts for all victims on board, except for the young man who was able to crawl outside. The chicken farmers even tried to revive him, but he was long gone. He had struggled heroically with his killer: his shirt was ripped and bloody at the elbow, and his face was gashed."

Struggled? I *struggle* not to roll my eyes at his faulty reasoning. There was no struggle, Mr. Minister, just reckless biking and a collision that could've saved his life had he the decency to stop for a moment.

"And you've identified all of the victims?" asks Katia.

"They all had passports or ID cards, except the young man outside. He had no identification on him whatsoever. Therefore, we could assume he planned to disembark this side of the border since Syria requires Lebanese residents to carry either ID cards or passports to cross."

Nadine's face is a mess now. I ease closer to her. Her handbag juts into my back and the yellow folder crunches under me. I squeeze her shoulder, but she doesn't budge. Nancy doesn't understand my attraction to this young woman: she intrigues me, not sexually, not even sensually. Behind those black eyes, underneath that scarf, I can sense a world of secrets, buried histories that I wish I could unearth, learn, mend, and then put back. If the Acacia is my mission, Nadine is my pet project.

Doorbell. I release Nadine's shoulder and clamber to open the door. Nancy walks in, carrying a binder under her arm. She's brought her work with her.

Nadine looks up. "Hi Nancy," she says. "We're watching the Minister."

I avoid the spot where I sat, throwing myself onto the single sofa instead.

"That's nice," says Nancy as she sits on the sofa arm next to me, laying her hand on my shoulder. "I watched it earlier. They're all chicken shit."

"You mean chicken farmers," I joke, but it misses the mark. She's already noticed the depression I left in the sofa cushion next to Nadine. Sometimes Nancy can be a little too observant.

The Minister continues on the television. "We also cross-referenced this information with tickets purchased at the two stations at which the bus had stopped," he says. "The total was indeed six tickets."

"And that accounts for everyone then?" Katia asks, a leading question, redundant, but intended to prod the Minister for more information.

"It accounts for everyone, except of course, the killer. Since there are no other stops between the second station and the scene of the murder, this tells us he got on board without a ticket, probably at a traffic light."

The Minister turns to address the camera. "We're confident that we'll bring whoever committed this crime to justice." To Katia, he adds, "We're keeping no secrets from the public."

"One final question, Minister," she says. "Do you know why Mr. Doreid Fattal was on that bus? Someone of his stature, of his political conspicuousness, on public transportation? Surely under the circumstances he couldn't have been on an official visit to Syria? After all, it's said this ceasefire in Damascus is fictitious, with reports filtering in of sporadic outbreaks of—"

"Miss Katia," the Minister says, visibly irritated. "At this juncture we cannot venture a guess." No answer, then. "It's still very early in the investigation. All we know for sure is that Mr. Fattal was on that bus, alone, with no entourage. Except for a small briefcase, he had no luggage either. That'll be all for now."

As Katia thanks the Minister, Nadine hugs her handbag to her chest and gets up. "Alright, I'm off," she sniffles and opens the front door.

"Stay, we'll order a pizza. Make an evening of it," says Nancy. I hate when she does that. Condescension doesn't become her.

"Better not," answers Nadine with a straight face. The patronizing words are either lost on her, or she's too weary to retort. "I'm sure you're both busy."

"Listen, take tomorrow off," I say.

Nadine begins to object, but Nancy interrupts her. "Yeah that's a great idea. It'll do you good. Go study."

With a hint of a smile, Nadine nods her goodbyes and walks out, closing the door behind her with a sense of finality.

"Good luck!" I yell, avoiding Nancy's dirty look, which remains fixed on the closed door. Credit music rises on TV. "Well, Minister," says Katia, "you have your work cut out for you. As they say, dead men tell no tales."

"Indeed they don't," he says. "And they tell no lies."

◆

"Flowers are essentially tarts," I say. "Prostitutes for the bees."

Nancy laughs mid-gulp, coughs on her Merlot, takes another sip anyway.

"There is, you'll agree, a certain *je ne sais quoi* about a

83

firm young carrot," she says, continuing the famous line from *Withnail and I*. Then she laughs, loses her balance, and covers it by leaning down to adjust the strap of her heels. I lean on her shoulder, but it gives way and we hobble over each other.

"Man I love that film," I say, pulling us both back to our feet, swallowing the last of my wine.

Back inside, her research binder sits unopened on the kitchen table and the empty bottle of wine next to it. So much for busy. "Anyway, at least tell me a little about your thesis."

"You really want me to bore you with the fornication habits of the fungi kingdom, specifically those indigenous to the mountainous regions of the eastern Mediterranean?"

"Nothing would thrill me more," I say, swiveling around to face the city. I lean on the railing and take in the view. The lower parts of Achrafieh and the Beirut Port shimmer through a light layer of fog.

"It begins with this horny mushroom that has recently, well, mushroomed out of control. It procreated to such an extent that it's become a menace to its ecosystem, leaving nothing in its wake."

"Mushrooms gone wild."

"Decomposer, nutrient cycling, nutrition, whatever. Sure, it has its virtues. But if they're fewer than its vices, then science will consider it a self-serving parasite. Agriculturalists believe mushrooms that behave this way should be eradicated like weeds."

"Farmers, gardeners, they're quick to label anything they don't understand as a weed," I say. "But you know what? Even taxonomists, those bastions of objectivity, name and rename entire species based on sexual behavior. Judging, always judging. Fungi, mushrooms included, get a bad rep."

"What's it with you and taxonomists? Did one drop you on

your head as a child?"

"I can't remember. All I know is from every encounter with those namers, numberers, labelers, scorekeepers, I've come out with a splitting headache. Our work isn't about facts and figures. It's about stories. Look at my Acacia—one of its many great talents is producing its own nitrogen. It enters into a mutually beneficial pact with fungi. They invade its roots and feed on its excess sugar. In return, they provide the Acacia with nitrogen. It travels through grooves inside the tree's bark, creating a whistling sound. Ants live inside these grooves, and transport nutrients along them. That's called interdependence. Like a marriage."

"Like sex," says Nancy. "We're the sex therapists of the plant world. Everyone's doing it. That, we cannot and should not stop. The secret is how to make them do it without resulting in overabundance. There's a reason the verb 'mushroom' means what it does. We just want our mushrooms to control their libido."

"Genetics."

"Linnaeus had it from the get-go when he reclassified plants according to their lineage instead of their leaf patterns. Family name, first name. Right? You taught us that in 101. Strictly speaking no single creature needs to reproduce—it's not like if we don't make love we die, right? But if altogether a species abandons reproduction, it dies out. Just like us, plants are selective. Take your trees. Even while rooted to the spot, the female flower still makes choices. First it chooses not to be entered by pollen from a species too genetically different from itself. But it also rejects pollen from other trees that are too similar."

"Variation is the spice of life," I say, knowing Nancy will appreciate the pun. "It's natural selection."

"Sexual selection, yes. And plants, like humans, aren't self-compatible. Nature made sex the dominant form of reproduction because it mixes genes from different organisms, and so produces variation."

"Naturally."

"My thesis argues that rather than curbing sexual reproduction, what my mushroom needs is proper sex-ed. If for genetic rather than social reasons, it should avoid being incestuous. I've found signs of inbreeding, with wildly unpredictable results. We're talking freakish stuff here. Marry within your sect if you must, but not within your family."

"Sounds familiar."

"Ha ha," she says dryly, nudging my elbow with hers. "Sexual politics are necessary for plant survival, and are what my thesis is all about. Of course it'll state the case in dry academic bullshit phraseology."

"I like how you presented it just now. I think that's exactly how you should state the argument."

"Maybe. I still have a lot of work to do on my case study at school. I sectioned off a square in the field by the girls' dorm to try out a couple of things." Her voice trails off. "Anyway, how was your afternoon?"

"Different."

"Care to tell me more?"

I scan the skyline for Tony's building, but it's only visible from the bedroom. "I did some," I hunt for the word, "sleuthing."

"Ooh. Botany's so fucking sexy."

"And fucking dangerous," I add.

She turns serious. "What on earth do you mean?"

"I'm not sure."

She sets her wine glass on the railing and draws herself behind me, clasps her hands onto my chest. "I'm not letting you go until you tell me everything." She puts her lips to my ear and whispers, "*In vino veritas.*"

◆

"All that happened while I was snoring?" says Nancy. "I should smack you for keeping it from me."

I press my eyelids, but the drowsiness sticks to them like moss. I replace my glasses and say, "I didn't want to worry you. I didn't want to worry myself. I thought the whole thing would come and go. But Nancy, he knew me. My name. My process. He watched me through that telescope. I can't get that out of my head."

"Then do something about it."

"Like what? He was a strange man, and he's dead."

"What was strange about him? He looked normal. His house sounds normal. By all accounts, he seems like he was a perfectly normal guy."

"And that's what makes him strange," I say. "His neighbor called him messy, but his place was spick and span, everything in pristine order. Only the insides of the closets were messy as hell. His name was Tony, yet he spoke with a heavy southern accent, like he's from Saida or Nabatieh. Where would you find a name like Tony in those Muslim places? And his last thought on this earth was that his cat be well-fed."

"Was he delirious?"

"Maybe he really loved his cat. I think it's Persian. White, beautiful, with strangely colored eyes," I say, feeling quite wasted. "Or shit, who knows? Maybe he was delirious. But even so, that doesn't explain the rest. And if he wasn't, that could mean he wanted me to find that journal among the cat food; that maybe there's something important inside. Something about me."

"So who is this guy? You've never seen him before?" says Nancy through wine-stained teeth, which I do not mention. She gets a little crazy with her teeth.

"No, but—" I rush into the bedroom and pick up the picture frame. "Here. I found this by his bed."

"Tsk, tsk, Professor. Stealing?"

"No," I say. "He was spying on me. So I'm gonna keep an eye on him until I find out why."

She takes the frame and squints into it, even tipsier than I am. Then her face contorts and I take a step back, worried she might throw up on me. I don't need any more red stains. But instead she looks up at me with a renewed urgency. "I know him! Shit, I know this guy. He's Nadine's friend. I've seen the two of them skulking around the university."

"Huh? Him?" I say. "I've never noticed him."

"That's because you never notice anyone, Professor. Jesus, that girl, I should've never introduced her to you. I just took pity on her, you know? Thought she could make some extra pocket money, cleaning for you. That little spy. What else do you think she has planned?"

I remember Nadine's flustered search from yesterday morning. "She was looking for someone yesterday. I thought it was a female friend, but it could've been him."

"See how broken up she was about that news report? You don't think she knows that the unnamed victim they were talking about is her friend?"

"She might have a hunch," I say. "But she can't be sure yet. I think she's just worried. He was her friend, and he just disappeared. All over the country everyone's calling up everyone else to make sure they're safe. Brothers to sisters, girlfriends to boyfriends—wait you don't think that's what he was?"

"Her boyfriend? What do you care? And if everyone was

worried about everyone else, why didn't you call me?"

Obviously because I was there and knew you were here, I should say, but I let her question linger, burying my nose in my wineglass.

"Anyway," she says. "I've only seen this Tony guy a couple of times on campus. He used to limp, and was always with *her*."

She tosses the "her" off her tongue like a nasty glob of phlegm. Maybe in Nancy's eyes, that's what Nadine's always been since she first set foot into this house, instantly switching from an apprentice to a nuisance. Before I can ponder that little tidbit further, Nancy makes her way to the sofa and leans against its back near the spot where Nadine sat a few hours earlier.

She pulls out the yellow folder Nadine had with her earlier. I didn't even realize she left it here. The thing is a positively garish pattern of petals, very much at odds with Nadine's austerely elegant fashion. I take an immediate dislike to it and whatever it might contain.

"She forgot this earlier," says Nancy with a touch of malice as she pulls out a stash of printouts. "Maybe there's something here."

"Come on Nancy, let's not go through her stuff."

"No, let's," she says. "It's not as bad as your stealing. And certainly not as bad as her boyfriend's spying."

6
Yellow Folder

I was born in Tartous, a port town on the east coast of Syria. Though I didn't know it at the time, my country was witnessing a period of great flourishing. Lebanon, our neighbor to the south, had been ravaged by its ongoing civil war, so my hometown was the new portal into the Levant.

But with economic growth came a rekindling of an old rivalry between the town's two largest Sunni families, the Toumas and the Akkads. It had ripped through every household, splitting the one-hundred-thousand-strong population in half. As alliances grew more and more rigid, the feud threatened to spark a small-scale civil war.

Ten months before I came to be, a fight between the two families led to the burning down of a house on one side and a death on the other. The heads of the two families realized that drastic measures had to be taken. One moonless night, they met in private with the aim of arriving at an amicable, mutually beneficial arrangement. For several hours, the two men convened, and at the threshold of the locked room, members of both families, weapons drawn, waited with barely suppressed rage. Everyone clamored for blood. As the two men inside negotiated in hushed tones, outside some bet on peace, but most on full-blown war.

When my two grandfathers emerged from that room to announce their peacemaking deal, my fate was sealed. One week later, Zeinab Touma and Mahdi Akkad were wed and exactly nine months later, I was born.

With their union and me as its fruit, Tartous finally emerged from its feudalistic past into the twentieth century, less than two decades before it ended. For four years, Tartous prospered beyond its townsfolk's most outrageous dreams. It's said that for the first time, Toumas and Akkads were seen facing off at backgammon tables at the same *kahwas*, praying in the same mosque, and brokering shipping and import partnerships that minted everyone's fortunes. Profit was shared fifty-fifty, and for once no half was bigger than the other. And before everyone's eyes, my mother Zeinab blossomed from a timid young girl into a matriarch whose household was the hearth where everyone congregated.

I don't recall much from that time, of course, but the few afternoons that I do remember saw our villa vibrate with guests debating the latest import tax increases, their heated but jovial words perfumed with my mother's cooking. My father was there too, always commanding the corner seat like a sphinx. He was the true *assad*, a sage with spectacles halfway down his nose, a silent observer from his corner vantage point. He only ever entered a conversation when it reached an impasse, and with a few choice words he'd steer it in a direction that in hindsight would seem so obvious that the matter would appear to resolve itself. To a child's ears, his words were lost, but the silences in between carried the weight of his wisdom. When he spoke, everyone else shut up and listened.

All the while *Mama* Zeinab would perch in the opposite corner of the *majlis*, surveying it with a prim smile, making sure every plate, every glass, every seat was full or being filled.

Between those two corner sentinels, the entire house was my playground. I bounced from knee to knee, my hair ruffled until my braids would come loose under my veil. I always landed on my father's knee last, for when I did he wouldn't let go. Even in mid-sentence, and without the slightest annoyance, he'd reach under my veil and adjust my hair. The Akkad house may have been Mother's domain, but when it came to me, I was strictly my *Baba* Mahdi's.

He was Sultan and I was his princess. To him, I was the perfect little girl and his embrace was my perfect little world. That the vast unknown outside it was less than perfect, held together by the taut strings of a precarious peace, was a fact my eyes chose to be blind to. Wherever Baba Mahdi went, I went too, trailing behind him like a shadow. No, not like a shadow. I *was* his shadow. I wanted to be his shadow. Everything he did, I did too. Every move, every gesture that was my father's became my own. And as soon as my lips could form them, his every word became mine too.

But Baba had another shadow. Like a tree lit by two suns (and who's to say the universe of Mahdi could not have two suns?), his massive figure was flanked by me on one side and by his younger brother Maurice on the other. Although only two years his junior, Maurice looked nothing like my father.

Their father, Mahdi Sr., who had died long before I was born, made his elder son his namesake—and for good reason. Not only did Baba inherit his name, but also shoulders broad enough to eclipse two men, or as it were, a young man named Maurice and a little girl. To Maurice, on the other hand, my grandfather gave a name that many years later I learned referenced Shakespeare's *Othello*. Mahdi Sr., it's said, publicly joked that Maurice wasn't his son, but rather a fatherless Moor left at his doorstep by the dark-skinned patron saint of infantry soldiers from Egypt, who had favored the Akkads for their fiery power.

That's the stuff of legend, but every myth carries within it a grain of truth, and though no one in Tartous claimed to take his father's words at face value, Maurice lived with their dark undertones. He learned to stare people down with his black Akkadian eyes until he reminded them that he was every bit a part of their line as Baba Mahdi and me. And soon, despite it all, he came to resemble Mahdi, who, hearsay notwithstanding, never made him feel like anything less than flesh and blood. By the time Maurice was an adult, Mother says, Maurice's frail figure and hunched shoulders commanded as much respect as Mahdi's did. And so, the man who could have been my rival for my father's affections came to share them instead. And I loved him for it.

◆

My affection for Maurice grew even more when in my fourth year, I realized that the dignified aura that surrounded him and my father didn't extend to me. Even as a toddler, I knew in my heart that without my father or Maurice, I was just a little girl. An Akkad, for sure, but not an equal. Just as he did his brother, Baba insulated me from the dawning realization of my place in the Akkad world.

Many years later, I learned why.

Mother would tell me the bedtime story of how she and Mahdi came to be husband and wife, how the fabled union buried their parents' strife, but I knew mine was not a story out of Shakespeare. As a Scheherazade living each of her one thousand and one nights as her last, my survival depended on the mercy of the men around me. What my mother failed to mention, or what her lyrical storytelling glossed over, was that even as a seed in her womb, I was already flawed.

I was a girl.

My biology lacked the crucial chromosome that would seal the unwritten treaty between the Akkads and the Toumas and would smother their hatred once and for all. For until Zeinab Touma could give Mahdi Akkad a male child, the bond between our two lines would remain loose. At almost four years old, my 1001 nights were coming to a close and we were all living on borrowed time, on the palm of a demon, as the Arabic saying goes.

"Time is God's greatest gift," Baba would say. "And man must repay Him with patience." In Mahdi's stoic silhouette, the two Tartous families invested all the patience they could muster, and for the first years of my life, we lived in peace.

But if Mahdi was kind to time, time was not kind to him. As our families gathered in the center of Mother's majlis to help me blow out my four candles, from the corner of my eye I could see Baba in his usual spot. Uncle Maurice had his hand on Baba's shoulder, and it might have been a trick of the flickering candlelight, but for once Baba was sunken in his chair, the slight Maurice almost towering over him. He had a handful of crumpled tissues to his mouth and coughed incessantly as we sang.

A few weeks later, most of his jet-black hair had fallen out, and what remained was streaked with a ghostly silver. Over that month, Mother aged several years and a thick fog of melancholy descended upon our house. It grew thicker day after day as our house echoed with the absence of guests. Those weeks should have been the longest of our lives, but instead they rolled by as one foggy dusk rolled into the next. We lived in many days of night, until one morning our house was once again filled to the brim with visitors. Even during Mother's most bustling dinners, her majlis had not seen so many faces and bodies—such that the late arrivals brought their own plastic chairs with them.

But my mighty Baba Mahdi was bedridden, and as, one by one, the guests tiptoed into his chambers to pay their final respects, they were greeted by a face as emaciated as a dried prune peeking from under the blankets. It was the dead of August, yet I could see his lips tremble with every smile he proffered onto his visitors.

Seated on plastic chairs at his bedside, my mother and Uncle Maurice looked Herculean in comparison. Careful not to disturb the delicate silence, as if every breath I took would rob him of his, the bedroom corner was now my haven: from there I watched as Tartousians (both Akkads and Toumas; only for now one and the same) and other assorted relatives from far and near, some familiar some strange, came and went. And to everyone, I was invisible—to everyone but Baba, who between every departure and the following arrival would fix on me an unwavering gaze, still as black and rich and sharp, deep from within the folds of his sunken cheeks. I had not completed my fourth year of being on this Earth, yet already it was shifting under my feet. The only constant was that gaze, and being Baba's daughter was all I knew and could hold on to. In it an infinite power raced against finite time. To me God's greatest gift was a curse. My true gift lay there before me, sinking into the bed as my spirit sank into my stomach.

When the final guest left, Mother closed the bedroom door and reassumed her position at his bedside by Maurice. The two of them then leaned forward, and for several minutes Baba whispered to them. I knew I shouldn't move. Even if I wanted to, I couldn't lest I disturb the delicate stillness that surrounded me. I just squeezed into my corner and watched.

Perhaps Mother is telling him one of her bedtime stories,

I thought, the same story that she's told me since, of the perfect young man and the blushing maiden clutching love from the snares of hate. But she and Maurice were quiet. Only Baba's lips moved, but his voice was gravelly and distant, like a majestic hearse disappearing over the horizon. In the end—for it was the end—Uncle and Mother rose and as they walked out, she turned to me and with a wan smile beckoned me toward her. I freed myself from the corner and leapt onto the bed, half-expecting Baba to catch me. Instead, he gave me a pained smile as he pulled up the covers and I slid underneath them.

I buried my face into his hard moist chest. His raspy breathing mixed with Mama's and Uncle's voices from the other room as they melded together. I didn't care then, but I do now. What they were announcing was that Maurice would take Baba's place as head of the household. He would be Mother's husband, my new Baba, the next link in the chain between the two families.

But at that moment, all I knew was the sweet smell of my father's sweat, his heartbeat against my cheek, and the tender voice of the Sheikh who now sat at his side, reciting verses from the Koran.

And again, the world was perfect. I nuzzled my nose in my father's chest and drifted into a sleep as deep as time.

7

Hypothesis

Indigo creeps through my kitchen window as I rinse out the wine glasses and set them in the sink, too drunk to wash them properly. Nancy's been gone for a few minutes, yet the story we've just read swirls through me with the spell of ages, a faithful companion to my inebriated insomnia.

Leaving my eyeglasses on the countertop, I scratch my head and drag my feet to the CD rack in the bedroom. *Time Out*, no. *Mingus Oh Um*, too close to home. I need a mood-changer. *Lady Sings the Blues*, not today. Then, I find it. I pull a silver CD from a jewel case and stick it in the player. Bill Evans' piano trills out the first notes of *So What*, the opening track of *Kind of Blue*, as I make my way to the Acacia. I slump onto my chair and spray its leaves to keep my mind from wandering.

For Nadine's story to be real, for it to be more than a work of pure imagination, she'd have to be five years older. The timeline is too uncanny, like it belongs to another reality. Nancy would call it a lie. I'd call it fiction.

Paul Chambers' bass thumps onto the soundtrack as I lay down the water sprinkler and study my reflection in the window-pane, a perfect mirror against the approaching dawn. My eyes seem sunken, like a whole lifetime has passed since morning. I reach into my jacket pocket for the yellow sheet of paper, and lay it flat on my desk. "Come, he hath hid himself among these trees," read Tony's cursive.

Bass and piano enter into a call and response, singing back and forth to one another. I lean the photo of Tony and the woman in the wheelchair against the Acacia pot. The window frames my own face with the laughing duo in the photo, but I switch off the lamp and the reflection fades into the Geitawi skyline. Tony's apartment window flickers across the "humorous night" as it too melts into another dawn.

But the telescope persists, eyeing me like a rifle as Miles' muted trumpet floats through my bedroom. No time to sleep.

◆

Two hours later, it's raining again and I roll up the windows of my Volvo. The wipers work overtime, screeching against the windshield. It's Wednesday morning, but traffic is light—after all the country is in mourning—which keeps my unease in check. Water pellets the sunroof, counterpointing the piano trill of *All Blues*, the fourth track on my *Kind of Blue* cassette. I've had the album on repeat, first at home and now in my car, as I struggle to focus more on task and less on consequence. Action now, thought later. Again and again I play this mantra through my weary mind, trying hard not to let it fall back on my neglected article.

I make my way up the hill and pass ABC Mall, a slight turn off Sassine Square brings me onto Istiklal Boulevard at a steady pace. As the track ends and the tape pops out, the radio comes on automatically. A laconic voice filters through the car speakers. "But the question remains," says the man. "Why was a prominent figure like Doreid Fattal traveling on a public bus, so early in the morning, and without his bodyguards? This suggests he acted under duress and then was ambushed.

We must concentrate on this angle, that whoever is behind the murder knew the particulars of his itinerary."

Then a female interviewer takes over, "We're always quick to point the finger at the Syrian Secret Service, but every time it's the prime suspect in an assassination, subsequent investigation always reveals it was innocent."

"It depends which investigations you mean, Miss. In politics, the notion of 'innocent until proven guilty' doesn't exist, and furthermore—"

I turn the dial. Another voice, "Israel is the prime beneficiary. The Mossad—"

Passing Baydoun Mosque to my right and Nazareth School to my left, I spin the dial again. "The most obvious suspect in a murder is usually not the one behind it. That's a game that—"

Switch. "And then in 1982 when Israel—" switch "—and so Syria is—"

My cell phone rings and I switch off the radio. "Hey. Yeah, I'm driving there now," I say. "Hold on." I hit the speakerphone button and stick the phone in my dashboard ashtray just in time to avoid the policeman in his impermeable overcoat loitering by the side of Chili's restaurant.

Nancy's enthusiasm crackles through the phone's jangly speaker. "Don't you fucking love Beirut when there's rain and no traffic? We found a taxi in, like, an instant!" she says. "Wait, my brother makes me put two thousand in the pretend jar every time I curse. Plunk, there. Yeah okay, Jesus, Rony! Hey Professor, I'm putting you on speaker too."

"Hello there Rony," I say. "How's my man doing?"

"Professor," he says with a timbre that could almost be Nancy's. "There's a lot of rain today, twelve centimeters. That's double the amount we had last week, two and a half times more than last summer."

"Twelve centi isn't enough. Too much for driving, too little for drowning."

Nancy comes back on. "I'm gonna take Rony to afternoon school later, so he'll be tagging along until then."

"Tag along tag along," Rony echoes in the background. "Tagalog, tagalog, Filipina!"

"But you know what?" Nancy interrupts.

"No, but I'm sure you'll tell me," I say.

"You bet your ass I will. Hold on, Rony, that's not a swear! So Professor, good news. When we got to Charles Helou Station, the police had just left. The teller was all greased up and ready to talk."

"Great. So what did you find out?"

"Wait, I'm putting you on Bluetooth," she says, her voice now more full. "Turns out you were right. Our friend Tony didn't board from Charles Helou. He got on at the second stop, closest to his house." Her voice lowers to a whisper and I strain against the rain to hear her. "But guess who was on the Charles Helou roster?" she says. "Doreid Fattal. Things are crazy on this end, but that means the second station should be fuzz-free."

"That is good news," I say, coming off formal. It may be fun for Nancy, but I fail to see the humor of the situation. "I'm almost there."

"The police confiscated the roster but the teller had a carbon copy. He said Fattal arrived on foot all alone and just bought a ticket like a normal civilian. He was so nonchalant the teller didn't even realize who it was until the news broke."

"Fattal was hiding in plain sight."

"Doesn't sound like someone under duress," she says. Her taxi must have been playing the same news reports.

"True," I say. "It seems he was calm and collected. Very good, Nancy."

"Elementary, my dear Watson," she says.

I laugh. "So I'm the sidekick in this detective game of yours?"

"Hey! Whose idea was it to stake out the stations, huh? And who used her deadly feminine charms to get you the intel on Fattal?"

"You, you. It's all you," I say, feigning exasperation. "Okay, I'll see you two this afternoon. I've arrived."

◆

I find a spot near the station and park the car. The rain has subsided to a light shower now, but I still wish I left home with an umbrella. Hitching my jacket above my head, I jump out of the Volvo and pass a sign reading "Damascus Road" and an olive-green bike secured to its post. Nancy was right: Tony was here.

I cross the street into the station, wipe the water off my shoulders, and lean against the counter of the ticket booth. "Good morning," I yell into the window in the most buoyant tone I can muster.

A teller looks up. "This line's closed today," he says. "I'm on my way out." He's as uncomfortable as I am.

"I just have a question," I say. "A friend of mine bought a ticket yesterday morning. Damascus bus."

The teller's face sags. "Damascus," he says. "That bus. That. Bus. I know nothing."

"The police took the roster?" I say, wishing Sherlock was here to work her charm.

"It's not that. The police weren't interested in the list. They just wanted the number of passengers."

Face-to-face with the ineptness of Lebanese public service, my fervor takes a blow. "Please," I say. "I lost someone on that bus. A skinny, darkish young man. Anything you can tell me about what he did, or maybe said? He has a southern accent."

At that last bit, the teller's eyes light up. "Yeah. The guy from Nabatieh, my hometown! Nice fellow," he says, as I realize the teller has a faint accent, but then his eyes fall again before I can capitalize on the unexpected stroke of luck. "God, I just can't believe... You're not from there too, are you? You don't sound southern."

"I was born in Nabatieh," I answer candidly. Never lie more than you need to. "But when the war broke out, my parents sent me to boarding school here."

"Those were hard times for the South," he says, and, noticing my restlessness, switches gears again. "Your friend rode in on that green bike out there. Caught the first bus in the nick of time."

He pulls out a clipboard, flips to the previous page and slides it across the counter. "Here," he says, pointing to the roster. I scroll through the list. Among the four names, one catches my eye. "Tony," no last name. It's barely a sign-up sheet at all.

The teller cuts through my reverie. "Is he on it?"

I nod.

"Smart of you to come here," he says gravely. "Easier than going through the official channels I suppose. Wait, one more thing." He disappears into the room and a moment later emerges through the door. "He forgot this," he says, handing me a dark brown blazer. Ripped and bloody at the elbow, a fact that if the teller notices, he doesn't mention. "It rang a second after he was gone," he says instead. "I chased him but he was late. Ran after the bus and I couldn't keep up. God knows, if I caught him he might still be alive." The teller loses his train of thought again. Twice the kid had a chance to forestall his fate, and twice it found him.

"Did you say 'it rang'?" I ask, but the teller just gazes into the distance.

In a daze, I grab the blazer and step out. The sky has cleared and the sun has broken through the clouds. I unfurl the blazer and inspect it front and back. As I lower it, I catch another glimpse of the olive-green bike, once Tony's, now a piece of wet junk with a bruised basket and a crooked wheel at an obscene angle.

From the blazer pockets, I pull out a half-open pack of Lucky Strikes with a cigarette missing, a Bic lighter, a passport, and a dead cell phone. I flip through the passport to the front page. Under Tony's familiar face, I read an unfamiliar name: Tariq Mahmoud Jaber.

◆

Classroom 2B is empty. I wipe out the notes next to my Acacia chart, then write "Tony (Tariq)" and inscribe it in a green rectangle. On the desk behind me sit the items I picked up this morning, the passport open to the photo and the name of one Tariq Mahmoud Jaber, age twenty-one, born in Nabatieh.

No surprises there. Correction: no new surprises, only the fact that he had intended to travel with his passport that morning and that his final destination could very well have been Syria. While this is perhaps insignificant as far as the media is concerned, it might help in unraveling the ball of thread this young man's final moments are turning out to be.

On the other side of the desk, Tony's (Tariq's?) blazer lies crumpled with the dead cell phone. Back on the whiteboard, I draw another box, label it "Syria," and connect it to the first. He was bound for Damascus, but we don't know if that was his final destination or not.

And on the way he was intercepted twice by—"ME," which I capitalize and label with a large question mark. The door to the classroom opens and Nancy walks in quietly, followed by her brother Rony. "Exam study week and national mourning," she says. "It's a fucking ghost campus, huh? Can you hear the silence?"

Rony promptly shatters it. "That's eleven curses. Twenty-two thousand liras today!" he yells, arms raised in triumph, and runs to the workbench in the back of the classroom. "I'm rich! I'm wealthy! I'm independent! I'm socially secure!" He does a decent Daffy Duck impression, but more than cartoons, he loves beakers, especially the graduated ones. He grabs one and ogles its numbers with delight.

Everything that is countable, he counts. Anything that isn't, he can't be bothered with. If Nancy says she loves him, he's unmoved. If she says she loves him as much as there are fish in the sea, he's enraptured, then feverishly explicates that fish are being depleted, so instead he loves her as much as there are mollusks, a much more populous phylum than fish. I used to believe Alfred Nobel's wife had an affair with a mathematician, until I looked it up and learned he was never married. Either way, history has shortchanged Rony, because if the prize did exist for mathematics, he'd have had a fighting chance one day. As it is, he's resigned to wasting his teenage years at an afternoon school for gifted children, watercoloring pitched-roof houses and playing Twister.

"So, what did you find out?" asks Nancy.

"As we expected, Tariq boarded from the Basta station, apparently in such a hurry he left his blazer behind." I nod toward the desk. "But check it out."

She finds the passport and lifts it to her face. "Holy fuck," she says, her cheeks quivering. "Are you shitting me? A secret identity." Nancy checks Rony at the back of the classroom, but he's too distracted by the workbench and lab equipment to fine her for swearing. She flips through the little booklet. "And look at these pages. All empty, but for a single entry stamp to Syria four years ago."

"What do you make of it?" I say. "If he's only been once, why go again after all this time, under these conditions, in this lousy weather? It can't just be for fun. Trade? Or some affiliation, maybe?"

"Hmm. I'd like to think there's something besides money and politics left in this country." She lays the passport back on the desk. "Another girlfriend perhaps?" she says, her tone almost hopeful.

"Maybe. I found some girl stuff in his apartment, but no clothes, no toothbrush. Nothing suggests she lived there or visited him for any length of time. So my guess is, the girlfriend's local."

Nancy picks up the cell phone. "Did you go through this?"

"It's dead."

"A Nokia huh? Hold on," she says, then rummages through her handbag and pulls out a charger. "When you spend as much time as I do in the field you learn to stay equipped. Just give it a few minutes." The phone beeps as Nancy circles toward me and rubs her forehead. "I've got a headache from all that radio in the cab," she says. "This thing's turned everyone into conspiracy theorists. Us too."

"Maybe."

"What do you mean?"

"We're scientists," I say. "And what do scientists love?"

"A good hypothesis."

"Exactly. Now let's hypothesize for a minute. What if Doreid Fattal wasn't the target?"

"But who else would it be? They're saying he was shot point blank. That it was a precise, professional job."

"Or maybe a clumsy, amateur job. People only see what they're looking for. They all see one thing…"

Nancy finishes my thought, "…because they're all looking in the same direction."

"Neither of us is an expert," I say. "But even experts make mistakes. Since the civil war Kalashnikovs are everywhere. Even my father has one—a gift from a satisfied patient if you can believe it. Throw a stone in Lebanon and you hit someone with a Kalashnikov, who'd then probably shoot you." Nancy laughs as I add, "One thing about those guns: they're very imprecise."

"But the news said Fattal was shot once," she says, tapping her forehead emphatically. "Clean between the eyes. You know, execution style."

"We interpret an incident not from what it is, but from what we assume it is," I say, squeezing Nancy's arms. "If something happened a certain way once or twice in the past, that doesn't mean it'll happen the same way a third and fourth time."

Nancy studies my face intently, egging me on.

"So if we let go of our assumptions for a moment," I continue, "this same incident could mean something else entirely." I release her arms and clutch a whiteboard marker; a pointing device comes in handy when I lecture. "If you want to shoot a big guy like Doreid Fattal with such a messy weapon, to guarantee a fatal shot you'd have to—"

"Pakhpakhpakhapakh," she mimics a machine gun. "I'd let the goddamn thing rip! All over him. Several rounds." I enjoy her little demonstration, but an instant later she seems to remember we're talking about a real person, and she drops her arms.

"That's right," I say. "However in this case, the Kalashnikov could've been a weapon of opportunity,"—I heard that expression on a police show once—"something the killer was just able to get his hands on at the time."

"You suppose the murder was a spur of the moment thing?"

I point the marker in her direction. "That, my dear, is a distinct possibility."

"So you think someone else was the target?"

"No, not just 'someone' else," I say. "My hypothesis is that the target was none other than Tariq Jaber, the man of multiple identities."

"The man who was watching, stalking, notating you," she says with dramatic flair. "The man who died in your arms. Egotistical theory, even for you, Professor."

"Maybe, but it makes sense. Of the countless murders in recent memory, how many were performed this way? In Lebanon, when it comes to solving problems, the method of choice is usually a bomb. Both Fattal and Tariq were in the back of the bus and the door in the front was open, so the killer had to go through everyone to get to them. That makes one of them the primary target. According to the news, Fattal was only shot once. I saw Tariq; he was shot several times in the chest. He had no chance of surviving."

"That makes sense," says Nancy. "Imprecise, but a sure way of killing someone."

"But there's one more thing," I say, then instantly regret it. I'd rather keep something this uncertain to myself, but Nancy is too excited to allow me to renege mid-sentence. "Tariq said 'Where is she?' *She*. I'm positive. It's clear on the tape."

"Yes, but?" says Nancy, hanging on every word. I like that.

"But yesterday," I continue, "even the neighbor knew the cat is male. If he loved his pet so much it was his dying thought, would he call *him* a *she*?"

"You're right, he wouldn't. We usually refer to cats as 'she,' but only when we don't know their sex. But if the neighbor wasn't close to Tariq yet knew his cat was male, it's likely because Tariq referred to it as such, not because she, you know, happened to check its balls."

"I thought that Tariq was just delirious at the end," I say. "I thought that his dying wish was simply that the cat be full and well-fed, silly as that sounds. But now, I think his last words were perfectly lucid."

"Which would mean the 'she' is someone else, not the cat," says Nancy. "But how can you be sure he was aware of what he was saying?"

"I can't be sure, but I believe he was," I say. Believe—the dirty word that only two days ago I mocked Chairman Ramala for using, has now escaped my own lips. Nancy doesn't take note of my slip, but I feel like I've slipped out of myself with it.

"He knew his request would lead me to his house, to that armoire," I say. "He wanted me to understand something crucial, something hidden in his journal." I phrase my words carefully—I got myself into this minefield of fancy and should now get myself out. "There's a reason he died on that road, and there's a reason I was there."

"*Et tu*, Professor? You speak of destiny? Really? Imagine if it turns out the fate of the world really does hang in your balance."

Click, I've stepped right on a landmine. "Forget fate. That's just a mumbo jumbo excuse people use to blame an invisible entity for what happens to them. No, this is destiny. We make it happen ourselves, and we take full responsibly for its cause and effect, its action and reaction. One naturally and scientifically follows the other. But if this 'she' isn't the cat, then who—"

The cell phone beeps.

"Hey, it's on!" says Nancy and hops toward it. "Let's see

what secrets Miss Nokia's been carrying inside her." She goes through the phone listings. "Hmm. Take-out pizza, pizza, and more pizza. He was a bachelor alright."

"Not just a bachelor. I'm a bachelor." She gives me her signature dirty look and I immediately correct myself. "You know, I mean an unwed man, but I still have a pot and pan. You should've seen the man's kitchen. Bare. His entire apartment was bare. Like he's a sniper stationed at a post."

"His call log's pretty bare too. Dialed numbers, nothing. Received calls, nothing. Not a very sociable guy. Made no calls."

"Or a very careful guy. Made calls then wiped them clean. Check the text messages."

"Already on it," she says. "Sent messages, nothing. Received messages—holy crap." She drops the phone to her side and looks up at me, blood drained from her face.

"What?" I snatch the phone. No name, just a number and a date: November 16th, 4:32 a.m., the morning Tariq Jaber died. I read the text message below it, "Leaving home now. We meet first bus, back seat. D."

"Doreid," says Nancy.

I turn back to my chart and write "Doreid," then next to it Tariq's last words. As I circle the "she," Nancy snatches the marker. "Would you leave that board for a second?" she says. "Can't you see how huge this is? A man's life isn't a chart of facts and figures."

Turning to Tariq's journal, I flip it open and indicate the charts. "Then what do you make of these?" I say.

Nancy snatches it from my hands. "Hey, Rony," she says. "Come here for a sec."

He returns the measuring glass to the workbench and approaches his sister. "Let me see, let me see," he says, closing the journal and reopening it to the front.

One by one, he leafs through its pages, running his index finger along the center of each, then pinching each corner with the precision of a pair of tweezers and flipping to the next. Nancy watches with pride as he goes through the whole thing, then closes it and says, "Constellations, star constellations."

I know that, but don't interrupt. And as I expect he has more—much more—to say. "These are maps of the sky, star triangulations. In search of Maurice. Maurice, Maurice, Maurice, Maurice. Twenty-two times. Different space, but same time. You and I, Professor, we cannot exist in the same space. Space is unique. But we share time."

Nancy edges closer to her brother, "Your mind works fast, Rony. But try and speak slow, OK? So we understand what you're saying."

Rony reaches for a beaker sitting on the windowsill and turns to me. "See these?" he says, pointing to the scale. "Here it says 500 milliliters. If I fill it with water, I have 500 milliliters of water. 500 units. But if I erase the numbers and change the scale to centiliters, I'll still have the same amount, only now I'd say I have 50 centiliters. 50 units. Fewer numbers but no less water."

He glances at Nancy, then back at me and continues. "Even if I lie, or even if the numbers change, the volume of water inside remains constant, because I've established that the beaker can contain a certain volume, no more, no less." Having served its purpose, he returns the beaker to the windowsill then takes the marker from Nancy and turns to the whiteboard. It seems I'm not the only lecturer in the room.

"That beaker is like a clock," he says, sketching what could be a beaker or a clock, but looks like neither. "Space is a thing, but time is just a measurement, a number. Einstein said we only need it so everything doesn't happen at once." He taps his watch. "Right now it's 4:33 in the afternoon here, also in Nicosia, even

Istanbul, but it's later in other places. It's 8:03 in the evening in Mumbai, and 11:33 at night in Tokyo. At the South Pole, it's past midnight the next day."

Nancy and I nod in tandem.

"So if I ask a Cypriot or a Turkish boy to meet me at my afternoon school at 5:00 p.m., we'd all arrive on schedule. But if I ask an Indian boy, a Japanese boy, or a boy from the South Pole, we'd arrive at different times and miss each other, even though the learning center is the same school. I'd have to tell all the boys to meet me in 27 minutes, then we all get there together."

As I grin inwardly at the image of young boys from various cities all over the globe converging in that one shoddy schoolhouse, Nancy pats her brother's shoulder and says, "Space can be absolute, but time is always relative."

Rony beholds her with love, like a stranger meeting a compatriot in a foreign land. "Now is simply the time you utter the word 'now,'" he says. "Paradoxically, because of this relativism, time is a more accurate method of measurement than space, which is relative to nothing, with no frame of reference." He turns to me. "Would you mind some history, Professor?"

He sounds just like his sister. "Not at all," I say.

"Astronomy was born in the Fertile Crescent many years BC, during the Akkadian Empire," says Rony. "Along with mathematics, it's one of the oldest sciences, but it was only used to observe the stars and mark time. Their calendar was based on both lunar and solar cycles, and was so complicated that each year the total number of months was decided by royal decree."

Nancy takes a seat in the front row, and I watch Rony in complete astonishment as he lectures on.

"It wasn't until the fifth century when Muslim scholars became folk-astronomers. They were distinct from the royals and officials, just people like you and me. For them the stars were a blessing, and a clear, star-filled sky was a good omen. They dreaded empty space, a peculiarity called *horror vacui*, and took an interest in the stars not to divine their cosmic fate, as the Akkadians did, but to regulate life here, on earth, in our daily lives, every day as we live it."

He taps the whiteboard with the marker, leaving a cluster of tightly spaced green dots. He's come undone again, like he's stuck. But Nancy knows what to do: she springs out of her chair and lays her hand on his, until his grip on the marker relaxes and his white knuckles turn pink.

"So these are people, right?" she says, indicating the dots. Then hovering her palm over the whiteboard she adds, "And this is the world."

"Yes," says Rony. "Muslim astronomers developed a system of spherical geometry to determine the qibla direction toward Mecca and the prayer timetable. If you know those two things, you can pray in the correct orientation and at the correct time wherever you are and whatever time zone you're in."

I pull up Tariq's journal. "The charts in here, is that what they're for?"

"Yes," says Rony. "With Islam, astronomers were no longer just hocus-pocus fortune tellers, but useful members of society. Folk astronomy is actually quite easy, as you can see in that journal. You use your location, your qibla orientation, and the time you pray. If you have two of the three, you can find the third. All you need is simple observation and a few calculations."

"So which two did the writer of this journal have?" I ask.

Rony takes the journal and flips to a page in the middle. "See this diagram here? That's the answer." He sketches it on the whiteboard and taps one of the vertices. "Suppose this is Maurice's location." He taps another vertex. "And suppose this is the writer." Rony flips to another page and reads from it and says, "There's a passage of text here, 'I kneel to pray, toward the Ancient Road, where God planted us but four minutes apart.'"

"It's beautiful. Do you know what it means?" asks Nancy from her front row seat, looking very much like the studious college senior she was less than a year ago.

"I think it's from a poem or a letter," says Rony. "See? It says Maurice again next to it. But to the journal's writer, it's more than that. It's directions. The writer starts from the poem to search for Maurice."

"How?" asks Nancy.

I'm stumped, but Rony has already figured out the answer. "In the absence of a proper reference, one would pray toward the main road leading to Mecca."

"The Ancient Road," I say. "The road to Damascus."

"Yes. That was Maurice's qibla orientation," says Rony. "Then using the relative time mentioned in the poem, the 'when,' the writer sought out his location, the 'where.'"

I take a step toward Rony. "The 'when' was the poem's four minutes, right?"

"Yes," he says. "The most accurate way to determine someone's location is with time difference. Official time zones are practical but sketchy. In reality, for every shift in degree of longitude, time shifts precisely four minutes."

Another digression. Eyes fixed on him, Nancy walks to the whiteboard in another effort to keep him on track. "What does that tell us?" she says.

But this was no digression; this time Rony knows exactly where he's going. "In the 'when' and 'where' equation," he says, "Damascus is the 'where.' That's where Maurice is."

"Stunning," says Nancy. "Rony, you're stunning."

I agree silently: if Tariq Jaber intended for me to discover something, this is it.

Rony sets the marker down and shrugs off Nancy's compliment. "Beirut is located at thirty-five degrees. That's the longitude. Damascus is in the same time zone, practically speaking, but it's four minutes later, one degree away. There are two people in that poem, the writer and the recipient. Time moves from east to west, but since the poem only says 'apart,' not later or before, we don't know who's east and who's west. So if the writer is here, the person he wrote to is there."

"Tariq was on his way from *here* to Damascus to meet a man called Maurice *there*," I say.

Rony lays the notebook back on the desk as Nancy watches him proudly and says, "It's written in the stars."

I nod. "It doesn't sound as saccharine when it's literal."

"Professor, Rony and I are off to the learning center, then I'm heading back to collect some more mushroom samples before dark. *Bshufak bukra*. See you tomorrow."

As they walk out, she ruffles her brother's hair and says, "Whoever said you're incapable of lateral thinking is a dick."

"You said dick," says Rony. "But this time, you get it for free."

◆

On the whiteboard, a line connects the word "Doreid" to the word "Tariq." He was on a journey to Damascus to meet a man called Maurice. He'd been searching for that man for many months. We know that now, but Doreid's involvement remains a mystery.

I walk around the desk for a broader view of my handiwork. Without Nancy and Rony, the classroom is empty and clinical: the Acacia chart on one side, the Tariq chart on the other, and the late afternoon sun streams through the line of windows onto the desk between them.

Chewing the tip of the red marker, I scan the classroom. Just yesterday it was filled with students: some attentive, some lazy, some dozing off. Young men and women of different colors and shapes, skin tones and hair shades. Eyes blue, green, brown, black, and hazel. Noses Roman, Greek, Arab, even Jewish. Breathing patterns thick, thin, fast, slow, and nervous. My classroom is a melting pot of national identities. Even now in its silent emptiness, the walls echo with their motley voices. Sir this. Sir that. Peter, Rawia, Ahmed, Souraya, Omar, Janette.

"Sir," asked Janette. "If the Acacia is so well connected, then why is it never seen in this region?" I repeat her question, and in my own voice I take it more seriously. Yesterday I gave her a generic throwaway response. I bite down harder on the nib of the red marker.

Today, I should have a more relevant answer. With that, I turn back toward the board and look down at Tariq's possessions: the passport with its alternate name, his brown blazer, and the cell phone, which Nancy left on its sleeve.

"It rang a second after he was gone," I speak the bus station teller's words. Yes, that's what he said—in my confusion I didn't pay much attention. I set the marker down on the desk, pick up the cell phone, take a deep breath, and hit Menu. I scroll down to the appropriately named Missed Calls, the one thing Nancy and I missed.

One person had called. Three times. All missed. "Nounz." I hit the green button and the phone dials. It rings a long time. Through heavy background noise, a female voice answers, "*Allo? Meen?* Who?"

"*Allo,*" I say, my voice breaking. For a few seconds, the background noise comes through again. It sounds like traffic. Then she hangs up and I lay the phone back on the desk.

"Where is she?" I echo Tariq's final words. Better not call again just now. My chart is filled with squares, circles, and lines, all leading to Tariq. "A man's life isn't a chart of facts and figures." I repeat Nancy's words as I wipe Tariq's half of the board clean and sit at the desk. From my messenger bag at its foot, I take out my memoir and pen.

I open to an empty page and start to write, "On the morning of November 16th, Tony awoke from a bad dream…"

◆

"He climbed onto the bus, made his way to the very back and took a seat next to a heavyset man."

Setting my pen down on my memoir, I slide my fingers under my glasses and push into my eyelids. When I open them I find myself back home at my desk. The window reflects the same face, but now sunken and morose. To my side, sit my tape recorder and the framed photograph of the two smiling people at the foot of my bandaged Acacia, today looking a little better.

Its branches partly obscure the doorway and through them my TV flickers with a blue hue. At a low volume comes the frantic overlap of dialogue that only a pack of clamoring reporters could produce. At the center of all the noise and people stands a woman in her forties, her face a subtle canvas unmarred by makeup, cheekbones chiseled and lips heart-shaped—all features that would suggest a staggeringly beautiful woman to a less indifferent eye. However, the upper half of her face is obscured by sunglasses, completely at odds with the setting, and a thin white veil characteristic of Arab women in mourning, which leaves much to the imagination.

But even with so much of her concealed, I recognize her immediately. As she speaks, I walk through the doorway into my living room. I pick up the remote from the arm of my couch with my half-eaten cornflakes-with-milk dinner and raise the volume.

"And I'd like to thank both the Lebanese public and the media for your tremendous outpouring of condolences and support," she says. "Doreid Fattal was a son of the South and of all of Lebanon. The funeral will be held tomorrow in Downtown Beirut, the heart of our Nation, followed by a private reception at the Mansion."

A hand shoots through the thicket. "We learned that your daughter Miss Lama canceled her flight back to Paris," asks a young reporter. "Are there plans that she run for office?"

Mrs. Fattal replies in the manner of a seasoned politician, accommodating but never to a fault. "Lama will pay her final respects to her father," she says. "But she'll fly back to Paris immediately afterwards. I believe the Parliament will meet on Monday to name a candidate to fill my late husband's seat." She glances over her shoulder at the Minister of Interior, standing right behind her, and he nods in confirmation. "But no, in light of these events, we've made our decision. It will not be a Fattal."

Another reporter follows instantly. "Mrs. Fattal, what do you say to speculations that Syria is behind the murder?" she says in rapid fire, squeezing three words in the space of one. "And if so, which one? The Syria of the regime or that of the Free Syrian Army? What if—"

Another younger reporter cuts her off. "Following the public outcry for sanctions," he says, ramming his microphone a few inches past her nose, toward Mrs. Fattal. "We expect more than one million Lebanese to hit the streets tomorrow in protest." Suspended between a declaration and a question, the reporter's voice trails off as the crowd mumbles in apparent agreement.

Once again Mrs. Fattal glances at the Minister, who

shoulders his way forward and leans over the podium into the microphones. "We understand everyone's devastated," he says. "Everyone's angry. But as the face of the government, it's our duty to keep a clear mind. It's our duty to keep the peace. We don't create lack of order. We preserve it."

The crowd snickers at this and the voices begin to rise again. Realizing his mistake, the Minister shrinks behind the microphones for an instant but then reemerges, his face softer and his tone more casual. "I mean, well—listen, we've all suffered a great loss, Syria included." He hushes the outburst of objections—perhaps to his ambiguous use of the word "Syria"—with a wave of his hand and continues. "We all know that as a young man Mr. Fattal made his fortune there in the Syrian mining industry and was a close friend of both the Syrian ruling party and the Syrian people. Of Alawites, Shias, and Sunnis alike."

The mob of reporters goes wild with protest at his speech, but the Minister's amplified voice drowns them out. "Still, we're not ruling out any possibilities. We have new evidence, and believe very soon we'll have all we need to bring the culprit to justice. Whether Israeli, Syrian, or whatever, Maltese. Yes, final question."

A red-faced male reporter presses his pen into his cheek and with a faux-intellectual grimace asks the Minister if he'd mind sharing some of this evidence with the public?

The Minister collects his thoughts then speaks in a single, well-rehearsed burst of verbosity. "We have reasons to believe that Mr. Fattal was meeting someone that morning. Whether on this or the Syrian side of the border, we cannot be sure yet. However, we have a name and we believe this person is the key to the ambush. Thank you."

He wraps his hand around Mrs. Fattal's forearm and

escorts her away from the podium as the pack of reporters bark questions. "Who is this person?" "Why was Mr. Fattal on that bus?" "Why was he alone?" "Was he having an affair?"

At this last question, Mrs. Fattal breaks away from the Minister's grip and edges back to the podium. She cranes her neck toward the microphones as the hubbub subsides. "I ask for your discretion," she says. Her voice betrays a note of the sorrow concealed behind her sunglasses. "Early on November 16th, my husband left the house unescorted and drove our daughter's car to the bus station. He then took the bus, I believe, to shed the cover of diplomacy that shrouds the car, his person, and our lives. My husband was on a private mission, of what nature, I don't know. But it was not an affair."

A babble brews in the crowd again, but the Minister silences it with an authoritative glare. Mrs. Fattal continues. "All we ask for is your respect as his family mourns. For everyone else, it should be midweek business as usual. No amount of idle chatter or lurid gossip can bring him back, or change the facts: Doreid Fattal gave a lot to this country, and finally, he gave his life." She wipes her nose and concludes, "He was a faithful husband and an honest man. Honor the man by honoring his memory."

Taking over Mrs. Fattal's microphone, the Minister squeezes in for a coda. "The past is always distorted by the lens of the present," he says. I think that rather poignant and make a mental note of it, but the Minister immediately follows it with a tired cliché. "Remember Doreid Fattal not by how he died, but how he lived. That's the true measure of a man."

The TV image wobbles, shrinks, and disappears into a dot as the remote hits the couch with a faint thump. Back at my bedroom desk, I continue writing, "With a puff of black smoke and the first roar of thunder, the bus toward Damascus began its journey."

Scratching a line across the bottom of the page, I lay my pen down on the desk and flip back a few pages. The pages I just wrote fit neatly in succession to my own account of November 16th as I experienced it. Now the two coinciding versions of the same day, Tariq's and mine, follow each other.

Someone—I think it was Kierkegaard in one of Nancy's books—said that life can only be understood backwards. Tariq died on the road to Damascus and I was there to see it happen. From that certainty, the road splinters into two uncertain paths: mine proceeds toward the future, his recedes through the past. His life ended just as my investigation into his life began. At the instant of his death, time fractured and folded back onto itself. The farther into my future I go, the further into the recesses of his past I enter. What led to the solid fact of his death and what will follow it are fragile reckonings. Why and how Tariq died are as much a riddle as where and when I might learn the answer.

For now, the memoir flips shut on the question, sealing it between its covers for another day, as the two faces in the picture frame gaze back at me from a different place and time. The photo is only slightly yellowed and the glass cracked in the corner, but it's otherwise pristine—a fraction of a second plucked from memory and encased in wood and glass. Tariq, the woman, and one more person: the photographer, who I now realize casts a diagonal shadow across the corner of the photo, where a signature would be.

Laying the frame face down on the desktop, I unhook the rusty metal hinges holding the frame and pull it off. The back of the print says "Kodak Kodak Kodak" in diagonal letters, and within it a printed set of numbers that dates the photograph at four years ago. One corner of the print remains tucked into the edge of the frame, so I scrape at it until it comes loose but my finger slices open on the cracked glass, tingeing it with a streak of red.

In the revealed corner, a line of ballpoint cursive letters reads, "My morning star, your evening star, forever one, forever light. M."

Flipping the photograph to the front again, the young man and woman now strike me as serene, at peace, luminous. But, like a distant star that has burned out many years ago, their light is delayed and portentous. In the photograph, the blurry line separating earth from sky undulates above their faces along three valleys and two hills. My finger follows its soft contour up and down, then up and down again. As I recognize the rhythm from a distant childhood memory, blood drips from my finger and smears the glossy surface of the photo. I watch it for a moment then pull out my phone and hit the green button twice.

"Done with the mushroom hunt?" I say. "Good. Get some rest. Tomorrow morning, we take a road trip."

8
Righting Reflex

He loaded the last box onto the back of the truck as the young man went back into the house. He blew out a puff of smoke and limped into the middle of the yard. The spring landscape stretched out before him, several meters below. This was Ibrahim's favorite season of the year, harvest time. Of course it's been years since he's farmed his own land, since the accident that almost cost him his life. A small price to pay. This land has paid much more over the years.

But now there was peace and quiet, at least for the time being. A good day for a drive, he thought, as he lit another cigarette with the dying tip of the first. The swing, a few meters away, creaked on its hinges as it blew gently in the wind.

"I think that's all," said Tariq Jaber as he lifted another box labeled 'books' onto the back of the truck. "But Ibrahim, I need your help with something in the—"

A sound interrupted him. Ibrahim had lost most of his hearing in the explosion many years ago, so all his senses could do now were piggyback on Tariq's. "Look," said the young man, and Ibrahim's eyes traced his outstretched arm toward the tree by the archway.

And then the sound came again. He heard it now. A meow. Both men looked further up and indeed, there on the treetop was the cat. It was stuck there helpless, the branch quivering with its frightened body a few centimeters from the third-story window.

"Why doesn't it just jump in?"

"It's too timid," said Ibrahim. "It doesn't know how."

"Wait," said Tariq as he disappeared back into the kitchen.

Ibrahim looked up at the terrified cat and in a few moments he saw Tariq's head poke out from the window at the top. He reached for the cat, his fingers almost touching it. "I. Can't. Quite..." he heaved, his upper body leaning perilously out of the opening.

"Hold on," said Ibrahim. He dropped his cigarette, pushing it into the dirty asphalt with the heel of his shoe. He limped to the pickup truck and reached into the back, easily pulling out a queen-sized mattress. He was glad his upper body strength still served him well as he laid it flat at the foot of the tree under the window.

"Okay, try again!" he yelled up to the young man. "Careful now!"

Tariq stretched his torso as far as it would go, but his fingers barely reached the cat. "Come on, just a little bit more."

But it was still out of Tariq's reach. No other way except for it to—"Jump!" yelled Ibrahim. He pressed his weight against the tree and shook it lightly as he looked up. "Come on, kitty!" Tariq joined in.

Ibrahim watched the cat's face as it gathered its courage and arched its head upwards. It crouched onto its hind legs and in a graceful motion stretched its tiny body and leapt off the branch. It flew through the air and grazed Tariq's fingers, just a few centimeters short of his grasp. "Meeeeeaaaaaaeeeow," shrieked the cat as it came tumbling down, landing on its side in the center of the mattress.

Ibrahim crouched down onto the cotton surface as the cat rolled up. It meowed at him, alive.

Tariq reappeared by his side in a few seconds. "Is it okay?" he panted. Both men looked down at the cat on the patterned mattress.

"Looks like the poor thing's broke its paw," said Ibrahim.

Tariq crouched down and lightly stroked the feline. "There, there, you'll be okay, Tarboush."

◆

Back inside the house, Ibrahim hugged the cat as he yelled up to Tariq. "So what did you want my help with?"

"I'll be right down!" yelled Tariq from inside the tower staircase. "Grab that axe from under the sink." Ibrahim set the cat down and walked into the kitchen. He reached into the cupboard and pulled out the axe. He returned to the hallway as Tariq emerged carrying a wooden easel.

He took the axe from Ibrahim and set the easel down. Then, with a few powerful swings, he chopped it into smaller planks against the expensive marble, cutting savage cracks into its surface. The cat jumped up startled as it watched.

"Why don't you do it in the kitchen?"

"Because I don't give a shit about all this," was Tariq's abrupt response. "That up there is the only room that matters," he said, using his chin to point to the open staircase. Then he added, "Hand me that."

The cat followed him with its eyes as Ibrahim brought him a toolbox from under the sink, set it on the scarred marble tiles between them and popped it open. Tariq reached down and put a few nails between his lips then pulled up his hammer. Ibrahim held up the wood planks as he nailed them across the door.

"There, that should do it," said Tariq. He tossed the hammer in the box and shoved it with the axe back under the sink.

The two men and the cat walked out and, after they had put back the mattress, Ibrahim climbed into the driver's seat of the car, the cat curling in the back. "You ready?" he asked Tariq. "Almost," he said, as he walked back in and reemerged a few seconds later with a long metallic case.

Ibrahim watched him through the side mirror as he carefully set it in the back. A few seconds later he climbed in next to him and said, "Okay, now I'm ready."

"Is that for your spying glass back there? To watch people?" asked Ibrahim.

"No," said Tariq. "It's to use against those watching me."

Ibrahim switched on the ignition and steered the truck along the hillside. Tariq scratched his forehead to avoid looking back, Ibrahim supposed. Once the truck was on the dirt road the young man asked, "How's the road to Beirut?"

"Clear and long as day," said Ibrahim.

9

Stones Unturned

Nancy and I argue most of the way to Nabatieh. Traffic may be a factor contributing to the rising tension between us as the Volvo weaves through a Beirut in political turmoil, escaping the vice of cars that threatens to squeeze the life out of my earth-colored vehicle. Carefully avoiding the downtown area, we exit Sodeco and—thankfully—swerve left, away from the city. Behind us, we leave two million Lebanese, close to one third of the population, fresh out of mourning to flood the streets in protest. Everyone is everywhere: one group protests another's presence, another protests for it, and others protest the protestors.

Nancy and I emerge from the flood as the Volvo makes a left onto Damascus Road. From the passenger seat, she watches a solemn line of cars, which inch through the adjacent lane like a funeral procession. A six-wheel pickup truck (what any Lebanese who's been in a car wreck knows as a *blata*) tentatively positions itself on the far side of the road while behind it a crane lifts the fallen bus onto it. The bus creaks and moans under its own weight, a beached whale in its final throes, visible agony that calls to mind Tariq Jaber's dying refrigerator.

I slow down and the Volvo tires make a crackling sound on the gravel as they come to a stop. Nancy leans across me for a view through my window. A crowd of onlookers do their best to spectate around the bus as the *Darak* police, part-army, part-militia, perform some amateur orchestration. One of them yells directions at the truck driver and another at the crane operator. Even from our obstructed vantage point, the lack of coordination between the two men is painfully obvious.

"Why don't they just drive the bus away?" Nancy asks.

"No practical reason. Superstition maybe?"

"Or maybe to preserve the evidence."

"Good luck picking evidence off a public bus. That thing must be a jungle of DNA, and with how seldom they clean the insides of those things—"

"Looks like they did a good job cleaning the outside, though."

She's right. The area around the bus has been flushed clean, and the spot where Tariq Jaber spoke his last words has no traces of that day—blood or otherwise. Puddles of crimson water line the edge of the highway, seeping into the soil where I stood witness just three days ago.

"They've got public perception to worry about," I say. "I'm glad they have their priorities straight." Disgusted, I shift the car into first gear and hit the gas. And that's when Nancy and I hit the first bump in the road, so to speak.

"I've been meaning to ask you," says Nancy, as the bus shrinks in my rearview mirror. "What happened after you pulled Tariq Jaber out of the bus?"

"I told you. He was about to take his last breath. He just died."

"No, I mean," she's drowsy, but won't let this one go, "what did you do after?"

"Well you know, as much fun as it was cradling a dead man while I got slathered with blood and rain, I didn't stick around."

She looks straight ahead. "So you left," she says.

"Yes. I got in this car, and drove away."

The wordless moments that follow a bout of talking with Nancy are one of the wonderful perks of our relationship, but now the emptiness weighs on me with brutal force.

"They were dead, Nancy," I say, cracking under the load. "Fucking blown to bits, every last one of them. Neither I nor anyone else could've done much to change that. So I split, okay? With the law in this country, anything else would've made things unbearably complicated."

"Complicated…"

"If I had said anything, my life, our lives, would've been blown wide open, while those people, Fattal, Jaber, everyone on that bus, would still be—"

"Dead."

"Nothing would've changed that."

"Correct," says Nancy, as if arriving at some conclusion. "But something inside you should've changed."

"Maybe."

"Not enough."

"Maybes are all we have."

"Then you should give it all up. This, your research, everything in our lives. It's all a worthless pursuit. Because nothing will ever change unless you change first."

I remain silent as the Volvo growls into fourth gear and eagerly swallows the road ahead.

A moment later she lays her hand on my bandaged finger. "Does that hurt?" she asks.

"No," I say, wincing with pain. "It doesn't hurt one bit."

♦

We leave Beirut behind us, and Nancy naps all the way to Khaldeh, but as we pass the suburb the Volvo hits a nasty bump

131

and the morning scales fall from her eyes in one fell swoop. "Boo. I've had it!" she says as she balloons with energy and pops out the cassette tape. *Birth of the Cool* cuts off, instantly replaced by "Darum dum doowop. Darum dum doowop."

"Ooh! You kick the gray skies out of my way," she sings. "You let the sun shine brighter than the brightest day! Don't you just love eighties pop?" She punches the air and then my arm, flailing about too widely for my Volvo's snug interior. The Swedes built the most practical car on earth, but dancing was probably not among its usage scenarios—or, what they call its *användningsfall*. Driving to Nabatieh, away from the pivotal article that in four short days will make, or most likely break, my career is definitely not among my *användningsfall* either.

"Wham!" I say, resigning myself to the fact that there's literally no turning back now.

"Can you believe these roads? I think that bump back there was the last one. How did they fix them so fast? Wasn't this highway bombed in the last war?"

"Yes, it was."

"Come on, Professor. I know you're not a morning person but it's good to get out of the city on a day like this. Away from the crazy traffic and demonstrations and shit. And look! We're making good time." She points at a sign that reads, "Welcome to Damour."

A few kilometers ahead, we stop at a bakery. Nancy instantly grabs a basket and disappears into the chips and candy aisle as I yell out to her "Cheese or *zaatar*?" Before she can reply, I turn to the baker and say, "Give me two of each please."

As the baker hands me the piping hot *manakeesh*, I turn back to the register and find that Nancy has beat me there, already emptying her basket of junk food.

"All set?" I ask.

"We're gonna have us a Volvo picnic!"

"And what do we have here?" I say, waving a pack of Marlboros and wagging my bandaged finger at her. "No, no, no!"

"Do not scold me, for it tempts me all the more," she says, quoting the poet Abu Nuwas as she snatches at the cigarette pack.

"Cure me rather with the cause of my ill," I continue the verse, avoiding her claws. The lady behind the cash register looks mildly amused as she beeps through Nancy's selection of oily snacks.

"Put it back," I say. "When we get to Nabatieh, if you're still dying for a smoke I'll bum you one. You'll never quit if you keep testing yourself."

"Fine, fine," she says. "But I want this awesome-cool lighter." She sounds like a twelve-year-old and she knows it, as she slams a cheap fake-gold Zippo on the counter painted with a blue palm representing the Hand of Fatima.

Nancy skips back to the car and I trudge to the driver's seat, then steer the Volvo out of the bakery parking lot. Back on the highway, Nancy remains quiet for a good kilometer and a half as she munches on her *zaatar mankoushe*. She feeds me the last bite with a "Yum," and as the oily morsel slides down my throat she turns serious again.

"Anything stuck in my teeth?" she says and her mouth spreads into an eerie grin, exposing a line of perfectly clean teeth.

"Your teeth are perfect," I say as we pass under a bridge marked "Oceana Beach Resort." She plants a lopsided peck on my lips, and then drops the empty *mankoushe* wrapper in the plastic bag under her feet.

On the radio, the DJ with a colossally annoying faux-British drawl announces the end of the Eighties Retro Megafest.

"Awww!" says Nancy, rolling her window open. Her hair flies into her eyes and mouth in wayward fronds. She picks it out strand by strand, but it goes every which way again.

But now that Nancy is all breakfasted and music-ed out, she picks up our morning squabble where we left off—same melody, different lyrics. "What time are your parents expecting us?" she begins tentatively.

"I didn't tell them."

"So we're just gonna drop in?"

"We're not gonna do any of that."

She frowns. "Come on, this Tariq Jaber business won't take all day. We'll just say hello and make your father's day. Don't be a prick."

"We're going to Lower Nabatieh. They live on the upper side."

"And those are, what, ten minutes apart?"

"Twenty, actually. I don't even know how to get there."

"We can ask," she says timidly, but she lets it go.

I don't. Instead I think it over then add, "We had a reunion in Beirut last year. He was fine."

"Fine? You call one night at a hospital a reunion? Sure the whole family was there, but so? And sure he was fine, medically speaking, but what if his biopsy had come out positive, then what? His funeral would've been a reunion too?"

"Believe me, that man will live to be a hundred. Doctors know how to take care of themselves."

"Then think of your mom. I miss her too."

"We'll see," I say, focusing on the road, still a good way from our destination. "Look, we're almost there."

We exit the highway and circle the roundabout marking the entrance to the city of Saida with its marketplace and elaborate mosques. We have plenty of road to cover but the streets are eerily empty for a weekday. Nancy surveys the vistas of the ancient city like a tour guide at a theme park, talking about this mosque and that *masjid*, regurgitating everything she studied in history class.

All over we see banners eulogizing Doreid Fattal as "The Son of all Lebanon" (quoting his wife), "The Giver," "Taken before his Time." I'm amazed at the almost endless ways Lebanese rhetoric can spin death into an epic act in and of itself. For my own epitaph, I want "Mighty Dendrologist, Martyred in the Name of Photosynthesis, so that Trees May Live, for All of Mother Nature."

"Look at this!" says Nancy, cutting into my daydream. She points at a stout structure to our left. "My dad and I went there to visit Rony. He was stationed in those barracks for his mandatory army service! Youngest kid in his contingent. Look, his dorm was in that building over there, but wow it's changed a lot! It was nothing back then, completely run down."

"The Fattal Organization rebuilt most of the city, starting with the official buildings and working its way down the social strata. They ran out of money before they got to the low-income housing though."

"Ha! But look, the ice cream store's still there!" she says, now pointing to the right. For her, Fattal could do no wrong. "I remember it was famous for its special banana flavor and for its owner with massive toes! Rony said his feet looked like banana clumps and his banana ice cream tasted like feet!"

"Sounds delicious," I say. "Maybe we'll stop on the way back."

We make our way through the outskirts of Saida and then we're back on the highway, climbing the hillside that marks the entrance into Lower Nabatieh.

We overlook a sun-kissed valley so tranquil, if it were not for the trees whooshing by, we might think we were rooted to the spot. The trees are leafless, still recovering from being burned during the last war to prevent infiltrating soldiers using them for cover. Nancy shows her true colors as a hard-boiled city girl as she watches the deceptively serene landscape, giddy with amazement. Soon we cut through the mountain and now the highway banks along a view of the Nabatieh hillside. It's not immediately obvious how high we are, but the air grows chilly. When there's not much more for her to see but more nature, Nancy sticks her head back into the car with a shiver, rolls up her window, and turns to me. "So, Professor, what's our first stop?"

"That'll be the Nabatieh Citizenry Electronic Database."

"Hilarious," she says, not buying my fib. "So you have like a mega computer with records of everything and everyone."

"Nope. Better."

◆

A giant sculpture of a two-pronged sword marks the entrance to Nabatieh. As we approach the roundabout that circumscribes it, I turn to Nancy and say, "That sword belonged to Imam Ali, the Prophet's cousin and founder of the Shia sect."

Nancy nods. "I took him in Cultural Studies last semester. He was a philosopher too. We read parts of *Nahjul Balagha*, his advice to his son. 'You have two lives: the one you seek and the one that seeks you.'"

"My father likes that quote. You and he'd make a good pair."

We circle the roundabout and descend to the coastal road to avoid central Nabatieh traffic. "We're taking the scenic route," I say. "I'll give you the grand tour of our market after we're done." I won't, actually, and she laughs knowingly. The sooner we're done here, the sooner I can head back to Beirut and my article.

We pass an intermediate school with its caged playground.

The high-pitched squeals of running children greet the ten o'clock recess with glimpses of gray-blue school uniforms swishing along the inside of a fence as the children run around.

Next is a mosque; its tiled minaret branches out to four geometric hands cradling a chrome loudspeaker, teasing glimmers from the morning sun. Daring imagery for such an iconoclastic religion as Islam. I point at it and remark, "Islam always finds ways around depicting nature."

"A search for perfect geometry, the world in lines, angles, and shapes," Nancy agrees as she switches seamlessly into intellectual mode. "Nature, the body, everything, really. Islamic art is non-figurative. Look at the Arabesque of the tiles. They could be, I don't know, flowers, birds, crescents. For Muslims, only the Creator can create. Everything man-made is an abstraction of God's ideal."

"Perfectly half-done," I say.

"The worst thing to be."

I can only think about my article, but one of us must lighten the mood. "You sound like you left all your fucks and shits back in Beirut," I say.

"Shit, no!" she says with only a hint of a grin, which vanishes into a persistent frown. "But this is serious."

"This?"

"You know," she says, molding the air in front of her into an invisible ball. "This."

Whatever this is, neither of us knows. I nod in response.

We pass a public park, its ground covered with layer upon layer of orange and brown leaves. In the far corner I spot a tree—one I remember well—its bark inside the iron fence and its branches spreading to the outside. In its shadow, two children, both too young for school, toss handfuls of the autumn leaves at their young parents. The leaves cling to the mother's scarf and father's stubble. Nancy laughs along with them; I've never seen her mood swing with such high frequency.

We drive silently past the park. Finally I slow down, make a turn into a dirt parking lot and switch off the ignition. Along a blind wall at the edge of the lot, a banner reads, "Ramadan Official Soccer Tournament." In any other context, there would be nothing about the bombed out parking lot that could be official in any sense of the word. But Nabatieh is a town that has made peace with war. In this town, war is not the opposite of peace, but its lining—and every hour spent in ceasefire is an hour spent living, going to school, and holding official soccer tournaments in bombed out residences-cum-parking-lots.

As we get out of the Volvo and I stretch my arms, Nancy points at a makeshift rectangular frame made from metal pipes. "Look! Fucking cool, huh? We used to play soccer too. I was goalie and my brother striker."

"Nice! When I was a kid here we used rubble from bombed buildings to mark the goals. Good to see technology's moving forward."

I lead her by the arm and we walk to a shack made of concrete blocks and corrugated metal. A thick cigarette-stained mustache peeks through the window, then the sinewy man attached to it steps out. He's dressed in a wool hat, which his rosy cheeks seem to agree is a tad too warm for this weather.

"How much?" I ask.

"*Lira w noss*," he says, and as I pay him the fifteen hundred liras he indicates a makeshift arrow-shaped metal sign that reads, "This way." Under it Nancy reads, "*Mukhtar.* Mega computer." She laughs as we walk out of the lot and make a left at the sign. It leads us along the back edge of the park.

"See that tree over there with the family?" I say. "It's been there for as long as I can remember, even before the park." We pass another sign; this one has printed letters. "My aunt—my father's sister Jamila—used to wait under it every day to pick up her children from school."

"That school we just passed?"

"Back then it was an elementary school. One day during the first invasion, the shelling had started and all the parents came out at once to collect their kids. She picked up my two cousins, carried the boy in one arm and the girl in the other and ran back. As soon as they got into the car, a rocket landed on the tree. The shells fell everywhere, killing five people around it."

Nancy doubles back around the tree. I stop and watch her. "They were badly injured and the girl almost died," I say. "But if not for the tree, they'd have been ripped to shreds. They lived out the rest of the war here, only moving to Beirut much later when the girl Aida got married and the boy went to medical college. I was twelve when it happened and my father was stricken with such paranoia, he sent me to boarding school in Beirut with barely a schoolbag and the clothes I had on. To my friends and classmates back here, I just vanished."

The mom in the park laughs. "*Bas ya Mama*. Stop it, kids," she says, but then proceeds to smother the children with a fresh handful of leaves as they all shriek.

"Who knows," says Nancy, rubbing my arm. "Perhaps that decision saved you too."

The family's playful chatter seems louder now, even as we walk further into a wide alleyway. On the opposite pavement a boy of fourteen spills water with one hand and mops with another, turning what could have been an awkward maneuver into something of a dance. Behind him, *Kahwa* Abbas, a traditional Nabatieh coffee shop, begins to fill up, starting at a line of tables along the sidewalk and spreading inside.

We arrive at a residential building with no signage. Well-trodden and dusty, the ground floor is clearly designed for public use, in distinct contrast with the apartments above. Fluorescent light spills from an open doorway by the entrance, and there a granite sign, this one with elaborately engraved Arabic letters, once again reads, "Mukhtar" and under it, "District of Nabatieh."

"Welcome to the Mayor's Office," I say, gesticulating to Nancy ceremoniously. She pauses at the threshold to thoroughly wipe her shoes on the doormat, releasing a cloud of dust that settles back on her shoes right where it was. She then walks inside with a failed attempt at a smile.

We're in a clean waiting room permeated by the scent of fresh gardenia. Its white plaster walls are clear except for a calendar with a photograph of the Byblos temple, which lies several kilometers to the northwest, filling the page. In the center of the room sits a Formica countertop, which makes up for the bareness of the walls. It's lined with a plethora of Lebanese memorabilia—a cedar tree carved out of cheap oak, several brass trinkets, a rosary made entirely of evil-eye beads, a miniature coffee pot with three bronze cups—leaving no room to rest my elbows. This space is clearly rented and instead of damaging the walls, the Mukhtar chose to express his Lebanese-ness with every loose trinket he could collect. Behind this showcase sits a dusty CRT computer monitor and behind it a purple-veiled head bobs up and down as a woman types at a keyboard.

"*Asalam alaykum*," I say in my most formal voice.

"*Ahlein*," says the woman politely, though visibly annoyed at the interruption. She's in her early thirties, fully made up in purple eye shadow to match her scarf. The only hint of character is a dark beauty spot in the center of her cheek, with a recently trimmed black hair poking out of its center. I can't decide whether it's real or fake (the spot not the hair), but it nevertheless gives me something to focus on amidst the rest of her carelessly painted visage.

I nod toward the calendar and say, "Next month it's Beaufort Castle." As I hope, mentioning Nabatieh's only monument of some historical value (itself a point of great contention among its inhabitants) elicits something resembling a wry smile. "Yes," she says. "All of us here are very excited."

I pretend the ice has now broken. Over my shoulder I beckon Nancy, who's been lingering shyly a few steps behind me. She approaches the counter as the receptionist's smile widens. "So how may I help you?" she asks.

"Is the Mukhtar in?" I ask in return. Smiling at Nancy, I add, "It's a family affair." My choice of words forestalls any further questions.

"Follow me, please," says the receptionist, as straight to the point as could be. In Nabatieh, family matters are safely guarded secrets (and, either as a result or as a cause of that, the fodder for endless gossip).

Nancy's warm breath tickles the back of my neck as she follows me into the adjoining office.

◆

The Mukhtar's office is a room-sized version of the receptionist's counter. The phrase "and then some" was likely invented for places like this: there's probably every piece of Lebanese memorabilia I've seen in the thirty-six years I've lived in this country. Every single one, and then some.

If there ever was an example of the Islamic fear of empty space that Nancy's brother Rony spoke about, then this office is it. Fatigued by an overload of sensory information and badly in need of a reboot, I roll my head and blink several times. As I do I notice in the corner from which we enter a man in a tan suit and sky-blue shirt, sitting with feet flat on the floor staring intently at the TV. He's in his mid-sixties, judging from the deep wrinkles cut through his clean-shaven face and collected in a whirlpool around his eyes. His cheek stretches under his knuckle, which supports the weight of his vapid head as it hangs cocked to one side. With that sight, I also become conscious of a scent of washing detergent laced with a vaguely familiar mélange of musky cologne and sweet tobacco. If the man sees us, then he doesn't show it; the TV continues to flicker in his unwavering gaze.

"Mukhtar?" I ask timidly. He looks up with only one eye, while the other barely moves. The man is beyond cockeyed, the only blemish in an otherwise impeccably neat exterior. With a lazy finger, he points over my shoulder past Nancy at a similarly aged man who shoulders past us, carrying two steaming hot glasses of red tea. He hands one to the cross-eyed man, carries the other to the desk and plants himself onto its corner.

He sniffs his tea then hitches his leg against the desk, showing his polished black leather shoe tapering toward a silk sock which itself is held in place by a leather strap disappearing up his pants—pinstriped and perfectly ironed with a fine crease running up to a belt buckle made of sparkling gold. His shirt is tucked in tight around a bulging belly, and along it dangles a pointed red tie from a tight knot wrapped under his Adam's apple, which bobs up as he takes a sip of tea. I recognize his face from the photographs, now around twenty years older, mustache lined with strands of white. Above it a broad nose almost completely conceals his eyes. Atop this package sits a full head of hair, dyed jet-black, or perhaps a toupee, I can't guess which.

"Have they done the Fatiha prayer yet?" he says toward the TV, clearly not addressing us. The man in the corner clears his throat in affirmation as he sips his tea.

I exchange glances with Nancy then take a step toward the desk. "*Marhaba* Mukhtar," I say, and then wait until he looks up at me from the corner of his eye. "I—we've come from Beirut to inquire—to ask you about someone. A woman."

Visibly amused by my loss for words, he cocks his head toward me and asks with exaggerated seriousness, "A woman?" He smiles. "What kind of woman?"

I fumble for an answer, buying some time by looking over my shoulder at the man in the corner. His cockeye remains unmoved, watching the TV and us. I reach into my pocket.

"I mean, here. I have a photo." I pull out the photograph of Tariq Jaber and the woman in the wheelchair and present it to him. The Mukhtar grunts, and instead of looking at it, turns his attention back to the TV. "We have a *baladiyya*, a town hall. Go now and you might find it's still open."

I notice my right shoelace is undone and have a sudden urge to kneel down and tie it, but instead I just shuffle my feet then stare back helplessly at the Mukhtar. Nancy brushes past me and takes center stage, directly between the TV and the Mukhtar. The cockeyed man follows her with his half-gaze and even the Mukhtar, his line of vision now interrupted, swivels his entire body toward us for the first time.

"Mukhtar, we're from the Lebanese University of Science and Technology in Beirut," she says in a single breath. She holds the Mukhtar firmly in her stare. "We've taken half a day out of our busy schedules to come to your town—personally my first visit— to conduct research about one of your constituents."

The Mukhtar's mustache twitches in—could it be?—the beginnings of a smile. Nancy continues to spin her prolix charm, unimpressed by how obviously taken with her the Mukhtar is. The inane smile spills over his face, even as he drowns in her deluge of words. I throw another glance at the cross-eyed man, and now he too has not one, but two eyes glued to Nancy.

"Now sir," she says, sliding the photo from my fingers, holding it with both hands, so close to the Mukhtar's face that he'd need to be superhumanly myopic to see it. "If you'd kindly take a look at this photo and tell us if you recognize this woman?"

He hops off the desk and lands on the plush carpet with a silent thud. His belly follows a second later, bouncing up then settling into place. Nancy traces his trajectory with the photograph, which she keeps a few millimeters from his face. The Mukhtar takes a step back and focuses on it for a split second before stretching his smile to such a cartoonish extent, the gold fillings where his rearmost molars once were glisten with fresh saliva.

"Yes *matmozeil*," he says in a typical mispronunciation of the French *"mademoiselle."* "That's Balkees, widow of Mahmoud Jaber, one of the best men Nabatieh's ever known, God rest his soul."

"You know her well?" Nancy asks and then, more tactfully, "I mean, the Jabers—you know them well?"

The Mukhtar squeezes his hands together and grins. "Everyone in this town knows me, and it's my job to know everyone back. The Jabers are one of the biggest families in Nabatieh. Mahmoud Jaber himself had five brothers, all fine men."

Now he's just showing off. "And sisters?" asks Nancy.

"One or two sisters. Mahmoud Jaber inherited the iron ore business from his father. Back then it was already big, but he grew it into an empire. It turns out this town rests on a thick bed of iron. He mined it and used the profits to build half of Lower Nabatieh. He brought electricity to the streets, water to the fields, coal to the houses. Genius, the man was. And generous too. Loved this town. After he passed away, his brothers sold their shares of the business to the eldest and the youngest, and moved to Ghana with their sisters, wives and children to run their own trading company."

"What about the kid here?" asks Nancy, indicating Tariq Jaber in the photo.

The Mukhtar's smile disappears. "That's Tariq," he says with a huff. "Always been an oddball that kid. Like his mother. Imm Tariq, we called her. All his life Mahmoud prayed for a strapping son. He wished upon a miracle, of course; we all knew Balkees was barren. Many years he was married to that woman, loved her like I don't know what. And in return, she gives him the broth of a man, a premature peanut a few weeks too late."

"What do you mean 'too late'?"

"I mean Mahmoud died before his son was born. He never met him. And what did the little nipper do for his mother? Nothing. A burden, that's all he ever was. She kept him away from the townsfolk, like our eyes would scorch him. Strange, strange kid. Top of his class at school, that's all I know. Never played with the other youngsters his age, never saw him at the store, and later never at the *kahwa*, never anywhere. Then last year he just vanished, left to study abroad maybe. All the rich kids of this town do."

"Rich?" asks Nancy.

"The entire mining fortune went to that tyke. First to his mother, then to him when he was of age. Every drop of toil from his father's brow went to Tariq Jaber. Mahmoud's brothers saw nothing, not a lira. They're still well off, but nowhere near what they deserve."

"One more thing, Mukhtar," says Nancy. She throws me a coy smile, and then turns back to him. "We'd very much like to visit Mrs. Jaber. Can you tell us where to find her?"

"Yes," he says. He looks down toward my undone shoes, then as he raises his head he mimics Nancy's smile and adds, "She's at the Hussainia."

"The Hussainia!" she repeats, turning to me, smile frozen on her lips. "Where's that?"

"The cemetery," I mumble.

Nancy's smile thaws. I take my cue. "Thank you Mukhtar. You've been most helpful."

He nods to me and says kindly, "You're welcome."

As he turns his attention back to the TV, he leans to the side of his desk and pops open the bottom drawer. In it sits a pile of loose cash and on top of it, a paper folded into a reverse-V, marked 50,000 L.L.

"Price has gone up," I say as I pull out the requisite bill and drop it into the drawer.

"Inflation," says the Mukhtar, eyes still on the TV.

I take Nancy by the arm and, as we leave, the Mukhtar adds, "And by the way, Miss, that nonsense about the demographic research, very entertaining. Thank you."

Nancy gives a wan smile, and under the stare of the cockeyed man, we walk out of the office.

◆

"A solid brick wall," says Nancy, twirling her arms around my coffee cup. I peer into it but instead of a brick wall, what looks back at me is a moiré pattern etched along the white porcelain.

"I didn't know you could read coffee cups," I say.

"Ah, no," she says, her weary eyes catching the light with an incandescent twinkle. "I'm talking about that." She points toward the Mukhtar's building across the street.

Kahwa Abbas bustles with men aged sixteen to sixty-six drinking tea, smoking hookah water pipes, and slapping their backgammon pieces with Persian exclamations "*Sheesh juhar! Benj yek!*" A few others play cards, and I associate the game with spending hours, sometimes days, huddled with twenty other schoolmates in a bunker, whiling our time between ceasefires. Maybe here too in Nabatieh, the game is too wedded to memories of the war to hold as much sway over its men's leisure time as it did. Sparser still is checkers—perhaps it caused one too many bar brawls with its pesky rule that a player must capture when he can, which often forces a winner into a severely compromising position. My favorite board game is the scarcest of all; as far as I can see it's only being played at the table next to ours. I toss a brief glance at it.

"Mate in three," I say.

Nancy tilts her chair perilously close to the table. She surveys the board and the players frowning over it, then tilts back and says, "You're right. Looks like white's in bad shape."

"Actually it's white's game."

"How do you know?"

"Black captures the queen with his rook, white recaptures with his knight, black averts check by moving his king, then white brings in that pawn for the kill."

"All that's in your head?"

"Elementary," I say. With an exaggerated wink, Nancy swings back to the table to check my claim. The players take no notice of her. Some things haven't changed since my childhood; this and other *kahwas* in Nabatieh remain strictly male establishments, by unwritten social norm if not official decree. That Nancy remains un-ogled here (and as a result completely unselfconscious) is a testament to her city-girl conspicuousness (and resulting irrelevance) to its clientele.

A dense layer of smoke fills the room, but it seems to settle on our table. "Let's see what the rest of the day holds," she says as she covers her coffee cup with the saucer and flips it over. "Give it a minute."

I continue my survey of the *kahwa*, this time starting at the opposite side with its main feature, a ceramic-tiled counter running along the entire length of the back wall and ending in a door leading to the back. The same kid who was cleaning the sidewalk earlier, now festooned with a white kippah, pops in and out with trays of tea and coffee, fresh hookah, and cradles of coal, all at once. The manager, presumably Abbas, hollers curt but not unkind instructions to him, always starting with "*Ya walad!*"

As she gazes into space, a lullaby escapes Nancy's lips and floats above the chatter of the *kahwa* across our table, drawing my gaze back to her. "Alright Imm Ali," I say, using a possible fortune-teller name that comes to mind. "Tell us what my future holds."

She snaps out of her reverie and her tune segues into a schlocky thirties Hollywood B-horror theme. She squiggles her fingers and flips over my coffee cup. Fully in character, she lifts it with the tips of her fingers and tilts it toward her eyes until the window light caresses its lip.

"Ooka pooka, smoke and hookah."

"Pooka?"

"Ooka Pooka," she says. "I have a fictionary of rhyming words, OK?"

"A 'fictionary'?"

"Shush. Let me concentrate." She squints into the cup, rolling it between her fingers, then says, "I see a... garden. Green trees. Long, thorny branches. Wild flower buds. And a... giraffe."

"A giraffe," I say, careful not to raise my intonation into a question. That would only encourage her—even in jest, superstition falls outside the realm of practices I can condone.

"Maybe a swan," says Nancy earnestly as she rolls my cup between her fingers like a street magician's coin. "Wait, I think it's a gazelle, with a slender neck. It tugs a branch from the tree, reaching for a wildflower. The branch cracks, and the tree is in pain."

"Aha. So what does the tree do? Does it just take it?"

"Hell no," she says shoving the cup toward me. "It gasses the gazelle. See this cloud here?"

The thick coffee stench tickles my nose as I look inside, but again there's nothing there but a moiré of powdery brown. "Gasses it?" I say. "You mean like with oxygen cyanide?"

"Maybe!" says Nancy with a laugh. "Something poisonous. See here on the other side, the story continues. The gazelle is sick, curled into a ball."

"That thick glob there is a sick gazelle, huh?" I say. "But what does it all mean?"

"It's your cup. I only know what I see. What it means, Professor, only you can know," she says, looking up at me expectantly, like I somehow have the answer to her implicit question.

At the next table, the white pawn advances for the win, and its owner exclaims "*Shah mat*," Persian for "checkmate." Black tips his king over and swears under his breath.

Nancy smiles, face filled with the same glowing pride she accorded her brother when he wowed both of us by cracking Tariq's coded astronomical research. She puts my cup in the muddy coffee puddle left on its saucer. "Let's do my cup next," she says, repeating the motions from earlier, first draining the dregs into the saucer, then flipping it on its lip, belly up. "But honestly, I have no idea what I'm doing."

"Come on, it's a good fantasy," I say, stroking her wrist. "You know what, instead of looking into the future, why don't we both look into the past." I pull out my memoir from my coat pocket and lay it on the table.

"Excellent!" she says, reaching for it. I pull it back and loosen the rubber band, then pull out my notes of Tariq Jaber's last day. I only hand her those.

Nancy slides her fingers under them and lifts the papers with grace. "Chapter Two?" she says.

"Yes, Chapter One is just my own notes, never mind those."

"Okay," she says glumly. Back to the pages, she runs her eyes across the first one, and her face lights up with giddy excitement. I watch her like a chef would a food critic sampling a specially prepared signature dish.

"You ran Tariq Jaber over! Really?" says Nancy.

"That morning he was just some idiot on a bike who happened to whoosh by my car. Only later did he become Tony, the man who died on the bus. And now, again, he's transformed into this Tariq. At least that much isn't fantasy, but it's not science either. I'd love to see the taxonomists try to wrap their thick heads around this one."

"No, it's more than science," says Nancy. "Imagine if you had hurt him worse, like broken his leg or something."

"Then he'd have missed the bus and would still be alive," I say rubbing my chin. "As you might say, it was a curse, disguised as a blessing. In this text, that's the only thing I know happened. The rest isn't my account of what happened, but—"

"What *could* have happened. What's definitely possible."

She smiles then hides her face behind my notes as she continues to read. The events of that morning, now three days old, play across my mind. First come the recorded sounds—

thunder, squish, metal-on-metal, then the remembered images—lighting, mud, bus. Contrary to the laws of physics, I recall the sounds first and then the images. The reel in my mind rattles to a halt as a familiar man in a tan suit bypasses Abbas, crosses to the counter of the *kahwa* and gestures directly to the waiter boy.

Nancy sets the notes on the table between us, and repeats the closing words "…the bus toward Damascus began its journey." She folds the loose papers and tucks them back in the memoir, politely resisting a peek at the rest. "Will you write more?" she says.

"The more we learn about Tariq and the people in his life. If we can't know who he was, then we sketch in everyone else. The empty space that remains is Tariq."

"Empty space," she says, looking up at me. "Do you think they'll throw him into an unmarked grave?"

Even if I don't quite share Nancy's empathy, the thought is vexing. "If no one claims his body."

"Then someone should claim the body. We should. Let's go tell that high and mighty Mukhtar that he's an idiot who knows nothing. And what about that crazy buddy of his? Did you see how he kept staring at me?"

I glance past Nancy at the ceramic counter, its owner now gazing straight at me with skewed eyes. When the waiter reemerges, the man receives a pack of red Marlboros, tips him, and turns toward our table. He drags his left foot behind him, though the dignified uprightness of his upper body camouflages most of this imbalance. I recognize him, but he also reminds me of someone else, though, of whom and why, he leaves me no time to guess before he's upon us.

"Not at you, Nancy," I say. "He was staring at me." She follows my gaze, then perks up as the man comes to stand directly behind her.

"Hello again, Miss," he says. "Sorry to intrude on your coffee time." His amiable demeanor contrasts sharply with his mad-eyed look, which he turns to me and adds, "You're the doctor's son. The obstetrician doctor from Hikme Hospital."

"Gynecologist, yes," I say, unsure whether it was even a question, then add unnecessarily, "He oversees but doesn't deliver."

He nods politely, but then his lips pinch into a grimace. "A word of advice," he says sternly. "I've known you since you were this high." He hovers his hand by his waist, parallel to the floor. "You and my son the engineer played football in our orchard all the time. And you boys attended to it whenever I was away in Syria."

Both his typically Nabatieh manner of denoting his offspring by profession and the scene he invokes unearth memories of growing up over many summers in this town. As Nancy engages him in small talk I won't even recall minutes later, memories flood my senses: he was a widower and he was always traveling. With only nannies around and undeterred by parents, his son and I would build fortresses in his modest house like it was our castle and run through his vast field like it was our fiefdom. There, I learned to use a spade, not like an axe, but a scalpel. And there, his son, deeply religious even at that tender age, would explain that, even in nature, everything is written, or as he'd say, *maktoub*. To nature, human beings were but a whim that would come and go. But trees, my playmate would proclaim, are Truth itself, and as such were timeless. While other religions wouldn't decide whether we live according to a prescribed destiny (*musayyar* was the word he used) or whether we were free to make our own choices (*mukhayyar*), Islam says we are both, the future engineer would explain. As whims, he'd say, we could only grasp the Truth by clinging to the trees. Nature's greatest creature was our one and true covenant with eternity. From conception to the grave, he'd say, we were in constant dialogue with all that surrounds us: through the trees we encountered minute by minute, we spoke to the air and water and sun, and in return the whole universe spoke to us.

Over many adolescent summers, my friend would regale me with magical lessons which he in turn had learned from his father, the man who now stands before me. The years have since pulled the old man's eyes into a grotesque squint and carved crow's feet into the corners of their sockets, but behind them I now recognize the man from my youth. Like all parents, he used to scare me then, but now, even under a face ravaged with scars, I see my boyhood friend's face. I rise and shake the man's hand. "Of course, *Ammo*," I say. "Nancy, this is Ibrahim. Sorry I didn't recognize you earlier at the Mukhtar's office."

Nancy smiles politely and extends her arm, but he courteously taps his hand to the chest, a gesture in lieu of physical contact across the sexes. Her smile unbroken, Nancy retracts her own hand and brings it to her chest. I don't even try to hide my amusement at her adorable mimicry, but then the man abruptly cuts the pleasantries short. "The Mukhtar back there is a good fellow," he says. "But someone in his position owes the people of Nabatieh certain courtesies."

"I see," I say, but I really don't.

"The Jabers," continues Ibrahim, his voice reduced to a whisper. "That family is poison." He peels the plastic wrapping off his Marlboros, and whacks the pack onto the back of his palm five times, each with a sharp crack. Like me, he's a creature of habit.

"Poison," I say. "How do you mean?"

"Mahmoud and his brothers did a lot for this town—that

153

much is true. The Jaber brothers, especially the two who stayed here, are much more in the money business than the mining business. They just hide it better than Mahmoud ever did. When he died, he left a fortune to all of his siblings, but those two sliced it up as they pleased."

"You mean they bought the others out?" Nancy asks.

"We here don't deal in fancy city talk," he says, not without kindness but with a certain degree of emphasis. "If those other brothers and sisters in Africa ever saw a lira, I'd chop my right arm off."

As he speaks, Nancy studies the man with intense concentration. When she was a student in my class, while her classmates frantically transcribed my every word, she did it with her eyes—the note-taking equivalent of photographic memory.

Ibrahim continues, "They left the country the only way they could, with barely the skins on their backs. They made do with peanuts and signed off their shares of the actual businesses to the other two. Jayjay and Barcode."

"Who and who now?" asks Nancy with a half-laugh.

"Jaber Junior, the youngest, and Yaqub, the eldest," he says, fully serious. "We just call them Jayjay and Barcode, the one who barks and the one who bites."

Ibrahim looks like he's ready to leave, but Nancy has him caught in her stare. "Barcode. Why do they call him that?" she says.

"Some say because he lives and breathes money, but you'll know why if you see him. And I hope to God you never do."

"The Jabers I've known over the years are good people," I say.

"Like any family tree, there's the good and there's the rotten."

He leans onto his cigarette pack and it buckles between his palm and the tabletop. "Mahmoud's widow Balkees was worth her weight in gold," he says. "And they say that's exactly what she was—the final chip her father paid Mahmoud Jaber in a game of poker. He bought her for a wife, and when she fell sick, she became his only losing investment. Crippled with a sickness of the spine, they say, it left her paralyzed by the end. Because after Mahmoud died, the town didn't see much of her. And until her own funeral, some even thought she had died with him."

"A queen burned alive on her husband's funeral pyre," Nancy remarks dryly. Her words linger in the cloudy air of the *kahwa*.

I cut into the awkward silence. "Ibrahim, I owe it to her son Tariq. I can't tell you why—I myself don't know for sure—but he led me here to find something. That family has a secret, and I promised myself to leave no stone unturned until—"

"No!" he cuts me off with a frantic wave of his hands. "The young lady here," he says, indicating Nancy. "She said you're a farming professor."

"Dendrologist," I interject, but it goes unnoticed.

"I'm a farmer too," he continues. "You know what I find when I look under rocks?"

"Moss," I say.

"Maggots. Those creatures don't get sunlight because they don't need it. They're blind to your noble intentions. Best leave those stones unturned, young man." His one good eye looks straight into mine. "Tariq is where he should be. Please leave him and his family alone."

I break the stare and turn to Nancy, who reciprocates with a sad look. Ibrahim opens the cigarette pack, tears off the silver lining, and pulls out a cigarette. "Enjoy our last week of autumn, and say hello to your father."

He nods politely to Nancy. Then, as abruptly as he appeared, takes his leave. His limp seems more pronounced, as if the secrets he divulged to us have done nothing to unburden him. He takes a single puff of his cigarette then tosses it on the sidewalk as he steps out, a sliver of smoke trailing behind him.

Nancy palms her coffee cup and flips it over.

"What does your fortune say?" I ask.

She brings it to her eyes and looks inside. "It says what we started, we must finish."

10
Bark and Bite

He leaned onto the stone balustrade to get a deeper look into the grounds of the family estate. The trees, grass, and hedges had grown wild over the past few months and his brother asked him to come over today to oversee the gardening crew they had commissioned to deal with it. For most of the day Jayjay had chosen to overlook it instead.

A few years ago, his brother wouldn't have let it pass, but recently his omniscient eye had become less watchful, leaving Jayjay much more leeway for creative interpretation of the family responsibilities assigned to him. Even though his share in those responsibilities had grown exponentially with the departure of his two other brothers to Africa, his share in the estate itself had grown even more, and with that, his pride. He was his own boss and soon Barcode—though he'd never call him that to his face—would retire on a self-allocated pension, leaving him in complete control.

But now that he found himself on the terrace, he saw no harm to cast his own eye over the minions below, who, like a school (or was it a colony?) of ants, scurried around from one hedge to the next until each was pruned to perfection. It was like they ate the excess leaves and, when they were done with each, left nary a twig of refuse behind. Ants they were, very efficient ants.

From the busy workers immediately below his feet, he cast his eyes beyond the estate, to the house on the hill with the tower-like eyesore attached to it. He ran a hand through his curly hair, still thick and the object of men's envy and women's desire—not the village idiots and harlots of this town, but real men of stature and women of esteem from as far as Monte Carlo (where he once came close to doubling his own fortune before losing half of it).

That house belonged to that cripple woman and her son, who he was convinced was no nephew of his. But now she was in the ground, and soon he would take the boy under his own wing and shape him into his own image. Men in their twenties were soft as putty: the harder you pressed, the more you impressed. He flashed his teeth and ran his pinky nail between the front two, smacking his lips against them until he was sure they shined with their signature gleam. He was a man whose own reflection cowered before him, and he hardly ever needed to use a mirror anyway.

He slid his eyes along the swells and crests of the hills, scanning their undulating surface for one more ant, a very specific type of insect—he knew that was the real reason Barcode had summoned him here today and he was anxious to see the boy after all these years. He looked over his shoulder at his elder brother, who patiently sat on his favorite sofa, plucking at his rosary with stubby digits. He now spent more and more time in this position, until Jayjay and everyone else saw that sofa as an extension of his body. Indeed, on the few occasions he did stand up, even his hefty stature appeared minuscule without that thick chunk of wood and leather attached to his behind.

The two brothers gazed blankly at one another—they were well rehearsed and until their guest arrived they had little more to say to one another. He turned his attention back to the hills and, like clockwork, a green dot appeared on the horizon. A glint of metal hit his eye—who buys a green car? But this was no car—it slid along those curves with a speed and breeziness that were way too agile for a car.

Then he realized what it was: a bicycle? A shiver of repulsion ran through his body. What disrespect. What nerve. Who would visit his uncles, the patriarchs of the Jaber family, on a rickety bike? This brashness will not be tolerated, nor will it be forgiven. But all in good time.

Jayjay adjusted his collar and slid his hand along the stone balustrade as he walked down the grand staircase. He took his sweet time to get to the bottom. It was crucial that the boy arrive before he reached the ground, that he watch Jayjay in the act of descending to his level. Too late and the boy would feel unwelcome. But worse, too early and the boy might think himself some important piece of shit.

In perfect synchronicity, the moment Jayjay's heel struck the cobblestone path at the end of the staircase, the boy had made his way up and was laying the bicycle on its side right there at his feet.

"Welcome," said Jayjay, flashing his favorite smile, the one that extended all the way across his face to his mother-of-pearl molars.

"Hello, Uncle," said Tariq Jaber, extending his hand. Jayjay shook it eagerly, laying his left palm around the handshake and squeezing it. Yes, treat them as equals—they like that.

"Come in. Your uncle's anxious to meet you." Two uncles, one Tariq. Make them see what they're up against right from the get-go. The boy didn't stand a chance.

The two men climbed the staircase, the younger one a step ahead, but the older one making it clear who was really in the lead with a firm hand on the boy's shoulder. As he had rehearsed it. As it should be.

◆

The boy was late, and the room now seemed dimmer. Good. This was their lair and Jayjay was glad it looked the part. If he could be anyone (and he knew he could), his last choice would be the boy whose shoulder he now gripped, Jayjay's pinky talon digging deep into the boy's blazer.

They now stood in the center of the living room, with the light from the window behind falling just short of Barcode. He looked up from the sofa and eyed the boy intently, his comb-over neatly pressed against his domed skull.

"You'll excuse me for not getting up, my boy," he said without smiling. "These legs aren't what they used to be."

Jayjay gestured to the boy to take a seat opposite his brother Barcode, as Jayjay circled the room and stood behind the sofa. He felt more comfortable there, the plush leather covering most of his body as his eyes grazed the shiny black and pink dome of Barcode's head and traced the backlit outline of the skinny boy.

"And you. Still riding that dinky thing? How about Jayjay here take you to Sour to pick out a real set of wheels? Our gift to you. How about that?"

"You asked to see me," said the boy with very little tact.

"Yes," said Barcode. "A man who doesn't beat around the bush. I like that." He swung the rosary around his fat fingers until it wrapped around them twice, then continued. "Losing one's mother, the breast that fed you. That's when a man becomes a man. We wouldn't have missed the funeral, understand. Nor the *Arbeen*, of course. The forty-day memorial is hardest."

The boy said nothing.

Barcode continued, "But when you're my age—God give you many years—you'll learn that time is unkind to the Jaber gene."

Redundant, of course, what he just said. But Jayjay

160

understood well what his brother had in mind and he studied the boy for a change at the mention of the Jaber lineage, but the mongrel face before him betrayed nothing. Jayjay decided it was time to depart from the script a little, to take matters into his own hands, but he resisted the temptation for now.

"As you know," said Barcode quietly, "our brother Mahmoud left your mother considerable assets, which we—"

"He didn't leave her any assets," the boy interrupted. "They were already hers when he was still alive."

"How do you know that, boy?" Jayjay blurted out. "You were barely a fart in her belly when he died."

Such nerve! Jayjay squeezed the back of the sofa, wishing very much that it was the flimsy shoulder he had in his grasp just a moment ago.

"There, there, Jayjay," said Barcode softly, gripping his brother's wrist over his shoulder. "That's no way to speak to our nephew." And with a voice as sweet as dew, he spoke again to the boy. "Listen, my son. We have no… issue with that. We want you to… understand."

He paused, but again the boy said nothing. It seemed that impetuous piece of horse dung only liked to speak out of turn. *Interrupt him one more time, you microbe. I dare you.*

Barcode released Jayjay's wrist and clasped his palms together, the rosary dangling between them. Then he continued, his voice carrying more weight but no less kindness. He had heard his brother, the accountant who carried that name even before his hair turned into a visual emblem thereof, use that tone when he was ready to make an offer. "We asked you here today, to this house, to your grandfather's house, to teach you a simple lesson. Even if you leave with nothing else, I hope you take what I am about to say to you, and carry it inside your heart for the rest of your days."

161

The boy raised his eyebrows, and to Jayjay's surprise, he seemed intrigued. He even spoke in line now. "What's that, Uncle?"

Jayjay could feel his brother shift slightly on the sofa. They were finally getting somewhere, back on script, and he was glad he had held his anger in check earlier.

"Family, my boy, is everything," said Barcode. "It's all we have. It's all you have. Your father knew that. I know that. Jayjay here knows that and so should you."

Jayjay felt a lump gather in his throat. He had to hand it to old Barcode—there was still something to learn from his brother after all. He watched the boy run his hands down the creases of his pants. Good, he was squirming now and they had him right where they wanted him. The boy's face broke into a smile. Ah, the naivety of youth, one word swings them to and another fro. Very good.

Tariq leaned forward until he was halfway out of his seat, his stupid smile suspended unbroken over the table between them.

"Thank you Uncle," said Tariq quietly. "You'll be pleased to know, I agree completely."

Excellent. The boy paused for close to a minute. He was off-kilter now, improvising. He had no script and he knew it.

"The only problem is…" Tariq stood up, still smiling broadly. "…You're no family of mine."

Motherfucking son of a whore.

"Motherfucking son of a whore! You're no Jaber! You b-bastard swine!" Jayjay bumped into the sofa, knocking his brother forward, sending his rosary flying from his grip and his comb-over flopping across his face. "Come here f-fucker! I'll rip your throat open, you f-fatherless piece of shit!"

Jayjay reached for the spineless twerp, but the sofa, Barcode and the table were all in his way. He tripped over each one of

162

them, and by the time he straightened, the boy was already halfway across the room, his frame now looking several inches taller against the opening behind him. His smile had grown into a full-blown laugh as he turned to leave.

But then Barcode bellowed, "Tariq Jaber!" The room shook and rattled Jayjay to the bone. The boy stopped dead in his tracks, and his smile vanished. Then, in barely a whisper Barcode said, "Careful riding that bicycle. A fall could snap you in half."

11

Synthesis

"Surely we belong to God and to Him shall we return," reads the Kufic engraving on the tombstone. Above it, a crescent engulfs a five-pointed star and under it, her birth and death in lunar dates.

The main part of the inscription reads, "Wife of the late Mahmoud Jaber, mother of Tariq Mahmoud Jaber." I run my bandaged finger along the ridges of the engraving, following its angular lines.

"Balkees died in the month of Muharram," I say. "January of this year."

"Young. Fifty-six," says Nancy, brushing her hair from her face.

"That's the forbidden month, second most sacred year in the Hijra calendar. Its tenth day is the *ashoura* mourning for the martyr Hussain."

"This place, the Hussainia, was named after him?"

"Yes. He was the cousin of the prophet and his significance in the religion is one of the most contested points between the Sunnis and Shias. Many believe it's what drove a wedge between the two sects."

"Where's all this coming from, Mr. Agnostic?"

"I'm not agnostic, Nancy, just scientific. Every year, the

kids in my town—the town I grew up in—would shave their heads and slit the skin above their noses with a razor blade. Nabatieh men paraded the streets, pounding their bloody foreheads for a full day. My father never let me partake in it. I'd march after them and chant along and as they got high from the loss of blood, I'd work my way through the ranks until I led the procession."

We watch the tombstone in silence. The afternoon breeze plays through the cemetery behind the Hussainia structure, ruffling Nancy's hair. Muharram is the month of peace, during which Muslims are forbidden to engage in war of any kind, even holy war. I recall the serenity painted on the faces in the photograph of Tariq and his mother. I press it against my chest behind my jacket.

In the distance, a turbaned head bobs up and down, skirting its way between the tombstones. Nancy and I watch as it grows larger, revealing a bearded face, eyes fixed to the spot where we stand.

"*Asalam alaykum*," says the man.

Nancy returns the greeting as he approaches, a man of about fifty with rosy cheeks and a hooked nose. "Balkees, God rest her soul. You're her first visitors ever."

"We come from Beirut to pay our respects," I say.

The man extends his hand, and when I take it he lays the other on top of mine. "I'm Sheikh Faqih. I presided over the funeral. But how do you know her?"

"I know her son," I say, realizing that's the truth. I really do know Tariq now, perhaps more than anyone we've spoken to yet.

"What was she like?" asks Nancy.

"Alas," says Sheikh Faqih with a knotted brow, like he has just lain the woman in question to rest again. "Balkees kept to herself. I cannot tell you much."

I release one hand from the Sheikh's warm grasp and pull out the photograph, laying it on his palm. Recognition flashes in the Sheikh's eyes, then turns to a jolt when I flip the photograph around and read the dedication on the back. "My morning star, my evening star, forever one, forever bright. M."

"Maurice," says Nancy.

The Sheikh raises the photo to his eyes, as if weighing it against the name inscribed on the tombstone. He exhales sharply and drops his arms to his side. "Please, come with me," he says.

We follow him to the edge of the cemetery, then around the main building of the Hussainia's terraced courtyard. He leads us up the staircase to its entrance, we walk inside, and continue down a corridor to a flight of stairs. Nancy follows his upturned turban as we climb three flights and I trail closely behind. At the top, he pushes an oak door until it creaks open, flooding the stairs with light. We step outside.

The Sheikh leads us to the edge of the roof and leans against the stone balustrade overlooking the cemetery below. It's a magnificent view for such a low structure, spanning not only the grounds of the Hussainia all the way to the main road we drove from, but a lot of the surrounding neighborhood. The lines between nature, town, and nature etch all the way to Upper Nabatieh, which extends to a hilly landscape dotted with sporadic limestone houses.

A few moments later, Sheikh Faqih turns toward us and rests the small of his back on the balustrade. The sky backlights his black turban as he studies Nancy and me, then breaks the silence. "I gave Tariq that photograph the day his mother passed away. Against her dying wish."

He cannot stand to face Balkees; even in death, his back

remains firmly turned away from the cemetery and her tombstone below.

"Tariq has no other photographs of his mother," I say. "I'm sure he was thankful for it."

Sheikh Faqih shakes his head. "Tariq's father was a tyrant; he ruled over his family with an iron fist. He died before Tariq was born, but even from the grave, his grip remained tight around Balkees and her son."

He looks down at the photograph in his hand and continues. "You're right, Miss. That 'M.' on the back is Maurice. Balkees kept him a secret, even from her son. And when her time drew close, she begged me to bury this photograph with her."

"But why?" says Nancy.

The Sheikh looks up. "When Mahmoud was gone, Balkees wanted a father for Tariq, a real father. Maurice was a young engineer from Syria, a good man, but Balkees knew the Jaber family would rob her—would rob her son—of the inheritance should their marriage be discovered."

"Marriage? Balkees and Maurice were married?" asks Nancy.

"Yes," says the Sheikh. "I performed the *katb kitab* ceremony right here after Mahmoud Jaber died, shortly before Tariq was born. I haven't seen Maurice since. They say he went into hiding."

"Why?" I ask.

"The Jaber brothers had it in their head that he caused their brother's death. When the mine caved in, taking the life of Mahmoud Jaber, they were out for justice. So after the *katb kitab*, Maurice was never seen in this town again. This photograph is the only sign he's ever been back since."

He straightens its dog-eared corners like a page out of a holy book. "In the Koran," he says, "God willed man to be born free and to die free. Sourat al-kahf says, 'Then whosoever wills, let him believe, and whosoever wills let him disbelieve.' If belief itself is a choice, then we should be allowed to choose our own destiny as well. Tariq had a right to meet the man his mother loved, the caregiver his biological father never was."

The Sheikh turns toward the view, lost in thought, but Nancy leans against the balustrade and brings her eyes in line with his. "If Balkees and her son were the rightful heirs," she says, "why was she so afraid? The law is clearly on her side."

"My daughter," says the Sheikh. "The law of the land is one thing. But *sharia*, Muslim law, has precedence over that. A man is not allowed to bequeath his fortune to his wife. God is forgiving, and when man is too, everything works. But the Jabers have no mercy in their hearts, only pride. With Balkees remarried, they had a religious right, if not a legal one, to the inheritance. And if Maurice were found legally responsible for the mining accident, the Jabers could have gotten everything. Thankfully that didn't happen, but the fear remained."

He raises a finger to a hill on the horizon. "That big house over there," he says. "That was Mahmoud's. Balkees lived out her days there with her son and kept him safe. After Balkees passed on and Tariq left, the Jabers locked it up. They still can't agree who it belongs to. Only rats live there now."

"And secrets," Nancy says whimsically.

To my surprise, the Sheikh smiles. I guess he's a romantic. "Yes, my dear," he says. "Secrets that only a handful of people share. We even burned the marriage certificate."

"The *katb kitab* must've been attended by witnesses, right?" I ask.

"Yes. Two witnesses. The only other partakers in this secret marriage. One alive and one dead."

Nancy ventures a guess, but makes it sound like a certainty. "The first is Ibrahim," she says. "But who was the other?"

Her subtle ruse works; the Sheikh thinks we know more than we're letting on. "And the second witness, God rest his soul, was Doreid Fattal."

◆

White noise crackles and pops on the Volvo's radio. I rotate the dial away from the Beirut channel to some reception—a news report covering the Fattal funeral procession lists the other victims of the bus, reminding whomever is listening that a certain young man among them remains unidentified. I turn it down a bit and ease the car around the park and up the boulevard connecting to the main street.

"What do you make of all that?" I ask.

Nancy has her chair reclined all the way, so she leans forward and brings her face on level with mine. "What I make, Professor, is that when God closes a door..."

"...He opens a window," I finish.

"Sheikh Faqih pointed us to the house on the hill."

"Yes. Let's go."

I downshift the Volvo and make a sharp right turn up the final stretch of the steep boulevard onto the main street. We're now in the beating heart of Nabatieh and the sights, smells, and sounds seep into the car's every pore.

The traffic by any other standard could be called gridlocked, but by Nabatieh's standard, is quite normal. We're in no hurry and from the looks of it neither is anyone else. Still, the town's clockwork is in motion and I wonder if that may be the more efficient way of doing things. The best way to avoid bottlenecks when you can't reduce volume is to reduce the speed of flow. I make a mental note of that.

I hit a lever and the Volvo spits out a few pathetic spurts

of water, making the windshield even muddier. Nancy sticks her head out of her window instead and I look in the same direction to watch the slideshow of Nabatieh town-life scroll by. As an accompaniment, I blindly pull out a tape from the glove compartment and replace the one sticking out of the deck. The radio's Koranic funeral chant is immediately replaced by a Latin rhythm and raspy male vocals singing about *amores y pasiónes*, et cetera, et cetera.

We pass the meat house with five full cows stripped of their hides, turned inside out and hung on hooks, their marbled fat glistening in the afternoon sun. Next up is a toyshop, the centerpiece in its window: a golden remote-controlled Mercedes Benz flanked by Barbie dolls both blue-eyed, blonde and brown-skinned, veiled. Next is another *kahwa*, this one more ornate with stained glass windows and hookah pipes lined like sentries along the front display. Another butcher, grocery stores, more toy stores, and yet more butchers. While this commercial reel unspools across the car window, another residential reel flickers through the Volvo's sunroof: homes cap the ground-floor marketplace, laundry hanging from the balcony railings, women and men popping their heads in and out, some conversing with each other from one balcony to the next like bees in a latticed beehive. A middle-aged woman leans out of a second-floor window and dangles a yellow bucket from a rope to a grocer below. It's filled with a bag of vegetables then pulled back up. The Latin melodrama, joyous and sad, busy and slow, plays along.

We're now at the outskirts of the market. As we turn a bend Nancy points at a single house perched on the top of the hillside. "This must be it, huh?" she says, and I have to agree; it's the only one that matches the house Sheikh Faqih indicated earlier.

"You're right. Look at all the others," I say, nodding my

chin toward the other hills. "They're clustered together like neighborhoods. I think that one over there is ours, where I grew up. But yes, this one here is on its own."

Nancy slides her head back in and I watch her delicate shoulders sway as I swerve off the main road onto the rugged hillside. Her eyes remain fixed in the direction of my own house as we make our way up the hill, the turns in the road getting steeper as we ascend. The Volvo cuts through the hillside effortlessly, leaving a cloud of dust in its wake, and as it settles again the town we just drove through reveals itself more and more, now a vista of a day running at half-speed, as Javier Álvarez's *Por Qué Te Vas* plays on the cassette deck. Nancy sings along, tapping her fingers on the armrest between us. "*Junto a las manillas de un reloj, esperarán. Todas las horas que quedaron por vivir, esperaran.*"

The house disappears behind the hillside as the road gets steeper, then reappears behind some trees only to disappear again—a house less of stone and brick than memory and mirage. It flickers between them like frames from an old film, neither here nor there, always somewhere in between. Nancy has her back to me, her head once again sticking out of the window. But from the reflection in her side mirror, I catch a familiar look in her eyes—her mind is sifting through ten, maybe even twenty thoughts at once. Until the perfect ones align across her cerebral cortex like cherries on a jackpot machine, she will not rest. And neither will I. This Tariq Jaber business is getting close to home—in more ways than one—and Ibrahim's maggots and the Jabers' barks and bites be damned, I will get to the bottom of it.

We make a final turn as we land on a plateau and the house reveals itself to us completely, sitting in the middle of an open field. Silent, austere, venerable.

The Volvo comes to a stop on an incline where the gravel ends and the soil begins, or, as Nancy might put it, where civilization stops and nature starts. A brisk jangle of keys kills the engine and brings Álvarez's melodic voice to an abrupt halt. We step out of the car, I on the side of gravel and Nancy on the side of soil, my shoes with a clunk and hers with a squish. She throws me a breathless "wow" over the top of the car like she had hiked the whole way up on foot.

"Balkees Manor," she says.

I lean against the trunk of the car and study the house: it's different from the other architecture in the area, though not at odds with it. Mahmoud Jaber must have had a say in its design, with elements of Lebanese rustic architecture in its pitched brick roof and limestone walls, but with porch columns that are clearly ornamental and structurally unnecessary, resembling Totem poles. The house itself is unfenced, just surrounded with light forestation, a somewhat West European style common to isolated properties that do not expect frequent visitors or trespassers. All in all, the house exterior suggests a well-traveled eclecticism, certainly uncommon amidst the cookie-cutter vernacular of the Nabatieh upper class.

"This Mahmoud Jaber was a man of specific taste," I say.

"Many different specific tastes," says Nancy over the Volvo, then she starts her descent toward the house. She casts her eyes along the green grass surrounding the mansion, careful to stay on the cobblestone path that begins a few feet from the car.

"What're you looking for?" I ask, trailing behind her.

"Sprinklers. The grass is young, but I can't see any irrigation. I think someone's been watering this grass by hand."

She's right. The ground is healthy for an abandoned house. "Come here for a second," I say, kneeling on one knee. I grab Nancy's foot, set it on my other knee, and tie her shoelace.

"Damn, Professor. Down on one knee. For a second there I thought you were gonna pop the question."

I tap her sneaker. "There. You're all set."

As we approach the entrance, I read an engraving along the top of the porch, "God bless this house and all who enter." We arrive at the front door, a massive panel of rich African mahogany, engraved with an elephant. Brass tusks protrude from the face, the trunk curves out and connects with a hinge to a massive wooden knocker. "House of the Honorable Mahmoud and Balkees Jaber," Nancy reads the brass plaque bolted to the right of the entrance. I lift the knocker, but Nancy yells out "Don't!" Then to my startled jump more apologetically, "Don't, please. There's no worldly reason to knock at an empty house." She smiles nervously as I release the knocker onto the brass base with barely a click. "What? It's not superstition. Really, it's not! I'm just... it's just good manners."

"They have, you know, passed away," I say, trying hard to avoid sounding sarcastic. "The owners, Tariq, Balkees, the father, they're all gone."

"So let's show them some respect, huh?" She shivers as she says this, but tries to hide it as she hugs herself and takes a few steps back. I follow her, the house looming over us, now looking much more voluminous than it did from our outpost behind the Volvo.

Unlike the traditionally symmetrical massing of the houses clustered on the other hillsides, this structure was built to fit snugly into its site, looking very much at home with the valley on one side and the mountain on the other. The house just exists; it simply is.

We stand in front of the entrance, marked by a two-story cube. It's flanked on one side by a single-story cube overlooking the valley below, and on the other by the tallest volume, three-stories in height, hugging the hillside and towering over the house. A dendrologist once wrote that trees are able to carry themselves throughout their life, even at birth, needing no external support. The house appears that way: rather than being built, it looks like it grew out of the land here. Its contours follow the natural rise of the hillside, with the only sign of man-made intervention being the tower.

It's the only part of the house not capped with the typical pitched roof, but rather with castle-like crenellations more typical of European Bastille-type architecture than of the softer more Riviera-influenced style of the Mediterranean coastline, of which Lebanon itself is a part. It's the only unnatural addition to the volume.

At its base, an open arch cuts through the front of the house. I step off the path onto the grass and walk over to it as Nancy follows. As we get closer, her pace hastens and she skips ahead of me to the opening. "Neat! It's a tunnel! Check it out!" she sings without a trace of her previous reserve.

I look through the mouth of the opening: the inside is dim but it's clear that the tunnel cuts through the entire mass of the building to the other side, ending with another archway, the silhouette of a leafy tree branch peeking into it. Nancy clasps my wrist and pulls me in.

As my eyes adjust to the dank darkness, I avert them from the glare of the opening to speed up the process. The tunnel reveals itself as a flat, rectilinear corridor; whoever built it marked the two ends with archways but didn't build a barrel vault to connect them, an amateur job at best in both concept and execution. This seems at odds with the rest of the structure of the mansion, which exhibits a higher degree of architectural expertise.

Nancy's anxious tugs throw me off balance, and as I lean

against the wall, it feels smooth to the touch, unlike the rough corbeled stone of the exterior. There are no other openings along the length of the tunnel—and as far as I can tell, it serves no other function except as a passageway from the front to the back. The glare from the back opening spills onto the floor and walls, revealing a dampness unseen anywhere else so far—must be a loose pipe somewhere, with water running through it.

"Funny an abandoned house should have running water when many inhabited houses in this town don't," I say. But Nancy's too excited to pay heed to my words, even though her tightening grip on my hand tells me they don't go unheard.

After what seems like several minutes (though it can't have been more than a few seconds) we exit through the archway on the other side. My right shoulder brushes against the bark of the tree guarding the mouth of the tunnel. I lean against it just as my eyes adjust to the midday light. The yard where we now find ourselves ends on the left with the hillside we drove around and opens into a field on the right. "The grass is always greener on the other side," I say. Then I instantly regret uttering such a banality, even though the grounds really were greener here than they are in front of the house.

"And wilder," Nancy adds. She's right: the green ground here has been allowed to grow naturally, several centimeters plusher than that on the other side. Flowers too, geraniums, lilies, sunflowers spurt out here and there in clumps, swaying to and fro in the light breeze. Nancy releases my hand with a yelp and sprints diagonally across the unkempt garden.

My adjusting eyes take a moment to realize her destination. The adjacent forest and the fenced ridge of the plateau overlooking the valley form a corner about ten meters away, embracing a cozy playground. There's a seesaw, a cube of monkey bars, a pair of swings and a merry-go-round. This last ride is what catches

Nancy's fancy, and she squeezes into one of the seats.

"Come on!" she says.

I trot over and without even thinking push her seat with all my might. She circles around twice, and before coming to a complete stop she grasps my hand and yells "Get on!" which I do, again without much thought. We each dig our heels into the ground and heave ourselves forward with our legs. I lift mine up as her words slur into a "Whee!" The house, the archway, the forest and the valley blur into streaks of color. We give ourselves another shove as we circle around again. I look up to avoid getting dizzy and catch the midday sun. It smiles down from the center of the sky above us, the only constant in a swirling world.

◆

Nancy hops off the merry-go-round. We catch our breaths as she hugs me and buries her face into my chest, her moist forehead rubbing against my cheek.

I stroke her hair then squeeze her hand as we walk toward the back wall of the house. "Let's see if we can get in," I say as we approach a wooden door. A thick-padlocked chain runs through the handle, but doesn't connect to the jamb on the wall. I give the handle a tug and then another, and the door swings open with a burst of dust and wood splinters. Nancy rubs her nose with a half-sneeze.

We take a few steps into what looks like a pantry. Light streams through the doorway and reflects off lines of shelves along both sidewalls. Besides overlapping patterns of circular rust stains probably made by years of canned goods, the shelves are bare. In the far corner of the room another doorway leads into the kitchen, not quite as bare, though as austere as the pantry.

It's filled with kitchen items and remains seemingly intact from when it was used. Pots and pans, rusty but otherwise in pristine condition, hang from a line of hooks on a wooden bar along the wall. Next to it stands a glass cabinet filled with porcelain plates, cups and—"Wine glasses," says Nancy. "Not your typical Muslim family, huh." Along the other wall, a countertop with rich black granite ends in a modern aluminum sink. Next to the sink is a niche where a fridge once stood. "Nancy, look at this," I say and crouch down to inspect four rusty markings. "Fridge legs. Tariq's General Electric fridge in Achrafieh had them. Who'd carry such a load of junk all the way to Beirut?"

"For a sentimental type, maybe it's not such a load," says Nancy. "How long after his mother died do you think he left?"

"Let's find out," I say, standing up. I traipse through the kitchen door into a vast hallway. The ceiling here is much higher, and on one side a staircase connects to the upper levels. My footsteps echo against the high walls and Nancy's sneakers squeak against the fine marble tiles. A fine veneer of dust spreads across the floor, but otherwise the room is quite—"Clean," says Nancy, completing my thought.

We continue ahead and the hallway opens into an even larger room, this one three floors high.

"Fancy," I say.

"Especially for a non-politician," Nancy says in agreement and swirls around as she looks up. Where a chandelier must have been now remains a chain with a bare bulb attached. "This was the salon, huh? And here must've been the dining room," she says as she strides across. "But look!" My echoing footsteps sound like I'm moving at double-speed, adding a sense of urgency to my approach toward a rickety cot. Next to it sits a table with a gramophone, and next to that a pile of children's astronomy books is topped with a throwaway Arabic paperback.

"We were right," says Nancy.

"More than right," I say flipping through the book. "There's no dust on these books. Somebody has a vested interest in maintaining this house. I should've known—his neighbor said Tariq was messy, but he'd never let his mother's house fall into disrepair. He, or someone he knew, has been here recently."

"But how recently, we can't know."

I set the book down and look around. Yes this space's been used as a bedroom of sorts. "Close to the kitchen and bathroom, but why sleep here?" Pointing at another doorway, I add out loud, "Let's check the upper—" but of course Nancy is already halfway up the staircase.

I follow her up the staircase, which ends in a wide gallery overlooking the lower level. There's a door at one end and a sliding glass screen on the other. We're closer to the door, so I walk toward it past Nancy, who leans against the railing and looks down at the space we just left.

I open the door and look in: it's dim, stuffy, unused for many years, the only heavily dusty room yet. I take a few steps inside. A plush bed occupies most of the space, the only piece of real furniture we've seen. I lean onto it and press into the mattress, releasing a fog of dust. I sneeze.

"Bless you!" says Nancy from the gallery. I sneeze again. "Bless you!" she's now closer, and then "Oh wow!" she says as she walks in. I look around too. Wow indeed; this is quite ornate. An oak wardrobe almost touching the ceiling occupies one wall, and on the other an elaborate night dresser and mirror with an old fashioned flamingo-shaped perfume dispenser sitting atop it. A broad window covers the third wall. Sunlight filters through the edges of the curtains, bathing the room in a dim glow. I notice the walls, wallpapered with a gold and turquoise baroque pattern. A doorway leads into a pink bathroom at least as big as the kitchen.

"Who'd sleep on that shitty cot with a bedroom like this?" asks Nancy.

"Don't you think sleeping in your parents' bed is a little, I don't know... I wouldn't do it. Could you?"

"When it's this gorgeous? Fuck yeah!"

"His mother had just died. We can't pinpoint how many times he's been here since."

My allergy makes my eyes well up and my nose sniffle. Nancy pulls off my glasses and looks up at me, preparing for another "Bless you," but it's a false alarm. Instead, she leans toward me and brushes her lips against mine, then pulls me back onto the bed. In the thick darkness of the room eroded by secrets, she rolls on top of me, the small of her neck teasing my eyelashes, her tender shoulders outlined by a ray of light that slices through slits in the shutters.

"Those squishy eyes," she says. "I wanna squeeze them with my thumbs and tickle your brains."

We're on the merry-go-round again, the Nabatieh landscape blurring around us. Faces from my childhood mix with Tariq's final words and the inscription on Balkees' grave as a macabre dance lifts us in its jazz, suspended between here and long ago. Nancy tugs my clothes off and I strip her naked. I stroke her chest until it quivers with every breath that was ever drawn in this room. Her fingers tighten around my eyeglasses until one of the lenses pops out.

She falls onto me and I lose myself into her.

◆

I squint through the slits in the bedroom window, pinching my glasses until they rest precariously on the bridge of my nose. Nancy buttons her shirt on the bed behind me, then smiles up at the crooked glasses. I'm sure they twist my face into a permanent pre-sneeze. "Let's go," she says. "Before you're hit by another avalanche."

Outside the bedroom, I ease the door shut and we walk along the upper gallery, away from the staircase, to the other end. Nancy unlatches the glass screen and it slides open without a squeak. We are outdoors, on a terrace above the dining room. "Nice," says Nancy, as she stretches her arms and spins around. Indeed the view is breathtaking, high above the terraced valley. In the distance lies the town center we drove through, and beyond that, the gleam of cars along the seafront. A thin layer of fog blurs the horizon, making it appear like the sea and the sky form a seamless blue gradient. On the west side, the three hills from the photograph, and from my memory, huddle together to form the town of Upper Nabatieh, an organic landscape of green and brown, salted with limestone white and peppered with brick red. A layer of dry mud decks the terrace under my feet, bare except for a plastic chaise longue and a matching plastic table like a set you'd find on the beach—minus the parasol. Nancy crouches toward the table and picks something up. "Hey," she says beckoning me over, and twirling the object between her fingers.

It's a long cigarette stub. She holds it up to her face and gives it a squeeze. "Marlboro. Soft," she says, then holds it to her nose and adds, "three, maybe four days old. So somebody was here."

"Yes," I say. "But not Tariq. He smoked Luckies."

"I know who it could be, though."

I cock my head toward the smelly cigarette. "Ibrahim. He smokes Marlboros. I noticed it too. But come on, that's probably the most popular brand. Even I know that."

"Yeah, but look. This one, all of them. Just one puff. And look how packed it is. Remember how Ibrahim whacked his pack?" She squeezes it again between her fingers then tosses it back into the full ashtray on the plastic table. "Of course, I'm just guessing."

"At this point, all of this is guesswork. Holmes, looks like you've done it again."

She lays her arms on my chest and smiles. "Told ya. Seems Ibrahim's as worried for Tariq as he is for us. And he was closer to him than he pretended to be."

I nod. "So Tariq finds out his mother was married to this Maurice," I say. "Then he leaves the house in Ibrahim's care, and moves to Beirut. But why?"

"Maybe something in this house will tell us," says Nancy. She kisses me and my nose sniffles again. She smells her fingers, "Ugh, sorry," she says with a grimace, pushing herself away. "Stale cigarettes. Worst stench ever."

◆

As we descend the stairs, Nancy takes another look down then says over her shoulder, "We missed something, I can feel it. There's the tower we saw from—" She turns away, trips, and goes flying over the last three steps with a "Shitfuckgoddamn," landing knee-first on the marble below. In an instant, I'm at the foot of the stairs kneeling next to her for the second time today.

"It's those fucking laces again," she says, but when I reach for them she waves my hand away, slumps flat on her butt, and curls her leg toward her. "It's fine. I got it."

She ties her shoelace. Her jeans are now ripped at the knee and two thin slashes cut through her skin, punctuated by beads of ruby red. "Come let me take a look." I tug at her arm to pull her closer to the light, but she doesn't budge. Staring ahead, she says, "Wait."

I follow her gaze to a door on the back wall. We somehow missed it on the way in, but its position makes sense because I now realize the tower outside doesn't connect to the house at any other point. "It's boarded up." I walk toward her, and tug at the wooden planks crisscrossing the surface of the door. "Strange, huh," I say. "Out of place with the rest of the house."

"Messy," Nancy says, clawing stubbornly at the planks with the tips of her fingers.

"But newer." I run my hand along its hinges, paint only partially peeled off. "And look at these nails," I add, stroking the heads of the metal studs attaching the planks to the door and wall. "No rust. Couldn't be older than a year. Hold on."

I make my way to the kitchen as Nancy's voice trails behind me. "They've been hammered in recently." I look under the sink and open a cupboard there. "So," Nancy adds, the voice rising in pitch. "It's house, extension, boards, Tariq moves, Ibrahim turns caretaker. In that order." The voice now comes muffled as my neck cranes further under the sink, my head boring deeper into the bowels of the cupboard. "Hmm, a definite maybe," I yell back, fumbling among a trough, a broom, a spade, an axe—why do they need an axe in a house that has no chimney and no need for firewood?—and there: a hammer.

I grab it and rush back to Nancy, then with a few yanks use it to pry the planks right off. Nancy opens the door and looks into the pitch darkness.

"Stairs," I say.

"Alright, up we go," says Nancy, brushing off my concerned glance at her knee with an "I'm fine." She slides past me and takes a few steps up.

We feel our way against the walls, step after slow step.

183

"Concrete," I remark. "Not stone like the rest of the house. This was built separately."

Nancy stops and I bump into her. "Hold on," she says a second too late, as I feel her rummage through her pocket. The darkness emits one flinty sound followed by another, and then explodes with a spark. The flame flickers hesitantly then grows as she winds the widget along the barrel of the gold Zippo lighter with the Hand of Fatima, a distant memory from the supermarket just a few hours back.

"Hey, you said you'd bum me a cigarette," she says, the flame twinkling in her eyes. We continue up and as we arrive at the landing a slit of light falls on us. We get to the second landing and approach it. It's a door, and when we swing it open light streams through. My eyes adjust to reveal a room stocked with wooden frames, canvases, paint buckets, used palettes, and other assorted art supplies. A window facing the door opens onto the earthy hillside just a few meters away.

"Great view for a storage room," Nancy says popping the lighter back in her pocket. "Yeah they could've used one of the lower spaces," I agree.

We leave the door open for the light, ascend the second flight, get to another door, and open it. Right on cue, Nancy and I turn to one another, her face reflecting my own surprise.

It's like a hall of mirrors, or a visual echo chamber, filled with living epitaphs. Along the walls, across the walls, spanning the walls, hanging from them, propped against them, leaning in their corners, large, small, square, rectangular, and in every other conceivable position, stand paintings, all of the same landscape. And in the center of the back wall, facing the door across the room, a window opens out to the Nabatieh hillside, that very landscape.

I survey the paintings again, taking a few steps closer to the nearest one. Nancy follows breathlessly as I realize my mistake: the paintings might seem like they're of the same view, but only to undiscerning eyes. The window shows the hillside as it is today, now, this very instant. This painting shows the hillside in the summertime, with its infinitely richer variations of oak green, sky blue, and sun orange. The next painting shows the same landscape in late spring, probably a few months earlier, or a year and a few months, or ten and a few months.

"Balkees," says Nancy, hovering her hand a venerable millimeter across the winter canvas a few boards from mine. "Her landscapes bloomed, withered, died, and then bloomed again. They circled from life to death and back to life."

An art expert would date these paintings along a timeline of paint and canvas erosion. A botanist would date the landscape depicted in cycles of Summer, Autumn, Winter, and Spring. A dendrologist like myself would study the trees in the paintings and combine the line and cycle: while the rest of nature lives in seasons, trees also live in years. Every tree is a story of time told in spirals. "Her body wound down," I say. "But it seems Balkees' mind was good until the end."

Nancy pulls out another painting, one of the very few that aren't landscapes. "Is this Tariq's cat?" she asks, pointing to the feline in the center of the canvas.

"Yes, that's Tarboush. One and the same."

"He's not a Persian. See those pointy ears and big almond eyes? That's a Turkish Angora. It has a body shaped like a ballerina, long limbs, very agile?"

"Something like that."

"Yeah that's definitely an Angora. They say the Prophet had one. He named it Abu Huraira, the Father of Cats. Loved it so much that one day the cat was napping on his cloak, and at prayer time he cut the fabric around it to avoid disturbing it.

Those things are very fragile and need constant care. They make good pets and don't do well in the wild. That's why they love family and are friendly, even to strangers."

"Didn't seem so friendly to me. It took me thirty minutes to find him. I called out and he just wouldn't come."

"Does Tarboush have blue eyes?"

"Actually yes, he does. One blue and another green I think. The painting doesn't show that. How did you know?"

"Because that means he's probably deaf, at least in one ear. It's said that when the Prophet's cat once saved him from a snake poised to bite, he thanked it by stroking its back, which, by the way, is why no cat ever falls on its back. But the Prophet also left marks on the top of the cat's head, so every Turkish Angora with those marks is perfectly healthy. Now see how the cat in the painting here has no marks? If this is Tarboush and he has no marks either, it means he's partially deaf."

"I don't remember seeing any marks."

"Then, my friend, Tarboush is hard of hearing. And most likely lactose intolerant too."

"There was milk in Tariq's kitchen. It was all over the place."

"Well then," says Nancy. "Whoever left it there knew nothing about this cat."

She paces along the series of canvases, most of the same landscape. She picks up another painting, this one of the same Nabatieh hillside, now with its swirling clouds and undulating valleys, smattered with white stone houses capped with red brick. But something in this particular painting is unnerving— what, I'm not sure. Nancy sees it too.

"See how the sky is clear blue, with just a few clouds," she says.

"Summertime, around midday."

"Yes," she nods then runs her finger down the painting to the landscape at its bottom. "The back hillsides catch a bit of that light around the horizon line, and get darker the lower we get."

"Nighttime. You're right, look the windows in the houses are lit."

"Aha, and see the landscape is wet in some places. Look at those puddles, they're reflecting a very different sky. A stormy sky, with clouds and darkness."

"What does it mean?"

"Your guess is as good as mine," she says with a shrug. "Freud calls it 'the uncanny,' the unfamiliar in the familiar. The bizarre in the commonplace."

"The bazaar in the marketplace," I say, but Nancy's having none of my smartassery, certainly not at her expense. So I revise my stance. "Art class?" I say, recalling how she filled all her elective credits with humanities classes, which I used to doggedly insist were an utter waste of time.

"Yup," she says as she twirls her finger through her hair and pulls her face into a theatrical smirk. "But not just that. I was obsessed with the idea for a while, and studied a lot about it. In art too. Surrealist artist Magritte has a similar painting, *Empire of Light* I think it's called, of a house at night with a daytime sky. But Balkees here, she's taken it a step further. You're right, this is definitely the work of a thinking mind."

"Look at this one too," I say, wondering how we could have arrived at the same conclusion through such divergent lines of reasoning: I, through observing the trees in the paintings, she, through studying their content. The painting is set during winter. The landscape is barren and bare, and at first glance seemingly just a representation—if a very good one—of a real Nabatieh, although one I've never experienced. However, in the corner a tree clearly depicts the outline of a man, his arms twisting and winding into branches. And the highest one cradles

187

a half-formed fetus, anatomically correct except for clear facial features that smile healthily. But then I notice another oddity, which I point out to Nancy. "These white strokes running down his face," I say. "He's been crying."

"Man, child, storm," she says, in a poetic mood again. "And Balkees had a steady hand. Takes a lot of control to paint lines as fine as those."

"Look at this tree," I say. "It looks different without its leaves, but can you tell what it is?"

Nancy squints at the painting then turns to me and says, "An Acacia of course! But why? There aren't any around here, no?" She continues to browse through the paintings around the room.

"Maybe there were at some time," I say. "This gallery is her life's work—"

"Flashing before her eyes like a series of memories," adds Nancy lyrically.

In another corner of the room sits her wheelchair, stainless steel frame, leather seat and armrests, and behind it another line of paintings propped against a piece of furniture. I pull away the canvases to reveal a bed. "It was also her bedroom," I say as Nancy pushes her palms into the single mattress, comfortable-looking but a far cry from the plush king-size in the other bedroom.

Above the bed hangs another painting from a hook. The smallest yet, but also the only one in a frame, it's again a simple rendition of the same view, now at night with stars and a crescent moon. Another aspect of this work makes it unique among the others: it's captioned in the corner with white, delicate, childish letters. I read the words out loud, "My mother cried, but then there was a star danced, and under that was I born."

"Shakespeare," says Nancy. "It's from *Much Ado About*

Nothing." Then, to my impressed look, she adds, "What? I like the movie."

"Stars," I say, looking out of the window. "Mother and son were both stargazers."

"Yes, yes, yes," says Nancy to the rhythm of her sneaker tap, tap, tapping against the wooden floor. "These three markings. You think they belong to a tripod?"

"Probably," I say. "I bet that's where Tariq set up his telescope."

She tugs the bed cover and leans her face into it. "It makes me sad when a dead person's scent lingers onto their fabrics. Makes me feel like they're still here."

"Speaking of fabrics," I say, following my words to a wardrobe in the corner. It creaks open and several dresses sway to and fro on their hangers. "For a woman who rarely went out in public, she dressed up."

"I have a feeling this wasn't just her gallery or bedroom," Nancy says. "It was her home. Her whole life."

Nancy runs her hand along the bed sheet, "Look at these pockmarks," she says. I approach her, careful not to bump into the wheelchair—I feel it would be sacrilegious to. "They're cat claws," she continues. "I had a cat and she used to get a spanking from my mom when she sharpened her claws on the sofa."

"Looks like our buddy Tarboush lived here too."

"Does it matter?" asks Nancy.

"I think it does. If the cat was a part of Tariq's life here until his mother died, then it makes sense it was precious enough to mention in his dying words."

"Which also means," Nancy continues my thought with her Nancy's onto-something smile, "that the rest of those words made sense too, and we're not on some delirious trip. He wanted you to find that journal, and to find Maurice. We're here now because that's what Tariq wished. I'm convinced of that now.

But then why did he leave?"

"I don't know," I say. "But I think it's time we leave too."

"Not until we find an answer. Why did Tariq move to Beirut?"

"Think about it," I say. "With his mother dead, he was the only thing standing between the remaining Jabers and their inheritance."

"But I don't think he'd just run away, leaving all this behind."

I sit on the bed with an exasperated sigh. "What's 'all this,' Nancy?" I say, running my hand over the pockmarked bedsheet. "It's just mementos."

"It's all he had. No, I'm sure there's something else. It's here somewhere..."

As Nancy wonders out loud, I slide my hand further along the bed sheet, under the pillow. My thumb hits a small metallic object. I grip it and pull it up to my face. "Such as this?" I say.

"Oh my God, a key!" says Nancy. "Yes! Exactly 'such as this.'" She snatches it and flips through the standing canvases, peeking behind them, looking for something to open. As I watch her, I remember something I saw under Tariq's bed. It was a long metallic case. I lean forward and look under the bed and sure enough, I pull out a small wooden box, locked with a golden clasp matching the key.

"Here you go," I say, pulling it toward Nancy.

"Professor!" she says. "You're the man." She scurries over, sits on the floor and props the box on her knee, then unlocks it and looks inside.

"Letters," she says with a smile, fanning out a handful of envelopes. "Let's see. One, two, three, four. That's it. She must have kept the photograph here too. But why not just hand the whole lot over to Sheikh Faqih?"

"I suppose she wanted to keep some things to herself," I say.

"Some are addressed to her, and some from her. Wait!

Maurice. That's the name signed on the ones to her. The envelopes themselves aren't postmarked."

I slide off the bed, lean against its edge across from Nancy and flip through the letters. "The ones from Maurice must've been hand-delivered. And the ones from Balkees, she never sent."

"You're right," says Nancy. "They were hand-delivered. I think Ibrahim was the go-between. He said he worked in Syria for a while. The newer ones are dated a few years ago, the older like maybe ten, fifteen."

She reads through them then says, "They're strange, all written in the third person—he felt this, she thought that. Balkees writes about the tower, how Maurice himself built it with Tariq. They call each other morning star and evening star."

I remember the photograph, which I pull out of my jacket and flip around. Nancy reads the dedication on the back, smeared with dry blood. "Yes. Morning and evening star are both Mercury, one and the same," she says, stroking my bandaged finger. "You see planets are divided into two groups, morning and evening. Except Mercury. It's neutral."

"That can't be your brother talking. I get astronomy. But this is pure astrology. As a kid my father taught me the difference: one begins with 'astro' and the other with 'ass.'"

"They both begin with 'astro,' you ass!" says Nancy. "Anyway it's not just astrology. It's also politics."

"How so?" Now I'm intrigued.

"You see, those two groups, morning and evening, are called sects. The only planet which belongs to both sects is Mercury."

"A non-sectarian star," I say. "Could be. Maurice is from Syria, Balkees from here. They were probably from different sects, which couldn't have made their lives any easier."

Nancy turns back to the letters. "They mention no one by name," she says. "Not even Tariq. They just refer to him as 'the boy,' maybe encoding the letters in case they fell into the wrong hands."

"Like ours," I say.

Nancy clearly doesn't share my reluctance in reading someone else's mail. "But I think you should read them," she says absently, and then snaps her eyes back to mine. "Please."

She hands them to me and I arrange them in chronological order. Recent events are more relevant, more concrete, so I read the last one first. It's from Maurice, chronicling the exact day the photograph was taken. Poetic, whimsical, completely empty of anything we don't know already. The second to last, sure enough, is about the building of the tower, this time from Balkees. She writes about watching the two men bring her dream to life. The earlier one, also from Balkees, is dated many years prior, at a time when Tariq must have been no more than five or six. It tells the story of a stubborn boy, on the monkey bars, refusing to come down. It's followed by the oldest letter, one from Maurice.

I was wrong. Whatever answer we've been looking for is right there, not in the most recent, but in the oldest, most distant, most whimsical letter of them all. I read a passage out loud.

"It felt like many years, four years to be exact, the four years since he saw Balkees last. A lot had happened in that time. A new life had entered his. A daughter, who one day he'll send here. But not to Nabatieh. That would be reckless. To Beirut maybe. Maybe one day she could be a companion to the boy he's here to meet. Then they could be together, as it should be."

"Maurice has a daughter," says Nancy. "That's why Tariq left, to seek out Maurice's daughter. Ibrahim urged us to leave them alone. 'Them,' he said. He meant Tariq and this companion."

"Maybe," I say, curling my arm around her waist.

"You said it yourself, Professor. Maybes are all we have."

"It's getting dark," I say, scooping her toward me. "Let's go."

Nancy returns the letters back to the box. She locks it and slides it back under the bed, where it should remain. As I watch her, a breeze floats through another window by the door. The garden below is partly obscured by the tree we passed when we exited the tunnel. I reach out and tug at the rustling branch. It quivers in response.

Nancy shuffles over to the window and looks out, then turns to me and says, "That tree over there. That isn't an Acacia, is it?"

"No," I say. "It's not the one in the painting. That's an olive tree. You should've paid more attention in my class."

As I slide my fingers into my pocket, the cut stings, but I'm careful not to allow Nancy to see it on my face. She's suppressing much more pain, and her footsteps echo clumsily down the stairs.

"How's the leg?" I ask.

"Heavy," she says. "Imagine how painful it must've been for Balkees to climb up and down. I think the three of them avoided the rest of the house and just lived in the tower."

"The three of them?" I ask. "You mean the cat too?"

"Yes. Looks like she was a proud woman who wouldn't sleep on that pecked bed sheet unless the cat was her roommate." We reach the foot of the stairs and as we exit the house through the kitchen I notice Nancy's shuffle has turned into a full-blown limp. I try to keep my hand on her shoulder for support, but she stubbornly trudges ahead, a step out of reach.

She's already outside as I cut through the hallway. I catch a glimpse of a moving shadow on the wall and freeze. I look over my shoulder, but no one's there. Then a few steps forward and I realize what it was: a large mirror covering almost the entire wall, and in it my own reflection. I inch toward it and there I stand, dwarfed by the emptiness of Tariq Jaber's house.

With an immense effort I finally tear myself from my reflection and step over the threshold once again to the exterior of the house. It's darker now. Nancy scans the garden, her hair blowing in the wind. "I wouldn't leave this place either," she says as I lean my hand against the tree at the mouth of the tunnel. "I mean even to go to town. Those two, they lived in a paradise."

"Or in a prison. Look, a gate." She turns as I show her a metal gate at the mouth of the tunnel, partly obscured by the tree. "This looks like it hasn't been used for a while, maybe not since Tariq was a child," I add, pointing to the pattern formed by the iron bars of the gate: a crude rendition of Mickey Mouse, with big round ears and whiskers, but with a clown nose and a big toothy smile.

"Maybe it's to keep people out," says Nancy.

"No, it would've been on the other end of the tunnel if that were the case. I think it's to keep them in. Doors work both ways."

Nancy hugs herself. "I hate clowns," she says with a shiver.

"Who doesn't?" I say. My voice is cold and distant.

◆

As we emerge through the tunnel onto the front lawn, Nancy's left step sounds heavier than her right, harmonizing with the asymmetrical drip-drip behind us.

"Why didn't they just call or email each other?" I say. "It's a little paranoid and archaic to write letters, don't you think?"

"They weren't writing letters," Nancy says. "They were exchanging handwritten mementos. She didn't even send hers, just held onto them as tightly as she did onto his. Empathy,

Professor. You could learn some."

She grins, but then I remember something, a loose thread. I take Nancy's hand and carefully walk her along the front of the house, past the main porch, across the grass, and to the edge of the plateau. "According to Balkees' painting, it should be right… about… here."

I stop, and look down. I slide my shoes across the ground, brushing away the grass. As I expect, the stump of an Acacia sits half-buried in the soil.

"It's been chopped off," Nancy says angrily.

I squeeze her hand then let go and crouch down for a closer look. "It was one, two, three… fifty years old. Probably was in the Jaber family longer than the house itself."

"That's crazy. Who would… why would anyone want to kill a tree like this? Can you tell when it was done?"

"Only if the bark were dead. But no, it's alive. Stunted, but still kicking. That's one stubborn stump. There's no way to—unless, hmm… wait here."

I stand and walk closer to the edge. Never one to take orders, Nancy follows close behind. "What're…? Careful!" she yells.

I lean over the edge and look down the hillside. There, the bark of a fully-grown Acacia tree lies on its side. "Christ," says Nancy. "Even dead, it's so… majestic. What? You're insane! Careful, goddamn it. Hold on, I'm coming with—ouch, shit my leg."

"I have to find out," I pant through her objections as I slide off the edge and start my climb down the hillside. I grip the weeds, thankful for their resilience. As I keep telling my students—and they love the irony—even weed has its use. But even after losing five kilos to my Acacia research project, it's impossible to carry my own weight and I lose my grip. "It's okay, it's easier than it looks!" I yell up as Nancy continues running through the entire range of her colorful vocabulary "Goddammit you crazy sonofabitch watch out Jesus Christ wait until you get back up here you fucking lunatic. Damn my shit-for-leg."

Sliding down the slope, my feet come to a stop against a pair of wooden poles lined with green moss. They've been here a few months, a year perhaps, but not much longer. "Balkees' crutches!" I yell back to Nancy, but if she hears me, it doesn't register through her anxiety. She knows I'm not a man of action.

I get to the bark and stop for a few seconds to catch my breath. I look up toward Nancy, but the sun blinds me. "It's fine! I'm there!" I yell out in her general direction, and then turn toward the fallen tree as I clap the dust off my hands.

Nancy's right. Even dead—and now my first impression tells me for many years—what's left of the tree itself is a proud specimen of foliage. Most of its branches are crushed by its own weight or by the impact of rolling down the hillside. Still, several thorns stick out of them. I lean onto it and walk along its length for a closer look, careful not to cut my chest on its branches or prick my palms on its thorns.

"What do you see?" Nancy's voice pierces through the ever-stronger wind.

I run my hand along the bark, paying special attention to the broken joints with the branches. There's no sap, no moisture left in the wood. Time of death: around twenty years ago. Even the moss along the branch is withered.

I run my hand along the entire length of the bark, careful not to lose my step. I walk around it and repeat the motion all the way from the highest branch down its length. Close to the truncated base, I come across an engraving. I wipe off the years of dust, moss and grime. Yes, there it is, as clear as day. A beautiful, delicate, geometric engraving inscribed in a circle. "Found it," I say.

"What? What is it?"

"I'm coming up!" I croak, as I make my way back. Anxious to share my discovery with her, but afraid my voice might not handle the windy distance, I scramble up the hillside. I lose my footing once ("Jesus watch out Goddamn it!" she yells) but make it quickly to the top.

"I hope you've saved some curse words," I say, smacking the dust off my pant legs. "You're gonna need them when I tell you what I found down there."

"Well?" she says.

"Well. The Acacia departed this world a couple of decades ago, around the time Tariq entered it."

"Uh, huh. And?"

"And there's an inscription carved into the bark. A star inscribed in a circle."

"The morning star?"

"Or the evening star," I say.

"Both. Balkees and Maurice."

"Do you think Tariq did it?"

"No. For one thing, the timelines don't match, right? You said it's definitely been chopped down after the engraving, and before Tariq was born. People might lie, but trees don't. I'm sure you agree, Professor?"

Smart.

"It was done with an artist's hand, which we know Balkees had," I say. "Still, it's strange."

"What is?"

"That compared to everything we've seen, this seems... childish."

"Childlike," Nancy snaps back. "And what's love if not a return to childhood? To being capricious, naive, filled with dreams and secrets?"

I pull out the photograph again and hold it up against the backdrop. "I think this was taken right here, where the tree was. You can even see the clump of grass here where the shadow falls."

"The tree was replaced by Maurice's shadow," Nancy says wistfully.

I lower the photo. "This confirms what the Sheikh told us, and more. Balkees and Maurice were lovers while she was still married to Mahmoud Jaber. He found out, flew into a rage, and chopped down the tree."

A layer of clouds blankets the valley below as a chill tugs at my chest. The sky fills with rain, but it's not ready to spill out yet. The first stars of the day twinkle dimly through the clouds above, while their secrets lie buried at the foot of the hill on which we stand.

"Tariq's story ended three days ago, on that bus," I say. "This is where it began. These are his roots, right here."

"The sins of the father shall be visited upon the sons," says Nancy, quoting *The Book of Exodus*. "I think it goes deeper still. We should trace those roots to their origin." She turns back, her steps brisk but now more labored. I follow her, trying to catch up.

"What do you mean?" I ask. There's no trace of the giddy Nancy of a few minutes earlier. Her face is the same, but her brow seems heavier, weighed down by a past rolling into the present.

"You know," she says, less as a shrug, more as an accusation. "We're living Tariq's life in reverse. You witnessed his death. And here, this was his home. It's time we learn about his birth."

I stop in my tracks, a few meters from the Volvo.

"Yes, Professor," she says, ignoring my demurral. "You must pay the doctor a visit." When I bare my teeth in protest, she adds

198

casually, "I'll ask him to take a look at my knee too."

Vetoed by my own sense of chivalry (the rascal!) I follow her to the car.

◆

My girlfriend is beautiful. I watch her from across the room and remember when she first walked into my classroom. I couldn't keep my eyes off her. I still can't as she stands in the doorway to my parents' garden almost a year later. A halo of light caresses the top of her head, and in her hands a silver tray with empty wine glasses reflects and refracts the light back onto her face. We could be the only two people in the room, as the babble of the twenty other family members and friends of friends mix into a blanket of white noise that carries only Nancy's voice across the vast living room.

She stops by the dining table, lays the tray on it, and leans over the girl at its head. Zeinab has taken charge of a game she plays with the three other children: her younger sister Sara to one side, and next to her my youngest cousin Nour, facing her brother Karim on the other side. All the children are about the same age, yet the three girls have teamed up against the boy in a card game that seems to be a variation on the old *Tarneeb*, but with rules Zeinab makes up on the fly. Nancy rubs the girl's head, but moves over to Karim, who beams at having an adult by his side like he now actually has a chance to win. Nancy points at a card, which Karim instantly slaps on the table, raising his arms in victory before Zeinab can twist the rules again.

Leaving the kids' laughter behind, Nancy carries the tray to the center of the room. She passes my uncle Kamel and aunt Jamila, she the paranoid hypochondriac who, upon hearing a crash in the kitchen jumps up nervously before her brother assures her it's probably just a metal tray, and he the father of the two girls Zeinab and Sara who were just defeated at a game of their own creation back at the dinner-cum-card table Nancy just came from.

Smatterings of his fascinating Islamic theories about science and medicine gather like scraps of dust in my nook by the entrance hall. "…And no one was able to interpret that passage from the Koran," he says, nodding to Nancy then throwing a disapproving glance at the wine glasses on her tray, but then continuing to direct his conversation solely to his sister Jamila, who's only partly listening, still distracted by the crash from the kitchen. "Until one day marine scientists found a subterranean river that connects to the sea, but doesn't flow into it. There was a sharp line between fresh water and salt water, and the two didn't mix."

I recognize the same conversation from many years ago, one Uncle Kamel repeats over and over to illustrate the prescience of the Koran, written a thousand years before subterranean exploration was even possible. Nancy comforts my aunt until she regains her composure, and makes her way toward the kitchen door, throwing me a wink as she passes by. Before she gets there, my cousin Aida, Jamila's daughter, intercepts her close to the other end of the dining table and, in true Lebanese fashion, tries to wrench the tray from her hands with a "*Ma bi seer*, it shouldn't be, please enjoy yourself, I'll take care of it." It's a polite, but fierce, battle of wills: Aida treats Nancy like a special guest, while Nancy responds to Aida like a close relative.

Aida is a jovial young woman who people say has a pretty face, which of course is a euphemism for being morbidly obese. As we grew up, our parents assumed we'd be married one day, which was never a likely prospect. How could it be? Regardless of what tradition says, we were like the fresh and salt water of

Uncle Kamel's parable. Instead, she married Socrate (as strange a name for a Muslim as Maurice is). He's probably in the garden outside taking charge of the carcass grilling (my sniffling vegetarian nose is a sure indication of that), a family ritual in which most of the fathers partake. There's my father of course, Socrate's own drunken, profane, and well-loved father, and then there's his father-in-law Salim (Jamila's husband). Besides that bizarre meat-eating ritual, and contrary to their operatic names, Aida and Socrate live a dull, urbane and, by Nabatieh standards, quite westernized life in Beirut with their two kids, Karim and Nour from the card game.

As I ponder the mathematics of family—its members interconnected like star constellations, and how every few years one either fades away or explodes in a supernova that rocks the entire family—Nancy finally wins the battle of pleasantries with Aida and retains possession of the tray, which she carries through a swinging door into the kitchen.

I'm glad no one seems to notice me. The corner is a good position to just stand and observe. However, the serenity is broken a few seconds later when the kitchen window slides open and a mascaraed eye peeks through it before it slams shut once again.

Through the swinging door Nancy just disappeared behind, a heavily made-up Layal bursts out with outstretched arms. "*Ahlan, ahlan, ahlan,*" she says, jogging toward me with such velocity I take a step back to avoid a full-blown collision and hug myself to cushion the impact as she wraps her arms around me in a hug. She withdraws, her elbows barely missing a startled Aida, then squeezes my face against her bosom, throttles me back and forth, and plants the customary three Lebanese kisses on alternating cheeks. She repeats the motion, this time sniffing me as she does until I'm left with, I imagine, six lipstick marks on my face to commemorate the special occasion of my visit.

"*Wlik*, my darling son! Nabatieh has never shone so bright," she says. "When I saw Nancy in my kitchen a second ago, I wished I could do a *zalghouta!*"

It's been years since I've seen my mother ululate, and I'm glad to keep it that way. That custom of Nabatieh revelers where a woman wags her tongue at an astonishingly high frequency while sounding a shrill shriek has never been my mother's forte, even if in all other respects she's as ear-piercingly affectionate as ever. I'm sure she spent all day (maybe even all week) at home, yet except for her squeaky golden sneakers, she looks and sounds like she's just come back from a wedding. "*Keefik Mama*, how are you," I say through a nose teased by her flowery perfume.

"I'm great *hayete,* light of my life. Wish you'd told me sooner, I'd have made *mulukhiyya*. Except for the *tabbouleh*, it's all meat tonight, I'm afraid. Hold on, I'll whip you up a nice vegetable stew." Then to Nancy, who's just stepped out of the kitchen, she says without a hint of exaggeration, "I make the best *mulukhiyya* ever, but the leaves need to be soaked overnight." Then she pulls Nancy by the fingertips and looks down at her knee. "*Yih, yih, ya dille*. What do we have here?"

"I just tripped, it's nothing," says Nancy. "But tell me. How have *you* been, *tante*?"

"It's not nothing. And I told you last time, it's Layal. None of this *tante* nonsense."

"Okay, *Tante* Layal," says Nancy.

"Good enough, good enough," my mother says, never one for small talk. "We'll get you as good as new in no time. Go wash it in the kitchen and I'll meet you there in a second."

Turning to me she adds, "But first, I'm taking my boy to see his father." She grips my hand, and as if we were crossing the street, we cut through the living and dining rooms. I nod greetings to my uncle and aunt when I walk past them, I blend into the scenery of the house, instantly familiar and unchanged since I left it years ago. My parents have minimalist taste (or what visitors from Nabatieh might consider "minimal" taste). The modern philosophy of "Less is more" is something my mother always preached (except of course when it came to her clothing). She also practiced the Lebanese philosophy of "Eat to your own taste, but dress to that of others."

We make our way past the heated card game taking place at the dining table ("*Yalla* kids, wrap it up," says my mother to the dueling card players as we pass them. "We must set the table for dinner.") and exit through the glass door to the back porch.

The deck of our back yard extends until the edge of the valley, overlooking Downtown Nabatieh in the distance. Balkees Manor isn't visible from here, maybe from the front side of the house though I suppose the hill isn't high enough to offer as clear a view of it as it has of us. Beyond the yard on two sides extends a newly plowed strip of land, its ridges freshly harvested but sown again and already sprouting something, but it's hard to be sure what they are in the incandescent light.

My father commands the center of the yard with his brother-in-law Salim and Bu Socrate on one side, and Uncle Kamel's wife, Amal, on the other. As I expected, Socrate is off at the third side of the garden, against the exterior wall of the kitchen, grilling, from the smell of it, *kafta* and *shish taouk*, minced meat and chicken kababs. Thankfully, my mother leads me upwind of the fumes, then clasps her hands against her back as she drops me off in front of my father's group like they were nursery teachers and this were my first day of school.

Bu Socrate is drunk already and is in the process of spitting out an Abul Abed joke, which my mother has no qualms interrupting mid-punch line. "Look what the cat dragged in," she says.

"Thank you, dear," says my father, very matter-of-factly. It's like he knew I was coming. He draws my mother toward him, and right then and there in the garden, he passionately, scandalously, dips her and squeezes his lips against hers. The guests cheer.

He lifts her back up and she tosses her hair, loses her footing, and stumbles back upright.

"Just in time, son," he says, as he watches her swoon with a naughty smile. "Listen to this one." But before Bu Socrate launches into his joke again, my mother takes her leave. "I must see to Nancy," she says. Then stopping by Socrate, who's sweating profusely over the grill, she adds, "Smells lovely."

My father's eyes linger after her as she disappears into the kitchen, then turn back to the sloshed man at his side as the audience listens intently to Bu Socrate. "'I've had it with my dog,' says Abul Abed to his neighbor one day. 'I've just had it. He'll chase anyone on a bicycle.' 'Hmmm, that is a problem,' says the neighbor. 'What are you gonna do about it?' Abul Abed shakes his head and says, 'I suppose the only thing to do is to take away his bike.'"

The group laughs, but none more heartily than Amal, who breaks into a gummy guffaw. As for me, all I can hear, once again, is the "See you later, Professor!" from three days ago.

Still bubbling with frivolity, Amal turns to me and says, "Now you're a sight we don't see every day!" She pinches my cheek and adds, "And don't you think you're too old for that."

Though I could live without the cheek pinching, I've always liked my uncle's wife. "This and that," I say. "Nancy and I've been working on a project for a few days and we've come to pick Father's brain."

Bu Socrate raises his glass and says, "Looks like you've caught him at the right time. Brain's oiled up." He gulps down the glass and follows it with a neat little burp. Then, apparently surprised his glass is empty, he turns to the liquor table by his grilling son as Amal watches him with good humor.

"So did you bring her with you?" she says. "Haven't seen Nancy since—well, since the hospital." She must realize that even euphemistically, bringing up my father's cancer scare last year would put a damper on the mood, so she corrects herself. "I'll go find her. Sweet girl, sweet, sweet girl, sweet…" She continues mumbling as she disappears into the house in search of Nancy like she were some kitty cat.

"So Father, as I was saying I'd like to—"

"Yes," he says. "Let's have a chat."

He leads us to the corner of the garden, diametrically opposite from the grilling activities. I'm thankful for that small gesture of kindness; my father knows that gatherings rival burning flesh for the top spot on my little list of horrors.

The plowed field stretches out before us on two sides, and now with our backs to the party and my eyes adjusting to the indirect light, I recognize the shoots bursting out of the earth as baby tomatoes. My father clasps his hands behind his back and surveys the field proudly.

"When did you take up gardening, Father?" I ask, careful not to startle him. Since retiring, he's found ways to replace surgery with manual labor. The land that has evolved from the neglected nullipara of my memory into the life force we now look over must be his handiwork.

"It's not gardening," he says. "It's farming. I have no time for idle flowers. This is food."

He crouches and strokes the ground with hands unmarked by the gardening (or farming as he'd call it) he's apparently taken up as a new distraction from unemployment. Leaving work must have left him with more time than he knows what to do with, so when my father says he has no time for something—or someone—it's more a statement of opinion than one of fact. "Looking good," I say—not sure if I direct it to him or to the tomatoes. Indeed, for a man of sixty-seven, even his crouching posture commands a palpable authority over me. He soon straightens back up and gestures us to an outstretched chaise longue in the corner. We sit side by side and look into the field.

"Thanks, son," he says surveying the land, missing, or pretending to miss, my point. "Last season was tough. Been working double-time for the next one." My father has never been one for personal compliments, but his work, on the other hand, he takes great pride in.

"Winter is upon us," I say, doing my best impression of farmer-speak, which he dismisses offhandedly.

"I don't work in cycles of seasons where we sow then harvest," he says. "I pull a few weeds here, pick a few ripe crops there, and plant new seeds directly above them. You could say that when it comes to farming, my method is quite surgical." He leads me to the edge of the garden, pulls up a foldable chair resting against the wall, then asks, "So what brings you to Nabatieh, son?"

"We wanted to see you," I say vaguely. At the mention of "we," I look over my shoulder for Nancy. Where is she when I'm cornered?

"Must've been a nice drive up here with the empty streets the past few days," he says as he unfolds the chair and sets it in front of me. "Of course with the new highways, it's not a bad drive on a regular day either."

He lays his empty glass on a plastic table to his side and continues. Behind him stand half a dozen folded chairs, perhaps set aside to make room for the party underway.

"Must be a whole other story in Beirut," he says, gesturing vaguely behind him, to a distant, perhaps in his mind even imaginary, Beirut. "They're saying riots have broken out."

His old radio is propped on a plastic table. The day my father switches it off is the day he dies. The news is playing inaudibly, but I know it's there anyway. We chitchat to smother the silence, which screams with every unspoken word.

"Riots?"

"Yeah. The people are out for blood. That man's barely in the ground and they're already calling for a conviction. The Minister's holding another press conference tonight. He's promising 'concrete results.'"

"Concrete, huh?"

He laughs. "Concrete my ass. Blockheads, the lot of them. I'll chop my hand off if they get anywhere." I never understood that idiom that Nabatanis use so much, especially when it comes from a surgeon. He knows I'm here for something, which gives him the upper hand to dillydally for as long as he likes, suspending the point of the conversation tantalizingly in front of my nose and taking his precious time to get to it. So I attempt an indirect strategy. If he won't let me get to it, maybe I sneak up to it from the side.

"I stumbled into Ibrahim earlier," I say, sounding, at least to myself, like a true Nabatani. "Remember? The engineer's father."

"Oh yeah? How's that old cockeye doing?"

"He spoke highly of you."

"Well he'd better. That guy owes me his balls."

"His balls?" Now that's an idiom I've not heard before.

"The right one to be exact. The left was beyond repair. During the Israeli occupation, poor guy stepped on a land mine planted in his field. Damn near blew half his body off. You should've seen the rake he was farming with. Burst into splinters the size of toothpicks. I was on call at Hikme Hospital when it happened and had him under my knife before the anesthesia even kicked in."

"Didn't know gynecologists did testicles too," I say, hoping my grin doesn't look too silly on my lipstick-dotted face.

"Bah! It was war, son. Orthopedic surgeons did appendectomies, cardiologists applied casts, dentists barely out of medical school did amputations. We even had mental patients. Never knew if the howling in the hallways was from women in labor, children whose limbs were blown off, or paranoid schizophrenics ferreting around for something they had lost years ago. Nurses were careful not to switch epidurals with sedatives. But I can't say accidents didn't happen. And whatever the emergency, whoever the victim, it was first come first served, by whoever was on call."

"Do no harm," I mumble, repeating the only part of the Hippocratic oath I know.

"Same with plant doctors, right? In times of crisis, you just do what you have to do."

Plant doctors. Now that was definitely a direct jab, and I choose not to ignore it.

"Father, a PhD in Dendrology doesn't make me a plant doctor."

Nancy finally appears, carrying a tray with two glasses of tea. "*Keefak Ammo*? How are you, Uncle?" she asks.

It's just their second encounter, and she's already comfortable using that term of endearment with my father. He doesn't seem to mind. There are many things my father isn't, but a gentleman is not one of them. A double negative? Perhaps, but that's all I'm willing to give him. My father is (not, not) a gentleman. As soon as Nancy appears, he rises to his feet with a "*Tameim*, perfect." In spite of myself, I find my father's youngish response to Nancy both awkward and endearing.

The stretch of Nancy's leg from her thigh to her knee is neatly wrapped in a bandage. She carefully brings the table over, the radio wobbling slightly, and props it between us. My father sits back and nods toward her. "What's going on there?" he says.

A smile breaks across Nancy's face, "I swear to God that *Tante* Layal would make an excellent nurse," she says. "I didn't feel a thing."

"Whatever she touches, she leaves in better shape."

"Alright you two, I'm needed in the kitchen."

"Nancy, *habibti*," my father says. "Ask Layal to fetch us the table."

My heart shrivels inside my chest as she throws me a watch-me-play-doting-daughter-in-law wink, and turns back to the kitchen.

"So," says my father suggestively. And here it comes.

"So."

"You two?" He opens the sugar bowl and takes out a cube.

"It's good."

"Good," he says. I'm not sure if that's what he thinks or if he's just repeating. In other words, I don't know if he thinks my "good" means what it means or the exact opposite. My father's good often means bad. As I search for more ways of saying the same thing, he holds up a cube between my eyes. "Sugar?"

"No."

He plops the cube into his own glass as I watch his hands intently. I respect my mother a great deal for using natural tea herbs, not those lousy tea bags. And I resent my father for defeating the purpose with refined sugar. I watch closely as it plunges into the brown water, disrupting the Zen of the floating tea leaves. I can barely stand to look at it, but still prefer it to the inquisitional face above.

"I'm a modern man," he says, breaking the silence and I look up, not quite meeting his gaze. "And when it comes to men and women, we—your mother and I—know that times have changed. Even here in Nabatieh, if you can believe it. Different religions, we don't mind."

"Progressive," I mutter with uncharacteristic sarcasm, which I instantly regret. When I'm around this man, I'm never quite sure who I am.

He doesn't hear it, or he ignores it. He just takes a sip of tea. "But people find things to talk about, even when I shut them up," he says through moist lips. "You think down in Beirut, who cares, right? No, there they just talk behind your back. It doesn't matter that you're not one of those professors who only use their fast internet connection to surf for vacation photos of their students in bikinis. They'll assume you are anyway."

"No one assumes that."

"I do."

"Of course," I say, looking away. "Anyway, Nancy's no longer my student."

"You'll always be her professor. And God forbid she gets pregnant. It'll be worse."

Bile rises up my throat. I swallow once, twice, but the bitter taste lingers on my palate. That lump of sugar would have been a good idea after all. My father leans forward to grip my palm clenched tight on my knee.

"Much worse," he repeats. His hand closes tighter around mine. I watch the creases along his forehead deepen. "We had a word for children born out of wedlock back at the hospital," he continues. "There weren't many, just a handful. And even as Head of Gynecology, I wasn't above using that word. You know why?" His palm sweat mixes with mine as his clasp tightens.

"No, Father. I don't."

"Because it was the only word. I never thought twice about using it. If I didn't, no one would know what in God's name I was talking about. You know what that word is, don't you?"

210

"Yes."

"Good. Because I don't want a grand-bastard."

He pats my hand, clasps his fingers behind his neck, and leans back. As he contemplates the full moon, Nancy returns, the tip of her tongue peeping through her lips as she carefully balances the chess table. My father and I slide farther apart, and she places it between us.

He chitchats with Nancy, something I've never known him to enjoy, let alone with someone he's only meeting for the second time. Perhaps he believes the son's girlfriend should be offered a treat, or perhaps even a peace treaty.

The problem between him and me was never a lack of affection. In fact, as an adult I grew into a solemn acceptance that it's quite the opposite. Love is a good thing, to be sure, but it comes with a mutual sense of entitlement that often leads to disappointment. My father wants a son who's just like him and I want a father who accepts that I'm not.

Build bridges, Nancy always says. Water under the bridge, he might say. I prefer a third metaphor: you never wade in the same river twice. Even though the issue between us has never changed, it has always found new and exciting ways of manifesting itself. And over the last few years, he's allowed those ways to sink past subtext to a deeper, much murkier level. We no longer argue about the justifiability (or foolishness) of Lebanon's latest border skirmish with Israel. Nor do we debate this or that politician's astute (or infantile) speech. Nor do we bicker over the nobility (or futility) of a profession that dedicates itself to caring for flora, rather than (or even at the expense of) fauna. Instead, as our encounters have dwindled, we've discovered in chess an efficient way to skip to the head-bumping portion of the program.

Admiring the time-honored effigy of two men on opposing sides of a chessboard, Nancy glances from me to my father then leans forward and kisses his forehead. The slightest hint of a blush glows across his cheeks, but before I ask her not to go, she does. As he turns to me, I watch the tendons along my father's neck tense like ridges along an iceberg.

"Tell me why you're really here," he says tenderly.

•

Chess allows us to lock horns in a manner where no one else can mediate—not my mother and not Nancy, who even after just one meeting takes my father's side.

The table between us was a gift from Uncle Kamel, initially intended to help my father through his recovery from deeply invasive surgery to remove a cluster of tumors from his colon. This particular game had begun on his second day, dark and groggy in a Beirut hospital bed. By the middle of the game, however, it grew into a test of determination (his word) and stubbornness (mine). And now, closer to the end, it's become a confirmation that his iron grip over life and death is as tempered as that of the young surgeon he once was.

The game is frozen at a critical point where perhaps, just maybe, I might defeat my father at a game he taught me. I'm surprised he even asked Nancy to fetch the table, given his precarious position on it. But right now he's biding his time—either in tacit admission of defeat, or in anticipation of my story.

Like all stories, it starts simply. "I was on the side of Damascus Road that morning," I say. "I saw everything, except who did it."

I search my father's face for signs of emotion. The silence between us thickens with the voices of new guests, now not just family, but relatives, then friends of relatives, then relatives of friends. But all I can hear is the four dreadful words echoing through my mind as they did throughout the drive up here,

"See you later, Professor!"

I turn back to the chess table. Last year at the hospital, he had offered me white, an empty gesture at best. It's believed that early on, white pieces have a slight offensive edge, but any seasoned player knows that the advantage quickly evens out. So I declined his offer, and he opened with his king's pawn, which I followed with mine. The two pawns stood like sentinels in the center of the hospital room, while chess pieces and visitors gathered around them.

Last year we each followed our openings with our knights, he on the kingside and I on the queen. This allowed him to sacrifice his pawn, and I gladly obliged, capturing it with mine. I remember my father's neck tightening at that point, a subtle but undeniable sign that I got his attention.

Years watching him hang up on rambling patients then swear into a dial tone have taught me doctors prefer facts first, emotions later. So I present my account of the events that led me here, in a way I hope my father can relate to. "When I got to the bus, Doreid Fattal and those other people were already dead, but one man was still breathing. I can't imagine what could've brought him and Fattal together on that bus, but he was there—the man you, and everyone in this town, knew as Tariq Jaber."

From there, my mind returns to that game at my father's bedside, to the fourth move where, in standard fashion, he brought his white bishop side by side with our pawns. I did the same, and that's where we had left the game back at the hospital, and where it stands right now, with our four pieces in a stoic frontier along the fourth rank.

And now, like the line of chess pieces, my father watches me patiently. "This game is mine," he says suddenly and makes his first move, bringing in his pawn to block my bishop. "When you captured that pawn last year, I knew I had you."

I ignore his taunt, capturing his pawn with mine. But somewhere in the recesses of my father's mind, deep under the unperturbed surface of his face, my story must have had an effect. He passes the chance to capture my pawn, and castles kingside instead as the tendons along his neck pulse. That's my cue to continue the story.

My words carry us from that damp road where Tariq Jaber's pallid face uttered its final rain-soaked words, through Madame Bogosian's house of wonders in search of the cat, and up the mountains of South Lebanon to Nabatieh. With the facts thus laid out before my father, I avoid following them with emotion. Instead, I choose intellect. "I believe Tariq was the real target of the attack," I say.

I instantly wish I had chosen another word: think, posit, hypothesize, anything but *believe*. All that word does is throw a stark spotlight on the glaring absence of fact, bringing it back to the realm of emotion. Then I make it even worse by saying, "I've learned much about Tariq over the past few days. I see a bit of myself in him."

My father smiles and brings his fingertips together. "I've never known you to take an interest in other people," he says. "And now you've come to Nabatieh to trace his roots, so to speak." The metaphor sounds tired when I hear it from someone else's lips. He drops his hands into his lap and leans forward to study my face. I can't stand when he lays the melodrama this thick, like a B-movie villain.

"So to speak," I repeat, taking another pawn: three fallen soldiers. The old man is losing his touch.

He finally retaliates by capturing my heroic pawn with his bishop and castles kingside, but now he's right where I want him.

He begs to differ. "Instead of playing your bishop," he says, "you played it safe."

"I forced your hand," I say. "I made you take my pawn with your bishop."

"What you did there is a *zugzwang*, a wait-and-see," he says, articulating the German word with meticulous eloquence. "Classic you. Predictable."

I'm baffled, but hope my face doesn't show it.

"You put yourself in a comfortable position," he continues, smiling. "And chose to play into a position you think you can maintain. But you can't, see, because everything around you changes while you sit there."

"What do you mean?"

"I play chess because it has no dice, no chance or fate. In this game, when your turn comes, you can't pass. But sometimes the move you make works against you. Here you spent the middle-game building toward a comfortable position that you wish you could hold forever. But now you have to move, and whatever that move might be, it compromises your perfect position."

Damn, the old man has a point.

"That's the weakness of the *zugzwang*," he says. "And that's your weakness."

From here the pace quickens, no time for existential dilly-dallying. The loss of my pawn forces my bishop to retreat, and another pawn exchange eventually leaves my queen hanging on the d-file in a gambit. We're both at risk, but a queen exchange would put my father at a serious disadvantage. They say play the player not the table, and I know my father never likes to play without his queen. Once again, if only for the moment, I might have the upper hand.

"Who else have you talked to about the bus?" he says—could he be stalling?

"About the bus, just Nancy," I say. "But today we ran into

Ibrahim and learned a few things about the Jabers, Barcode and Jayjay. He seems to think they're, I don't know, evil or something."

"Evil, no," he says. "But those two are definitely something. There's a—what's the medical term?—*crazy* streak running through that family."

The chaise longue creaks under me, but I swallow my distaste at his vocabulary.

"You didn't think doctors use that word either?" he says teasingly. "We'd just have you believe that. We do it all the time. Good umbrella word. Bu Yaqub, Tariq's grandfather, wasn't just crazy. He was a madman who went hunting one day and shot himself. I was a kid at the time, of course, but I remember we heard the blast all over Nabatieh, and the tale that followed."

"Which is?" I ask, intrigued.

"Word was he thought his left hand tried to strangle him, so he blew its thumb off. The man was insane, I tell you, but he was also a genius—maybe the first this town ever knew. He started that mining business from scratch. They say nothing comes from nothing, well he proved otherwise."

"And when he died, it all went to Mahmoud, his eldest son," I say.

"Right. Mahmoud Jaber is the father of the Nabatieh you see today. He took the nugget he had inherited and turned it into a goldmine. Well, an iron mine to be exact. He employed the youth of Nabatieh, and the old loved him for it. You see, the craziness had died with the father, but he passed the genius gene to the son—only to that son, and it caused a lot of animosity in the family."

My father turns back to the chess table, but he refuses the gambit. Instead of exchanging queens, he captures my e-pawn with his knight. I take the offensive and capture his queen anyway. He's crippled now and I'm in position for the kill: a smothered mate, which would trap his king behind his own pawns. Victory is within my reach, but it's not a sure thing yet. All he has to do is capture my queen with his rook to avert it.

Except he doesn't. Instead, he reins in his bishop along the white diagonal, placing me in check. This throws me off, but my queen remains strategically positioned to checkmate him in one move.

"From what I gather, that Mahmoud Jaber was just as crazy as his old man," I say, taking the time to plan my next move. "It sounds like the whole lot are."

My father's brow knots into a frown. "Don't believe everything you hear," he says.

"I didn't just hear it. I saw traces of it in that house."

"Don't believe everything you see either. That's even more dangerous. Mahmoud Jaber was much more nuanced than his father or brothers ever were. Sure, he had a temper, a voice that shook an oak until it shed its leaves. But everyone loved him. On the other hand, he only ever loved one person. He called Balkees the apple of his eye, even if that apple often got bruised."

"So he went to her father and bought her."

"That poker game is the stuff of legend, one that may be true on the surface. On the other hand, I judge a man not by his actions but his intentions. Things were different in those days, understand. And that particular day, the money Mahmoud paid Balkees' father was dowry. Back then every marriage was a transaction between the groom and the parents of the bride. Mahmoud plucked his wife from a tree but he fed her parents until the last days of their lives."

I finally make my move, advancing my king out of check along the e-file.

But my father smiles wickedly; I must've played right into

217

his hands. Ignoring his threatened rook, and still dangling checkmate one tantalizing move beyond my reach, he advances his knight, placing my king in check again. "Anyway, Mahmoud Jaber ended up paying the price," he says.

"Money is nothing."

"Son, money is only nothing for those who have it. And in the end the price turned out to be about much more than money."

"Ibrahim called Balkees a losing investment."

My father nods. "Perhaps in everyone else's eyes she was— a crippled, barren woman who bore Mahmoud Jaber no children in his lifetime," he says, but then his tone falls to a hush. "Every father dreams of having a son to follow in his footsteps. It's a man's second chance to make something better of himself even after his own time runs out. To be robbed of that opportunity is nothing short of a tragedy."

I understand, but just nod.

"Mahmoud and Balkees Jaber were my patients," he continues. "They came to me trying to conceive, and they tried everything. But the worse her condition became, the less likely it seemed Mahmoud would ever have a son, to the joy of those brothers of his. They barked and bayed at his feet like rabid dogs."

"So he stayed with her, and he never took a second wife?"

"Out of respect for Balkees, he never did. In the end, death made sure of that."

We sit in silence as I save my king by capturing the threatening bishop. I've alleviated the threat and gained a piece with a single move. Now I hold my breath in anticipation of my killing strike, still one move away. Does he not see it? Can I win this one? Could it be so easy? Maybe if I distract him. "So how did Mahmoud Jaber die?" I ask. "Was he sick?"

"No. Just unlucky. The Lower Nabatieh mining project was supposed to be his *coup de grace*," he says. He then pauses, for dramatic effect I suppose. My father enjoys telling a good story. "Instead, it was his swan song. He hired the biggest contractors from Saida, Beirut, Damascus, Amman, everywhere, and he personally supervised the groundwork. Then one day they were blasting through that mountain over there."

He extends a delicate finger in the direction of the valley separating our hill from the Jabers', then continues, "Mahmoud just showed up in a grip of lunacy looking for some man. They say he was out for blood, ignored everyone's pleas, and just barged into the mines. He was struck by falling rubble; a fragment of rock hit him clean between the eyes." Beads of cold sweat form on my forehead. He sees my anxiety, but forges on. "And the engineer in charge at the time was a certain up-and-comer by the name of Doreid Fattal."

My father fixes his eyes on the table until he's sure I'm watching, and then gently and with great precision, captures my rook in the corner. "Checkmate," he says.

I stare at the table as the air escapes my lungs in a gasp. I've lost the game.

◆

The gathering has grown close to fifty people. Strange faces: some I recognize, most I don't. My mother weaves in and out of the kitchen, setting trays of food on the dining table. He watches her through the window with a tenderness I've always admired.

His face now softer, he then taps my knee and says, "Come with me."

Dinner must be ready because the crowd has now assembled in a neat line, making their way indoors toward the dining room table. We follow them, my father ushering his guests inside until we're the last two left in the garden.

The scent of cooked *kafta* wafts into my nose as Nancy and my mother set the table with all sorts of barbecued cuts, *mezza*, *tabbouleh*, *fattoush*, the works. In the corner stand half a dozen bottles of iced arak surrounded by tens of small glasses. My mother walks out carrying a platter of pastries.

"Don't worry, these have no meat. I whipped up your favorite potato *kibbeh*," she says, smiling proudly, and scanning the table for an empty spot to set it down.

"How on earth did you fix all this?" I say.

"*Walaw*?" Nancy sings from the kitchen window.

My father takes the platter as we walk in. He lays it on the dining room table where some guests sit and others stand with empty plates held to their chests, waiting to serve themselves. "Save us this corner," he says to no one in particular, then to the guests he adds, "Please everyone, help yourselves. We'll be back shortly."

We leave the clattering cutlery behind us, cross the living room, and climb the stairs above the entrance. I find myself wishing I was back there watching everyone from a safe distance. We pass the master bedroom into his study, as pristine as I remember it, but lined with books on agriculture, replacing the medical tomes that now sit in neat piles on the floor. The yellow garden light from below floods my father's eye sockets like a crazed scientist, and a smaller antique desk lamp in the corner glints along his straight white hair.

He gestures for me to sit on the leather chair, then crouches by a stout cabinet and opens it. Inside, a set of black dossiers lines the upper shelf, each marked with a series of digits. "Let's see, that would be 198—" he says, voice muffled by the oak doors. I sit down dutifully and watch as he runs his fingers along the spines, pulls out a dossier, and sets it on the corner of the desk before me. "There. This should be it," he says as he leans into the pool of light. "So, did you go to the *baladiyya*?"

"Not yet," I say, unsure why he'd ask that out of the blue. "The Mukhtar suggested it, but—"

"Don't bother," he says proudly, opening the dossier. "The *baladiyya*'s come to you."

He flips through the pages and I realize what I'm looking at. "Hospital records," I say.

"Not just that," he says. "Birth certificates, death certificates, it's all here, every record of every soul born into Nabatieh and every soul that departed over the thirty years I ran its only proper hospital. You wouldn't find any of this at the *baladiyya*."

My father's burst of words leaves us both breathless. "How is it possible? Is that even legal?" I ask.

He turns to me, a page in mid-flip between his delicate fingertips. "No. It's not legal. But it's ethical. And it's possible because we were at war, son. Nabatieh was ripped apart. Raped. They went into every house, opened every closet, looked under every bed, even the civic buildings were ransacked, desks flipped over, chained cabinets blasted open. They looted everything, but I'd have died before they got their hands on our records too."

He pounds the half-open page with his other hand as he speaks with rage that fills me with a strange pride. "The *baladiyya* only has whatever copies we gave them," he continues. "Most of them counterfeits and decoys anyway. Every night we spent hours forging documents, creating one fiction after another. By the end I was a master conjurer of people out of thin air."

He catches my admiring smile, perhaps mistaking it for bemusement at an image which, in hindsight, is deliciously gothic: a doctor on a cold dark night leaning over his desk, ink-stained fingers scratching a quill across yellowed documents like a medieval dramatist.

"There," he says, returning to the dossier, flipping it over, and stabbing it with his finger. "Tariq Jaber. Born to Balkees Jaber, widow of Mahmoud Jaber. I was probably right there in the next room pulling a piece of shrapnel from someone's lung."

The page reads, "Tariq Jaber. Born at 1.9 kilograms. O Negative."

"Same blood type as his mother," he says. "Continue."

Years of experience have taught me to make sense of a doctor's chicken scrawl. "Brown eyes, black hair. Incubation recommended. Mother suffered blood loss, now stabilized."

"Notice something odd?"

"He was born premature."

"He was born severely underweight, was in the incubator for weeks, and yes everyone thought he was premature," says my father. "But in truth, Tariq Jaber was no preemie. He was a weak baby, but one that had spent ten full months in his mother's womb. Now look at this." He flips to a page stapled directly to the birth certificate. It's from Mahmoud Jaber's medical records, dating back to a few years prior to his son's birth certificate. My father points out a pair of letters, "AB."

"You know we didn't have DNA testing back then," he says. "But do you know the chances of a child with blood type O being born to an AB father?"

"Nil," I say.

"Close enough," my father says. "Mahmoud would've had to be an A, B, or O. Even though ABO blood-type sampling has been discredited since then, with such extreme odds one still has to wonder."

"So there's almost no way Tariq is Mahmoud Jaber's son."

My father nods. "And now for the final piece of the puzzle," he says, pointing to another piece of text. The heading reads,

"Fertility report for Mahmoud and Balkees Jaber," and under the subheading of "Mahmoud" are the words "Sperm Count: ten million per milliliter."

"Ten million sounds like a large number, but that's another way of indicating…" he says, voice trailing off expectantly.

"Sterile," I say, now in complete awe.

My father agrees with a satisfied nod. "My guess is it's from working in his mine all those years. The explosion that killed him also killed the mine itself, saving countless young men from sterility and with them countless Nabatieh lineages from extinction."

"Then Tariq's birth was no miracle. Balkees Jaber was fertile."

"As fertile as my tomato patch will ever be," he says closing the dossier.

"And if Balkees was pregnant for ten months, that means that she must've had an affair, even before her husband died."

"An affair, a fling, immaculate conception," he says, tossing his arms in the air. "Who knows? The mismatched blood types, the fact that Balkees carried her child to term, and Mahmoud's sterility together mean one thing. The odds that Tariq was a son of Jaber are in the stratosphere. Only the late Balkees knew for sure, and her secret died with her. But facts remain and numbers never lie, my son. That's all a man's life is: facts and figures."

"Father, you said the mine died with Mahmoud. Why didn't his brothers Barcode and Jayjay take over?"

"That was the question on everyone's lips," says my father. "Even after many years of marriage, Mahmoud Jaber died childless. Therefore, his estate indeed should have gone to his siblings. But if that had happened, the Jabers would have taken the money and thrown his beloved Balkees out."

"That's a huge assumption, no?"

"Not an assumption, a fact. Behind the closed doors of my

clinic, Mahmoud and I spoke about more than just methods to impregnate his wife," he says with an adolescent smile. "He knew that even in his final will and testament, he couldn't go contrary to the tenets of Islamic Law. So he did all he could to prevent that from happening while he was still alive: he signed his entire estate over to Balkees. And when the mine exploded, the shock of Mahmoud Jaber's death was followed by the even bigger aftershock that he had given everything to his wife."

"And the Jaber brothers assumed it was all Balkees' idea," I say. "The black widow who bled her husband dry then watched him die."

"To them, that's exactly what she was. She was banished from the family, as was her son. All that and the Jabers didn't even know Tariq was likely a bast—"

"She must've been terrified for him," I say, cutting him off. "That house is a fortress, but she couldn't stand to live in it or sleep in Mahmoud's bed, even years after he had died. She had a tower built so she wouldn't have to."

My father listens.

"Her secret didn't die with her. It continued to live in her son," I continue. "As a child she kept him locked up safe, but then he must have learned the truth, and it killed him."

"You kids love absolutes, don't you?" he says.

"Black and white, good and evil. Everyone thought Tariq Jaber was a weakling, that he'd never outlive the Jabers. That boy was like a cancer to that family, sure. But what on earth would drive them to murder their own nephew?"

"How about greed?" I say. "They want the money. Balkees died a year ago, and now with Tariq out of the way, the estate automatically returns to the Jaber brothers, right? Fine, let's assume they weren't involved, and that they don't know Tariq is dead. It would still be a matter of time before they find out.

And when they do, what if it turns out Tariq had left a will of his own? That would be their greatest fear realized."

My father's neck is pulsating rapidly.

"But one thing is absolute: the information in there," I say, pointing to the dossier. "Even if you don't think the Jaber brothers killed their nephew for the money, they might kill someone else for their legal right to it. That dossier proves that after Balkees' death, the estate was always theirs, and never Tariq's. It's their only safeguard against his will, and for that, Father, it's an extremely dangerous thing to have."

I'm suddenly glad I didn't tell him about visiting Sheikh Faqih, which I initially thought was irrelevant. The Sheikh had burned the marriage certificate, but now I remember the two witnesses to the ceremony. Doreid Fattal was one of them. I keep that knowledge to myself; the less my father knows beyond this, the safer he is.

"This dossier will never see the light," he says. "I promise you that."

"Then keep it with me."

◆

I follow my father into the gallery and he leans against the railing to watch the crowd assembled in the dining room below.

"The day you passed your entrance exam to medical school was the happiest day of my life," he says.

I remain silent as my father looks straight ahead.

"Instead you let my nephew, Kamel's son—a failure by any standards—become the doctor of the family, while you watched from the sidelines."

"Is that what you wanted for me?" I say. "To be a general practitioner who graduated from some buttfuck Eastern

225

European country, and who has hack diplomas on the walls of some ramshackle clinic he shares on the first floor of a walk-up apartment building?"

"Of course not. But at least it's something I understand. You were—you are—the most promising member of this family, the most brilliant person I know. But as it is, only I know it. It would break my heart to see you fail."

"Father, my greatest fear isn't failure. It's mediocrity. And one day I'll make you proud. You'll think it happened overnight, but I'd have been working everyday for it."

He glances at the dossier under my arm. "But no more wait-and-see. When you make your move, make it a checkmate."

I hold onto an emotion for a few seconds, mulling it over, weighing it, testing it in my mind. Then I turn to him and put it into words. "Father, I'm glad to see you in good health."

"Yup. Nipped it in the bud," he says laying a hand on my shoulder. I follow his eye-line to my mother and Nancy, clinking their arak glasses near the empty head of the dining table below. "A man spends his whole life attending to his garden," he continues. "Never allow a weed to grow there, or it'll eat it alive." He looks up and adds, "Before you go back, have something to eat."

I nod, knowing full well that "back" is not where I'm going next.

◆

Finding our next destination is almost too easy. Practically every other road sign on the east side of Nabatieh is directed toward it, as Nancy first helpfully and finally redundantly points out with a finger quivering with excitement. And when I hit the Volvo's brakes at the top of a steep slope and kill the engine, she adds an utterly superfluous "This must be it."

Partly to shut her up, I pull up the handbrake with a loud creak, harder than usual, for the slope we find ourselves on threatens to overpower even a truck, and force it crashing down into the rocky valley. With the Volvo's headlights out, we're in the pitch darkness of the dark side of the Upper Nabatieh hillside. But we might as well be on the dark side of the moon, which now hides behind the mountain range embracing three sides of the trapezoidal piece of earth on which we so precariously rest.

"Watch your step," I say as I sling my messenger bag on my shoulder—better to be armed with something, even if it's just a plush leather bag. We step out of the cushy confines of our car and find ourselves on the short edge of the trapezoid. Beyond us the expansive grounds straddle the foot of the mountain range all the way to another steep hill, on top of which looms the mansion we seek. The grounds are strung with what look like Christmas lights, but as we walk closer Nancy says "Construction." I nod and grip her hand, pulling her forward at a clipped pace.

As we approach, the *trompe l'oeil* makes the grounds expand and the unmoving mansion, defined only as a silhouette against the cloud-streaked indigo sky, appears even more distant. After Nancy's clumsy step causes me to lose mine for the third time, I look over my shoulder. "Maybe no one's home," I say, but rather than dismay I catch a smile cut a crescent across her face.

"No," she says. "There's someone there. Look."

I follow the line of her extended arm and spot the outline of a figure, reclining vapidly on a chaise longue in the center of the grass fields. The construction lights zigzag away from the figure, so I cannot make out its features. But as we approach, a glowing ember pulsates like a fiery heartbeat, lighting a cherub face with each rhythmic inhale.

The figure's hand, tanned and masculine, dangles by its side, as if the ridged tendons that line it are off-duty. When it lifts the cigarette stub to its face again, the pungent fumes of burning hemp fill my nostrils. In the glow, the lined features of the visage that now surveys us reveal themselves as those of a man of about forty, hair a thicket of blonde curls. A gold ring, which could have been a wedding band were it not on the wrong finger, catches the waning light of the ember and ricochets it into a pair of sharp but vacant blue eyes, pupils as dilated as the invisible full moon.

"Hi," says Nancy, and the man nods in acknowledgment, the only movement we've seen him make outside the mechanics of smoking his joint. Pretty potent stuff. I can already feel the sickening euphoria of a contact high creep up my arms, filling my chest with dread.

Nancy, however, is immune. She pulls up a dusty plastic stool lying on its side, and without wiping it invites herself to sit down until her eyes are level with his.

"Jayjay," she says.

"That's what they call me," comes his reply. He flicks the still-burning stub in an impressive parabola, ending in a bush a few meters away. I make sure it doesn't burst into flames, and thankfully, we're spared the biblical image to go with our nighttime rendezvous—uninvited, perhaps, but a rendezvous nonetheless.

Tariq's name derives from the Arabic word for "nocturnal visitor," the morning star that guides the way before light breaks. Tonight I take on this very role, toward a meeting that must happen, of that I'm sure. I turn back to Jayjay, who produces two fresh joints from heaven knows where and points their twisted tips in our direction.

"Hmm?" he says. "Good stuff. Got it fresh from Beirut just this week."

Thankfully, Nancy declines with a wave of her hand.

"We must talk," I say.

Jayjay looks up and smiles, his turquoise eyes burning through me with a cold iron stare. "So talk," he says.

I throw Nancy a helpless glance, but she doesn't take the cue.

"Is your brother around?" I say, turning back to Jayjay but not quite meeting his stare. Too casual. Damn it. My eyes rest on his lupine smile, then dart around for a better place, settling on his fair eyebrows. At least they don't bite.

"He's busy," he says, eyeing my messenger bag, smile unwavering.

"At this hour?" Nancy says.

"He's resting."

"You said he's busy," I say, catching Nancy's lob.

Jayjay ignores our two-pronged attack and his gaze remains fixed at my chest, but focused at a point several miles beyond it like a stake driving clean through. Several decades later (now I must be intoxicated), his smile broadens. "Yes. He's busy resting," he says.

Smart. I shift my weight but my ankle twists on a rock under my sole. I'm in pain, but try hard not to show it. And if I don't act now, we might as well circle back. Time to go for the kill. I clench my fist around the car keys in my pocket. "It's about Tariq Jaber," I say.

Jayjay's pupils snap into focus. He looks up, his smile gone. "What about him?" he says, his voice down to a subterranean grumble.

Nancy adjusts herself on the stool but says nothing. I study her, aware of the silence between me and Jayjay. I turn back and finally fix my eyes on his. "Take us to your brother," I say.

A hint of the earlier smile plays on his lips—I'm a worthy opponent. Holding that half-smile, his pearly teeth glinting through his parted lips, he curls himself upright with the grace of a Doberman. Nancy's neck cranes up with him, eyes mesmerized by the *contrapposto* David who unfurls before her.

The heavy air around us sinks to my feet, as Jayjay pulls out a Davincian hand toward Nancy. "*S'il vous plaît*," he says and I watch with horror as she takes it and allows him to lift her to her feet. He continues to pull her toward him, but she wraps her other arm around mine and he lets go in one continuous movement. The whole thing could've been a ballet.

I'm not sure if the tremor that runs between us starts with Nancy or me, but we shake it off and nod to the nonplussed Jayjay, who spins around, lights another joint, and starts toward the mansion. Eyes straight ahead, we follow him wordlessly.

◆

Metaphors compete as we tread two steps behind Jayjay, but none can adequately describe him. He's a bit of everything, and I catch myself falling for his charms. Could the rumors be false?

We're now a stone's throw from the mansion, and I imagine the elder brother Barcode behind one of those windows waiting to throw literal stones at us. I wish I could read the thoughts running through Jayjay's frizzy head, but not once does he stop or look back at us. He just marches on at a steady pace like a theater usher leading us, his spectators, to our seats. The mansion ahead is as opaque as it was from the distance. If Barcode is really in there, there's no trace of him on the exterior. All the windows are curtainless but it's impossible to perceive anything through them except more black, and as we inch closer to the house, even the construction lights fail to brighten the way ahead.

Nancy tightens her grip around my arm and she looks up at me for the first time, eyes filled with doubt. My trepidation rises too when instead of leading us by the staircase to the main entrance of the house, Jayjay makes a sharp turn to the right and walks around it. I look up at the mansion now behind us at such an acute angle I get a crick in my neck.

But then from the second story, a red light pierces the darkness of the facade, and we finally ascend a smaller staircase leading toward it, keeping a two-meter gap between our host and us. When we get to the top, Jayjay steps aside and gestures to Nancy. "*Après vous*," he says and opens a side door. Nancy steps into an orange glow and I follow as Jayjay closes the door behind us with a loud clunk. No turning back now.

We find ourselves in a Baroque hallway, the dim light turning the furnishings a deep shade of burgundy. Jayjay brushes past us to the center of the room and stretches out his palms like a court jester. "This is it," he says, but I'm not sure what he means. A few centimeters above his head hangs a crystal chandelier, its two-dozen candle-shaped lamps blackened with age. Those still alive stutter, casting Jayjay's eye sockets in reluctant shadows. Several sofas, golden arms and backs, plush blood-red cushions, line the walls. I notice the gold peeling in scales, and here and there tufts of cotton sticking out of holes in the sofa cushions.

I then realize what "it" is: this is the Jabers' inner sanctum, where guests are rarely allowed. Everything they want to hide, they bring up here. We must be in the upper hallway—three closed doors punctuate the wall closest to us, all probably leading to bedrooms, and a wooden balustrade connects a staircase down to the first floor.

On the wall immediately facing us is the portrait of a man with a thick mustache, and a pair of turquoise eyes that look down on us. He holds a cane between his ringed digits, one of them just a stub wrapped with the thickest ring of all, crowned with a blood-red ruby. My father was right, the senior Jaber had lost a finger, but what is surprising is the portrait makes no attempt to conceal that.

"Bu Yaqub," says Nancy.

"My father, God rest his soul," says Jayjay. "Wait here."

He makes his way past us toward the stairs, but then I notice a fourth door on the wall through which we entered, this one ajar. I'm careful not to budge—Jayjay shouldn't presume we'd follow him uninvited.

Light pours through a crack in the doorway and I realize that there's a woman of around sixty cowering at the threshold, a tray with a bowl of soup between her hands. She grips its lips with her thumbs and wafts of smoke dance in the faint light, as reluctant to pass through that doorway as she is.

Jayjay waves his palm a few inches from her nose and pushes the door open just enough for his thin frame to slide through. He swings the door behind him until the opening is back to a slit.

I fight the numbness in my feet and take a few timid steps forward. Nancy's arm is still wrapped around mine, but I release myself and lean over the old woman's shoulder. We both sway to the same side, left and right, at the same time, to and fro, I trying to catch a peek inside the room and she rebalancing the tray to prevent the soup from spilling. She succeeds but I fail—Jayjay must have his back against the inside of the door, his voice down to a muffled whisper.

Then just a few seconds later, the lull breaks as the door shudders like rice paper with the raspy baritone that bellows through it. "I told you not to smoke that goddamn thing in the house," it says. Jayjay's ringed hand juts through the opening, puts out the joint in the old woman's soup, and slams the door shut.

She's clearly had to endure more vicious antics from Jayjay, because she remains nonplussed. Instead, she tosses Nancy a helpless smile, revealing a set of buckteeth too large to fit into the tiny frame of her jaw, so that they've buckled over each other. She then turns around and disappears down the stairs.

Nancy smiles like a kid who's just overheard the class bully get burned by the school principal, but I frown back at her like a kid who knows he'll be next. Jayjay may be nasty, but on the other side of that door he's the lesser of the two Jabers—his morbid curiosity about Tariq makes him our wartime ally, the keeper of the Barcode fort—and knowledge about Tariq arms us with a weapon that remains concealed from his master's omniscient eyes.

The windows of the hallway clatter with the night wind, marking the seconds, which now roll into minutes, as Nancy and I wait in silence. Not a single murmur escapes through the oak door that separates us from Barcode, who unlike us, has revealed that he's quite immune to his younger brother's charms.

"Hey," whispers Nancy as I try to hide the painful stab of the broken silence. "Maybe we should've told him Tariq's dead."

"Shush. Not yet. That's the only ace we can play."

"But that might be the only thing that would get us in."

"And once we get in, then what?" I say. "Let's wait. Jayjay'll come through for us. He can't afford not to—"

The door clicks open and Jayjay steps out. "My brother will see you now," he says. He then swings the door open, his wary eyes avoiding Nancy and fixating instead on me.

We walk into Barcode's bedroom.

◆

A king-size bed stretches before us, hooded by a canopy of the same velvet that adorned the hallway outside. It's empty, but from the near corner of the room by the headboard, a veiled nurse rattles pills from assorted containers into a segmented medicine box on the side-table, a hooded lamp outlining her delicate white shoulders.

In the far corner at the foot of the bed opens a bay window, and next to it another nurse rummages with the catheter of an intravenous drip. It hangs from an aluminum stand like an overripe fruit waiting to be plucked. A hand clenches its lower third, with stubby fingers and white over-stretched creases. A thick gold band wraps around the middle one, encrusted with the blood-red ruby I recognize from the portrait of Bu Yaqub guarding the hallway outside. Even from our distant vantage point by the door across the room, the stone dazzles me as it glimmers against a second lamp positioned on a stout coffee table by the window. This must be the light we saw earlier from outside the mansion.

The body attached to the hand is Barcode, very much as he was described to us. He sits in a corner armchair among the shadows, chin to his chest, bald head lined with a thinning combover. His face falls into deeper darkness as he turns toward us, his floppy cheeks following a fraction of a second later.

"Have a seat," he says, gesturing toward a smaller armchair angled along the wall next to his.

Jayjay stays by the door as I approach Barcode, passing a long ornamented mirror on the wall, reflecting the room, doubling its size. I ignore my tiny likeness, which stubbornly follows me to the armchair and sits down with me in tandem. It's got my back, I think, but what use would it be in the face of the mound of flesh opposite me?

He takes no notice of Nancy, who tiptoes behind me and half-sits against the foot of the bed facing him, but I admire her insolence.

"I've been told you have news of Tariq," he says, setting the formal tone of the conversation to follow. His voice rasps with the corrosion of six decades, but rings an octave mellower than the rumble that emanated through the door moments earlier.

I nod, unsure how to proceed, the sweat scent of malady and decay making it even harder for me to think.

"What's my nephew done now?"

"Not very much," I say.

"Then we have nothing to talk about. The imp disappeared a year ago, like the earth cracked open and swallowed him."

I look up at Jayjay, but he remains stupidly stuck to the door, gripping the handle. If Barcode's portentous words struck a chord with him, his blank expression remains unaltered. They do register with Nancy, however, and she nods to me to soldier on.

"Not yet," I say. "But soon." My voice breaks and I hug my messenger bag to my chest. "Mr. Jaber, Tariq's dead."

To my left, one nurse rattles her bottle of pills, and across to my right, the other drops her catheter.

"*La hawla wa la quwwata illa billah*," he says. His head snaps toward Jayjay. "What have you done?"

Jayjay releases the door handle. "Nothing, Barcode, I swear." He leaps toward me and grips my lapel. "What the hell do you mean, dead? Where? When?"

I yank off his wrists and flatten my collar.

"And who are you? H-h-how do you kn-kn-kn-know all this?" His words break into a stammer as he gyrates in a wild dance. His stammer must come out when he's riled up, just like a school bully, just as I imagined. But is there more to it? Does he know more than he's letting on? Barcode seems to share my thoughts for a second, but then regains his composure as abruptly as he lost it.

"Shut up, Jayjay," he says. "Everyone. Out."

Visibly relieved, and without as much as a glance toward him, the two nurses slide past Jayjay around the bed and walk out. Barcode looks up at his brother. "You too," he says.

Jayjay's face pinches into a childish scowl. "But," he says, jabbing a finger toward Nancy, "w-why does sh-she get to sta-ta-ta-tay?"

She pushes herself off the bed and squeezes his arm. "Come on," she says. "We'll wait outside."

Tears well up in the corners of his eyes, now reduced to tiny specks of blue in cheeks as red as my father's tomatoes. He glares pleadingly at Barcode, but the elder Jaber remains motionless. Jayjay hangs his head and allows Nancy to pull him out of the room, closing the door behind her.

Barcode now turns toward me as the light falls onto his full face. If the Jaber line had a limited quota of beauty, then Jayjay has gotten all of it. Barcode runs his palm along his bald dome, and flattens the black strands that have earned him his nickname.

"Same questions," he says. "Who are you and how do you know." He makes them sound more like statements than questions.

"I teach Dendrology, the study of woody plants, at a university in Beirut. The day before yesterday, I was collecting samples on the side of Damascus Road and I—"

"The bus."

"Yes. I saw nothing," I say. "But I was there at the end."

Barcode rubs his hands together, transferring a veneer of

sweat from one onto the other. He wipes both on the knees of his pajamas with a scrape that fills the silence between us. "So he was with Fattal," he says. "That scheming bastard was on his way to Damascus."

I'm not sure which of the two men he meant by the designation. "Do you know anything about that?" I say.

"I ask the questions and you answer them."

"I can't tell you more unless I know more."

Barcode exhales. His massive lungs carry a lot of air. "I don't know more," he says. "But I know why. Jayjay, the kid's as dumb as a tree stump. But he has intuition. He felt—he knew in his heart—something was amiss with that boy Tariq."

"And you?"

"As I grew old, I grew a conscience. The problem with that, mind you, is it makes you think. And while you think, you cannot act. I could've squashed Tariq when he was a kid, or I could've taken him in and raised him as my own. But by the time I chose which to do, I could do neither."

"So which choice did you make?"

"It doesn't matter. Either way, when my brother's wife Balkees died last year, we had Tariq over. Kids these days, they have no… finesse. Just like Jayjay."

"And what about Fattal?"

"Doreid was a politician. They're another breed."

"But why was he on the bus?"

"I suppose he saw an opportunity and took it. I can't say for sure."

"Can't or won't?"

Barcode's temper remains in check, but his ruby hand tightens its grip on his knee. "What difference does it make?" he says. "He was preparing for next year's elections, planning an official trip to Nabatieh. I hadn't seen him in years, but last week, he sent me an olive branch."

"A peace offering," I say.

"No, literally an olive branch," says Barcode. He reaches toward his chest and flips over the lapel of his pajamas, with a golden olive branch pinned to it. "In the end, *he* was the one who needed *me*. My brother died in a mining explosion. His own mine fell on his head. Some lowly worker from Tartous caused it, everyone said. But just as Jayjay had his doubts about the boy, I had mine about Fattal. *He* was the one responsible. My brother Mahmoud wasn't supposed to be there. They say he showed up suddenly. Fattal failed to do the final check. He killed my brother."

"Why did you let him get away with that?"

"Because he covered it up. I had no proof and he made it so that a worker at his company took the blame. But for all those years, I've known. And I've never forgotten."

"And Jayjay, did he know about Fattal's message?"

"No. Only I did. And only I know what it meant. Jayjay's a gambler, but he's a lousy one. Gambling needs patient men like Fattal and me."

"So was Fattal dirty?" I ask.

"He may have been a clean politician, but he was a dirty human being. We were young men back then, but he had more power than I did and he used it."

"And now?"

"Listen, Professor," he says, wetting his lips with a pointed tongue. "Even back then, Doreid Fattal was untouchable. After the accident, he moved to Beirut, and with the war raging, it was like he had moved to another country. I became king of the hill here in Nabatieh, but what power does a king have outside his kingdom? So I used the only power not limited by place."

"What was that?"

"Patience. I waited for him to need me. And when he sent word the other day I knew the time had come."

"For what?"

"For reckoning. The olive branch meant Fattal was finally willing to give me the one thing I wanted."

The door opens and we look up. The old lady from earlier walks in, and from the hallway outside I hear Jayjay yell at Nancy, perhaps thinking he could slip back in, but neither of them do. Instead, the lady approaches Barcode and leans toward him with a fresh bowl of soup. His hands remain on his knees.

"Bring me a cigar," he says.

"The doctor said no more," she says, the D from "doctor" sounding more like "dizz" through her jumble of teeth.

Barcode turns up his palm. "See this hand? If there isn't a Cohiba number five in it in the next thirty seconds, I'll have Jayjay toss you out that window. Jayjay!"

Jayjay sticks his head through the doorway, but the lady has already slipped past him and left the bedroom.

"Close the door," says Barcode.

Crestfallen, he does just that.

"That's terrible, what you said to her," I say.

"Efficient," says Barcode. "Change requires energy and time. I have neither. She's the only person in my will. Soon this house will be hers, then she'll discover where the last nine years of her life went."

"It's all about money."

"They say you have everything if you have your health," he says. "But, failing that, money is a good alternative. If Jayjay knew where all this is going he'd maul that woman with his bare teeth. But I'll die before he and his Spanish prostitutes get a piece of this house."

"Looks like you'll get your wish," I say. "Maybe that's what

Doreid Fattal had in mind as well. A monetary gift in return for forgiveness and political support."

"That bastard wouldn't spare a lira unless the entire country knew where it went. As I said, for me it was never about the money."

"What then? What could be more important?"

"My brother Mahmoud was duped by that woman he married, and the stain will remain in our family forever. Doreid Fattal was their friend. If anyone knew, it was he. Mahmoud had the family fortune. He left it to his wife, who left it all to Tariq. That bastard imp got it all."

"A bargaining chip. That's what Fattal had for you. Proof. He was planning to sell Tariq out."

"It's too late now. That boy's going into an unmarked grave, where he belongs."

"If that happens, if no one knows Tariq's dead, you won't see a lira of that money."

"So be it."

I look into his eyes. "Mr. Jaber," I say. "Did Jayjay shoot up that bus?"

"It's time for you to leave."

I stand up. "Well then," I say. "Before I do, let me say you're right. It is too late. Now you have to live with Tariq's death on your hands." I reach into my messenger bag. "But I want to make a deal."

"I make no deals," says Barcode.

"You'll want to make this one. You say it was never about money. Then this is your chance to prove it. All you have to do is claim the body, and in return I give you this." I unzip the messenger bag.

"What's that?" asks Barcode.

I reach into the bag and place my father's dossier into

Barcode's outstretched hand. As he opens it and peers inside, I make my way to the door and open it. "Professor," says Barcode, holding my gaze for several seconds. "Please send my brother in."

Nancy and Jayjay watch as I cross into the hallway. "He wants you," I say. Jayjay looks vacantly ahead and trudges into the bedroom. As he closes the door behind him, I feel like I've just sent a helpless mongrel to slaughter.

Nancy and I step out, the walls resounding with the deep baritone of a caged hound. We stumble away from the mansion, down the marble staircase as it trembles with Barcode's voice.

12

Empty Home

"I'm sorry, Mother," said Tariq, realizing his entrance had woken her up. He set the hot tea on the table by her bed. Balkees lifted herself and looked at her son. His timid features beamed back at her with infinite care.

"I've been sleeping more than I should. Where's Tarboush?"

"Right here at your feet, Mother," he said, sitting down near the spot she indicated. The cat lay curled up behind him, by her motionless legs. The sun caressed its white fur, painting its tips a golden hue. She loved these quiet Friday afternoons, when a breeze carried the song of prayer across the Nabatieh hills into her tower window. Tariq rested his palm on hers, as sleep lifted itself from her eyelids, replaced by the tenderness of the young man for whom she had lived her whole life. The pain was back, now crawling down her arm. She swallowed her wince and reached for the tea.

"Ibrahim will be back soon," he said. "He went to town to get groceries for dinner."

"Listen to what he says." To the confused look her son returned, she added, "Ibrahim is a good man. He'll be all you have."

Tariq had learned not to retort with "You are all I have." He simply nodded, accepting her instructions like the man he grew up to be, taller than his father, more handsome, yet just as kind. On his eighteenth birthday, she had pleaded with Maurice not to come to Nabatieh again. Two years had passed since then, during which her son, in her mind and heart, had become his father—his scent, his dark skin, his brown eyes. "How do you feel now?" he asked.

"Much better," she lied. "But I'm out of medicine and I forgot to tell Ibrahim."

"He wouldn't know how to read the prescription anyway," said Tariq. "I'll walk down the hill. It's a nice day."

"Don't hurry back."

Tariq kissed her forehead, then slowly, reluctantly, rose and straightened his pants. Balkees knew the only request that would wrench him from her side was one that she made for her health. She had to take this journey alone.

"I won't hurry," he said. "But I won't be late. Down to the pharmacy and back." He cast a smile that filled her soul with light, then made his way out of the room. As his footsteps disappeared down the stairs, she tugged at her thighs and brought her feet flat to the floor. Tarboush twitched awake, stretching his legs into a yawn. The room was tidy and everything was in order.

Almost everything.

Balkees slid her fingertips into her pillowcase and pulled out the letters as Tarboush hopped off the bed, as if he, like her, knew where those letters belonged. Now and for eternity. She pulled the case from its secret place under the bed and put them gently inside, then locked it tight. She exhaled and replaced the case, then mustering all the strength in her upper body, pulled the crutches from their leaning spot against the headboard and hooked her elbows into them. Then in a colossal effort that left her chest pounding, she yanked herself into a standing position. Tariq would be back soon with her medicine. A small waste, a white lie. She reached again into the pillowcase and took out the capsules she had hidden from him, and buried them in her bosom.

The first step is always the hardest, she knew that, the second difficult too, but somewhat lighter, then third and fourth brought her to the door. Down the staircase, she let her crutches lead the way, slowly, deliberately, carefully. Fifth step then sixth. The tower staircase unfolded before her, as austere and beautiful as the day Maurice and Tariq built it. She dragged her legs down the first flight, then the second and finally onto the ground floor of the house. The realm of Balkees ended here and opened into Jaber territory, ornate, ancient, archaic, distant.

The weather was indeed beautiful, the breeze soft and fresh against her skin. She took a deep breath as a raw pain ran up her arm, making the little hairs on the back of her contorted neck stand straight up. Balkees made her way around the bend of the garden through the tunnel, her crutches clumping against the stone path, then out the other end onto the front grounds. Nabatieh, the most beautiful place on earth, the only home she ever knew, stretched before her. She had many good years with Tariq here, in their own reality, the world outside but a distant nightmare. These had been the physical boundaries of her life, but with Tariq by her side and Maurice on the other side of the mountain, her life was limitless. *Alhamdulillah.*

As she arrived to the Acacia stump, Tarboush, her constant companion, brushed past her and climbed onto it. God willing, by the time Tariq returned, it would be over. She pressed forward and slumped down against the amputated tree. Tarboush curled his tail against her shoulder as she gripped a crutch and, with all her might, heaved it off the edge of the hillside. It went crashing down below her with a crack. Another heave, and the sound told her the second crutch landed by the first.

The grassy walls of the upper hillside embraced her view, lined by the path that many years ago Maurice had climbed to visit their son for the first time. She could see him now, walking toward her from the distance. Was it the young Maurice, or was it perhaps Tariq returning from town? Time folded into itself as she winced in agony. Tarboush purred behind her and the pain crawled from her fingertips and gripped her heart in its claws. She breathed in and held it inside her. Let there be no more pain, let there be no more pain. She breathed out, and all the pain was gone. All gone.

Balkees closed her eyes onto the world.

◆

Sheikh Faqih's cello-like voice slid up the Arabic scale, plucking at its quartertones with melodic precision as the rain tapped against his umbrella. "*Ya ayyatuhal nafsul elmotmainna, irjai ila rabbiki radiya mardiyya.* O content spirit, return to your Lord with your blessing and mine."

The Sheikh watched the rain slide against the young man's profile, dripping from his eyelashes and the tip of his nose. Ibrahim, the family friend, watched silently, helpless against the boy's grief. The tree above them sheltered the boy's head, but leaning forward got his entire face drenched, until the Sheikh was unsure which of it was rain and which was tears. As he chanted, he wondered if the young man was crying at all. How else would he release the immense sadness he must feel right now? Not in prayer, it seemed. His hands lay flat against his body, and his lips didn't move. Maybe it was a silent prayer, the kind the Sheikh himself was unable to do even after all these years and even after committing most of the Koran to memory.

Or maybe the young man felt nothing. After all, his mother

had been sick all her life. He must have relived this day over and over in his mind. He must have known it would come soon. And with their family history, he must have been prepared for death to invade his life at any moment, as soon as he turned his back to it.

But today death did not invade. It just crept up on the woman silently and snatched her soul from her as she slept outside. It came in a daydream as her son went out to buy her medicine.

Of all the ways Balkees Jaber could have left this world, this was the least likely.

"*Fadkhuli fi ibadi, wadkhuli jannati.* Enter into My realm, and enter My paradise." As the Sheikh brought the funeral verse to a close, he opened his Koran to the first verse and read the *Fatiha*.

Ibrahim opened his palms into the form of a book before him as his lips mouthed the words. The boy remained motionless. From behind the gold-leaf pages of the Koran, he watched Tariq Jaber and understood that whatever words of prayer he might have for his deceased mother, they would not come from the Holy Book. The Sheikh closed it, careful not to drop or crease the precious piece of cardboard he held inside it. He shut the umbrella, feeling the last remnants of rain drop from the tree and onto his brown *abaya* with a splat. He took a step forward and laid a hand on the boy's shoulder. To his surprise the boy lifted his own hand and clasped it tightly. The two men stood like that for several minutes, looking down at the fresh marble slate with its epitaph.

But the real epitaph was the shoulder he now gripped. This man had an entire life ahead of him. A life sentence in solitary, pronounced by the woman they just buried. She too knew full well this day would come soon. She had pleaded with him to bury the secret with her, that piece of cardboard within the folds of his Koran.

Ibrahim squeezed the boy's shoulder, nodded to the Sheikh, and walked back through the cemetery into the distance. As he watched Ibrahim disappear among the tombstones, Sheikh Faqih thought back on the months of solitude he'd suffered since he lost his own wife—he could not bear to think of that immense sea of time multiplied twenty-fold for this young man before him. Allowing that to happen would be a sin, and for the first and last time in his life, Sheikh Faqih broke a promise.

◆

Very few words were exchanged between the two men as they crossed the wet grounds of the Hussainia cemetery, but by the time they got to its entrance, Sheikh Faqih knew that he had set the boy's life on a new course, one that his mother had never wished upon him, or even imagined. She had spent a lifetime burning every piece of mail she received. Every letter was read and instantly destroyed. Every word committed to her infinite memory, set down with her paint and brush in a new codified form that only she could decipher.

But now between his fingertips he held a memory that the Sheikh could not bear to see go up in flames. He thought of it as an occupational hazard, one of the many perils of being a vessel between this world and the other. He pulled out the photograph from the folds of the Koran and slid it into the young man's hand. And the young man understood its meaning.

"Maurice," he said. And with that, he unlocked his bicycle and pedaled away. Sheikh Faqih clasped his Koran shut as he watched the man disappear into the rain-drenched Nabatieh traffic. Then he turned around, adjusted his turban, and walked in the opposite direction.

13
Nocturnal Visitors

"Nancy?"

No answer.

"Nancy."

The side mirror catches her blank face sticking perilously far out of the passenger window. Her hair flutters toward me but she doesn't budge.

"Goddamn it, Nancy!" Still no answer. "Fine, give me the silent treatment but don't get your head chopped off doing it."

A pair of high beams overtakes us along the right side, just to prove my point. I turn my attention back to the road, squinting into oncoming traffic. Apparently the highway reconstruction budget fell just short of installing streetlights.

"Fuck it," I grunt switching on the radio. "Let's see if anyone else has something to say." I make as much noise as possible as I click through presets of static.

Radio Mont Liban comes on with Reporter Katia's distinctly raspy voice. "...And so ends November nineteenth, a day that'll live in infamy in the history of our nation. Emotions ran high in Downtown Beirut today, three days after the tragedy, as one-point-five million people, practically half our population, watched Doreid Fattal laid to rest in the heart of the capital. But what started as a peaceful vigil rapidly turned into an angry riot as the crowd demanded justice for his blood. Justice for the indignities that our Nation has suffered over the last thirty years. Justice for…"

I tune out and turn to Nancy, whose face still sticks out of the window. I stroke the back of her head. "Nancy, come on, you'll catch a cold," I say, though I know she won't. Either way, I get no reaction.

"…Justice for the red blood that floods our streets," Katia waxes on, "which early this evening lit up with the orange flames of anger, only to darken again with the black smoke of rage. The Darak police have spread out and are on high alert all over the city to extinguish the fires in time for the Minister of Interior's press conference, scheduled to begin in less than half an hour, and promising to announce major developments in the investigation that has rocked—"

I pop in my tape and lower the volume as bebop plays over the whooshing cars. I rub Nancy's back, and this time try on my kind voice. "Come on Nancy, this is silly. We have a nice lunch, we get in the car and then what? Ten minutes later I'm in the doghouse?"

For whatever reason (I can never guess with these things) this gets her to talk, and talk she does, even before she's even finished turning all the way toward me.

"I'll tell you what's silly. Doing a half-assed job is what's goddamn silly."

"I see nothing half-assed about what I did," I say. "As far as I'm concerned, the matter is done. Tariq will now get a proper burial. Isn't that what you wanted?"

"But at what expense? The killers go free. And you just handed him that dossier like it didn't matter?"

I gesture absently toward the radio. "Nancy we've both lived in this country long enough to know it. The killer always goes free."

"Christ, Professor, we drive all the way to Nabatieh, which is a lovely town by the way—I have no idea why you don't ever come here—and we learn all there is to know about Balkees Jaber and Tariq Jaber and Mahmoud Jaber and their dead tree and their pet cat. Hell, we even find the house where she spent her life and where she died and where, for all we know, Tariq was reborn as Tony, and no, wait not only that, you actually get his birth certificate, and your dad—by the way you should treat your parents like royalty because that's what they are—he opens up this chest of secrets. And—" she stops to catch her breath.

"Thanks for the recap," I say, grabbing my chance to squeeze a few words in, but only a few because with a new batch of oxygen in her lungs she continues.

"How can you be so obtuse? Could you really be so blind to everything that's not you? That miner from Tartous that you told me Barcode spoke about, that was Maurice, Tariq's biological father. He shouldered the blame for Mahmoud Jaber's death and was fired. Remember Nadine's yellow folder? Don't you think the two are connected?"

"Perhaps, but a lot of things aren't. For one, we know she's born in Damascus, right? She said so herself. The papers say she was born in Tartous. And her age doesn't fit either. She'd have to be around five years older. And didn't she write that her father's name is Mahdi?"

"Yes, and she said her uncle's name is Maurice. She's lying, Professor. She left those notes, those neatly typed out pages—who types out their diary, all grammatically correct and clearly legible?—so we'd find them. She's toying with us, having fun at our expense. She's a liar. All to throw us off track. Why else do you think she was acting so weird the other day when we watched the news report? She's covering something up."

"What, you think she's involved in Tariq's death?"

"Well, she was involved in his life. Much more than she wants us to know. When Maurice was fired, he must have returned to Tartous and when his older brother died he left a widow and daughter behind. Maybe Maurice married the mother and adopted the daughter as his own."

"Muslims don't adopt."

"Raised her then, became her stepfather," says Nancy. "Here's how I see it. Without a job or a son, Maurice had no way of keeping the two feuding families together—the Akkads and Toumas, right? Only a male child would ensure the peace. He lost his job at the mines, and he had one, of course, in Tariq. But he kept that a secret. Then as the family got poorer, he took menial jobs to support his daughter and bourgeois wife. The Lebanese war was seeing its worst days back then, which made it impossible for him to visit Balkees and Tariq in Nabatieh. And why would he? The Jabers wanted his head. If he showed his face there he'd be killed, or at the very least he'd risk revealing Tariq's true parentage."

"Yes. And if that were to happen, Tariq would've lost his right to the Mahmoud Jaber fortune," I say. "Broke Maurice could not dream of matching that life for his son."

"And the only two people who knew about Tariq's father were probably Ibrahim and Fattal. But Fattal was untouchable, right? But if the Jabers were watching him and they knew he was on that bus, they could have ambushed both of them with a single move, wiping him and Tariq out."

"Nancy, there's something I didn't tell you. Barcode seems to think Fattal was reaching out to him, trying to make some sort of a deal."

"I highly doubt that," says Nancy. "Fattal was a good man. And even if that were true, that dog Jayjay would've gone after Tariq anyway, given the chance. He killed them, I'm sure of it."

"Maybe," I say, but I have my doubts.

"And, and, and," Nancy says—there's no stopping her now. "Then after we come face to face with them, Barcode the Devil incarnate and his whipping boy Jayjay, what do you do? You thank them, get in the car, and drive off into the sunset."

I hum the theme from a Clint Eastwood spaghetti western, not sure which one, under my breath.

"Ha ha, cowboy," she says. "If you told me right then and there what had happened I'd have gone back into Barcode's bedroom myself. How do you know he won't come after us now to erase the last shred of evidence?"

"I'll tell you how I know. Because Barcode is very much the politician Doreid Fattal was. He'll put the matter to rest. It's not in their interest to come after us, or anyone else." I keep the detail of Fattal's olive branch to myself—no need to sully the man's legacy, unless it's absolutely necessary. Instead I say, "They're all dirty, and that's why they won't come after us."

"You know what? Fuck you. How about that? If you're such a mighty gunslinger why didn't you stand up to injustice? And I don't mean like those bullshit politicos on the radio. I mean really, really stand up and do something. Did you notice that bastard Jayjay said he was in Beirut this week? Right there on the lawn, casually reclining on his deckchair like it was nothing?"

"First, I didn't thank Barcode or Jayjay. We got what I wanted from that meeting, you know that. And second, so what if he was in Beirut? For all we know, he just went to party and score some weed. And also, what's this about injustice? What are we, Colombo all of a sudden? Or Perry Mason maybe? That's not what our project is about."

"Who the hell are Columbus and Perry Jason? And second of all—"

"Mason," I correct her but she ignores me.

"What's this 'project' about then, huh? A woman and her son, their lives destroyed by that crazy family. He was murdered right in front of you while you stood and watched. Jesus fucking Christ, no, worse. You walked away. Seven people dead and you didn't bat an eyelid. Three days ago and again, all over again today. Tell me Professor, what does this 'project' really mean to you, huh?"

"The guy watched me through that telescope. I wanted to know why," I say feebly, but she just stares back at me in disbelief.

"And do you know that now?" she says. "I mean really, even if that's all it was for you. Can you answer the question? Why on earth did Tariq Jaber have that telescope pointed at your window?"

Damn, she has a point. I still can't answer that question, so I set it aside and say, "So then you think his uncles got on a bus and murdered him—their own flesh and blood—and seven other people, including a national figure?"

"Duh!" she says. (I wonder how she can pull off her "duhs" so well. I never could, but I have very little time to think that over. Once Nancy starts, there's no stopping her.) "You don't think? First of all that Fattal was on the bus at all couldn't have been, I don't know, some freaky weird crazy coincidence. We know he was connected somehow, but why he was on that bus that day, we don't. And hey, we've already established that Tariq AKA Tony was very likely not the Jabers' flesh and blood. And most importantly, those people are crazy and we just left them alone and drove off like a pair of chicken shits."

"'Crazy' is correct, and all the more reason to leave them the hell alone, don't you think? Or what, you'd rather I waltzed up to the Jaber brothers and went 'Good day, kind sirs. I'm Professor Dickweed from Lebanese University of Science and Technology, or LUST for short. I also happen to be a wannabe private investigator on the side, you know just for fun, and I've come across some utterly inconclusive and totally circumstantial evidence that you've committed a mass murder. Yes, that very massacre that has half the country in grief and its top investigators chasing after their own tails. And by the way, I'm also a crusader for justice, so would you care to comment and maybe confess to these murders so my girlfriend can sleep at night'?"

"Yeah, something like that," Nancy says, though she's clearly subdued.

"Listen Nancy, what you may see as chicken shit cowardice, I see as plain old boring common sense."

"I never said cowardice," she says, turning to me. "It's just, I don't know, I'd like to see you care."

I continue to look straight ahead, not sure whether to avoid her scowl or to concentrate on the almost pitch black road ahead. "I do care," I finally say.

"About what?"

"About finding the truth, of course."

"The truth about what?"

"All of this."

"But what's 'this'?"

"You know. This," I say, releasing my ten-and-two grip on the steering wheel and waving my hands in a circle. But she's not buying it, so I add, "You know the man was watching me through his telescope. That's big. Huge."

"Aha, so that's what you meant when you told your dad you see yourself in Tariq. You were just speaking, umm, literally huh?"

"Did I say that?"

"You said it or not, I dunno. I heard it though. Yeah, I was right behind you collecting the teacups. I felt so…" she sways her arms theatrically, "proud hearing that. Like getting an insight into the Professor's soul. I was so blinded by the light, I had to walk away…" She's never good with sarcasm, so her voice drifts off, as she slips into some Nancy daydream.

"It's not just that," I say several seconds later and she snaps out of her private reverie.

"I sure hope not. For your sake. And mine."

"What's that supposed to mean?"

"I don't know."

"Tell me. It can't be worse than everything else."

"Actually, it is," she says with a sigh. "It's, I don't know, sometimes I feel like, like you're a vegetable."

"A vegetable." I can't help but laugh, but just for an instant because I glance at her and she's dead serious. "You mean like a tomato?" I ask.

"More like a cucumber. As cold as a cucumber. Like you have no soul," she says. I think she's done but as soon as I open my mouth to say something, she goes on. "I said you should treat your parents like royalty. I know they're not perfect—parents never are. But if you ever meet my dad, you'll know what I mean. You know the first thing I noticed when we walked into Balkees Jaber's room with all the paintings?"

"I don't."

"That there's no bathroom."

It's not the vegetable comment, but it's just as unexpected. So I ask, "No bathroom?"

"Balkees Jaber was almost crippled, right? There's no bathroom in that room. Just a bed and her paintings. Someone had to carry her up and down those stairs every time she had to go."

"Her son Tariq."

"It's those little things, Professor," she says, looking at me.

"It's not about 'big' and 'huge.' It's in the details."

She checks her watch, breathes out, closes her window and says, "It's been twenty minutes." Then nodding toward the radio, she adds, "Let's hear what that Minister has to say."

Wordlessly, I pop out the tape and raise the radio volume. Transmission is now much clearer since we're closer to Beirut. "One bullshit politico," I say, breaking the heavy silence, "coming right up."

◆

"I reach out to you today not as Minister of the Interior, but as a Lebanese citizen who with almost unbearable sorrow, watched a great man take his final journey. And who with almost unbearable anger thought back on the vicious crime that took his life and the lives of seven other innocent people.

"Yet bear my sorrow I did. And bear my anger I did. As I hope every one of you will. In this country, sorrow and anger are not calls for revolt, but for reform. Let's not allow our emotions to drive us to the streets but to drive us toward the truth.

"Under our clear directives the Darak police, with great care and precision, have collected the necessary evidence from the scene. And in record time cleared the road to Damascus of all reminders of this heinous crime in preparation for our workday tomorrow.

"And with that in mind, I reach out to you fellow Lebanese with a call to honesty and openness. A call not to point the finger of blame at this party or that before having all the necessary evidence. And today, my fellow Lebanese, I'm here to inform you that this evening, less than forty-eight hours after this heinous crime, we've completed the preliminary report and that we have an important lead, one that we're confident will steer us very soon to our destination: the truth."

Nancy turns to me with faux esteem, as the voice on the radio continues its verbose imagery and run-on sentences.

"Our team of experts has collected an abundance of sensitive data from Doreid Fattal's person which points toward the last person he spoke to."

"That just means they went through Fattal's phone," I say to Nancy.

"Our evidence clearly indicates that the person in question participated in, and very possibly orchestrated, the ambush that took the lives of Mr. Fattal and the others: Maurice."

"What the fuck?" says Nancy.

"What the fuck indeed."

"Motherfucking Maurices mushrooming everywhere."

"Try saying that five times fast."

"Hold on, let's hear the rest."

"…And while we're aware this announcement could compromise our investigation, we're keeping our promise of complete transparency. Therefore, we've made the name public. Anyone with information pertaining to this name in connection with Doreid Fattal should contact the Ministry at the numbers listed below. That's all we have, a first name, but as far as names go it's not a common one in this country. Maybe among certain groups more than others." He pauses, I suppose to select his words as he must now tread lightly, as must any Lebanese who commits the error of using the phrase "certain groups."

"We ensure total immunity and anonymity to anyone who comes forward," he says, closing with what has already become the slogan of the investigation, "All in the name of the truth."

I switch it off and turn to Nancy, "What do you think?"

"Like you said," she says. "Chasing their tails."

"There might be more to it. They can't be that stupid."

"No, they're not. But they think the public is." She looks at me then adds, "Today, in Nabatieh you know, I forgot this is bigger than the Jaber family. Bigger than both of us."

"That doesn't matter as long as we focus on what does."

"You're right but—wait," she says as she points into the rearview mirror at a blinding pair of high beams. "Look. Is that car following us?"

I squint into the mirror but before I can tell what it's doing I say, "Of course not," and as the lights get larger and brighter, I add, "Don't be silly." But maybe it is.

Nancy looks behind us and now the light fills the inside of the Volvo like a projector as it ricochets across the beige leather upholstery into a bluish tint.

Before she finishes yelling out "Keep to the right, let them pass!" I hit my turn signal and swerve into the next lane, careful to maintain our speed so we don't get rammed from the rear.

It's now half a car length behind us and I can barely see ahead. "Jesus fucking Christ do something," yells Nancy.

I stick my hand out of the window into the brisk night air and wave to them to overtake us, but instead, the car swerves into our lane and we're now almost bumper-to-bumper.

I downshift, hitting the gas all the way and the Volvo stutters as its engine catches up. The RPM needle bounces into the red.

Nancy digs her nails into the seat. "Damn, damn, damn, damn, damn," she says, her pitch harmonizing with the Volvo's.

The car behind us ramps up too, catching up with us to the right. Through Nancy's side mirror, an orange BMW 320 circa 1990 model, pimped out with spoilers, tailgates us. It must now be just a few centimeters behind us. If the engine stutters or we hit a bump, that'll be it.

I glance across to Nancy. Even with her closed window the drone of the BMW rattles our dashboard. I swerve to the left into the oncoming lane, and lift my foot off the gas. The car now catches up with us on the right. We're nose to nose.

Inside it are four men, two in the front and two in the back. It's too dark to make out their features, but they're glaring right at us. Then one of them rolls down the left rear window as Nancy screams, "Shit, they've got a rifle. Oh my God it's Jayjay. He's gonna shoot!" and I catch the tip of a shiny silver barrel poking out of the window.

I throw a quick glance at my rearview mirror and slam the brakes. Nancy and I jerk forward as the Volvo screeches down to half-speed. The BMW finally overtakes us, for an instant its busted taillights bathing our windshield in their weak red glow. As they speed off the silver barrel sticks out all the way, and from it a large white banner waves above the car, with Doreid Fattal's striated but familiar face smiling back at us.

"Look. It's just a flag," I say, pointing at the BMW speeding off. "It's not Jayjay. Just a bunch of nationalist idiots."

"Motherless sons of bitches," she pants.

As we pick up speed again, I squeeze the back of her neck lightly—mine's already stiff from the jolt. "You okay?"

"Just drive slow for a bit," says Nancy. "Don't want to catch up with those shits again."

"As slow as pie," I say and she smiles nervously at my meaningless idiom. She leans her forehead against her window and lets out a loud sigh.

◆

It takes Nancy all of five minutes to fall into a dreamless sleep, her light snores accompanying the caged growl of my Volvo. Without the finger-twitching characteristic of a dreaming Nancy, her hand just remains curled between the window and her cheek, motionless but for the heavy vibration of the engine. I shift it into fourth gear and it too hums a sigh of gratitude. Both have had a long day and have earned their rest.

But my day isn't over yet. In fact, it's just started. At this timid rate, we're still a good fifteen minutes from Beirut, so I roll up my window and relish my first moments of alone time in complete silence. I then reach for the glove compartment and pop it open. Keeping one hand on the steering wheel and both eyes on the empty Jiyye road, I pull out the jazz tape and toss it in the compartment, then take out my tape recorder, jack it open and pull out the tape. Years of doing this literally singlehandedly have made me quite dexterous and within just a few seconds the empty recorder is resting back in the glove compartment and its prior contents are spilling from the Volvo's metallic speakers. I glance at Nancy—she's a deep sleeper, one of her good qualities for sure—as I raise the volume of my own voice from that fateful morning.

I replay the events in my head, accompanied by my narration. But I feel distracted, not quite able to concentrate on the intricacies of my report. Another sound fills my head, a high-pitched squeak, no, more like a screech, from just a few minutes ago. Car brakes. Something about that sound is familiar. But being a careful driver, I think the last time I heard it was that morning three days ago when I almost ran over a man on a bicycle.

No, I correct myself, the last time was a little more recent. I shift to the right lane to allow another speeder to overpass, and they drive straight through, their taillights disappearing into the distance in a matter of seconds. I switch back to the left lane and hit the fast-forward button. My words squeak in that Mickey Mouse voice I love about tape. Nancy continues to sleep peacefully.

With absolute precision I get to the section I want: the dead silence between the end of my report and the start of the bus incident. I remember cupping my palms to my face during those moments when, like a blind man, the sensitivity of my ears and the tape recorder itself were heightened.

There it is. That familiar sound of screeching tires. But they're not the Volvo's. No, they're much thicker, more baritone, more desperate.

These are the brakes of the bus.

Nancy mumbles and shifts in her seat, then wipes her face with the back of her hand. "How long was I down for?"

"Fifteen minutes or so…" I say. "That's all the alone time I get today." I switch off the cassette deck and smile at her, but she looks ahead as her face brightens with an orange hue.

"Look," she says pointing, and for an instant I think she's caught in another thriller-movie attack of fear. But no, her eyes are wide with wonder, like a prophet haunted by a burning bush.

I look ahead too: the Beirut skyline glows with the flames under a cloud of thick black smoke. "Reports of peace have been greatly exaggerated," she jokes. From our insulated Volvo-cocoon we watch the city we left this morning loom closer, a much-changed landscape of fiery reds and charcoal blacks. We drive into the Ring Area onto Salim Slem Bridge, its sides lined with burning tires and men of all ages spilling oil into the flames. Even with our windows rolled shut, the fumes of revolt fill our car.

I worry Nancy might be frightened again, but no, she's exhilarated. "Let her burn," she says. Then her voice rising she sings, "Down, down, down to the ground. Weed the country out."

Her lips tremble as the flames flicker in her transfixed eyes.

◆

"I'm making a quick stop," I say as we get on Damascus Road.

"In this chaos? What the hell for?"

"Just a quick stop," I repeat, easing the Volvo off the lane. "Stay in the car."

"*Stofil*," she says. Nancy knows when not to argue. She also knows that cold word, meaning "do as you please," is actually my favorite in the entire Arabic language. She's doing me a favor; she knows that, and I appreciate it. Keeping the engine running, I raise the handbrake, grab my tape from the car deck and recorder from the glove compartment. "Keep your knee raised and hand me that lighter." I enjoy giving orders when she's in a timid mood. "And lock the doors," I say as I grab the lighter and hop out. I wait for the Volvo's safety lock to click behind me and make my way toward the "Beirut Night. LIFE!" billboard about ten meters ahead.

The full moon shines lazily through clouds of dust and the fumes of burning rubber make my nose twitch, anticipating a sneeze that never comes. The projectors hitting the billboard above also light the road under my feet with an electric-blue. It mixes with the intense reds and oranges of the nightlife scene advertised, together painting a reality much altered from the one we've just driven through. Same colors, different picture.

Wishing I were back home with my Acacia and jazz, I look down at the gravel where only this morning the bus stood, right where Tariq Jaber died against its front wheel. I flip the tape over and slide it into the recorder. I take a deep breath and hit the red Record button.

"November 19th, 8:32 p.m.," I say. "The road to Damascus."

My voice sounds distant and foreign, as if it were already on the tape, and I feel like a spectator watching myself from the back seat of an auditorium, the billboard as backdrop, and the gravel surface where I now stand as stage. I clear my throat and continue.

"I'm standing in the very spot where, three days ago, a bus crashed into a billboard. That day I heard a screech and saw tire marks ending here, but now the marks are almost gone, washed away by the rain and the police's commendable efforts to clean the street of all traces of the incident."

I step ahead and scan the stretch of highway visible under the billboard light. A few cars pass, but it's otherwise empty. Riots target busier neighborhoods than this one, districts where they can rally the biggest mob, which would then cause the biggest ruckus.

"The driver was already dead when I got here," I continue into the recorder. "And I didn't hear a gunshot after the bus crashed, so I assumed he had been killed with the bus still in motion, that the killer had jumped off further up the road. The fact remains, however, that the bus did brake right here. I didn't think much of it at the time, but now my assumption feels wrong."

A light trace of the tires remains, barely visible if one didn't know to look. I lean down and touch the spot with my fingers, rubbing the gravel between them. Gravel, like soil, doesn't lie—those brake marks are there, and I remember the screech. "It seems that the driver did in fact hit the brakes, that he was killed after the crash, and that the killer got off right here, after the bus had come to a complete stop. This can now be considered a fact."

But like any fact, it means nothing in isolation, unless I build a hypothesis upon it. That's why I'm sure those experts on TV will miss its significance. They just hop from one assumption to the next like a toad on floating lily pads, barely disturbing the surface of the pond. I too keep the surface undisturbed, but that's as deep as the similarities go. I'm like a mole tunneling through the soil, tracing the roots and the interconnections between them, while remaining completely invisible from the surface.

But unlike a mole, nighttime isn't my element. Like a tree, I need light to function. Tariq Jaber fancied himself a stargazer; on the other hand, the sheer effort I need to concentrate in the darkness makes my head throb. I throw a glance toward the Volvo. Nancy's silhouette leans against the window, with car lights on and the engine still running. Smart girl. In case we need to make a quick getaway.

The tape mechanism stutters, telling me to get on with it before the batteries die. "If the killer got off after impact," I say into the recorder, "it means he escaped on foot. I don't recall seeing any other vehicles on the road between the time the bus crashed and the time I got on it."

"Let's see, slipping away from the other side of the highway is impossible," I continue. "It's fenced off and there's a big drop to the streets below. No, the killer must have gone around the back of the bus as I approached it."

Retracing my path from that day I circle the outline of where the bus stood, like a detective following the chalk contours of a dead body. Starting at the front, where I laid Tariq down, I pass the front bumper touching the point of impact on the post of the billboard, making my way along the front bumper to the left side, then along its length, past the window where Tariq's bloody hand thwacked the glass, then around the rear bumper to where the taillights were.

"This is it," I say, right where the gravel ends and the soil begins. "This is the lowest point. It makes sense. As I approached the bus, the killer crouched in wait here by the tail lights, watching me. And as I entered from the front, he must have slid around the back, toward the field, through the field, and past the spot where I collected the Acacia. He then escaped along the very path I came on, the ridge, where the rainwater collects along the line of Acacias. He had no other cover."

Could it be? I follow the path into the field. The ground is now dry and cracked from the evaporated rain. Nancy always tells me to dry my face thoroughly after washing, and she's right. When excess water vaporizes, it takes with it the moisture right under the surface, a dehumidifying effect, causing cracks. I reach into my pocket and pull out her lighter, then stoop down and flick it, cupping the flame in my recorder hand.

I continue along the line of Acacias, the brothers, sisters and second cousins of the one I have back home. "Here." I stop. The flame shines into the gap left by the Acacia I pulled out, my Acacia. Sure enough—"The other Acacias here have been disturbed," I say into the recorder, but they weren't disturbed by me. I was careful. And they weren't just disturbed. "Trampled. Crushed," I say, my voice sounding angry.

"Dead Acacias," I say into the recorder. "The one I took, I probably saved its life. These others, their branches have been smashed, and have dried into the caked mud. They were crushed during the first rain, drowned over the day following the accident, and have since dried into the mud like fossils."

The killer must have trampled on them. He probably lost his balance as he fled, and fell into the grove. No one else would've had a chance or reason to cut through here in that brief window of time. Judging by the damage, the killer would have been injured too. Those thorns are sharp. There will most likely be defensive wounds on his hands and arms to break the fall.

Jayjay Jaber's hands had been clean. Manicured and delicate. No cuts. Not a scratch. As I run my own hand along the destroyed branches, the flame goes out. I look up toward the billboard, clearly visible from where I stand. "And if the killer got off here, that also means... that he saw me."

Electricity jolts through my spine. "So much for seeing without being seen," I say. The exact opposite happened that day. And I thought Tariq's "See you later, Professor!" was unnerving.

But then, closer to the edge of the field I notice—"Fresh buds. Barely a day old. How come? My Acacia was on its last breath, but these babies look healthy and new. How's that even possible? And what does it mean? That the new buds grew after the rain." Could these Acacia be the trees Nancy found in my coffee cup earlier today? Or maybe the gazelle? Could I really be wondering that right now, right here? As the night grows murkier than stale coffee dregs, I decide to keep that happenstance to myself. Nancy would have a party on my head should I give any credit for this shocking discovery to her fortune telling.

Feeling supremely silly, I find myself thankful for the darkness in which I stand, hidden from unseen voyeurs, lurkers, lechers, leeches, vultures, eyeing me, staring me down, boring holes through me. And my car's still there—small consolation— glowing like a straw lantern a few meters away from the billboard.

"This finding will alter the course of my entire research. It's—"

But wait, someone else is there by the Volvo. "Nancy! Nancy!" I yell, switching off the recorder as I run toward the car.

Yes, there's a figure there, leaning into Nancy's window. The car grows bigger but I can't tell what's going on. Shit, shit, shit. "Nancy!" Her window's open. She's got her head out. The figure is grabbing her wrist. I'm losing my breath, I trip, regain my balance, climb back onto the road. Hold on, just a few more seconds... It's a man, burly, dressed in a gray cape, his back to me. I reach out and grab his shoulder, make a fist with my free hand, swing back until my shoulder blade creaks. I'm ready to push my fist into his face.

The figure turns to me and as I'm about to feed him my knuckles, he shoves me in the chest. I stumble back a couple of steps, the front of the car breaking my fall. "What's the matter with you, brother?" he growls.

Nancy looks back at me shocked, but I swear I catch a twinkle of pride in her eyes. "What the—" I yell back at her before realizing what was going on. In her hand, sticking halfway out the window, is her driver's license. I look back at the grizzly man. He's a Darak policeman.

"What're you two doing here?" he asks me, already cooling off. I examine his face as I catch my breath. It's one of the traffic cops from this morning.

"We were just… admiring the scenery," I answer with the first thing that pops into my head.

"Yeah that's what the Miss here said," he says. "Tragic. Nothing left to see."

"As I said," Nancy says to the officer. "My friend here was just paying his respects, with Downtown crowded and all."

Paying my respects. That's almost true.

She turns to me and adds, "*Watan* here was concerned about me, a girl all alone in the middle of nowhere."

I've never understood why people use the word "w*atan*," which actually means "nation," to address Darak police. But Nancy apparently does, and she knows they like it. "Aha, good," I say catching on.

"Okay then," says Watan. "You two better go home. No one's allowed here."

"Yes, Watan," says Nancy with a smile.

"Let's go," I say, circling around the front of the car and getting in. Through the rearview mirror, Watan watches intently as we drive off.

"What was that all about?" Nancy asks with a broad grin, still looking mighty impressed.

"Had to check something before it rained again."

"What did you find out?"

"Acacia stuff," I say and leave it at that. She's had enough drama for one day.

◆

"I'll be working on my article until morning. Best I take you home now." I ease the Volvo up the hill and past my building.

"My father's at that Russian show at the Casino," says Nancy. "After that he'll hit the blackjack tables all night. I don't want to be alone tonight."

She speaks about her father, but in my mind it's Jayjay. She doesn't want to be alone because of Jayjay. I'm glad the edge in her voice has mellowed somewhat and the skies are clearing between us. We circle back toward my building and ease the Volvo into my parking spot. I take out Tariq Jaber's phone from the glove compartment and glance at its screen.

"No calls, huh?"

"Nope," I say and pop it in my jacket pocket. "We'll try that Nounz number again later." I hop out of the car, trot around the front, and catch her hand as she steps out. "Here, careful." Her limp's gotten worse.

The elevator button glows red with "*Occupé*," which means someone's in it or one of the kids in the building has been playing with the buttons again, so we just wait. "Good to be home," says Nancy with a sigh.

The elevator arrives and the door bursts open as my next-door neighbor and her granddaughter step out. "Hi, Tala," I say, leaning down to the little girl as I hold the door open for them.

"Are you being naughty or nice to *Teta*?"

"Naughty!" yells out the four-year-old as her grandma laughs. Nancy tousles her hair with a "*Yiii*" and we step in. The elevator rattles up to the third floor. I pick up the evening newspaper from my doormat. Since the bus incident, most newspapers have been running twice a day.

"You can get all that on this thing called the Internet for free," jokes Nancy as I open the door.

"The Internet doesn't have that crisp paper feel," I say as we step inside and I flip on the light.

Nancy limps across the living room into my bedroom and tugs at the chain of the desk lamp. The light glows brighter and through the doorway she rummages through her drawer and picks out her purple pajamas with some underwear. She takes off her top and tosses it on the bed and brushes past me. "Hey I'm gonna take a bath," she says. She heads toward the shower, then looks at me over her shoulder. "Wanna come?"

"So I'm out of the doghouse?"

"We'll see," she teases as she unclasps her bra and closes the door halfway.

"Be right in," I yell back over the running water.

In the bedroom I rub my neck and peel off my coat. The Acacia stands on my desk. More accurately, what's left of it stands there; the rest, withered and fallen, lies scattered around in a pathetic heap.

"That can't be."

My coat falls to the floor as I stroke its leaves. They're a darker shade of brown, and what remains attached to the branches has turned yellow-tipped and sickly. I scoop up some soil with my finger and rub it against my thumb. It's still moist—too moist— from this morning.

"Aren't you thirsty? If you don't eat you're gonna die."

I look through the window. The Achrafieh landscape shines before me with a hundred lit windows. Along the coastline a few spots burn with the last remnants of the day's riot, but otherwise it's quite peaceful. Another day has wound down. And there's Tariq Jaber's window, lit with its constant blue light. The man whose roots we spent the day tracing already feels like a ghost from the past.

Huh? What? A ghost?

There it is again. And again.

A figure. It crosses his window. Someone's there.

I run out of the room. Then I double back and stick my head through the crack in the bathroom door. The steam wafts against my face, carrying toward me a faint, out-of-tune melody. I yell out to her blurry outline behind the shower-screen, "Nancy, I'll be right back!"

She continues to hum.

No time. I have to run. I sprint across the room and pound and tug at the elevator door. It doesn't open. "*Occupé.*" The kid must have pressed all the buttons. Why does that darned grandmother let her do it? I run down the stairs, taking two at a time. Second, first, ground floor. I dash out the gate, almost knocking down the old lady and her granddaughter on their way back.

It's dark and I assume there are no cars. And if there's one with busted headlights, well then I get run over and it'll just be my luck. Theories upon theories run through my frantic mind, as I look up in search of Tariq's window. I can't see it from the street. I cross the street, not bothering to look, half-expecting a bicycle to run me over. Theories. Hypotheses. Banal, significant, Tariq, the Jabers, olive branches, Acacias. See you later, Professor!

I stumble, trip, topple, get up, wobble, continue down the

open staircase, too wide and cracked to take two at a time so I just zig and zag clumsily until I reach the bottom. I wind around the grocery store as "Kwak. *Manyak, manyak.* Asshole," goes Faris the parrot malignantly. "Donkey! Die, die, die! Donkey!" Is that what he says? How does he know those words?

"See you later, Professor!" says Faris. No, no. It's in my head, must keep telling myself that. It's all in my head. The dark figure in the window. It's all in my head. One block—come on!—two and three.

Why am I outside again? The perilous, dark outside. The Achrafieh buildings close around my heart as it pounds through my ribcage. Windows, windows everywhere. People watching. Every pair of eyes is on me. I look up, the one window I seek is out of view. A streetlamp casts a glare across my glasses. I'm blinded for a moment.

A right turn takes me into Tariq's building, through the layers of laundry, hoping I don't run into Bu Joseph. I hear the news blare from his shack and catch a glimpse of his potbellied outline through the window. Tiptoeing up the first flight, I confirm I'm out of earshot then continue up the staircase. I'm losing my breath but don't stop; instead I wonder if I should knock at his door or Mrs. Bogosian's again. Damn, so many questions. What to do?

On the fifth floor, the answer reveals itself: Tariq's door is open. Just a crack, but I can just walk in. I take a moment to catch my breath and collect the pieces of my scattered thoughts.

My breath quivers as I fumble through my pockets. Tape recorder, two cell phones, lighter, wallet. Dammit, all useless. And then… keys! That should do. I grip the biggest one and hold it up—not the most threatening weapon, but it's all I have. The door creaks open and I shuffle in, across the hallway, past the kitchen, and into the living room, bathed in its blue glow.

There it is, in the corner of the room, the shadow. Behind me I flip on the light. Startled, the shadow jerks around as my pupils contract with an audible snap.

"You!" I say.

◆

"You!" echoes Nadine. "What are you doing here?"

"You tell me."

"This is Tony Jaber's house," she says. "He's my... friend."

"What are you doing here?" It's all I can say, but that's really all I want to know.

"Well, umm. He—I mean I, I'm looking for him. I'm worried. He called me yesterday then hung up. I didn't know what to do so I came looking for him here."

"You're Nounz?"

Her face regains some of its color, but still looks pale in the blue TV light hitting it." Nounz, yes," she says. "That's what he calls me. But, what—"

I hold up Tariq's phone. "It was me. I called you."

She approaches me, reaches for the phone, and I loosen my grip. She scrutinizes it like a fragile historical artifact that might hold the answer to a thousand questions.

"Why do you have his phone?"

Wait, am I the one in the wrong here? "Listen, Nadine," I say, deciding to take control of this situation before it slips away completely. "You answer my questions first. How about that?"

She releases the phone into my hand and I slip it back into my pocket. "Tony's my friend," she says. "But I haven't seen him for two days. Not since... not since the murder. He just vanished into thin air and I'm so worried. And there's the young man on the news. No one knows who he is. I'm scared it might be Tony."

"So he's why you were crying at my house the other day, not Fattal."

"It's all very sad. Everyone. But Tony is—"

"Your boyfriend."

"What? No! No, nothing like that."

"And that morning at LUST, you were looking for him," I say. "Why didn't you just call him? I've had his phone all day."

Nadine hangs her head. Through the cacophony of her lies, shame is the one thing that rings true. "He says I should never call him. Ever. He just calls me. But why is his phone—"

"I found it," I say and leave it at that. "I take a step toward her and grip her elbow. It tenses under my fingers. "Come on. Admit it, you were lovers," I say, as if I were the third wheel in that proscribed affair. And why not? I feel betrayed, to the core. This girl, this devious woman, lied to me—in my house. But what was her lie exactly? I don't know.

Nancy might be able to explain; Nadine just shakes her head.

"I found some… feminine products here," I say. "They're yours, no?"

"What products? I've only been here twice." She reaches into her pocket. "And I have this. He left it on the electrical box outside. Just like you leave yours for me under your mat. Just like you." She holds up a key with dust-tipped fingers, corroborating that part of her story, but little more. "He said it was for emergencies, and I've never used it until now."

"What emergencies? What kind of paranoid game did you two play?" I say, not believing a word.

She throws my question right back at me. "You've been here before, then?" she asks.

Better not to lie to her more than I have to. "Yes. I came for his cat."

This catches her off-guard, and she doesn't even bother

274

asking why I'd do such a thing. "Tarboush," she says, glancing around. "I was wondering where he is."

"So I came in from the balcony next door to save the cat," I blurt out, but then realize how ridiculous I must sound. "Anyway, the cat's with the neighbor now." I over-explain the cat to avoid explaining the cell phone.

"I see," she says, eyes piercing through her scarved face, as white as a full moon. She's not scared anymore and now she's the one that's suspicious of me. I decide to tell her more, just enough to maintain the upper hand. "There's something I should show you." I grip her arm and lead her to the telescope. "Look through this."

She pushes her face into the barrel and squints through the eyepiece as I adjust the focus. I can tell she's not done this before, but I don't need to ask her if the image is sharp, because just then she jumps back with a gasp.

She clasps her hand to her mouth. "Oh my God," says Nadine through her fingers. She stares back at me, one eye marked with a deep red circle, the outline of the telescope eyepiece.

"That's why I got curious," I say. "He was watching me."

She lowers her hand. "You're wrong. He was watching *me*."

♦

I watch her.

It's probably the first time I really look at Nadine, and I realize something Nancy must've known all along: she's beautiful. Her dark eyes stare back, wide open, moist with tears of anxiety. Her thin nose begins with a delicate tip that widens to a recess that marks the arch of her thick lips, caressed by a perfectly pert mole in the corner. She's wearing no makeup, yet her skin emits a hue that I've only seen on newborn babies. Her mouth quivers

275

slightly before she finally breaks the silence.

"I have something to show you too," she says. "Come with me."

She makes her way into the bedroom as I trail behind her, past the record rack, open closet and a pile of clothes. She flips on the light and inches toward the bed.

"I've only ever been in this room once," she says. "I was looking for the cat."

"Aha," I say, still not sold on her doleful playacting. The cat is turning out to be the *prétexte du jour* in this charade, but I let it pass for now.

She kneels down, reaches under the bed and pulls out a long metal case. I remember it from the last time I was here, though I didn't pay it much attention at the time.

"Open it," she says.

On my knees, I unfasten the golden metal clasps. We exchange furtive looks, and I swing the cover open.

The case is empty, but the sculpted felt interior shows the clear outline of—"A Kalashnikov," I say.

"It was here before," says Nadine.

"And now it's gone," I add unnecessarily, not sure what else to say. "Is that why you were anxious the other day, when you watched the news report at my place?"

"Yes," she says. "When I heard the news about the bus. This rifle was the first thing I remembered. Then Tony vanished and I didn't know what to think. And when I found it missing earlier… They said it wasn't a murder-suicide. But I'm terrified he's the dead man on the bus, or that he was somehow involved."

"Let's get out of here," I say and slam the metal case shut.

◆

We walk down the night streets of Geitawi. Nadine turns to me and says, "I'm glad we left. The house is different. It feels cold."

"It's the TV," I say. "The cathode tube emits a blue—" but I know I should stop.

"The house is dead without Tony in it."

"Don't worry, my place is full and alive and Nancy's there. She'll make you some hot chocolate or soup or a salad, maybe." I have no idea what I'm saying, just trying to fill the silence as we leave Tariq's street. I'm playing nice, a page out of Columbus and Perry Jason, as Nancy would call them.

"Would you mind if we don't go back to your place?" says Nadine. I shouldn't have mentioned Nancy.

"Why not?" I ask anyway.

"There's a place I know, let's just go there for a few minutes if you don't mind."

We make a left and instead of climbing the staircase toward my area, we take the long way up the hill. I follow her up the slope and cut a sharp left before the grocery store. It's closed now, and I'm thankful for not running into that pesky parrot who knows too much for his own good. He's too much like me, I suppose.

At the end of the shortcut, we find ourselves in front of Beit el Kataeb, a satellite office for a political party that dates back to Lebanon's founding fathers. We leave it behind and plod through a silence so heavy, it weighs on my feet and presses into my shoulders. There's barely anyone around this time of night— people are either off rioting or tucked away at home trying to avoid taking a political stand one way or the other. Whatever the case, we walk ahead without event or incident, until we arrive at a park I didn't know existed. My face must betray the wonder of the sight before us.

"It's a secret garden," says Nadine weakly. A metal sign hangs crookedly above the gate, "Geitawi Public Park." If it's a secret, then it's hiding in plain view, much like the girl—or is she a woman?—next to me.

"How could I have missed this place?" I ask.

"I didn't know about it either. Tony brings me here all the time. I don't like to meet at his house just the two of us. An unmarried man and woman seen in public is bad enough, but it's worse if they're seen in private. Anyway Geitawi here is different from LUST. They talk less."

I can't agree with that. "But it's innocent enough, so why care?"

"Because. It's just... not decent," she snaps as we step inside. "Gossip is like Chinese whispers. It starts innocent, but Tony and I both know that a single word could change everything. 'Catwoman' is cool. But 'cat lady' is sad."

We stop at a bench in the corner.

"Here we are. Our spot," she says as we sit down.

"Yours and Tony's," I say, not sure how to continue.

"I wasn't his girlfriend. Whatever it might look like, it wasn't that. I met him a few months ago at the mini-mart facing the main gate of the university. It was one of those 'meet cute' incidents that only happen in romantic comedies, you know?"

I nod. Nadine continues. "We both reached for the same carton of Lucky Strikes, then we each insisted the other have it. You know, very Lebanese. He hummed a bit of Miles Davis' *So What*. I didn't know much about jazz, but I loved that tune. My father played it to me as a child. Tony and I continued to nod hello whenever we ran into each other at LUST. Soon we became friends."

"Does he study there?"

"No," she says. "But he likes the campus. He bribes an office boy, and he lets him in. He spends a lot of time there at LUST.

Makes him feel like he belongs to something."

"How so?" I ask, keeping my interjections short. She speaks about bribing like it's something you just do; maybe she'll slip up and reveal something relevant to our project. As the moon peers from behind a cloud and lights the top of Nadine's head, I can't decide whether she looks attractive or repulsive.

"When Tony is drawn to something or someone, he doesn't just like it. He makes it a part of himself. As he does jazz, as he does me, until I feel like we're one and the same person."

This level of commitment, this giving of oneself to one's obsessions, fills me with an intense longing. I know exactly what she means, but I just nod casually.

"For instance, did you know Art Blakey almost quit the Jazz Messengers several times before becoming the greatest drummer of his era? Or how John Coltrane composed the impossibly complex *Giant Steps* in one sitting?" she says.

This is small talk, perhaps the smallest possible in these circumstances, but I'm compelled to listen.

"Tony taught me how to live day to day, that whatever happens and will happen don't matter. A reporter once asked Miles Davis what he sees in the future. You know what he said?"

I shrug.

"Tomorrow," she says.

"Why didn't you ever mention Tony?" I say. "To me, to Nancy?" I'm surprised at my sudden sense of entitlement.

"Why should I? My life is my own. I'm just a simple girl from Damascus."

"I thought most of the Syrian... help in this country comes from the villages." I'm still playing nice, but it's my first subtle slight, to be sure. I recall Nadine's papers, which—much to my consternation—Nancy and I read the day before yesterday. They said she was born in Tartous, not Damascus.

She laughs like I said something cute. "It's fine," she says. "You can say maid. There's no shame in that. I don't mind taking care of people, of their homes. I do it to pay for my lessons." She indicates an iron ring twisted around her finger, embedded with glass stones.

"You made that?"

"Yes," she says proudly as she adjusts her scarf, and then allows her hand to fall into her lap.

"It's beautiful," I say, hovering my own hand over the ring until the stones tickle my palm.

"Thank you. It's my second one. My first is even prettier," she says, raising her hand again into the light and eyeing her artwork with a smile. "I'm learning metallurgy. My mother was against my moving here, but my father helped convince her."

She seems more relaxed. I decide to pursue this line of small talk a little further then segue into what I really need to know.

"We have a master's program at LUST. I work in science, but maybe I can pull some strings in applied sciences."

"That's very kind... but I can't afford it."

"Actually, I think they're offering scholarships now to disenfranchised Arab students."

"Disenfranchised?"

"You know..." I say, hesitating. "Poor."

"They're impossible to get if you're not Lebanese. And who are we kidding? These days 'Arab' means anything but Syrian. My sister tried at the nursing school and was refused. Not the right demographic, they said, whatever that means."

I'm surprised Nadine's so forthcoming, that I've earned some of her trust. Asking about her family has started to build a solid bridge between us. Soon I'll bring the conversation back to Tariq, but for now, I continue to pave the way a bit further. "Is

280

your sister here too?" I ask. "She's visiting. She was supposed to go back, but she got food poisoning."

Nadine reaches into her robe, pulls out a cigarette and lights it. "I've quit since meeting Tony, but I make exceptions," she says, and before I can capitalize on the mention of Tariq, Nadine then returns to my question.

"Nissrine lives—or maybe I should say 'lived'—in Damascus with my parents," she says. "But since the war, I try my best to keep her in Beirut with me. I want her to apply for a study-abroad scholarship at the Romanian embassy here. But those kinds of opportunities are impossible for us now."

We're getting way off track, but I can't see how to get back on it. Easy does it. "So why was your mom opposed to you studying here?"

"She's, how shall I put it, set in her ways. My mother wears a black hijab that covers everything. Nissrine does too, but as I got older my father and I managed to bargain me down to a scarf."

She laughs as a few lustrous black tresses fall out of it, and I find myself unable to picture them covered by a hijab. She takes another puff from her cigarette, and a wisp of smoke plays in the lamplight, throwing a dappled shadow across her crescent-shaped profile.

"I didn't know Syrian parents still demand that a girl wear a hijab," I say.

"Not so much in Damascus, but in the smaller towns and villages, yes. My parents are from Tartous, and they still carry a piece of that town inside them."

Tartous. Now we're getting somewhere. "So it falls on you to uphold the family tradition," I add, sounding very much like my friends at the Sociology Department, where I gave an elective last year.

"So to speak," she says in her Syrian accent, now more noticeable than before. "My father changed jobs all the time, took us all over. He wanted a good education for me. A better life. But he only had money to send one of us to college, and my sister Nissrine—God bless her—insisted it should be me."

"Have you ever been back to Tartous?"

"No. My parents are settled in Damascus, with their Damascus ways. Even today, my father refuses to leave. But I know my mother carries a piece of her hometown in her heart. She always tells us stories of the way things were back there—simpler, cleaner. If she saw me wearing this," she motions to her short-sleeved blouse, far from scandalous, "she'd go mad."

I just nod politely, hoping for a window of opportunity to mention Tariq, but don't get it.

"In Beirut, I even take my scarf off sometimes," continues Nadine. "And when my sister visits, I hide her clothes. I try to make her wear some of my stuff, dress a little more modern, you know. More becoming." She laughs. "I don't know why I'm telling you all of this."

"I don't mind," I say, but actually do. We're miles away from what I really want to know. Silence lingers between us but I'm unsure how to break it.

"I feel safe talking to you," she says, splintering the silence into something all the more awkward. "Like my secrets are locked up tight. Like you're not interested enough to repeat them." She looks down. "That's how it is with Tony," she adds. "Only different."

Her guard is down. Now's my chance. She's finally defenseless.

"How so?" I ask, taking her aback. Then less directly, I follow with "Besides jazz, what else do you two have?"

She crushes her cigarette against the edge of the bench then tosses the dead stub in the wastebasket. "I never had a brother," she says. "We're both from out of town. He's an only child. Secretive, warm. He watches over me. I don't need protection, but it's good to have a friend like that. But my parents would kill me if they found out. They wouldn't understand."

"I don't either."

"Why would you? You're not a girl living alone in a foreign city."

"Don't you have roommates at the LUST dorms?"

"But those girls are vicious. I bribe them with gifts and favors just so they don't rat me out when my sister stays over."

That's the second time she's mentioned bribing. "Go on," I say.

"But Tony's different. Unlike anyone. And he's always scared. For himself, for me."

"How so?"

"You should see him at home. As I said, I've been there twice, I swear that's it. But all he does is play his records, look through that telescope, and scribble in his notebook. Besides me, he has no friends."

"A telescope in the daytime? And doesn't that strike you as bizarre?"

"He says even though stars hide in the daytime, he knows they're there. But yes, I realized later that there was more to that telescope than stars. He'd know things about me, harmless things like what time I got to your place, which room I cleaned first, the plants on your desk. He phones me the second I finish. Like he's watching me. I didn't mind—I still don't, and I never bring it up."

"But you must admit that's unsettling," I say, more about the dreadful thought of Tariq Jaber watching me pamper my Acacia than anything else.

"Yes," she says. "The second time I was at his house, he started opening up. As long as I was at school, at your place, or at his, he says I'll be safe. I never understood what that means; and yes he frightens me a little. Since then I've only agreed to see him here or at school. But still, I like feeling looked after."

"You said he opened up. What did you he tell you?"

"I can't say."

Damn, that was too direct. Does she know about Fattal? About Tariq's parents? Just then, the park light dies.

"Power outage," I say, looking around at the surrounding buildings, all gone dark. "It's from the mains."

None of this registers with Nadine. Instead she gazes into the dark silence.

And then my phone rings. "Hello? Yes, Nancy. Yes, it's gone here too. Nowhere, I'm close-by. But you were in the shower! Listen, I had to leave. Something came up. No, not on the phone. I'll be right there." I think for a second and then add, "Listen, I'm bringing a guest. I'll explain when I get back. Bye."

Nadine turns to me with a shiver. "You haven't told me why you have Tony's phone," she says.

"I found it," I say. "He left it somewhere and I picked it up."

"When he—when you—called, I didn't know what to do. I couldn't come yesterday with the city so empty. And even today, with the riots, so dangerous. So I waited until the streets were empty. Until dark. I was scared for myself for the first time. I wished Tony were with me. I don't know what I came looking for, and now I wish I didn't."

"You'll be fine with Nancy and me," I say.

◆

Climbing the stairs is much harder than stumbling down them and I pant so hard I feel embarrassed. The electric generator's deafening growl sounds like it should be powerful enough to run the elevator or at least light the stairway, but it's not. Nancy's lighter comes in handy again as Nadine and I make our way up, and when she almost trips and I grip her hand up the second flight, things become as awkward for her as they are for me. But I'm not having one more injured woman on my conscience today.

We get to the third floor on my last breath and I pull out the keys by lighter light. Dexterity was never something I had any shortage of, just stamina. We walk into the hallway lit by the familiar blue glow of my TV. I worry that would bring the fears of the same light from Tariq's back to Nadine, so I distract her by yelling, "Nancy, we're here!"

That scares Nadine even more. We walk into the living room, and there stands Nancy in a white bathrobe, hair wrapped in a matching towel, both reflecting the flickering TV.

"Hey Nancy," I say.

She throws us a blank look then gestures toward the screen with the remote gripped in her hand. Katia the Newscaster's monotone greets us instead. We walk in and as Nadine simpers at Nancy, I gesture toward the sofa and we take our seats, a formal distance apart.

"...The stunning turn of events led to an urgent assembly at the Ministry of the Interior," says Katia. The screen is split with her in the studio on the left and a male reporter I recognize from the morning news in the marble echo chamber of the Ministry on the right.

He holds his hand to his ear and after a brief delay nods and says, "Yes, Katia. The Ministry has issued the following statement." He reads from a notepad, "In the interest of complete transparency, as promised by the Minister of the Interior, we've decided to share this information with you."

I glance at Nadine, who sits next to me, hands clasped in her lap, staring at the screen. Nancy remains behind the couch, a pillar wedged between us.

"Following the unfortunate incidents that broke out all over Beirut today, and following the press release made by the Minister earlier," the male reporter continues, "a witness has come forward. He contacted the Ministry first by telephone then spoke directly via conference call during their meeting. Katia, we were told his report is of a very sensitive nature, but it was agreed that the witness will be given the chance to address the public directly."

"Thank you, Nasser," says Katia. She turns to the camera and fills the screen. "Yes, ladies and gentlemen. In just a few moments, the witness in question will speak over our airwaves in an exclusive scoop." She holds her hand to her ear then corrects herself, "I'm being told the call's being patched through right now. Hello?"

"Hello, good evening," says another male voice. "My name is Samandal." No first name.

Nadine twitches on the sofa, her hands clasping tighter. Above us, Nancy's face contorts into a grimace, but she remains otherwise unmoved.

"Thank you for joining us tonight," says Katia. "We understand you do this at grave personal risk."

"Yes," says the voice. "But I thank the Ministry for taking all the necessary precautions, securing me a scrambled phone line and guaranteeing my anonymity."

The man's voice is assured and confident. He speaks in formal Arabic, and his accent is hard to pinpoint, especially by a non-expert like myself. He could be anywhere between 25 and 40, and his diction suggests a good education or social background.

"Please tell us what you can," says Katia. "The nation is

anxious to hear you."

"I must be brief, but I also must begin by extending my condolences to the Fattal family and to all the Lebanese for this tragedy."

The Lebanese? Isn't he one?

"We all share this burden of grief," he continues. "As an Arab first and a human being second, I felt the need to come forward today with what I know."

"Yes, please continue," says Katia.

"Around two months ago, I was approached by a young man. I was at a restaurant in an Arab capital, frequented by intellectuals, artists, and writers. The man knew my name and a great deal about my background, and asked if I'd be interested in attending a meeting organized by a leftist group. He explained it was part of a larger effort to reconfigure the Western mentality against Arabism, even in its benign form associated with politically neutral countries outside the Middle East."

"Did you know the man's name?"

"I just knew him as Maurice."

Nancy and I exchange glances. Nadine remains fixated on Katia's face. Samandal's voice continues.

"But I knew nothing else. I accepted to attend because it seemed like a worthy cause. Later at the meeting we did exchange names, but in light of what I eventually learned, I'm confident those were merely aliases."

So it's just an alias. Samandal, chameleon. How apt.

"I see," says Katia. "Please go on."

"I attended the meeting. It lasted about an hour, and was impressed by the group's knowledge of the history and politics of the region. There were five men, with me six in total, and they were all quite moderate in demeanor and ideology, so I decided to join the group. I attended five more meetings before their true intentions became evident."

"How did that happen?"

"I'm not at liberty to discuss specifics, and will leave those details to the discretion of the Ministry. However, it became clear to me that the group's political agenda was a cover for a deeper plot. The assassination of Doreid Fattal."

"Why?" says Katia, her heavy makeup adding a touch of melodrama to her otherwise professional ambivalence.

"Because of who he is."

"Can you be more specific?"

"No I cannot, because they weren't. Behind the intellectual facade, the group was just a bunch of mercenaries. Highly trained, professional soldiers."

"Why do you think they chose you?"

"Because of my military background. That's all I can say about that. I've disclosed everything to the Ministry. But on the air, I prefer not to delve into my own background, in the interest of personal security."

"Do you know who was behind the mercenaries?"

"If any of the group's members did, they shared none of that information with me. But they said Fattal was dangerous. That he was getting too close to the neighbors."

"Which neighbors? Syria? Israel?"

"Your guess is as good as mine."

"The assumption that the assassin or assassins were highly trained professionals is consistent with the findings of the investigation. Yet a certain kind of weapon was identified, one commonly associated with infraction groups. Were you made privy to the plan? What does your military background tell you about that?"

"A military background doesn't make me a criminologist," he says, sounding annoyed for a moment. "They assassinated

Mr. Fattal and with him all witnesses, disembarked the bus, and escaped in a separate vehicle. As for the uncharacteristic nature of the weapon, if I were to venture a guess I'd say it's a signature. Someone with that kind of expertise doesn't make mistakes."

"So did you break with the group before or after the assassination?"

"Before," says Samandal emphatically. "When I learned about their intentions, I attended one or two more meetings to gather as much information as I could, then I left. Not just the group or the city. I left the country."

"Did you learn when they intended to execute the plan?"

"Not the exact date. Just that it was imminent."

"And next, what did you do?"

"I went to the authorities."

"Which authorities?"

"The Lebanese, of course."

"And then?"

"Nothing."

"Nothing?" repeats Katia.

"That's right," says Samandal.

"Whom did you talk to? What level of command?"

"That information is with the Ministry. I gave them the names."

"Mr. Samandal, then what did you do?"

"I contacted him directly."

"Doreid Fattal?"

"Yes. It wasn't easy reaching him, but I finally did a few days prior to the assassination. He wanted to meet with me personally. In fact—and I've been given clearance to reveal this— that's where he was bound the day he was killed. Our meeting never happened."

"Where was it supposed to take place?"

"A private location."

"On which side of the border?"

"I cannot say."

"Is there anything else you can say?"

"That's all for now," says Samandal. "Thank you for the opportunity. I'll end by saying Mr. Doreid Fattal was a great man, a treasure to the Lebanese and all Arabs. It's a dark day for all of us, and like the Ain el Remmaneh incident, it will remain a stain on the white veil of Arab history until the truth is revealed."

"Mr. Samandal, thank you for your courage and candor," says Katia as she brings her hand to her ear. "Ladies and gentlemen, this just in. In what many have termed a 'symbolic' move, Mrs. Fattal issued a formal request to the Ministry of Transportation that bus service between Beirut and Damascus be resumed tomorrow morning. This will be the only bus, pending further developments in the Syrian ceasefire. To confirm then, the first bus will depart from Beirut's Charles Helou station tomorrow morning at 6:30 a.m. That's exactly ninety-six hours after the fateful bus on which Mr. Fattal lost his life."

Nadine studies her hands as Nancy looks on, face drenched with scorn. "Ladies and gentlemen," continues Katia. "With this open call to resume friendship between our two nations, we'll take a short break before returning with our political analyst for more. Please stay with us."

Dramatic music accompanies a garish video montage as Nancy abruptly (and thankfully) flicks the TV off and tosses the remote on the couch with a plop.

"This is bullshit," she says.

Nadine looks up at Nancy and me. "What's the Ain el Remmaneh incident?" she says.

"The bus massacre," says Nancy. "It started the war in Lebanon."

"The Civil War?"

"It was the first spark of what came to be known as the Civil War," I say. "But there was nothing civil about it."

"So what happened?" she asks Nancy directly, maybe preferring her more graphic version.

"Twenty-six Palestinians were gunned down on a bus on its way to a refugee camp," she says. "Some say it was in revenge for an earlier attack on a Lebanese politician."

Nancy looks like a guru under her towel-turban, and I enjoy her efficient account of events much older than she is.

"The politician was Muslim and the Palestinians Christian?" asks Nadine.

"The other way around," I say, "but it could've been either. It was an explosion waiting to happen. And soon it turned into a sectarian war, with lots of killing on both sides."

"And afterwards, the Israelis and Syrians, at different times and for different reasons, got involved too," continues Nancy, "and we had a regional gang bang. Lebanon was fucked from every side."

I throw Nadine a look, but she doesn't seem to mind the flowery language. I must admit Nancy's choice of words paints a vivid picture.

"I understand," Nadine says, with the hint of a smile.

Nancy runs her hand over her forehead under the towel. "Excuse my language, we had a long day."

"Yeah, you look tired," says Nadine. (Why can girls say that to each other without it turning into a fight?) "I'm sorry for dropping in like this. I can explain."

"No need. Actually, I think I'm just gonna head to sleep."

"But you'd find this interesting, Nancy," I say.

"I'm sure it'll be just as interesting tomorrow," she says, pulling off her turban and running her hand through her hair.

She picks up the yellow folder off the side-table, spraying it with droplets from her hair, and hands it to Nadine. "You left this here the other day."

"Thanks! I've been looking all over for this," says Nadine.

"I bet you were," says Nancy. "You know what you are Nadine? You're a fucking liar."

That catches us totally off guard.

"What? Why?" says Nadine.

"Your little story in there," says Nancy. "I read it. We read it. It's all bullshit. You pretend you're one thing, but you're really something else completely. Why hide it? You keep telling me about your father, Maurice. Well he's not your father is he? He's your stepfather. And you moved to Damascus when you were four. And you never mentioned your real dad."

Nadine says nothing. She just looks at me in complete shock, but Nancy charges on.

"That boy you call Tony, that was him on the bus, and you know it. Even before he died, you knew everything about him."

"Nancy that's enough," I say.

Nadine buries her hands in her face, and her shoulders bob up and down. But when she looks up, her face is dry. She snaps back at Nancy. "What do you mean, died? Who gave you the right to go through my personal papers? Just because I come here and clean your boyfriend's floors doesn't mean you own me! How do you know Tony is dead? Who told you that?"

Nancy makes a beeline for the bedroom and returns with the evening newspaper, open to the obituaries page. She pushes it into Nadine's chest and jabs it with her finger.

Underneath Nancy's fingertip I read the last line of the obituary. "Tariq Jaber (20?): Son of Mahmoud (RIP) and Balkees (RIP), Researcher, funeral to be held at Hussainia Nabatieh."

Barcode claimed the body after all. Tony's secret identity is out, not that it makes much difference now. The pseudonym only served Tariq Jaber inasmuch as it kept him safe. At least now he'll be buried near his mother, under his real name. Small kindnesses.

"See this man?" says Nancy. "That's Tariq Jaber. Your Tony. He was the man on the bus."

Nadine snatches the paper and scans the last line over and over, as if her eyes could somehow erase the words that glared back at her.

"I should go," says Nadine dryly, pushing the paper back to me. "I have a final tomorrow."

"I'll drop you off," I say sheepishly.

"Goodnight!" sings Nancy, waving a floppy backhand bye in response.

In a flash I pick up my keys and the Acacia from the bedroom and tug at Nadine's shoulder. Limp as a withered leaf under my grasp, she gives in and allows me to lead her to the door.

"I might stop at the lab on my way back," I say to no one in particular as Nancy tosses her towel onto the couch and turns into the bedroom.

"*Stofil*," she mutters and shuts the door.

◆

The Volvo's headlights cut through the narrow street past Beit el Kataeb and the secret park on the right hand side. I downshift to second gear and watch Nadine, who sits quietly with hands clasped in her lap, ring catching the streetlight bouncing into the car interior.

In the rearview mirror my *Acacia tortilis* pokes its branches between the two front seats, like an anxious child nagging "Are we there yet? Are we there yet? Are we there yet?"

I turn right onto the main road and at Leil Nhar crossing make another right onto Achrafieh highway, avoiding my normal route up the hill. This is where the posh part of town begins with a line of jewelry stores, which Nadine eyes as we stop at our first red light. I'm not sure how to break the silence, and am still out of ideas when the signal changes and we pass Sofil center on the right, followed by Mandaloun cafe with its upper class faux-bohemians smoking hookah on its open-air terrace. The view then opens onto Downtown Beirut, overlooking my favorite church with its square Orthodox cross, with the golden dome of the Downtown Mosque backdrop. The brightly lit nightclub area of Gemmayzeh separates the two religious edifices, though I doubt it'll see its usual bustle of partygoers tonight.

"I love this city," says Nadine. I notice she's teary-eyed but am thankful that one of us finally spoke. "This is a view you'd never see in Damascus. A mosque, church, and nightclub, a short walking distance from each other."

"Only in Beirut," I agree. "One of its charms, and all of its problems."

"I'd live with the problems for the charm," she says. "I wish I could stay here forever."

I should say something about what happened back home. "Listen, about—"

But she won't let me. "In my city you wouldn't even find a Sunni mosque on the same street as a Shia mosque," she says. "Can you believe that?"

"During the war, that was unheard of here too."

"Well my country had no war until now."

We take the underpass and the street dips as the view disappears. Another left turn under the bridge followed by a U-turn brings us onto a lower street. With nothing to add, I'm glad when Nadine is the one to speak. "When my parents moved to Damascus," she says, "my father had to find just the right spot to live. Money was tight and they didn't have many options. My parents were overprotective of my sister, and I didn't know until much later just how difficult things were."

"In what way?" I ask. This must be Nadine's defense to Nancy's onslaught.

She hesitates for a moment, perhaps unsure how much to reveal. "Well, you know. My parents' tribes are among the biggest in the country, and they're both in Tartous. Two big fish in a small pond. They were rivals for centuries, and each only married from within their own tribe. But then they made peace in spite of—or because of—my parents' marriage, the first inter-tribal union in generations. My father is a man of the world, a secular man. But my mother is Sunni by the book. Moving to the big city, she wanted to make sure we would be brought up Sunni."

"So they wanted to live in the Sunni part of town?"

"My father had no problem with that, except that it meant he was forced to live in a house that was more than we could afford at the time, just to keep my mother happy."

"Because of those problems you spoke about?" I'm not especially interested in knowing the answer, but I think the more I learn about Tariq Jaber's object of obsession, the better. Plus any talk is better than that awful silence. "It's okay, you can tell me. My family's not perfect either."

"It's not that. My family is happy, or at least they are now. Yes, my mother says it was tough at first, but as soon as they settled in Damascus and I was born, things got better. I had a very happy childhood and my sister took great care of me. My parents were there too, but it's her. I owe it all to Nissrine. She's very close to my father, and in a way she took over his responsibilities as he grew older and more depressed. She's a copy of him: Nissrine. When she was younger, they'd go on hunting trips to the outskirts of Damascus every month."

"Hunting," I repeat, emptily. I can barely keep my eyes open, but any conversation is better than nothing, given the circumstances. This must be how Nadine deals with denial, or uncertainty.

"Quail hunting, yes," she continues. "My father's only passion. And Nissrine was a bit of a tomboy, still is, so he'd take her with him. She's my father's, and I'm my mother's. That's how it is. When the two of them used to head out, my mother and I'd spend most of our time at the mosque. We live near the biggest Sunni mosque in the city. I used to play in the olive groves around it, then join my mom inside for prayer." She looks ahead, her dark eyes wide with nostalgia. "We went every Friday evening. And now with this rumored ceasefire, I'm visiting home the day after tomorrow."

I make a right turn and drive toward Ras el Nabaa crossing, my least favorite street in the entire city, and certainly the most chaotic. "*Harit kil meen eedo ilo*, to each his own," I mumble as I hit the gas and cut a narrow right through the intersection into Basta area. Every car has to find its own way to cross through the maze of intersections to the other side. The traffic police and signals only add to the confusion.

"Yeah, that's Damascus too," she says, getting my reference. "You know that was a TV show on Syrian TV. The main guy, Ghawwar, got into all sorts of trouble."

"Doreid Lahham," I say citing the actor's name. Then I continue, pressing on. "It's strange how names create these coincidences. Doreid Lahham. Doreid Fattal. And then there's Tony."

My throwaway comment takes her by surprise. "Is it true what Nancy said back there?" she asks.

"Yes," I say. "His real name was Tariq. He was on the bus."

"But how do you know?" she says, fresh tears welling in her eyes.

"I just do," I say. "He was a good man, and he died for nothing."

Is she truly unaware of all this? If not, it's quite a performance. "But how could that be?" she says.

My vagueness must be infuriating, but then so is her demeanor. I still cannot tell if she's being naive or conniving. Whichever it is, her performance doesn't falter, and I struggle to remain focused on the narrow residential road as more thoughts than I can handle compete for my attention.

"Nadine, why did you make up that story about your family in that folder?" I ask.

"I didn't. It's all true."

"But none of it matches what you told me." "That's because I haven't told you everything," she says, looking out the window, adding, "We've arrived."

It's like she can't wait to get out of the car. We're at the traffic light by the main entrance to LUST, possibly the farthest gate from the women's dormitory where Nadine lives.

"I can drive you to the dormitory gate," I say.

"I'll get off here. I don't want the guards to see me getting out of a professor's car. I'm late for curfew and there's gonna be hell to pay."

"Okay, hold on," I say, slowing the Volvo down, and after an oncoming car passes, I signal right and parallel park by the gate.

"Thanks," she says, in tears again.

"You're welcome. Listen, take the rest of the week off. The past few days have been tough."

"That would be good. I have finals tomorrow but afterwards, I want to go back home to my dad. He wasn't feeling well last

297

time." Her voice trails off.

I want to learn more, but don't know how else to steer the conversation. "Listen. About Nancy," I say. "She can be curt sometimes, but trust me, she's like that with all women. Likes to mark her territory."

"It's important that you… that both of you know I'm not that kind of girl. I come from a decent family. Even with Tony. It's not—it wasn't like that."

"I know," I say, though I'm not sure I know anything about this girl.

"The two months I knew him, nothing happened. Nothing. In fact, well… I think he had a girlfriend."

"Do you know that for sure?" I say, my ears perking up.

"The last two weeks or so, whenever we met he always smelled of alcohol, like he was out drinking all night. I didn't ask him, but he seemed distant, hung over, like he wasn't himself." She turns to me with a contorted smile, a hint of—what?—mischief playing around the corners of her lips. I watch the tiny mole there as she adds, "There's only one cause for that sort of behavior—even a young girl like me knows that."

"A woman," I say.

"See you next week, Professor," she says, sounding very much like Nancy as she steps out of the car. The yellow folder clasped tight to her chest, she runs through the Volvo's headlights, flashes her ID to the guard, and disappears through the university gate.

"Goodnight," I say through my window, but she's already gone.

◆

My head drums with a dull headache as I bring the Volvo to a stop in the lot marked "Faculty." It's empty except for another car, which I don't recognize but hope doesn't happen to be Chairman Ramala's. It's probably too late for that anyway, but with how the day's been going so far, anything is possible.

As I reach for the Acacia in the back seat, the wind rustles the trees outside. I step out of the car, Acacia under my arm, and roll up the window. The wind is strong tonight and at the head of my parking spot, the sign marked with my name creaks back and forth. I straighten it without any pride that my lot in life, at thirty-six years old, is just that—a parking spot marked "Assistant Professor."

As I step onto the concrete-tiled path, my footsteps echo against the modern walls of LUST, my home for the night. Two steps forward, then three. The echoes slow down, speed up, and then stop. I glance around me, but there's no one there but the trees. Another few steps ahead, a branch cracks.

"Is anyone there?" I yell out. No answer, save the rustling and some distant traffic. I quicken my pace toward the shadow cast by the bridge between the two main buildings. The cafeteria plaza lies gloomily ahead, a small stretch of concrete in an entire land of mourning.

The light from the cafeteria, empty but bright as a jewel, falls onto the Acacia as I reach into my pocket for my keycard. I beep myself in. The atrium glows to life and the door clicks open. The messenger bag slides halfway down my shoulder and I grip the door handle, but then a shadow cuts across the cafeteria light. I look up and catch a silhouette cross the plaza and vanish behind the far end of the Applied Sciences building.

"Hello?" I yell out, letting go of the door and crossing through the plaza. "Is anyone there?" I make my way toward the corner of the building in time to catch a glimpse of a flowery blue scarf disappearing further into the shadows.

"Nadine, is that you?" I say, stepping off the tiled concrete into a sandy patch planted with a thicket of bushes. Nothing.

Feeling colossally stupid, I reach under my glasses and wipe my eyes, and then head back toward the Botany building. I beep myself in again, and as I wait for the elevator a tremendous fatigue burrows through my bones.

Did Nadine lie to me again? Did she really go back to her dormitory or was that just an excuse to follow me back here? I must be more tired than I thought.

The elevator takes me up three levels and opens with a ding. As I get off, a muted hum greets me from the middle of the third floor hallway, and as I get closer a light alternates between bright and dim. It's like lightning, but more electric. I peek inside the room.

Garo, LUST's one and only office boy, looks up as the beam of the photocopier travels across his face.

"Working late?" I ask.

"Ah, *Istez*," he says. "Yes. Got these finals to photocopy for tomorrow afternoon. Does your class have any?"

"Not until next week," I say, and cutting the Q&A short, I drag myself through the remaining stretch of hallway to Classroom 2B.

◆

My Acacia is dying. What leaves that still cling onto its graying branches all point downwards, and many more have fallen onto the workbench within the short half-hour it's been sitting there.

A rack holds eight test tubes, each containing a sample thorn from the Acacia. With a pipette, I fill one with distilled water, another with saline and another with a diluted solution of hydrogen chloride. As my egg timer ticks, I make my notes, carefully watching each for signs of discoloration. This choice of solutions is arbitrary. I'm fresh out of hypotheses. I'd be embarrassed if one of my colleagues looked over my shoulder and found me dipping my precious thorns, as they cling to the waning hours of life, into what is essentially table salt dissolved in water. The remaining test tubes haven't even been filled yet—I just can't think of any liquids that could react, whether favorably or adversely, with the thorns. That's it. I'm stuck.

In the rear of the empty classroom, even the chairs have turned their backs on me. My tree silently mourns the dead fruits of our research, condemning our failure. I stroke the longest branch and like a razor blade my fingers shave off several more pathetic leaves, which cascade down to the workbench like shaved stubble. Crisp, brittle, dead. The unbearable silence presses down on me like a pile of dirt, and I feel like a corpse getting its first taste of soil tossed in by the gravedigger.

Every now and then, the window in the back door glows with traces of Garo's photocopier further down the hall. I pick up my tape recorder and hit the rewind button. The mechanism spins backwards and I hit Play at a random spot. I have only my own voice to keep me company, but instead it just echoes emptily, mocking me with its matter-of-factness.

"The killer must have trampled them."

From the open bag on the desk I pull out the newspaper. The front page headline reads, "Lebanese of All Sects Join Together in Peaceful Mourning."

How wrong the headlines were, printed hours too early. I can think of many adjectives to describe today's events, but peaceful certainly isn't one of them. I pull out a spread and return the rest of the newspaper to the bag. I flatten it over the desk and with the edge of my hand scrape the dead leaves off the workbench into my other hand. I drop them onto the newspaper surface

301

and repeat the motion. One, two, three.

Some needles bury themselves between the ridges of my skin, but I pull them out and flick them onto the paper. They bounce silently onto the printed words of the penultimate spread of the newspaper, picture-less, colorless. Just words.

Another flash of light travels across the window of the back door. I continue to scrape the needles as I absently go through the list. The headline in the corner of the newspaper reads, "Obituaries." At the bottom it has a separate listing entitled "Returned to God on the Deathly Bus" and under it seven names with brief descriptions of each. I scan them quickly, and as I expect, Fattal is not listed. This is the "others" list mentioned occasionally on TV, as in "The victims included Doreid Fattal and others."

Rubbing my hands together, a few more needles drop onto the paper. I wipe them off the column of text and lean in for a closer look.

I read the names.

– Mazen Najjar (32): Son of Mustapha and Lamisse, Engaged to Soraya Kamel, Engineer at CalcomCo, funeral to be held at Mosaitbe Church.

– Halim Ghulmiyyeh (47): Son of Hazem (RIP) and Taghreed, Husband to Nawal, Father of Suleiman and Samar, Teacher at Rawda High-school, funeral to be held at Al Sayde Hazmieh Church.

– Nasser Tabbaa (56): Son of Moein and Salam, Husband to Hadeel, Father to Moein, Ahmad, and Ramiz, Manager at Tabbaa Sales and Lettings, funeral to be held at Damour Mosque.

– Samira Sabbagh Kanafani (36): Daughter of Samir and Terese, Wife of Khalil, Mother of Samer, Sima, and Patrick, Employee at BLC Bank, funeral to be held at All Saints Church, Jounieh.

– Tariq Jaber (28): Son of Mahmoud (RIP) and Balkees (RIP), Researcher, funeral to be held at Hussainia Nabatieh.

– Maya Kawwas Maasri (30): Daughter of Kamal and Mona, Wife of Hisham, Mother of Mohamad and Jad, Pregnant with Julie—

"Pregnant," I say, my voice breaking.

The metallic voice from the recorder echoes mine. "Fresh buds, barely a day old." I stop it and pull off my glasses, holding my hand to my face, pressing into my eye sockets as hard as I can.

I leave it all at the workbench and make my way to the long window. I've always liked the Raouche area, and I don't think I've ever seen it look as beautiful as it does right now. Along the left side, the Ramlet el Bayda coast curves inland, lined with the twinkling lights of generic residential towers middle class Beirutis seem to love so much. But from my vantage point, high on the third floor of LUST, they could be twinkling stars or planets, maybe even distant galaxies that died a million years ago or are just being born.

"Pregnant."

I follow the coastline, empty except for a few figures speckled along the sand. They could be vagrants (though Beirut never had many homeless people) or maybe even lovers meeting under the cloak of darkness. Along the boulevard, sporadic headlights streak through the black streets like comets.

Beyond the shoreline is the sea, silently doing its to and fro dance under the full moon, now sharply outlined against the clear sky after the riot fumes dispersed. I've spent my life looking downward: at the soil, roots, plants spurting their first buds.

"Fresh buds."

Tariq Jaber looked upwards. Even at my own Acacia, he watched the world through his telescope.

"The star danced, and under that I was born," read the inscription on his mother's painting. And now back in the soil, he will spend eternity by her side.

"I was born."

I recall the young woman on the bus. She was scared for her baby. That was her final desperate attempt to save her unborn child. Her knees were curled to her chest in a fetal position, the same position as Julie, the life inside her she tried in vain to protect. Maya Kawwas Maasri was her name. She too died on that bus, a faceless woman I'll never know.

Tariq Jaber, Doreid Fattal. Those are names too. Not letters, or even words, but names. Proper nouns, people of flesh and blood. One, two, three, seven people. The reports are wrong. It was eight people, counting unborn baby Julie, as real as the fetus in Balkees' painting.

Nancy and I chose to trace the story of Tariq Jaber. The news chose to trace that of Doreid Fattal. But we could have chosen Maya, Mazen, Halim, even baby Julie's—any one of the eight people on that bus. Any one of those people would have been as crucial a story as any. Those people are as dead and gone as any Doreid Fattal or Tariq Jaber.

My head throbs again; my eye sockets fill with moisture, flooding down my cheeks. The salty taste stings my tongue like a thousand needles. My reflection is unrecognizable to me. I must be more tired than I thought.

Then I see it: a face stares back at me in the glass. I swivel around, and through the window of the back door, I spot a pair of beady eyes looking in. I'm sure of it. I rub the salty discharge off my face and look again. It's still there, a girl's face, Nadine? Just for an instant, then it's gone.

I rush to the door and swing it open. Out in the hallway, the photocopier from the next room flashes across the wall, blinding me. The hallway is empty.

"Garo?" I call out as I step into the office, another beam of light wiping across its walls. He looks up from behind the photocopier. "Garo, did you see a girl slip past just now?"

"I'm sorry *Istez*, I've had my head in this machine all night. Are you looking for someone?"

"Never mind," I say, and walk back to my classroom.

◆

"Where is she?" reads the whiteboard.

Then on a second line I write, "Feed the cat."

I step back for a wider view. Other fragments of colored ink streak the whiteboard, but these are the words that matter. Like lines in a jazz melody, they're where everything began, and where I must now bring it to an end.

A dying man who I believed was in the throes of delirium spoke these words. But no, he knew precisely what to say: in two brief sentences—one a question and one a demand.

On the right side of the couplet, I draw a bracket encompassing the two lines. At first I thought "she" and "the cat" were the same person, but I was wrong.

I was wrong about many things.

"Why the cat?" Nancy and I had wondered. Yes, there have been "motherfucking Maurices mushrooming everywhere" as she so aptly put it. A person might have many names, but they'd still be the same person, just as a beaker would contain the same volume of liquid no matter what numbers are marked on it. There was Tariq himself. And there was the cat, which I know was Tariq's masterstroke; it led me to his journal. And that in turn led us to a certain Maurice, who like a seasonal wind had quietly come and gone through Nabatieh. Few knew he even existed, but he did leave his mark on the lives of Balkees and her son, and on that fallen Acacia tree. That much I'm certain of. That much is fact.

Next to the first line I write "Nadine" and next to the second I write "Maurice+Balkees." I draw an arrow and write the cat's name, "Tarboush."

The rest is a question mark, but tonight we might have learned who the "she" could be. I draw another arrow and write her name again, "Nadine." Tariq was watching her, or that's what she claims—not as certain as the first fact, but definitely possible.

"It's all relative," I say, and with the sound of my voice Nadine's insistent words resonate through my mind. From them, I pluck the one word that matters the most and write it between her name and Tariq's, "Brother."

Then there was Samandal from TV, who, I believe, is but a yarn woven by the powers that be, an elaborate piece of fiction to keep us all busy, to milk Fattal's death for all its political worth. I keep that story off the whiteboard.

And then there's the newspaper obituary—that's fact too. It lists the names of all the victims side by side with those of their family members. It's all relative.

So finally there's Nadine's father.

I draw a circle around her and Tariq's names, and label it with the only word that could close the circle, "Maurice."

He was Tariq Jaber and Nadine Akkad's father. This is not a fact. It's not even a probability. But it is possible, what I like to call a hypothesis. And I finally know where to look for proof.

Where it began, there it must end.

14
Root, Stem, Fruit

Root.

He pressed the plastic toy to his face and looked through the eyepiece, but the sun burned his eyes. He wanted to get the hillside in the shot, the high wall of dirt that ran along one side of their world. This was their space. This was only the third time he'd been here, their niche in the universe: the flat stretch of grass on which he now stood, the mound hill and trees he so loved and the tower they built for her four summers ago were all theirs, and theirs alone.

He lowered the toy from his face and waved to them to move out of the way, to circle around to the other side. He knew he had to place the sun behind him, otherwise they'd just be silhouettes against it. He had to literally move heaven and earth for that to happen, but he felt that in a way he had already done that by the sheer fact of being here today.

She understood what he was trying to say with that wave, but instead of circling around, she spun the wheels and the chair catapulted straight toward him as the boy followed a few steps behind. He understood that silent pact that neither of them would push or pull her unless the wheels got caught against a shrub or rock, and even then they'd just give her the smallest nudge. But now the wheels spun around freely as the two of them moved toward him in a straight line. He approached too until the three of them stood face to face at the center of the front lawn. They exchanged smiles but no words as she wheeled past him, the young man trailing close behind. He took a few more steps toward the hillside and turned to face them again.

Balkees and young Tariq now stood at the edge of the valley, next to the tree stump and he had his back to the hillside. He studied the view, realizing this was even better than what he had in mind. His wife, their son, and the tree where they had inscribed their initials, and which almost got them both killed. Instead, the man she was married to cut it down in one fit of rage, beat her within an inch of her life in another, and sent out a pack of armed bloodhounds to hunt him down in a third. One week later, his rage unabated, he was struck down with the same fury, this one of divine proportion. The man was dead. And forty days after that, that same divine power blessed them first in marriage, and nine months later with the child who now stood eighteen-years-grown before him. A mirror of his own proud youth.

That's how things happened for them, always in threes. Three acts of rage, followed by three acts of mercy. And because of that trilogy of circumstances, he was only able to see them together three times. God works with great precision. That's why he knew in his heart that this day together would be their last.

She was now relegated permanently to that chair. The boy was of age. It would be unwise for him to be seen here ever again. Not for a long time. And that's why this photograph, the only one ever, had to be perfect.

He pressed the toy to his face, looked through the plastic eyepiece until he was sure they were perfectly framed: mother in her chair, boy standing behind her. "*Idhaku*! Smile!" He shouted out with all his might.

Click.

◆

Stem.

She leaned her arms against the crutches as she watched her son carry a bag of sand across the yard. He had fully recovered now. The injury to his foot left him with a limp, but Maurice assured her it would subside with time. They even joked about it now, Maurice and he. "How's the Wicked Toe?" Maurice would ask. "Still wicked," Tariq would answer, and the two would laugh until Balkees admonished them, reminding them that a near-death experience was no laughing matter.

Tariq's brown muscles gleamed in the sun, his T-shirt caked with muddy sweat. At fourteen, he was a man now. For the first time she noticed the uncanny resemblance between the two men as the younger one passed the bag of sand to his senior, who in turn passed it over to the first of the six workers he had hired for the job.

It was only the second time the two of them had been in the same space at the same time, like alter egos, reflections, ships in the night. The visual metaphors flickered through her head as she pictured herself at the top of the tower painting them onto her canvas. It was half-complete now. The assembly line of workers headed by the two men had turned her vision into a half-realized reality with great speed. Soon the structure would poke its roof beyond the veil of the hillside, visible from every corner of the town.

It was a bold and reckless thing to do by any stretch of the imagination, but the sheer pleasure of watching an abstract object of that imagination transformed into mortar, brick, and concrete was worth the risk. They had assured her of that, and as she watched them hard at work she knew they were right. They very clearly took as much pleasure in the work as she no doubt would in the end result.

But she also understood that it was the work itself that was the real purpose of this project. To see the men share in the creative and manual labor of making something from nothing, to see them as equals, was the quintessence of joy.

The distance between them, now reduced to nothing, would expand again. It was like the tide, closing down only to reopen. Today was but a droplet of time in the ocean between their encounters. But even if this were the last, the structure they now built would stand as eternal witness.

"Tariq!" said the first. "Hand me another bag!"

"Yes sir, Mr. Maurice!" said the second.

That even for a few seconds, she had to squint at them to make out who was who, that for a moment she couldn't even tell the two men apart, filled her with immense pride.

◆

Fruit.

"Tariq! Get down this instant!"

The child stubbornly refused to budge. How the four-year-old was able to climb all the way to the top of the monkey bars during the half-hour she had spent in the kitchen, she couldn't imagine.

"Come down! We need to get you cleaned up."

But no, he refused to move. He just sat on the iron joint and looked out over the hills like a conqueror surveying his spoils. She couldn't help but feel a tinge of pride at that, but this day was too important.

She reached out but he was a good meter out of her grasp, and her stiff knees ached with pain as she stretched onto the tips of her toes, but it was no use. Her body was as stubborn as the dirt-caked child above her.

On the other side of the house, the hike up the hillside couldn't have taken Maurice more than a few minutes. He knew that, because the sun had barely moved behind the antenna on the horizon, since he got out of the taxi cab on the road and made his way up the dirt path. Yet it felt like many years, four years to be exact, the four years since he saw Balkees last. A lot had happened in that time. A new life had entered his. A daughter, who one day he'll send here. But not to Nabatieh, that would be reckless. To Beirut maybe. Maybe one day she could be a companion to the boy he's here to meet. Then they could be together, as it should be.

No photos had been exchanged between him and Balkees. They were very careful. Instead, all that Maurice had to be able to imagine the boy were the words they had exchanged on the phone. Balkees painted a vivid picture, but nothing could compare to the thought of laying his eyes on his child for the first time.

He adjusted the long gift-wrapped package under his arm without pausing for breath as he cut across the front lawn toward the stone house, following the contour of the hillside. But as it opened to the backyard, he stopped. He could hear her now, her angry voice sweeter than a lullaby.

And there they were; she at the foot of the playground monkey bars, the stubborn child at the top. Maurice approached them, careful not to startle them, allowing his footsteps to squish through the grass until she turned to him.

He laid a hand on her shoulder as she smiled into his eyes. He then turned to the child and stretched his arms out. The child looked down at him for just a second. "What's that?" he asked, pointing at the gift-wrapped cylinder under Maurice's arm.

"You'll have to come down and see," he said.

"What did you get me?" asked the child.

"The stars."

The child released his iron grip from the monkey bars and free-fell into Maurice's outstretched arms.

15
"Where Is She?"

A loose page sticks to my cheek as I lift it from my memoir. Prying it off, I look down at my soggy words, trying to recall the final ones I wrote before I dozed off. "The stars," they read, but they've long departed the sky outside. In their place, the fluorescent light seems inconsequential in the glare hitting me through the classroom window.

It must be a new day.

The clatter of footsteps in the hallway count down the few seconds that separate me from appearing to the students like a turgid mole that just crawled out of the earth.

My throat tightens as I reach into my bag and pull out my comb, then hurry over to the door. Through its glass panel, hordes of students funnel through the doors down the hall. Young men and women of all groups and phyla, all forms and colors, close in on me, helpless in this empty room. I'm trapped: no mirrors, the morning outside too bright for the window-pane to reflect my face.

Even on the day of the bus incident, after spending a good hour in the bathroom cleaning up, Nancy remarked that I looked like shit. Nancy notices things, like (I'm sure) how I left her at home last night, angry out of her mind. But I can't think of that now, nor can I slink out to the bathroom without my disheveled appearance being noticed and noted.

I must make do with what I have to get myself in order. I can't let the students see me like this; despondent, shaggy, messy, my Acacia and spirit broken. To have that happen on the fifth day of a mindless quest, one with no rhyme or reason, would be unacceptable. I have no control over my own life, but to also lose control over my reputation would be disastrous. What would they think? What would Chairman Ramala say? How would my colleagues react? With the utmost glee, no doubt.

To the side of the door is a golden plaque. (I dislike gold. Too shiny. But today I appreciate its brilliant tackiness.) In my own tired reflection, the face of my father looks back at me with downcast eyes, disappointed, betrayed, dismayed. I wipe my eyes and adjust my glasses, then pull down the cuff of my jacket and wipe the golden plaque until its bold letters reading sparkle "Botany: Classroom and Lab 2B" and the surface glimmers with a mirror-like sheen. There, my father's face dissolves into my own: tired, no doubt, but nothing that can't be fixed. It's not as bad as I feared.

I run the comb through my hair. One, two, three, and part. Once more: one, two, three, and part. There, that should do it. I give my shirt collar a tug and my tie a pull, and make my way back to the desk. I glance at the charts on the whiteboard, committing the diagram to memory. (I'll never forget it anyway; it's etched there like cracks in dry soil.) I wipe the whiteboard clean.

Now it's really a new day.

In the back of the classroom, I pull at the edges of the newspaper on the workbench, allowing the Acacia needles to slide into the crease, then carefully fold it into a makeshift pouch and insert it into a pocket on the inside of my bag. I look at the Acacia itself, but something of this size has nowhere to go, so why hide it? I grip it under my arm, make my way to the front of the class and plop myself behind the desk. I'm at the helm again, and this classroom is my ship. Ahoy captain, ahoy. I clasp my hands on the table and wait through the dead calm that separates me from nine o'clock…

…Just a few seconds as it turns out. The well-oiled door glides open, and the first student walks in with a bright "Good morning, sir."

I try to echo his tone with my own "Good morning, sir," (I've taken the habit of calling my students, even the female ones, "sir" as a reminder not to call me that, even if none of them ever get the joke) but my voice comes out cracked and weary. As the next few students walk in, it livens up and by the time the class is half full, and enough sun has seeped into my body, I'm as perky as a daffodil.

But a soft voice over my head brings me back down. "Oh no, what happened here?" I look up at Janette, as her arm reaches out for the Acacia on my desk. She's right: I may look okay, but the tree doesn't. "Is it dead?" she asks.

"Almost," I say. She throws me a dark look and makes her way to her seat in the front row. I scan the class and then nod absently as a student politely walks over to the door and closes it. A few moments later, everyone has settled down—a full class, of course, on a day of finals. I have no exams scheduled, just term papers and a regular lecture for today. Then with all my energy I utter the most profound word that comes to mind, "Well."

"Well," someone echoes from the middle of the class.

I unclasp my hands and get up. "Well," I repeat, circling to the front of the desk and leaning against it. "We certainly live in interesting times."

The class mumbles in agreement.

"If this were a school in, say, the American Midwest, we'd all be in grief counseling this morning."

Mild groans.

"And you'd all have your finals canceled."

Louder groans.

"But this is Beirut," I continue. "*Harit kil meen eedo ilo.*"

The students laugh now.

"To each his own. I assure you, finals will proceed as scheduled. And for this class, please have your papers in my pigeonhole by the end of the day." I wait for them to settle down then continue, "We're all dealing with the events of the past few days, each in our own way. And please know that if any of you need to talk about it, or anything else, I and the rest of the faculty, and of course Chairman Ramala, are at your disposal."

The class responds with a smatter of unenthusiastic thanks.

"Alright," I say clapping my hands and making my way to the whiteboard. "With that out of the way, let's begin our—"

"Sir?" someone interrupts. I spin around and notice a fair-haired boy in the center of the room amidst the cabbage patch of heads. He never spoke out before. I think his name is Mazen.

"Yes, sir?" I answer (my "sir" habit comes in handy when I can't remember students' names by semester's end).

"Sir, what happened to her?" he asks.

"Her?" I ask the twenty pairs of eyes fixed in the direction of the Acacia like sunbeams. "Oh, her," I say as I buy some time. If I thought the empty seats last night were oppressive, they're nothing compared to a jury of students staring back at me. I hadn't planned to be cross-examined today, but I remember a line I once read in a legal drama: never say more than you have to, and my own version: never lie more than you have to. "I think she's dying," I admit.

"But why?" the boy presses on. "We charted the Acacia taxonomy down to the smallest species. We followed its life

316

cycle. You, sir, you know more than anyone how these plants survive."

Where was this kid hiding all semester? Was his great-grandfather, with those same blue-green eyes and sharp features, a member of the Ottoman Inquisition?

"True," I say, knowing full well how arrogant that might sound. But it's the truth—if anyone could've saved this plant, it's me. And like the expert dendrologist that I am, I flop my hands in the air and say, "I honestly don't know. I found her on the outskirts of the city, already in bad shape. All her siblings were healthy, and some still are. You'll read everything in my paper, but I don't know what else to do. Nothing short of a miracle would—"

"Sir," Janette cuts in. I turn my attention to her as she continues. "You know the Acacia is called Christ's Thorn. They say His crown, you know when He was crucified, was made of an Acacia branch because it has the sharpest thorns."

"Yes."

"Maybe you're right," she proceeds, her words overlapping with mine. "Maybe a miracle is what you need. They say the leaves continued to grow while the crown was on Christ's head. And they say that when He rose from the dead three days later, the crown had sprouted fresh buds."

"They say a lot of things," Mazen retorts.

This is going nowhere, so I intervene before things get heated. "Listen," I say softly, tiptoeing to the front of the class as if through a minefield.

As a rumble of unsettled voices rises in the room, I raise my hand. "Hush, hush now," I say. "Listen. All of you know I'm the first to agree that the stories we tell are crucial to understanding why we are what we are. History, even mythology, while pure fiction, is relevant at least in some way."

Janette objects with a stern look, quite possibly to the word "mythology." To a devout Christian, the life of Christ would be closer to fact than myth.

"The fact remains, we're scientists," I continue. "We draw a line between science and faith. Anything we can't prove by evidence in the material world has no place in our research. But consider this. It's not what we can prove, but what we can disprove. Sure, one could build an argument that a weeping virgin is proof that God exists. But can we argue against the existence of God in that manner? Does every virgin who does not weep prove that we live in a Godless universe? You don't need to show something is true. You just need to show its opposite is not. If you can't do that, then the basis of your argument is anything but science."

The class settles down. My students know not to belabor a point, but the walls continue to echo with discombobulated murmurs. They've invested an entire semester in our study and care of the Acacia genus, and I've come short, the dying poster child on the desk behind me a grim testament to my failure.

But now I realize the rumble of voices is actually coming from outside, and so do the students. Several leave their seats and lean against the long window. I follow them and look outside: in the concrete-tiled plaza below, students cluster around podiums and kiosks, all perhaps chanting in unison, but collectively forming an indistinct babble. Banners and signs of different sizes and colors—yellow, green, orange, blue, white, and black—shoot up and down through the crowd.

"Alright, let's all take our places now," I say, moving back to the desk. "We have a class to run, but I promise to let you out half an hour before lunch break. This isn't a good day to spend inside."

But in truth, I wish I could stay in this room forever. If twenty pairs of condemning eyes are harsh, that's still a world of mercy compared to the judgment that awaits me outside these walls.

◆

The slit between the elevator doors lights up and the carriage thuds under my feet as it stops between the lower floors. Today started later than yesterday, but I'm in no hurry.

Under my arm, the sickly Acacia leaves prickle my skin much more timidly than they should. I hitch the pot up a bit more, careful to keep it level as the tree's limp thorns bend miserably into my sleeve with no resistance whatsoever.

Through the slit window by the elevator cage, the crowds have thickened, but I'm happy they remain somewhat organized, if loud and unintelligible. The thought that in a few moments I'll have to walk through that rabble fills me with dread. Open spaces terrify me, but never more than when they're filled with this many people out for blood. Not mine, to be sure, but who knows? I might be trampled, like collateral damage on a bus riddled with bullets.

From here, it's hard to decipher what the many banners read, but I can guess. The colors are those of the parties that make up the Lebanese political landscape. And indeed, from up here, it does look like a landscape. In the background the Corniche Boulevard smolders while the emerald Mediterranean twinkles in the sunlight, especially strong for a late-November day. Life goes on, as Fattal's widow said. The only difference is that now it looks unreal, almost painterly, like a Monet, as Nancy might say, speckled with dots of bobbing heads and swatches of bright cloth.

Where could she be this morning? There's a lot to tell her. The crowd below speckles with mostly blue. The blue group. No, she wouldn't be there. The smaller orange one. No, she can't

319

be there either. Come to think of it, not once did I wonder or ask what her favorite political color might be. But I'm sure she should be down there somewhere.

A dot zigzags between the clusters, like a rogue cell avoiding the placebo effect of the groups, or the Ms. Pac-Man game I spent countless hours with as a child. It stops sporadically every few seconds before carrying on. It must be Nancy, caught in a challenge of wills against her own limp. Rush, ouch, rush some more, ouch some more.

I must catch up with her. Tap, tap, tap on the elevator button, decades newer than the one in my apartment building, but stubbornly reading the same "*Occupé.*"

I check the staircase—it might be faster. But no, office boy Garo has just emerged and if he sees me he'll want to chitchat. Dammit, come on!

Ding! Finally, it's here.

I get in and hit the GF button. Come on…

It grinds into gear, but then ding! It stops one floor below. The doors slide open. There's no one there. Good. I hit the Close button frantically and when the doors are a few centimeters apart, a high-pitched yelp goes, "Wait, wait, wait." Shit. No choice. I hit the Open button and a manicured, veiny hand sticks its resolute fingers in the widening gap.

"Good morning," the hand's owner pants.

"Good morning, Chairman Ramala," I say, as the doors click shut. Great, just what I needed.

No pause. She dives right in. "So, how's that paper coming along?" she asks in her thick Palestinian accent, stabbing right into the heart of the matter between us. The only thing I hate more than too much small talk is none at all. Who'd have thought that such a huge white elephant could fit into the tiny cabin of the elevator Ramala and I now share? For once I yearn for the open space awaiting me below.

"Good," I say.

"You sure?" she says, ogling the Acacia suspiciously, her high heels raising her eye level well above mine.

"I'm making progress. I know what *not* to do."

"I see," she says. The elevator dings open. Please let it be her floor. A brunette freshman throws a glance at us, and then very obviously avoids getting on by turning and yelling, "Yes? Okay I'm coming!" to no one. I'm sure it's not me she's avoiding. I suppose she doesn't like sharing tight spaces with the Chairman either.

"I'm glad to hear that," Ramala continues. "The review board is meeting today. We have a spot open for Associate Professor, I'm sure you know that."

"Aha," I say. Is this elevator always so slow?

"I'd like to toss your name onto the pile," she says. (I think she says "pile" not "fire," but with Ramala, one can never be too sure. It might even be "pyre.") She throws me her shiny-red lopsided version of a smile as she looks down from under her hooded eyelids, heavy with blue paint. "Of course, it all depends."

"On what?" I ask brazenly.

"Knowing what not to do is a good start," she says. "But that's all it is. What we're all anxious to hear is where it ends." Has she been talking to my father? Or was she eavesdropping on my thoughts last night?

Ding! goes the elevator. We're at my destination: ground floor, the lowest level. And that's where my heart has sunk, to the very base of my stomach.

"An academic of your caliber can't afford to miss this deadline. Not anymore. The hunt is underway and your reputation precedes you. It's your scent. The evaluation committee smells your fear. They're coiled and ready to pounce, to chew you up like a carcass. Wait, where did I get that expression? Is it one of yours? Hmm, I wonder…" The doors slide open. "Remember, Professor. Your final draft. On my desk. By the end of the week." And with that, she lizards out.

◆

The plaza is busier and more colorful than it looked from above. There's barely any wiggle room in these groups and groups of groups. From down here, they don't look like clusters, but a full-fledged jungle: broad shoulders hedge through the open space, forming a segmented labyrinth, arms and limbs branch over the paths like canopies, while legs stay firmly rooted to their spots. No matter how hard I flail my arms about, trying to push through it, I feel like a helpless Snow White in the Haunted Forest.

And above me—no sky, no clouds—banners and signs block the sun with slogans—subtle and direct, timid and profane, slang and poetic, but also:

Existential—
Death to So and So!
Long live So and So!
Referential—
"An Arab capital," says the Witness!
"An Arab capital," lies the Witness!
And biblical—
Rebuild the roads to Damascus!
Burn down the roads to Damascus!

Through the thicket, it's impossible to find Nancy, and as I hunt around, the Acacia and I get shoveled hither and thither like leaves carried by the winds of political dissent.

At a small clearing in the center of the ruckus, I bump into a massive tanned man with a TV camera on his shoulder.

"Cut, cut, cut," yells a familiar voice. It's Katia from the news, her makeup several layers thicker than on TV. "Let's do that again."

"And… go," says the cameraman.

"Today the nation wears its politics on its sleeve, in a patchwork of color. The air is charged, and Lebanese come together as never before against a common enemy. Though who that enemy is, remains to be seen. It's a faceless threat, recalling the invisible terror that gripped the world only a few years ago. A local breed, that took the lives of Doreid Fattal and a number of other citizens of various sects. Today we come together as one Lebanon, one hand against…"

I retrace my steps toward my department as the speechifying anchorwoman fades into the white noise. Back at the Botany building, I make a right through the alley, past the cafeteria, and into the parking lot. When I parked last night, the space was almost empty and, now in the daytime, the mosaic of cars is as colorful as the banners on the other side. It takes me all of ten minutes to find my dirt-brown Volvo, neatly sandwiched between two much larger SUVs. Invisibility isn't always a good thing.

The trunk pops open, and as I set the Acacia inside, it sheds more leaves. I lean against the open latch and think for a few seconds. No, I'll not lay it to rest just yet. I take it out, slam the trunk shut, and open the back door instead. I set it down carefully on the backseat and roll down the window just a crack so that my Acacia can breathe.

I look up and trace the path of the sun with my finger. It's bound to hit the car directly in an hour or so. I take out a bottle of water from my bag and empty its contents into the tree pot. It's the humane thing to do, though I already feel guilty as I toss

323

the empty bottle on the seat and close the door on her.

"*Keefak Istez*?"

I flip around with a start. It's Garo, in fisherman mode. That's what I call him when he's wearing his rolled up bermudas and plastic slippers. A cheeky smile cuts through his sweaty face, topped with his dirty "Gone Fishin'" cap. His entire outfit, down to his plastic slippers, is the same color as my Volvo. He almost disappears against its paint job.

"Hello Garo. How are you?"

"*Wlik, intawashna ma heik*? Noisy, noisy, noisy!" he says casually. He must have the morning off. "*Inno* what do they think they'll achieve?"

"They're just angry that's all. Have you eaten? Come, I'll buy you a *kaake*."

His face lights up as we cut across the parking lot to a van along the sidewalk. These "express vans" used to line the entire Corniche Boulevard when I was younger, and were a feature recognizable by tourists from all over the world. But when the fast-food franchises started invading town, a rumor spread that the vans were doubling as drug retailers, though I never saw any of that. Either way, they were banned and vanished almost overnight. Nancy and I found this one, the last of a dying breed, tucked into a side street just off the Corniche.

"How's the fishing?" I ask Garo as we make our way to the express van.

"Look!" he smiles, pulling a baggy from his pocket. In it three silver fishes squirm in some water. "Check this out!" He pulls one out by its tail, and sticks its head in his mouth. Its translucent fins quiver between his lips. He then pulls it out and plops it back in the bag. It goes back to squirming. "I have a whole freezer in the car. Good catch today."

"Yes. But don't tease them!"

"Oh no *Istez*. I saved these small ones. These'll go in my bowl. I have a collection! The bigger ones go in the frying pan."

We arrive at the van and I lean in. There are three other customers, and on the other side, I find her.

"One *kaake* with Picon and *zaatar* please," says Nancy. "And a Diet Pepsi."

"And for me a foamy Nescafé and..." I say, then turn to Garo. "What do you want?"

"*Kaake* with *halloum* cheese," he says.

"*Kaake* with *halloum*," I say to the seller as I catch Nancy watching me.

"Two!" adds Garo. "Been up all night. Photocopying makes me hungry."

"Two!" I repeat. "And a Pepsi."

I make my way over to Nancy as she watches her *kaake* being prepared.

"Hey," I say.

"Hey," says Nancy.

We watch the seller prepare three *kaakes* with amazing deftness. He slices each open with a steak knife, squeezes three triangles of Picon cheese directly into each, then spreads them with the knife, wiping it clean against the bread on the final stroke. He does the same with the *halloum* ones, but instead of spreading the cheese he slices it right onto the *kaake* without cutting through to the bread.

"*Zaatar*?" he asks me. "Yes!" yells Garo from the other side of the van.

The seller then sprinkles *zaatar* on all three *kaakes*, hands Nancy one and me the other two. I pay him for all as he hands us the soft drinks, and I notice that he handles the money with his other hand. I'm glad Nancy follows me over to Garo as I hand him his food.

"*Merci*," he says with a smile, then he points to Nancy and adds, "Be good to *Istez*, he's a nice man."

She laughs. "We'll see," she says, but when she turns to me all I get is a frown.

I take my cue and say, "Okay. You're mad. But I've got stories to tell you. So put it on hold for a minute until you've heard them." I catch my breath, and before she can retort I add, "Garo, walk with us."

He must enjoy playing Cupid, because Garo takes up my invitation with a jovial tap of his cap. The three of us cross the Corniche separating LUST campus from the reclaimed land on the other side, a concrete deck jutting into the Mediterranean. A rocky beach, part of LUST property by law for ninety-nine years, lines its outer edge. The three of us lean against the corroded white railing overlooking an emptied swimming pool below. Its white tiles catch the noon sun and bounce it back in a harsh glare.

I turn my back on it and face the Corniche. "Done with the finals?" I ask Garo.

"Only my part's done. The students take them all afternoon today and tomorrow. As you can see they're studying hard." He waves a hand absently at the LUST crowd across the Corniche. Oh, sarcasm. I get it.

Nancy just munches on her *kaake* and watches the passing cars.

"Garo, who was there yesterday in our building?" I ask.

"Besides us?" he says. "No one, *Istez*. I told you that."

"Then let me ask you this. You have access to the student records, correct?"

"Of course, *Istez*. I file them for Mrs. Ramala. But why do you ask?"

"Then you must know a certain Nadine Akkad, in Applied

Sciences. She studies Metallurgy."

Nancy looks up.

"I might," says Garo tentatively.

"And you must know she had a friend. A *boy* friend."

"I'm sorry *Istez*, anything that's not a matter of record, I don't know."

"Oh but you do," I say. "Tony something."

Garo remains silent as I continue. "A few months ago, Tony appeared on LUST campus asking about a student. Maybe he only knew her last name back then, perhaps her age too, and you pointed her out to him."

Garo turns away, tracking the passing cars like the beam of his photocopier, back and forth.

"Look," I say, positioning myself in a way so as to block his view of the Corniche. (Did Nancy just smile?) "I won't get you in trouble. I just need to know."

"*Istez*, please," says Garo with a whimper. "I caught him one night trying to sneak into the girls' dorm. I swear, that's it. The security woman was dozing off, and I just… happened to be there in the booth by the gate, where they have the umm…" Realizing what he almost said, he glances at Nancy, but she pretends not to notice. Good move.

I fill in the blank. "Where they have all the monitors?" I say.

So he's a sneaky little lecher. We have bigger fish to fry, but now that I have something on him, I won't let it pass unless he tells me more. "Those little screens are hooked to the security cameras at the women's dorms, correct?"

"Okay, okay you're right," he says, eyes and lips twitching. "That guy Tony, he was looking for someone, for Ms. Akkad. He said he'd tell on me. Get me fired. So I just told him her name and where she studies. That's all, I swear."

Last night Nadine mentioned Tariq had bribed an office boy.

Close. It wasn't a bribe, but a threat. "Good," I say. "So he came looking specifically for that girl, no one else."

"Yes, *Istez*. That's it. That's all. Please *Istez*, Professor, sir, this job's all I have."

I nod, but Nancy drops the *kaake* to her side and says, "Garo, don't ever let me catch you by the girls' dorms again. If the guard's sleeping on the job, you go tell Chairman Ramala, okay?"

"Okay, okay! I promise," he says. He stuffs the remaining half of the *kaake* into his mouth and mumbles something that could either be "*shukran Istez*" or "*gâteau aux fraises*." He checks again for passing cars, then in a single sprint skips across the Corniche back to LUST like Nancy had set his ass on fire.

She taps my shoulder and says, "Professor, let's go."

◆

Sunlight ricochets against the white tiles, forming a soft dapple of light and shade, which the dark blue tiles slice mercilessly through. We sit in the deep end of the empty LUST swimming pool, walls zigzagging around the slope. The lines converge to a single point at the tiled stairs on the other side, creating the illusion that we're immersed in an endless blank space. Yet the shadow cast by the high wall against which we lean forms an alcove that ends just at the tips of Nancy's extended legs, keeping us contained in our own private space.

Other than us, a few avid sunbathers stretch out on chaises longues, soaking up every last ray of sun before winter. Their bronze skin glistens in the distance, yet from our spot they could be inanimate objects, or distant stars like the ones that sparkled through last night's sky.

Nancy munches on her *kaake* silently, but her unopened

Diet Pepsi sits, baking in the sun. The light has moved quite a bit since we sat down, the seconds rolling into minutes as Nancy soaks in my stories from last night. I reach for her Pepsi, happy to find it still palatably cold, and set it down inside the shadow line.

"Thanks," she says.

"You're welcome. Now you can go back to being mad."

She wraps the rest of her *kaake* and sets it aside. She then wipes her mouth with a tissue and grins. "Anything stuck in my teeth?" she asks

"Your teeth are perfect."

Her smile disappears as she exhales and says, "That was quite a story."

"It's a hypothesis," I say.

She turns to me, looking straight into my eyes. "You know what to do now."

"Yes I do," I say. "I should go to Damascus."

"But?" she says.

"First, there's my paper. This whole business with the Chairman. Two days!"

"And second?" asks Nancy.

"Second?"

"You said 'first,' so I'm assuming there's a second."

"And second, I looked at the facts yesterday. The only thing we know for sure is the least important bit. The cat's name, that's it. The rest, it's just hypotheses. Nadine, his sister. Maurice, his father. And then the girlfriend, whoever she is. We assumed it's Nadine, but she, herself, brought up the girlfriend last night on the drive here, unprovoked. Everything we have is an assumption. All of it."

"True," says Nancy softly, but her gaze doesn't waver. Her eyes tell me to continue my line of thought to its conclusion, whatever that might be.

"Sure, all the clues are there, like Tariq being protective of Nadine. You know those notes he took, of my monthly routine, figuring out when I was away. He wasn't interested in me. He wanted to know when she was alone. At least when I was around, he knew she was safe. He didn't worry for himself. He worried for her. Whether he had reason to or not. Of course, that's assuming she's actually telling the truth."

"Who knows. Maybe she is," says Nancy. I'm taken aback. Not once have I heard her speak kindly of Nadine during the many months that she's worked for me.

"And maybe she isn't," I say. "I mean, who's to say this is the path to the answers? Those people on TV, they speak of the truth? And that witness. Maybe that's where we should've looked. Who's to say where the truth lies?"

"You just said it. The truth lies," says Nancy. "None of that TV shit matters."

"But yesterday. As we drove back, you were so upset," I say. "All that talk about injustice."

"I was upset because I want to know you care. Those yakkers on TV, even the few who aren't completely full of shit, they're only concerned with what happened on the bus because of Doreid Fattal, the politician. Watch how politicians from all sides will use every mention of that name. As a party line to hang conflicting agendas onto."

She lays her hand on my cheek. It feels warm and moist. I find myself wishing she'd keep it there forever. "For me, for you, it's the exact opposite," she continues. "It's not about politics, it's about people like Tariq Jaber, like that pregnant woman you read about, even like Doreid Fattal, the middle-aged man with a wife and daughter. You know I was glad when I heard the he might have had an affair? He's not the demigod everyone makes him out to be. He's just... people. That's what they all are. People. How they died isn't who they were."

Nancy sounds as if she were at my side in Classroom 2B last night, when I arrived at the same realization. Then in a final breath of quiet desperation, I ask, "Come with me?"

"I can't," she says. "Dad lost at blackjack last night. He came back home this morning and freaked the fuck out when I wasn't there. I had twelve missed calls this morning."

"Tell him you're sorry, and come with me."

"And I have to work with my mushrooms tonight while the moon is still almost full," she smiles, her hand cupping my cheek tighter.

"It'll be full again next month."

"And there's my knee..." she says.

"I'll get you crutches."

"Let me tell you a story," she says, dropping her hand from my face.

"You can do that on the way."

"No, listen," she repeats, her smile fading. "After my mother died, Dad took Rony and me to church every Sunday." She ignores my sigh and continues. "For many years, every Sunday we sat there and listened to stories. My dad finally got bored and decided blackjack was a better use of his weekends." She smiles ever so briefly. "But I enjoyed those mornings. Well, the hymns not so much. But the stories, those were the best part, and many of them stuck with me. My favorite is the story of Saul."

She looks at me and I shake my head. I'm not familiar with that story, so she begins. "Right after the time of Jesus Christ, there was this man named Saul," says Nancy. "He was known as a wise man, but no one knew that more than he. He was also one mean motherfucker. In fact he hated every thought of Jesus and whoever followed Him. He saw them as sheep, as cattle, and took it upon himself to educate them by force of torture or even death."

I watch her intently. In this white emptiness, we're the only two people in the world.

"He was obsessed," she continues. "He had to hunt down every last one of Jesus' followers. So he rallied up a posse of bounty hunters and set off from Jerusalem through this land en route to Damascus. He was determined to get there or die on the way."

I remain silent, mesmerized by her voice.

Nancy takes a deep breath, and continues, "Then one day, on the road to Damascus, he had a vision. Jesus appeared to him in a flash of light and spoke. He asked Saul why he hated him so much. 'I don't hate you,' Saul replied. 'I hate the people who follow you blindly. Who are too stupid to think for themselves.'"

"Good point," I say.

"And that's what Jesus thought too, so He said to Saul, 'Look around you. See those men with you. They hear my voice but they can't see me. Only you can. Only you can decide. Only follow me if that's what you want.' Saul looked around and saw that the men with him had no clue what he was looking at. It was Saul's revelation, and his alone."

She looks into my eyes then adds, "After that Saul went blind for three days. He had to be carried back to Jerusalem, deaf and dumb. He was dead to the world. Then, the story goes, he woke up from this catatonic state, and was rechristened as Paul. He made it his life's work to spread the message of enlightenment, not as Jesus saw it, but as each person did in his own heart."

"The Revelation of Saint Paul," I say, recognizing the title of the parable.

"Yes, that's what the Church calls it," says Nancy. "Since then, the 'road to Damascus' became part of our language, an expression of—"

"Change," I say.

Nancy pushes herself up and wipes some invisible dust off of her jeans. I recognize the look on her face, the matronly, admonishing, holier-than-thou look that tells me I should remain seated, like I had been caught stealing from the cookie jar.

"You're upset and you're disappointed," she says. "I get it. You thought you were the center of something significant, something that... matters to you. And then you had the rug pulled out from under you when you realized it was never about you."

The sun is right behind her, and I can barely look up.

"Well, Professor," she says. "To that I say, 'Boo.' Fuck it. You make it about you. You make it about that bicycle-shaped dent in your bumper. You make it about a telescope pointed into your bedroom. You make it about that favorite jacket of yours, ruined by bloodstains that just won't wash off. Tell me, why didn't you throw that away, huh?"

Clearly a rhetorical question. I remain silent.

"It's because the blood is on your hands too. You'll never be able to wash that off. Even if you don't see it, it's there. And it'll always be there until you do something about it. You. Not those idiots on TV."

I get up but, before I can speak, Nancy grips my arms and pulls me closer. Scandalously close, given that we must be visible from every point on the LUST campus.

"Look," she says, perhaps meaning it literally, so I fix my gaze on hers. "I won't use words like faith, fate, whatever. I'm not here to change your system of belief—or lack of one. God forbid I should pull out a brick from that monolith of yours, the whole thing would come toppling down on our heads. You say you're like a mole, huh? Well, I'll tell you what: you may be blind to a world beyond you, but you're worse than a mole. You're a hedgehog. That's all you are."

I don't laugh. In fact, sarcasm is the last thing on my mind as Nancy forges on.

"You're all about the big ideas. About systems. The problem is, when you only think in terms of big ideas, you miss the details. And God knows that's where the devil is. You can't see how one spine on hedgehog A's back connects with one on hedgehog B's. Me, on the other hand, I'm a fox."

I don't intend to, but I do laugh at that. Nancy is a fox, I happen to agree with that. She pushes me away, but to my surprise, she smiles too.

"Wipe that silly grin off your face," she says. "Not that kind of fox. Damn, can't you think metaphorically for once? I'm a fox in that I start from the details. My mind is turned upwards, to the sky, where thoughts are light and airy and volatile, and then I bring them down to the ground. Unlike you, Professor. You start from the ground up until you get to the top and realize that you've built your reasoning—if you could call it that—on faulty foundations and you must tear the whole thing down until there's nothing left. And then you have to start all over from the beginning. Even if you sit here and wait, the mountain won't come to Mohamad."

Nancy's right, it won't. Nothing will come.

"You think it's not about you?" she continues, and I listen to every word. "That's not an objective fact. It's a subjective choice. Tariq chose you. He fell under your car by some cosmic choice. And later he died in your arms because some benign force willed it. Who knows if those last words about the cat were the ramblings of a dying man or his last moment of lucidity. They led you to the notebook and to Maurice. And that's all that matters."

When she's right, I have no reason to disagree. This is no longer a battle of wills.

"And that girl Nadine, she said she's going home this weekend, right?" she asks. "Then if our theory's correct, time's running out. If you want to go, Professor, do it tonight. Or don't. Ever. It's your choice. You've been led this far—no, you've come this far by choice, now follow the road until the end. It might take you somewhere. And even if it doesn't, I know you'll find the truth along the way. But whatever you choose, whichever way you go, you are your own guide."

I don't argue. Nancy's right, time is running out. I have until tonight to make my decision, but in the meantime, there are a few practical things to take care of.

"Okay then," I say, handing her my keys. "I'll leave my car here in case you need it tomorrow. I don't want you chasing after taxis with that limp. Just take the Acacia out of the car, okay? And don't throw it out just yet, please. I'll grab a taxi back home."

She must've expected such an unabashedly pragmatic response to her sermonizing, because she smiles and says, "Don't worry. I'll take the Acacia back to your place tomorrow. And we'll both be there when you get back."

"Nancy, if I go to Damascus, I'll be looking for a needle in a haystack."

"Yes," she says. "But now you know which haystack."

◆

"It's right after St. Georges Hospital, above the Geitawi hillside." I clasp the phone between my chin and shoulder as I run the towel through my hair. Only a floor lamp and the window overlooking Achrafieh light my living room. The bedroom

335

behind me glows with its own desk lamp spilling onto the spot where I now stand just outside its doorway. Nancy's pajamas from last night lie carelessly on the arm of the couch. It's not like her to be messy—I suppose she must've been quite mad this morning before we met at the express van.

As I carry them to the hamper the phone slides off my shoulder and lands on the laundry with a poof. "Shit, I'm such a klutz. Just cleaning up after my girlfriend."

Girlfriend. "You still there?" I say into the phone. "I see. Will the traffic be better then? Okay then, two o'clock, in five hours. In that case, please pick me up from the entrance to Gemmayzeh by Paul's Cafe. Sure, I'll have cash. One passenger, no luggage. Thanks."

I hang up and toss the towel into the hamper, then slide the phone into my shirt pocket as I turn back to the living room. I pull my comb out of my pocket and into the mirror count OneTwoThreePart, OneTwoThreePart. Fast. A personal record. I tap the messenger bag on my shoulder a few times. Check. Everything's in there. Giving the room a final idiot-check, I make my way to the floor lamp and flip it off with the toe of my shoe. The living room falls into total darkness except for the window and the desk lamp from the bedroom.

In the apartment doorway, I throw a mournful glance at the empty spot on my desk where the Acacia stood, then, with a shiver, I step out and close the door behind me. Down the building stairs, then down the Geitawi staircase, and I find myself face to face with—"*Jagal, jagal,* playboy!"

"Shut up, Faris!" I yell to the grocery store parrot at the foot of the staircase, but I make a left, away from Tariq Jaber's house. Today's different. I seek answers, not questions. I start down another staircase leading into the heart of Gemmayzeh.

For a district whose death has been pronounced many

times over the past few years, it's quite alive. Even on a Monday evening, and even after the mourning of the past few days, the nightlife district of Beirut is busy, busy, busy.

At the foot of the staircase I'm almost trampled by a stampede of five girls in glittering stilettos, miniskirts, and ridiculous tops showing off shiny tanned shoulders, maintained well into November, and deep cleavages pushed up by bra engineering or plastic surgery. I don't make a conscious effort to examine them—they're just there. Everywhere. Were there so many girls around when I was their age? I find myself wishing Nancy were with me, if only for her profane commentary on the parade of tits and ass that marches past me to the brass rhythm of car horns and staccato melody of valet parking attendants rapping numbers to one another with the precision of a jazz ensemble.

I'm already well out of my element, in the midst of all these people. A fist of cold air grips my chest, and I take a deep breath. Must not let it take hold of me. I'm in control. It's me. I'm on a mission. This is my project. I'm here for a reason. But what reason? None right now, but soon enough. Five hours to kill. Where do I start?

I arrive at a red glass window with a DJ, headphones stuck to one ear, spinning records with one hand and smoking a cigarette with the other. This place is as good as any, I suppose. The door swings open and a young couple brushes past me as I step inside.

Drum and bass. Could've been worse. I feel my liver bounce up and down as I slide through the crowd to the bar. I sit on an empty swivel stool as the bartender pops up and asks in English, "What's your poison?"

"Huh?" I'm familiar with the expression, but I'm taken aback anyway. "Your drink, man," he continues with a faux-American twang, a silver ring swinging wildly from his nostrils. "What you having?"

"Mexican," I say and watch him pull out a chilled beer mug, dip it in salt until the crystals stick to the rim, fill it with lemon juice, pop open a bottle of iced Almaza beer, and empty it into the mug. He slides the drink over and slams the empty bottle in the garbage with a thwack. "Ten thou," he says and I lay a crisp ten thousand lira bill on the counter. I take a sip of the beer and then another. It's been a while and I enjoy the zesty mixture of salt and sour on my lips. I take another sip, and a third, pushing away the worry of what to do next as I enjoy the now of a light buzz.

The bar was built into the ground floor of a renovated stone building dating from many years before the war. No major changes were made to the original architecture, with the exception of removing the mezzanine. As a result, the ceiling is exceptionally high for a space this tight, and the rough surface of the barrel arch structure remains exposed, adding a degree of dignity and sophistication to the ambiance.

Waving the bartender over, I say, "Hey fella, can you help me with something?" but he already seems bored by my hip act, so I ask directly. "I'm looking for someone."

"We all are, man," he says with a smirk and slides away to take an order from a twenty-something bombshell down the bar. Great.

Something I read many years ago as a student comes back to me. I never had an interest in etymology, beyond the doggedly factual. If a word didn't denote a concrete object, or perhaps the genus of a plant with precise, scientific nomenclature, then it was, as far as I was concerned, too abstract. And who has time for abstraction?

Poets and romantics, perhaps, not me.

But the passage I now recall has stayed with me ever since. It was in the English edition of a book on Japanese chrysanthemums, neatly tucked into the fine print of the translator's footnotes. Apparently the Japanese language has two words for "heart": the first word "*shinzo*" is for the organ in the chest cavity that circulates blood through the body—the physiological object, as in "I have an abnormal heart rate." On the other hand, the word "*kokoro*," also meaning "heart," is used only in matters of emotion, as in "I love her with all my heart."

What then, I wonder, would a Japanese person say for "My heart skipped a beat?" Did the *shinzo* literally hammer a silent note or was the *kokoro* flooded with metaphorical euphoria at the sight of a beloved? I remember enjoying the entire book for the translator's choice, which favored the word "*kokoro*" over its more corporeal alternative, suggesting that the chrysanthemum is a sentient, perhaps even sensual being.

But which of the two words would I use to describe myself now? "He has no *shinzo*," perhaps? No, I do have a blood pump inside me—the biannual checkups attest to that. Rather, "He has no *kokoro*."

He has no heart.

A man without a heart. "You are your own guide," Nancy said. How, then, should I interpret that?

Within half an hour, two empty mugs stand between me and the bartender, with the third one closer to half-empty than half-full. I've killed two hours, with three more to go. At least the music isn't bad, this track is slide bass with a rapid cymbal backbeat. Reminds me of Jaco Pastorias, though not as good. And then a trumpet enters the mix. I tap my finger against the bar as the man behind it walks over and offers me a cigarette.

Glancing at the printed smoke-silhouette dancer swaying on his pack of Gitanes, I say, "No thanks, I quit," more to the blue dancer than to the man holding her up to my face. As he slides away I call him over again. "Know any jazz places along this strip?"

"Sure. Live jazz and blues. Two bars down that way," he says, pointing behind him with two ring-encased fingers.

I gulp down my beer, lay down some cash, and head out.

◆

Puddles splatter my footsteps and I feel a light drizzle on my cheeks, but neither seem to matter much to the partygoers, who have multiplied during the time I spent inside the bar. I wrap my jacket around my chest, feeling the chill of my thirty-six years and walk past the line of Gemmayzeh holes-in-the-wall. One catches my eye with its display of pressurized jars containing corn kernels, sunflower seeds, and lentils immersed in formaldehyde. It looks like a botanist and coroner decided to share a lab, but through the jars the space inside is indeed a bar, with a menagerie of faces distorted by the convex glass. The effect stretches the slightest motion like plasticine, contorting, twisting, and snapping back. I rub my eyes and look again, but the spectacle continues through the mirage of glass, alcohol, and lemon swirling through my mind.

The next shop is lit by a blue neon sax, and I know I've arrived. I pull open the thick glass door and walk into a dark lobby lined with f-hole guitars and a glass-encased poster of Buddy Rich, signed with a golden felt pen. As I wonder about its authenticity, a smartly dressed bouncer pulls open a blue curtain, and ushers me inside.

The opening shuffle from Charles Mingus' *Pedal Point Blues* makes me feel intensely happy. The bouncer glances around and leads me across the club. At the far left, a four-piece band breezes through Mingus' intro with great skill and the signature look of ennui for which I'm sure jazz musicians perform facial calisthenics until their eyes droop. There are around fifteen tables in the place, all occupied by a mixed bag of quasi-intellectuals, middle-aged couples, posh twenty-somethings, and buttoned-down office workers. All in all a familiar, if somewhat predictable, group of people. Even though I've never been here, I feel at home and my anxiety subsides.

We arrive at the bar and the bouncer gestures me to an empty stool. To my right, two men with their backs to me converse quietly, one of them tapping his foot on the rung of his stool and the other leaning against the bar, munching on wasabi kernels. To my left at the far end of the bar two girls in their early twenties watch the band play. I take my stool near the center of the bar, nodding toward them as I settle in. They either don't notice me or simply ignore me. Either way, I realize the only person I could possibly prod for information would be the bartender, a skinny man in a tuxedo vest and prim bow-tie. He stands across the bar from me, his back turned away, polishing glasses against a red lamp.

He brings a wine glass to a crystalline glisten with a lightness of touch that leaves me mesmerized and polishes the next glass, and the one after that, the motions of his white cloth streaked by the red light. The hypnotic dance makes me drowsy and I jerk my head up to stay awake. As I do, my stool lets out a clumsy squeak, which thankfully no one else hears over the music, save for the bartender. He spins around like a red Tasmanian devil, wine glass and cloth still in hand, and inches toward me.

"*Marhaba*," he says. "Something to drink?"

I yell to make myself heard over the music. "I'm looking for a man," I say. I reach into my pocket and pull out the photo of Tariq Jaber, hoping that it didn't come out sounding the way I thought. "He might have come here. His name's Tony." With much less effort and without looking at the photo the bartender replies, "The only men I know are Jack, Johnny, and Jim."

"What? Oh," I say, realizing what he means.

"Whisky or bourbon, what'll it be?" he clarifies anyway.

"I'll have a Jim Beam on the rocks," I say. I'm getting nowhere, so why not kill the remaining hours with some good liquor.

As he makes his way to the bottles I add, "Start a tab," and notice one of the girls to my left looking in my direction. Must be the mention of a tab. I turn away. I've been too blunt so far. Better ease into this one.

Mingus comes to a close with an enthusiastic round of applause. Then a woman in a strapless auburn dress and matching long hair knotted to one side takes center stage and adjusts the microphone. "This one's for Max," she says in a shimmery voice as the sax plays the opening notes of *All of Me*.

I usually prefer the melancholic Billie Holiday version, but the woman sings it in the upbeat vein of Ella, and by the time the trumpet enters with an actually-quite-good Louis Armstrong solo rendition, I'm hooked. Before I know it, I'm tapping my foot and singing along. I down my drink and the bartender refills it without asking. The two girls to my left get into it too and out of the corner of my eye I watch one of them get up and dance around the other as they both lip-sync. Being with Nancy has helped me perfect my peripheral vision, which I discreetly employ even when alone.

I have a theory that girls who go out in pairs usually consist of a pretty, introverted one and a not-so-pretty, extroverted one. These two girls are the exception that proves the rule. The red light caresses their outlines with a sensual sidelight, and as they groove into their duet I watch them perform a few not-at-all-introverted dance moves. It's all in good fun though. And soon

I find myself joining in as they sing to me and I sing back.

"All of me, why not take all of me?" sings one.

"Can't you see, I'm no good without you?" I sing back clasping my hands to my chest.

"Take my lips I wanna lose them," sings the other.

"Take my arms I'll never use them," sings the first.

Then all together, we harmonize. "Your goodbyes left me with eyes that cried. How can I go on dear without you?"

By the time the auburn woman on stage starts scat-singing (and quite well too), all three of us are jumping around "do-do-do-do-dee-ya doo-dee" until the trumpet, sax, piano, bass, drums, bourbon, Gemmayzeh, Acacia, Nabatieh, me, the girls, the universe, all come to a crescendo so huge it feels like the wide red world is crashing to an end.

◆

With that *petite mort*, as Nancy might call it, *All of Me* trills out, as I wipe my brow and the two girls hug each other, nuzzling one another's necks. The club breaks into applause, and one of the girls approaches me and leans against the bar on tiptoes, its edge digging into her stomach and pushing her breasts a few inches away from her body. "Can I have a gin and tonic, please?" she coos to the bartender as the club quiets down. "Put it on my tab," I tell him, then turning to the girl I add, "I mean, if you don't mind."

"Oh."

Gesturing toward the other girl, I ask, "What's your friend drinking?"

"She'll have a Bacardi Coke," she says and I nod to the bartender to get us the order. "Thanks. I'm Tanya, by the way," she adds, and holds out her hand. Palm turned upwards. I shake the tips of her fingers as she turns over to the other girl. She curls out her other hand in her friend's direction. "And this," she adds, "is my friend Ola."

"Ohla?" I repeat. "That's a Nordic name, no? It means 'relic.'"

"No, silly!" says Tanya daintily then follows it with the not-so-dainty "O. O. Ola," emphasizing the guttural "O" sound I've only ever heard in Arabic. She laughs at her own vulgarity while I enjoy her display of fake modesty, which does nothing to diminish her charisma. I must remember to take a page out of this young girl's book.

Ola walks over and extends her hand in the exact same way. I let go of the first and shake the second, both hands feeling like they belong to the same person. They sit down as the bartender gets our drinks. The band is on a break now and the DJ takes over, playing Horace Silver's *Song for My Father*.

"Good tune," says Tanya. A strand of dark hair teases her forehead, while the rest falls in tussles on a pair of delicate shoulders, nicely framed by her black short-sleeved top. O. O. Ola slides behind her and nuzzles her chin into a dimple in her friend's neck.

"I saw Horace Silver live once," I say in the general direction of the girls, who form a perfect Gemini. "He came to the Beiteddine Festival a few years back." I instantly feel old again, but Ola surprises me.

"Oh my God, yeah I was there!" she says. "That was a great year. They also had Branford Marsalis."

"I missed that," I say and Tanya adds, "Yeah I missed both. You lucky bastards! I was in Cyprus with my boyfriend that summer."

Ola cuts in. "Who, Karim?"

"Yes, silly. Silly Karim," says Tanya. Okay, so "silly" is a *passe-partout*, I suppose. How silly would I sound if I used it too?

"It was the summer that A-hole cheated on me." She stretches the A like it's the rude part of the word. "But hey, thanks to him I met Jeff. My *hombre* Jazzy Jeff. And if he does that, I'll kill him." She makes a pistol-shape with her thumb and forefinger, sticks it in my chest and goes "Pukh!"

"We've been getting good jazz in Lebanon lately," I say, changing the subject. "You two seem too young to be jazz cats. Of all the things in life, why jazz?"

"Because jazz is life. But beautiful," says Tanya.

Ola nods. "We're here every night," she says through a proud smile. "We know everyone here, but I don't think we've ever seen you around. You told Bob you're looking for someone, no?"

"Bob?" I ask.

"Bassem, the bartender. You showed him a photo?"

"Oh that Bob. Yeah, I'm looking for a guy who might've come here." I pull out the photo and hand it to Tanya. "Maybe you know him?"

She raises it to the red light as Ola leans over her shoulder. Tanya squints at it, then cocks her head. "I'm not sure." Ola isn't so quick to dismiss it, she studies the photo for a few seconds then says, "Umm. Maybe. This is an old shot right?"

"Yes," I say. "A few years."

"Hmmm. They weren't here tonight, but Tanya, remember that couple? They sat over there." She points at a booth in the farthest corner of the club.

"What, him and the lady in the wheelchair?" asks Tanya.

"No, silly! The guy in the photo and his girlfriend. He wore those chic blazers. Like three, four times, every time a different one. Remember? I said I wanna get Jeff one." Then she adds to me, "Jeff, that's my boyfriend." I get it already, but say nothing.

Tanya's face changes as she says, "Yeah," then adds to me, "she's right, they've been here a few times. Just concentrated on

345

each other. You know, didn't dance or anything. Kissed a lot. Ola here dared me to go talk to him—silly, you just did it for the blazers huh? Well anyway, I didn't. That girlfriend looked like she'd bite my head off if I did."

I laugh. "Can you tell me what she looked like?"

"Pretty, in a snarky sort of way. Long black hair, big eyes." says Ola. "Exotic, I guess. Don't think she's Lebanese. Arab maybe, but not from here."

"How can you tell?" I ask.

"I can't, really. Just a feeling, I dunno."

"Yeah that's about it," adds Tanya. "It's dark in that corner. Plus we don't like to ogle men, even cute ones," she says.

"Oh wait, wait. I just remembered something," Ola says, perking up. "Someone was taking photos a few days ago. I don't remember if they were here that night, but if they were, your friend and his girl might be in one of the shots."

"Where? What magazine?"

"No, no, not a magazine. It was instant photos."

"Polaroids?"

"Yeah. They're for the club. There's a collage outside the bathroom."

"Aha. Would you ladies excuse me while I go have a look?"

"They don't have them outside the men's room," Ola says with a smile.

"And how do you know that?" teases Tanya.

"Lucky guess," says Ola. She grabs my hand. "Come, we'll take you to the ladies' room."

"You two go. I wanna hear this song." It's Sarah Vaughan's *Moanin,'* which I like too. But this is more important. I smile at Tanya as I let Ola lead me away.

◆

346

Faces. Faces. Faces. "Every mornin' finds me moanin.'" Sarah Vaughan's muffled vocals seep through the club wall into the corridor where Ola and I stand.

It's a mystery how musicians can create an infinite variety of tunes from just seven notes. Jazz, blues, rock, classical. And that's just the broad strokes—within each there's an infinite number of sub-varieties. Even a simple melody can be rendered hundreds of different ways.

Faces. Those are even more complex, and with far less material to work with. Hair, nose, eyes, ears, and lips. That's it. Yet no two are the same, an infinite sea of features spreads out before us, covering the entire wall. It's the same with plants, but it takes an expert to recognize the minutiae in that world. Beyond a certain—still quite coarse—subdivision, most people can't distinguish one species from the other. And, for some, their ability to discern doesn't even extend beyond "tree," "flower," "vegetable," and "fruit." I think the laypeople jury is still out on whether strawberries are one, whereas they have distinct characteristics of the other. But we know strawberries. We know that the fleshy part people refer to as the "fruit" is really a receptacle for the tiny "seeds" that sit on it, and we know that those are really the strawberry's fertilized ovaries, each with an actual seed inside it.

Even in language. The word "*warde*" or "rose" in Arabic has come to mean all flowers, much like when I ask for a Kleenex, I wouldn't mind if someone handed me a Kotex (which also makes tissues but has become a generic word for something else entirely). I just want to blow my nose. And in Japanese, the word "*hana*" for "flower" is a homonym for nose. I recall reading that somewhere too.

Ola's own sculpted nose hovers a few millimeters from the wall as she scans the collage of faces. There must be close to a thousand, and the dim light casting our shadows over the mural makes it even harder. I move from one to the other, some captioned, others dated, but most unlabeled. And because the wall is so cleverly lit by indirect artificial light, there's no way to tell which were taken this week and which five years ago. I remember how the Polaroids I took faded in the sunlight. "Don't take the albums outside!" my father would yell whenever the pangs of nostalgia hit me enough to carry one of them out to the porch.

I try not to be distracted by Ola, still unsure if she's the outgoing one or the pretty one. Her long lashes cast a light shadow over a pair of deep brown eyes that catch just a hint of the light bouncing off the photos. As she moves, the colors change in her dilated pupils, a smile teasing her glistening pink lips now and then. But it's the faces on the wall I should concentrate on and I wrench my woozy eyes off her and onto the flat surface along which we stand.

"Ooh, ooh," she shrieks, pointing to a photo in the corner.

"What?" I blurt out, as I snap out of my Jim Beam stupor. "Did you find them?"

"Oops, sorry no. But check out her dress!"

"Dammit, focus, Ola!" I laugh, but I'm getting frustrated, more with myself than with her. Someone once said, the hours you lose having fun are not lost at all. True, I suppose. And I am here to kill the hours, but it would be a shame if I leave this place as empty handed as I entered. I lay my hands on the wall and lean in until my nose just grazes the laminated surface, as one by one I comb through the Polaroids starting at the side farthest from her. This tunnel vision makes the process easier, and I cover more ground.

Toward the middle of the wall, in a spot between us I focus on a cluster of photos that look like they could've been taken in the past few days; their edges lie over the others, some corners cutting into the faces underneath. I circle my eyes in a spiraling motion from the outside perimeter of the cluster, slowly zeroing in on the center.

"Ola."

"Uh huh," she says, her voice muted by the wall in front of her as the song behind us winds to a close, "Didaladada."

"Ola, come here," I repeat, tugging her gently by the hand. I raise my index finger to a photo. Like many of the others, it's undated and uncaptioned. The man wears a smart navy blue blazer, as the girls described, his glass raised in a toast to the photographer and partially obscuring his face. "Look. It's them, right?"

"Oh my God, yeah. That's him. That's definitely him." Her shoulder digs into my chest as we squeeze our faces together, squinting into the square frame of the Polaroid.

She might be right, although the face that looks back from the photo is happier than I remember it. The right (what Nancy would call "camera left") side of his face, the side not obscured by the glass, is pulled into a startled grin, a long tapered nose, and floppy black hair. His right eye looks straight at me. The blazer itself, while a different color than the one I found at the station, is of a similar trim. There's no question about it: it's him.

"She didn't seem so shy to me!" replies Ola, and in an instant I see what she means. The girl snuggling to Tariq's left has her hand raised to her face, palm toward camera. She has a deer-in-the-headlights look you often see in magazines when celebrities are cornered by pestering paparazzi.

Only her lips and hair are visible. Long black hair, silky smooth, just as the girls described. And her lips. Those lips. Something about those lips. Beautiful, thick lips. But more than that. There's something more.

"Shit," I say. "I think I know her."

"You do?" Ola's voice rises, but I can tell she has nothing but disdain for this girl.

"Yeah, but…" It can't be her. The top of her dress is barely visible, her shoulders mostly obscured by her long hair, but the space between her chin and the tabletop offers a generous view of her chest. A glistening white spread of skin that reminds me of melted butter. And the curl of her lip seems… vicious. Maybe it's just the surprise of being shot with a flash without permission, as photographers are prone to do. But no, it's just so… out of character.

And then I see it.

On her raised hand, reflecting the light from the flash, gleaming like the eye of medusa right back at me. How could I have been so blind? On her finger, a twisted iron ring, embedded with glass stones. It's her.

"Nadine," I say.

"Who?"

I take a step back. Nancy was right. "She lied to me."

Ola twists away from the wall and lays a consoling hand on my shoulder. "Women these days, huh. What's a man to do."

"I'm so stupid."

"There, there," says Ola, squeezing my shoulder. I'm too dazed to do anything about it and she smiles. "Tanya over there," she says, nodding toward the doorway. "You don't suppose… she thought we came back here to make out, do you?"

A proposition? She looks up at me, her doleful eyes inviting me take it or leave it. Right now. Decide, they say. I'm drunk. No, more. I'm hammered. But not so much that my body doesn't tingle with possibility. Take me away, say her eyes. Carry me through those drenched streets, through the Beirut night, out of this life, this crimson netherworld, on a jazzy lullaby, lay me down, and rip me apart. Tear it all to shreds, this wall, this wall of infinite faces, no one to say don't, don't, don't. No more blood, no more dying man, no dying tree, just you and me in this garish city. Then you wake up tomorrow, and it's a brand new day. And it's yours and you erase it all. And you write, not a paper, but papers, volumes, reams, and the LUST botanists scurry at your feet for many years, trying to understand but they're all blind and deaf and dumb and you assume your regal throne as King of all the Land, and with a mere twist of your ankle, you crush the lizard under your shoe and her bones crunch as they all hail the onliest Professor with eyes like sunbeams piercing the terrain, where Acacias shoot out of the earth and impale the sky. Forget it all, don't, don't, don't trouble your mind. Forget the Road, forget Saul and Paul, forget the journey of thorns and death and blood. Forget Damascus.

"Don't, don't, don't," I say, but it's just a mumble.

Then my pocket vibrates.

I pull out my phone and flip it open: Unknown Caller. I check the time. 2:03 a.m. "I gotta go."

"Oh. Okay," says Ola, dropping her arm to her side. I take it and pull her gently through the corridor and back to the bar, both of us tripping several times on the way.

"Tanya, Ola, thank you," I smile, my head spinning with anger and confusion and desperation and anxiety. Again, the anxiety. I must leave now. I should go. My ride is here and I must be on it. I set a few bills down and push them toward the bartender. "You've both been very helpful."

"Where're you off to?" asks Tanya lazily.

"Out of town," I say. "Keep it real, jazz cats," I add, sounding colossally idiotic even through my drunken stupor.

"Bye bye, Daddy-O," says Ola with a flick of her hand, which I'm unsure whether to take as sincere mockery or mock sincerity.

Faris the Parrot's words "*Jagal, jagal*, playboy!" squawk through my ears as the band comes back onstage with a piano trill.

The elegant bouncer holds the glass door open as I disentangle myself from the lures of the black and red behind me, stumbling forth into the vast unknown of a rainy night.

◆

I'm out of breath, gagging on the taste of beer and bourbon. "Wait, wait!" I yell, waving like a madman, my shoes splashing onto the puddled street. The taxi sign bathes the top of the car in a yellow glow as perfunctory rain pellets against its pearly metal surface.

"I'm here!" I dash across the street through the tangle of traffic, cutting in front of the cab so the driver sees me. I pass the entrance of Paul's Cafe, open the back passenger door and jump in. "I'm here," I pant as I slam the door shut. "You been waiting long?"

The driver inspects me through the rearview mirror. "Fifteen minutes," he says sharply, his thick white mustache twitching. "The traffic's still bad, but if we avoid driving through Gemmayzeh, it should be smooth sailing from here."

"Good, good, thanks."

"Luggage?"

"No."

"Here," he says as he reaches under the front passenger seat and hands me a wad of paper towels. I dry my face and the taxi reverses out of Gemmayzeh. Before another car can enter behind us, the driver makes a U-turn onto the main road, avoiding the drenched gridlock ahead.

The rain has done me some good. Besides soaking me to the bone, it sobers me up a little. But now I feel immensely tired, and I drift in and out of sleep as the taxi makes its way up the boulevard.

Several minutes pass.

The traffic light turns red at the Sodeco intersection, we pass through the street along where only last night I had driven Nadine to LUST, but instead of a left, we take a right. A shiver runs up and down my body. It could be the sting of cold or the bite of Nadine's deception.

My drenched jacket clings stubbornly to my body as I peel it off, careful not to drop any of its contents. I lay it on my knees to wipe off the excess water. Seeing this through his mirror, the driver switches on the heater and snaps on the dehumidifier with the agility of a pilot working his cockpit.

"Thanks," I say.

The light changes and the car eases onto Damascus Road. I slide down my seat, hoping the driver doesn't engage in any conversation, but all he does is drive along as he throws a glance toward his left where the bus stood and says something under his breath followed by a "Tsk, tsk, tsk."

Over the edge of the window, the only remnants from the bus incident are the damaged billboard post and the miserable Watan policeman (or his replacement) in gray waterproof overalls. The glare of the billboard strikes my eyes, and I turn away as we drive past, rubbing my aching forehead.

"Get some rest, sir. Seems like it's clearing up, but it's gonna be a good three hours to get there." His mustache drops into a more relaxed position on his face.

My consciousness flutters back to the tower in Nabatieh, the house of Balkees and Tariq, and to his father, the man she loved. Perhaps the man I now seek. The breeze of time carries my thoughts to a childhood long gone, the sweet sadness of days and faces past, they land on a broken Acacia and cling softly to its branch.

Everything I've believed was wrong. Life is not a series of facts and figures. All that matters clings to the spaces between the facts, beyond the figures. In Balkees' Nabatieh tower, Nancy and I had found letters exchanged between two people who knew they could never be together, and who yearned for each other all the more because of it. At the time, I thought them devoid of answers, flights of fancy taken by a pair of star-crossed lovers. If only I had known it was all there, on those pages.

Phone to my ear, I hit speed-dial zero. "Nancy, it's me," I say. "I'm going to Damascus."

The phone slides onto my lap as I lean onto the glass and fall into a dreamless sleep. Thoughts as light as breeze, as volatile and airy as a waft of nothingness, lift me onto a cloud toward that hidden room in Nabatieh, carrying me deeper into my sweet slumber.

16
Deaths in the Family

Drenched in cold sweat, her palm lay against the Acacia as her eyes shut. The moonlight contoured her shoulders with a scraggy silver edge. They heaved and shook, but nothing came out, just the sighs of a woman who knew deep in her belly that she had walked through an invisible tunnel, and that she must walk ahead, step by tortuous step. The Acacia tree sang with her, the wind whistling through a thousand invisible veins etched inside its bark. New life comes at a cost; it rips through the earth with the power of eternity, and presses upon its branches with the force of a thousand years. Their every ounce weighed on her pelvis, but her upper body remained as insouciant as a breeze.

The Acacia tingled against her fingers, just as the child twitched within her womb. The three of them were one. Layers of unknown lay folded inside her, warm and safe from the outside, the cold world that threatened to cut through her entrails like an iron sword. Again, another heave, but nothing. She straightened against her crutch and leaned her soaked back against the tree. Then he appeared. He carried himself toward her like a man on a mission, determined to reach into her womb and pull out her secret, even if just to smother it with his bare hands. He gripped her shoulders and pulled her toward him, spilling his menace into her ear. She withdrew, but her body failed to withhold the momentum of her motion as she came crashing down at the roots.

She curled herself around the bark, to the far side overlooking the lush hillside below. He followed her doggedly, pulling her upright by the cloth around her neck. She grasped for the veins in the wood and found a hold, but then he pulled her away. He had spotted it, the cuts on the bark she tried to conceal with the girth of her hips.

Two letters, separated with a heart shape. She and the other man, the softer, gentler, kinder, darker man had tattooed them into the tree many months ago. But now this man's gaze burned into them with the power of a thousand magnifiers, and with it the dawning realization—the letters, the dry heaves, her motherly gait, into a story that painted his face with anger and shook him to the core. He raised his hand to strike, but in an instant the moon hit his face with a blinding light, melting the anger into a silent sadness.

The man lowered his hand and released the woman, then walked away. She exhaled, but relief eluded her. Only pain remained. She brought her palms to her face.

But soon the man returned, and with him the glint of metal reflected in the harsh sun. She screamed, she pleaded, she clawed at him, but with a single swipe of his arm he wrenched her away and sent her sailing to the ground.

The Acacia didn't feel the first strike; it just landed into its bark with a dull thud. But then the second sent a bolt of electricity up its entire being. The third was just as painful as the fourth, but worst of all was the sound, the tortured crack of wood being cleaved. Splinters flew across the grass with the might of every blow.

Then gravity did its work, aided by the heft of his bulk against the tree. It swung back then forth. Another blow, another, and then a final crunch toppled the tree over the edge of the cliff, sliding down the hillside with the weight of its fifty score years.

All that remained was a stump.

The man tossed the axe against it, but it bounced off and landed by the woman, now crouched helplessly at its foot. The man growled words of anger and betrayal, not toward her, but toward someone else he was now determined to seek. He straightened and clambered down the hilly footpath, disappearing into the landscape.

The stump struggled to mark the seconds, minutes, hours the broken woman lay there. Clouds gathered in the distance as dusk gave way to night, slowly sealing its fate as the pulp around the stump coagulated. The Acacia was cleaved in twain, evergreen but for the act of man. Soon, it would wither and die. As the skies fell into an inky night, a mellow breeze caressed its jagged wound, and then a hand stroked its splintered edge, a soft touch, gentle, kinder. "Maurice," she said. The dark man lifted the woman into his arms and embraced her for a long time.

In the distance, across the gray-blue night skies, a blast shook the hillside. The wind carried forth a cloud of ashen debris and the scent of death. In its roots, the Acacia felt the life of the man that took its own snuff out in agony.

17

Paradigm Shift

"Lying is bad, Nancy," says Rony as I hang up the phone. "You said you can't go with him."

"I didn't lie!" I say. "I just told a few half-truths."

"A half-truth is also a half-lie. Dad's fine, your leg's better, and your mushrooms are done. That's a total of a lie and a half."

"Fine, I lied."

"And a half," insists Rony.

"Okay! I lied-and-a-half. It was for a good reason, and I'm not proud of myself, happy? Anyway, he's already in the taxi, and well on his way."

Rony clears some excess dirt and pats the earth down with his spade. He didn't seem to mind us getting drenched with rain, and now watches as the last of it pools nicely into the crevice he's created around the mushrooms in his cluster. It spreads across our little lot like incubated babies, tagged neatly with a little sign that reads, "Nancy, Master's Level I, Botany."

The LUST campus is all but deserted, a wonderful relief from the day's craziness, and the air has that stark clarity it only gets when washed by a generous downpour. Rony's voice comes through it like a songbird. "Good night my babies." He runs his fingers over the cap of a mushroom. "Look, Nancy. Some of them are out tonight."

"They're reproducing," I say. "Making babies of their own. Did I ever tell you that mushrooms are more closely related to us than to other plants? You know how a baby inside the womb first looks like a tiny shrimp? Well, the same kind of glucose that exists in shrimps and little bugs also exists in mushrooms. It's what makes them crunch when you bite into one."

"I stepped on a bug once. The crunchy sound made me sad. I think it made me think of a baby being crushed. Do we need to go home now?"

"We can stay a bit longer."

These quiet late-night moments with my brother are the best. He looks over my shoulder and keeps me on the straight and narrow, but since starting my master's thesis, I don't see him nearly as often as I'd like to. I've missed him the most the past few days, with Professor needing me more than ever. He's the angel over my other shoulder, though I'd never dream of saying that to his face. From the moment he set foot on that bus, he hasn't been well.

Professor is nearsighted. Soon after we started seeing each other, I made him finally get his eyes checked and get a prescription. I went and ordered his glasses myself, while he trailed behind me, almost literally kicking and screaming like a child.

The glasses force him to see farther, but he claims that's at the expense of what truly matters to him, what's in front of his knows (Freudian slip!)—nose. And boy does he see *that*—he sees the hell out of it, fixating on minutiae no one else would even notice. And whatever he sees, he obsesses over, dissects, kills.

With his imperfect eyesight, he can choose what to see and what to disregard. Near-sighted, that's his true nature, how he loves to be, how he wishes he could always be, oblivious to everything and everyone else around him. I wish I could change that. I wish he could acquire some peripheral vision, perhaps even learn some intuition, maybe have an inkling for a world beyond himself. I wish he'd believe what he feels, not merely what he sees. But that would be a leap of faith, something he's scorned all his life.

And when I bring it up, he brushes all this off as semantics, as if our different ways of seeing the world don't mean we have fundamentally different ways of being in it. He prides himself on being retro, but I love him for being old-fashioned. "I'm not agoraphobic," he'd say, for instance. "I just don't like crowded spaces." And Tariq wasn't claustrophobic, I'd say. He just didn't like closed rooms. Professor won't admit it to me, of course, but he gets heart palpitations, I know it, when the world around him seems to fall out of his control. And recently with Tariq Jaber knowing who he is, where he lives, and what he breathes, his fear of people and open places had gotten much worse than I've ever seen it.

Then there's Nadine, with her lies. Her fucked up, devious, malicious, lies. "There," I say, snapping out of my reverie. "Not bad for an evening's work."

"Yup," says Rony. "I'm proud of us."

Well, I'm not proud of me. I stand up and brush the dirt off my jeans. God, I haven't looked like a girl in so long, and for what? Across the plaza, a blonde student very much like a Botticelli cherub, waves at the female guard at her post then flutters into the women's dormitory. Three damn hours here and no sign of that nasty Nadine.

I wonder again about Professor. When he didn't call me all evening, I knew he hadn't decided yet what to do. He doesn't like to talk to me when he's all wishy-washy. Perfectionism is a disorder. He doesn't know it, but I do. I also know that our swimming pool talk this afternoon got to him. When I don't make sense, he just brushes me off. But today he listened. "You are your own guide," I said. He may not believe it, but I know it's true. And he'll know it too, in time. Always in his own time.

"Dad's late," says Rony.

I check the time on my cell phone. "Come, I'll take you home," I say. "Looks like the bird's staying in the nest tonight." There's no point waiting here for that stupid Nadine like some stalker. I pull out Professor's keys and we make our way past the dorm toward the faculty parking lot.

But wait!

Speak of Nadine and she shall appear. Sure enough, there she is. She's just popped out of the dorm.

"Quick, hide behind this tree," I say. Rony does exactly that, recognizing that the game's afoot.

Nadine walks past the security guard followed by a second girl wearing a matching scarf with a darker shade of blue. It's hard to tell from here, but the other girl looks slightly older, yet carries herself with the same confident gait. Her sister, perhaps? That must be her. She mentioned her once or twice. Besides a lumpy plastic bag Nadine carries, the two silhouettes look identical.

The pair of girls make their way toward the gate along the side street by the dormitory. "Hey Rony," I whisper. "Wanna go on a stakeout?"

He nods vigorously.

We slide back behind the tree and, avoiding the gravel, take the longer way along the grassy lawn toward the faculty parking. As we cut through the bushes, I feel like Susan leading Edmund through the magical wardrobe to vanquish the Ice Queen. Sure, why not.

"Quick, we must hurry," I say as Rony's palm grows sweaty

against mine, but when I unclench it he grips tighter as we exit the brush onto the gravel parking lot. It's pitch dark, except for a few scattered streetlights barely bright enough to light themselves. But with only a smattering of cars we easily spot Professor's light brown Volvo.

Jangle of keys, squeak of leather upholstery, click of the safety lock, growl of a disgruntled engine and before we know it I've eased the car out of the Assistant Professor spot, cutting diagonally across the others until we exit through the main gate as the wooden plank barely clears the car's roof. We make a quick left, then another, and we enter the side road just as the two girls get into a rickety Nissan taxi cab.

"Whoa," says Rony. "Are we gonna follow them?" He's not wary, or scared; quite the opposite, he's positively quivering with excitement, as am I, like I've just polished off a whole bag of jellybeans. "You bet. See that? That's one nasty little Ice Queen." Then just for good measure I add, "Bitch." But Rony's too adrenalinized to demand a coin into the fake jar this time.

We follow the Nissan onto the Corniche Boulevard, across which just this morning a scared-shitless Garo took a dash. I maintain a safe distance behind, now and then allowing a car or two to sandwich between us. Nadine knows the Volvo—she's been in the Volvo—but I'm betting its blah color wouldn't give it away too easily. Invisible, as Professor might say.

First out of the Raouche area, then past the Jamal Abdul Nasser monument, we climb the hillside toward Upper Ain Mraise area, and then make another right toward the American University. "Shit. Maybe they're just off to get a Zululu or some other fruit cocktail from Bliss Street," I say. That would be a stupid end to this chase, if it turns out they're just headed to the dessert capital of Beirut. But no, to my relief, the Nissan makes a turn ahead in the opposite direction, left toward Gefinor.

We remain hard on their tail; now only a few perilous meters lie between us, as the night grows thicker, all the way toward Gemmayzeh. But instead of entering the traffic-packed nightclub district, the Nissan makes a right toward Tabaris Boulevard.

The red taillights of the gridlock bounce off the rearview mirror as we leave their glare and the blare of horns behind us. The Nissan makes a left into Achrafieh and drives straight past Leil Nhar restaurant, then cuts another left into the Geitawi area.

"So," I say. "They're off to her boyfriend's house."

Rony looks up at me quizzically, and before I can venture an explanation, he dun-dun-darans into the theme song of his favorite retro cop show.

The Nissan comes to a stop in front of Beit el Kataeb, and the light inside comes on as both rear doors click open and one of the silhouettes ahead holds up a paper bill to the driver. Must be quick. I wrap my arm around Rony's headrest and shift the gear to reverse, and just as another car approaches I back up past it into a public parking lot a few meters behind.

Handbrake up, engine off and we step out. I drop a five thousand lira bill onto a stout table in the parking attendant's shack. "Keep it all," I say as Rony and I hop out to the street. The girls are already gone, but now that I know where they're headed and now that we're on foot in a quiet area, it's better to keep a bigger margin between us. Both Rony and I are wearing sneakers and with my leg much better now (Rony's right; I suppose it was a bit of a lie), we're as quiet as mice.

Through the street, past Beit el Kataeb, down the slope, and there, I catch a glimpse of the duo as they round the corner onto Tariq Jaber's street. I wait until they're inside the building then grab Rony's hand and we rush after them into the courtyard, past a line of laundry, and up the stairs. There's no light, save for the glare of the city shining through glassless openings, lighting the steps. The girls' voices echo unintelligibly down toward us, as we climb after them, keeping two flights between us. First floor, second, third, and we stop at the landing of the fourth. I put my finger to my lips, but Rony doesn't make a peep over my own frantic breathing. Professor is right: I should quit my two-cigarette-a-day habit.

Above us, the hems of their dresses ascend onto the fifth-floor landing. I don't know which one is Tariq's apartment, but I remember Professor saying it's that level. Rony and I crouch against the wall and wait.

A doorbell. What? Another. Could they be ringing Tariq's door?

But then comes the indistinct (yet Lord oh so high-pitched) voice of a woman. I climb up a few more steps with Rony trailing close behind, his chin resting against my shoulder. The door above clicks open and cuts a sliver of light across the girls' faces and into the hallway. I squint as we both squeeze ourselves tighter against the wall.

A woman dressed in a peacocky abaya pops her fully made-up face out of the doorway and sings a drawn out "Yes?" and with it a Fairuz melody harmonizes from inside.

Next, Nadine, barely audible, squeaks in reply. "We're sorry it's late," she says. "But Tony said you never go to sleep before four."

With that, the woman ushers the two girls into the apartment and closes the door after them.

Rony does a good Nancy impression, pressing his finger to his lips and taking my hand. Unsure what he has in mind, I let him lead me up the stairs to the door of the apartment the girls just entered. He presses his cheek against it, but then pulls back and shakes his head. Whatever's going on inside is inaudible through the door. I worry they're going to burst through any second, but instead of taking me back down where we came from, Rony leads me up another flight.

Of course! We should catch the tail end of this encounter, but when the girls come out they'd walk right into us if we remained on the lower flight.

No sooner do I finish ruffling my smart brother's hair that the door opens again and the two girls step out. Their backs are to us now, but Nadine holds her hands to her chest and the plastic bag she carried earlier is now with the woman, who rummages through it greedily.

"*Shukran, shukran*," she says, pulling a handful of lipstick tubes, then some eyeliner pencils, and a couple cases of blush. All used, but quite a loot anyway. Nadine turns in our direction, but remains focused on an object she holds against her chest. As the other girl reaches out for it and makes a stroking motion, its purrs fill the hallway.

Tariq Jaber's cat. A trade! A bag of makeup in exchange for Tarboush.

"Nununu," says the other girl, petting its head. "*Ahlein* Madame Bogosian," says Nadine, her Syrian accent thicker than ever. The lady closes the door behind them with a satisfied clump and the two girls disappear down the stairs with the cat.

We wait in silence until we see the girls emerge onto the street below. I turn to Rony, "Good work! Come on, let's go home."

◆

"What country is this?"
   "Still Lebanon, sir."
   "Where?"

"Anjar."

The dark landscape swishes by. With only us on the road I get that feeling again, of being on a fiery comet cutting through the night sky as Tariq Jaber watches us through his telescope. The taxi drives at a steady eighty kilometers an hour, along the middle lane of the highway.

Anjar. The eastern town marks the darkest chapter in the Beirut-Damascus love-hate affair, site of the mass burial ground discovered a few years ago adjacent to the infamous Mazze Prison run by the *Mukhabarat*, the Syrian Secret Service. A direct link between the two was never made and as abruptly as it was uncovered, the story was buried under layers of diplomacy. But the coal was not put out, and I imagine it still stings the Lebanese subconscious, burning quietly under the surface of current events.

"How long was I out?"

"A couple of hours, sir. We'll be at the border shortly." The driver's face remains unchanged in the mirror, without even the slightest trace of weariness. He flips through the radio channels, from classical music, to static, to Fairuz, to soft rock. Typical early morning fare. Then he comes to a stop at a song.

"The radio," I say, my voice still groggy.

"Oh sorry, sir," he says politely as he reaches for the dial. "I'll switch it off."

"No, bring it up," I say and he obliges, turning it the other way.

I tap my finger on the window to the familiar tune from my childhood. It's the folk Syrian character Ghawwar singing to his beloved Fattoum:

"Fattoum Fattoum Fattoume, hide me in your pantry. When the cold days come I will keep you warm." Ghawwar sings along, or rather Doreid Lahham, Nadine's favorite actor.

Nadine. The music stokes the anger in my belly, like the secrets buried under the land we now cross. But I cast my thoughts away from that as I tap, tap, tap against the streaks of muted colors flashing past the window. By the second verse I find myself singing along, and the driver joins in.

"Open my heart and take from it a flame. Search the village, you won't find a man like me. Fattoume, how I loved her. Don't look at her with your eyes. See her with mine."

The music plays like a lullaby, over and over, until once again I drift to sleep.

◆

I shuffle through the morning talk shows as a phrase from one broadcast fuses with a phrase from the next, like a game of connect-the-dots in which the numbers have been switched around. Sitting in the driver's seat of the Volvo I have a fresh perspective on the interior of our relationship, through the Professor's eyes. My own ghost sits next to me in the passenger seat and I wonder what it must be like for him, being pushed and prodded by that girl with pointy features. I never liked my chin, even though Mom always said my eyes were saucersful of secrets (she was fond of Pink Floyd) and my chin a dagger through the hearts of men (she might have gotten that from a Grimm's fairytale).

She lived in a daydream, Mom. That's why she died, my father insists—perhaps swerving off the road was her last act of revolt, like it would lead somewhere no one else had ever been, a place only she could know. "Just because she saw it and heard it, that didn't mean it was there," says my father.

At different times, Mom wanted to name me Cassandra, Larissa, and even Anastasia, anything but the perfectly unfantastical name I ended up with. My father had always wanted Nancy, a softy, a goody-two-shoes. She's not even a complete person, a diminutive Anna, a reduced Anastasia. Funny how things come full circle. So today, here in this car, that's what I am. Mommy's Anastasia, the Russian Duchess of lore, who escaped being executed with the rest of her family.

"And the first caller will win…" switch "…the new line of sensual lingerie only at…" switch "…light showers are expected later in the…" switch "…first concert at Biel for the first time in…" switch "…the Paleolithic Era, during which scientists believe a meteor wiped out all life…" switch and then "All yours, Babooshka, Babooshka, Babooshka-ya-ya!" Kate Bush pierces the morning with her rapturous soprano, somehow both denouncement and celebration, about a blind devotion that turns into blind lust.

The transformation is complete. Today I'm not the timid woman clinging to her man's whims like a cellist to her wood instrument. I'm a warrior princess, singing at the top of my lungs in my car under the shade of a tree, watching the dorm gate with laser eyes for the slightest sign of my prey.

The clock strikes 9:05 a.m. and the two girls emerge through the gate, bright and early. I slide down in the seat, gripping the steering wheel until my knuckles turn white.

The girls glide along the sidewalk, away from my spot. Wherever they're heading now, they're traveling on foot. I should allow them a head start as Kate Bush's voice rises, singing about the a wife who freezes on her husband, then as he loses interest, she disguises herself as a warrior princess and seduces him all over again. And as he falls for her, he shouts out, "I'm all yours, Babooshka, Babooshka, Babooshka-ya-ya!"

I switch off the radio and jump out. After the rain last night, the air is chilly. I wrap my pashmina around my shoulders. Once again today, the game is afoot and Anastasia is in hot pursuit.

Down the street they go, and I follow. Two shadowy figures in broad daylight, robes to their feet, indistinguishable from this distance, but an easy mark—two triangles against the light morning traffic. So this is what it feels like to be a stalker, fixated on every detail of your quarry. Or maybe I'm just like Professor, with his picayune attention to minutiae. But unlike either, I'm not scared of being out in the open. With my faded green T-shirt, my stonewashed jeans, and my limp-free lightness, I'm his favorite kind of invisible. They won't see me as long as I maintain the few meters between us.

Around the street corner and down the street, past Riviera hotel, and along the Corniche. This could be a morning stroll. The clean air feels good. The city is still in the lull of mourning, five days after the bus incident. Plus it's the weekend, so it's just me and a few passersby. Beirut feels very different outside the humdrum of its working routine.

The girls make another turn away from the Corniche, and up a hill into the Raouche inland. I tuck myself behind a tree and observe them walk into a store, unable to make out whether it's one of the faceless boutiques that line that block or perhaps a hair salon with faded posters of hairdos ten years out of style. A few minutes later they step out. One holds a plastic case, and the other reaches into her robe and pulls out the cat, placing him inside and closing the lid. A pet store then, that's all it was. Please let there be more. I slide behind the tree and prepare to duck into the entrance of an apartment building should they decide to walk back, but they've resumed their climb up the hill. So there is more. Good. I step out of my hiding spot and follow them further up the hill to the top.

There, at a large roundabout, streets spiral out in many directions: one past the mansion of the Head of Parliament, with a guard stationed outside, another down the other side of the hill to Verdun area with its cafes and marbled malls, a third crossing into the Sakiet Janzeer area with its cluster of residences. The duo cut through the roundabout and take the fourth path, further up the hill into the inner belly of Verdun, and when they're safely on the other side, I look both ways and skip after them.

One block later, they stop at a brown stuccoed entrance and walk in. I wait for a moment, making sure that they don't reemerge and bump right into me. When I'm sure they're staying inside, I approach the entrance and look up. Lettered metal plaques line the height of the seven-story building. The unmarked floors must be residential, while the balconies with plaques are marked with various names and vocations, mostly clinics: dentist, ophthalmologist, gynecologist, nose and ear medicine, pediatrics.

So barring a personal visit to one of the unmarked apartments, the girls are likely here with a medical matter. But what? Inside the hallway, I look up and through the elevator cage into the stairwell, but it's empty and silent. They must have taken the elevator. The panel above the door lights up as the elevator approaches each floor, stopping on the third and another time on the seventh.

Scanning the directory on the wall for levels three and seven, I narrow down their destination to two possibilities. They stopped at the third or the seventh floor, so they're either here for an optical or a gynecological checkup. Bad peepers or bad punanis—there must be a joke there somewhere. Fuck, I wish I could know which, but at this juncture all Anastasia, warrior princess, can do is wait. I sit down on the first stair, rest my face in one hand and fiddle with my phone in the other. "Crossed the border?" I type absently, and hit Send.

The elevator rumbles in its cage and I look up, but it just moves between floors. Twirling the tassels of my pashmina around my finger, I twitch like a caged beast, ready to pounce at any instant.

◆

I look up with a start. I'm on my side in the back seat. The phone on the floor before me continues to vibrate and bounce against the back of the gearbox. "Crossed the border?" reads its liquid crystal display. Kate Bush's *Babooshka* plays on the radio at a low volume. I must have dozed off again. As I lift myself up, the driver leans over his seat toward me, the dim light revealing the rest of his face. It's mostly mustache, but behind it I now notice a glimmer of warmth. Morning light washes through the car, painting his etched face a rosy pink. Behind his mustache, he indeed reminds me of a Russian Babooshka. I rub my eyes and ask, "How long was I out?"

"Several hours, sir," he says, and then his mustache arches up into a smile.

I lift myself and look through the windshield. "Syria."

"Well, the border, sir. Syria's on the other side." He brings the car to a stop as I'm gripped at the same time by both a yawn and a thrill. I pull the jacket off my lap, getting ready to step out.

"I just need your ID card and fifty thousand for the paperwork."

I hand him the items from my wallet. He takes them and steps out.

"What, no passport?" I ask.

"Just those," he says as he closes the door and crosses in front of the car into a booth at the side of the road. A striped wooden plank separates me from Damascus, one end hinged to the booth and the other tipped with a rubber stopper. I realize this is one of a string of tollgates under a brick archway spanning the entire width of the broad highway. Through the sandy smog ahead, the city twinkles with point-lights, remnants of the fading night, half-asleep half-awake. If I were a Bedouin in the desert, I'd have dismissed it as a mirage. But Babooshka has indeed confirmed that I've arrived.

A few minutes later, he reappears from the booth and crosses into the car, slamming the door.

"Thank you," I say as the plank swings open and the taxi crosses through.

"Sir, welcome to Damascus."

The car continues along the highway, its headlights piercing the smog, and in a few seconds I realize what I thought was a haze is actually a hillside, with the city of Damascus spread out before me. An immense stone castle caps the rise, its towers partly obscured in the haze, and from it a terraced landscape extends downwards as a smattering of stone structures grows denser along the outskirts, ending with the immensity of the city below. The dominant color is ash brown, limestone, and untamed rock, but a sprinkling of modern buildings catch the early morning sun, their glass and steel facades glimmering like pearls in a sea of sand. I open the window and a warm dusty breeze hits my face as I hear the echoing sounds of overlapping *adan* prayers from hundreds of minarets jutting out of the urban tapestry.

The city looks like it's slowly rising from a slumber of many months. Amidst the rubble of some buildings, others stand perfectly intact—like the battle was surgical, rather than random, aiming for specific targets and not blanket destruction. The only signs of the ceasefire's fragility are the military tanks stationed at every street corner, canons aimed at an angle, saluting the lazy sun.

Babooshka turns off the radio with an "*Ashhadu an la ilaha illa Allah*," and wipes his face with the palm of his hand. We continue along the highway for a few minutes, and as the city looms closer, we make a right onto an exit ramp and descend a boulevard lined with pine trees. Buildings here are sporadic, and we're clearly still on the outskirts, but a cluster of modern edifices mark the heart of the city, a handful of minutes away.

"So, sir," says Babooshka. "Where would you like to go?"

"A mosque."

"A mosque, sir?"

"Yes, a Sunni mosque. I believe it's the biggest in the city."

"I'm afraid I can't do that, sir," he says politely, continuing to drive straight ahead.

"Huh?"

"*Haram*," he says. "That would be a sin."

"A sin?" I'm not sure I follow.

"Well yes. You've been drinking." "Oh," I say. He's right, of course. Can't argue with that. "What should I do then?" I ask carefully. "I can wash outside the mosque. There are fountains, no?"

"Yes, sir. But that won't work."

"Won't work? What on earth do you mean?" I try to keep my voice calm.

"You have to wait forty days."

A fresh wave of anger rises inside me. "I don't have forty days. You know we're leaving today, don't you."

"I'm sorry, that's what they say."

They say a lot of things. I resist the urge to yell that out, but I say something even worse. "And what do you care?"

"I don't," he says, then eyes me through the mirror, his moustache shrinking into a ball. "But God does."

374

I sigh and wipe my face with my hand, squeezing my temples again. This can't be happening. An awkward silence hangs between us.

"Look," says Babooshka a bit more softly. "You can't pray if you've had alcohol. It's *haram*."

Ah. I look up. "But I'm not going there to pray. Just to talk to someone."

Babooshka's mustache and eyebrows twitch upwards. "Well then, that's a little different. You don't have to wait forty days."

"Oh good," I say, already feeling tired. "How long then."

"They say one day. It's dawn, so the day is new. But you have to do two more things."

"Which are?"

"First, perform ablution."

"Okay, and second?"

"Offer a *kaffara*." "What's that?" "*Kaffara* is from the Arabic '*kufur*,' meaning 'sin,'" he says. (Does he think I'm a foreigner? Perhaps when it comes to the intricacies of Islam, I am.) Babooshka continues, "You make a donation to the mosque for your sins."

"A *kaffara* for my sins," I repeat. "Okay." I'm not sure what kind of donation would suffice, but I'll cross that bridge when I get there.

"Very well, sir. So should I take you to your hotel?"

"Actually, I didn't think to book one. I'm just staying a few hours. Can't I just wash at the mosque?"

"With that amount of alcohol?" he asks, scrunching his nose. "I think not." He considers our options for a moment, clearly trying to help now. "Know what? I'll get you sorted out." He signals right, then moments later, the taxi takes us down a side street.

My phone vibrates again with a welcome message that I'm

now connected to the local cell phone network. I hit Reply to Nancy's message and type, "Crossed the border." But now it seems I've hit another border, between me and an acceptable level of sobriety.

The city that was but a few tantalizing seconds away disappears behind a line of trees.

◆

The elevator comes to life again so I take my place a few steps up from my perch on the staircase. It descends through the cage to ground level, and I hold my breath as the girls step out. They exit the building, and I tiptoe after them. My phone buzzes in my shirt pocket, but I ignore it. Must hurry.

The girls walk further up the hill, but I barely have time to consider the futility of this pursuit before they make their way into another building. This one has a blue exterior, and is in the international style of architecture, at least a decade older than the previous one, the precision of its construction belying an older time when quality mattered. In my head, I sound just like Professor as I loiter outside until the girls step into the elevator and it hums to life.

Careful not to make the same mistake this time, I'm already at its door by the time its orange 1 digit fades and the 2 lights up. Thankfully, it stops there; my breath is now in short supply and it gets shorter as I climb the stairs two by two and slink onto the second floor. A sign on the wall immediately opposite reads, "Manderley Clinics" and under it two arrows point in opposite directions, each marked with a list of doctors and their specializations. The one on the right reads, "Gastroenterology, Urology, Orthopedics" and the one to the left reads, "Gynecology and Endocrinology."

That narrows it down: the only one in common with their previous stop is Gynecology, so indeed one of the girls must be suffering from punani-itis. And Professor, if you're reading this, before you think me vulgar I should point out that word's root, which you may not be familiar with (since it's not a tree!). "Punani" is actually a lovely word. I believe it's perhaps one of the most beautiful ways I've come across to describe the female sex. What else could be more divine than the Hawaiian *pua* for "blossom" and *nani* for "heavenly"? Oh Glorious Flower!

But now, one of the girls has trouble in her paradise, and I must find out which girl and what kind of trouble. Shoulder to the wall, I follow the sign left, past the Endocrinology clinic and toward the Gynecologist at the end of the hall. Through the glass door I see a prim secretary behind a desk and facing it a line of chairs with only one occupant, a middle-aged woman with striking red hair coiffed into a mullet.

I must be careful. The girls might still be in the far side of the room behind the wall, and now would be the absolute worst time to blow my cover. I approach cautiously and as I push the glass door open, a ding dong announces my arrival. Damn, I hate those things. What is this, a patisserie? I'm already inside the room and two pairs of eyes are now on me, as the prim secretary and red-haired patient scrutinize the newest entrant into the club of malfunctioning women. Thankfully the two girls aren't there.

"Name please?" says the secretary over a Sudoku grid.

"Umm, do you take walk-ins?"

She scans me from head to toe, and then back up, her gaze resting at my pelvis. "Yes, we're having a quiet week," she says, flicking her pencil in the direction of an empty seat by the desk. "Sit down. Someone's already inside." She uses her pencil to point to a door along a short corridor behind the red-haired lady.

I sit down and the secretary tucks her strikingly manicured feet back under her desk and returns to her puzzle. From here, a massive box of Kleenex obscures the Sudoku and all I can do is sit there and try to figure out what to do next.

On the seat next to mine sits the girls' basket, and in it, behind a metal grill, the white cat naps peacefully. They are with the doctor, and whatever brought them here is hidden by the wall behind the red-haired lady, whose face is now curled into a grimace. If the girls walk out now, they'll run straight into me.

As I smile at the secretary for no reason, I notice another door at the end of the carpeted corridor behind her, this one painted a dark blue, the color of the building exterior.

"Miss, do you have a private bathroom?" I ask her.

Without looking up, she points her pencil in the direction of the blue door. I get up and walk past the red-haired lady, nodding back at her in thanks for her striking red hair, which led me to notice the blue door in the first place.

Right behind her is the examining room door, which does what doors do best, sealing the interior behind an opaque surface away from prying eyes. I'm careful not to linger; no need to raise eyebrows. Passing it, I slip into the bathroom and close the door, avoiding my reflection in the mirror above the sink. This isn't my proudest moment, pursuing two girls to a gynecologist's office, but there's no turning back. If I were a cat, my curiosity would surely have worked its way through my seven lives by now.

The bathroom is a ramshackle affair, tiled from floor to ceiling in stark white ceramic. It even has a curtained bathtub. Perhaps the clinic is part of a partitioned apartment, adapted for its current use. These modern buildings exist all over the city, partly converted from residential blocks to clinics and offices, which allow them to be leased at a higher rent.

Along the wall of the bathtub a window pane slants toward me on a horizontal hinge. First one then the other, I toe off my sneakers and slide my feet out of them. Stepping onto the edge of the bathtub, I allow myself to fall onto my palms against the wall and look out the window. It faces the blind wall of an adjacent building across a light-well, but to the left another window opens into a fluorescent-lit room.

I curl my toes around the edge of the bathtub and spread my feet further apart, adjusting myself to an optimal height to make out the white outline of the doctor standing above a girl. He has his back to me, and his figure obscures most of her reclining body. Her legs are tucked in, knees spread apart, dress hitched up to her waist, hand clenched around the edge of the examining table. Her face is turned away from the doctor and the window, and away from the other girl seated in a chair a foot away.

The doctor makes his way to the foot of the bed and ducks his head between the girl's legs. He then straightens for a moment and pulls out a metal utensil from a tray somewhere and then once again ducks back in, deeper between the girl's legs. She appears to be gripped in a spasm of pain as her hand tightens against the table and the other girl jumps up and strokes her forehead. With most of her body concealed behind the two standing figures (the girl in black at her head and the doctor in white at her feet) only an abbreviated stretch of calf with tensed tendons is visible.

Whatever the procedure being performed, it's clearly not a routine one, causing all three of them a great deal of distress. No girl wants to be in that position, regardless of the circumstances that led her to it. Is this the final outcome of love, of violence, or of recklessness? Whatever choices a girl makes in her life, this is one result she avoids at all costs. But what if it is love that carried

379

her toward this fate? Can love itself be avoided? Surely violence and recklessness are not paths one would choose to take, but love? Could one love too much, blind to its consequences?

The girl's calf jolts and she kicks the doctor in the shoulder, pushing him away. I snap out of my stupor as she pushes the other girl too, and then leaps off the table and across the room, disappearing past the window. Through the wall of the bathroom I hear the examining room door open and a second later a rustle outside, then a click at the bathroom door. Shit! Distracted by that stupid mirror I must've left the door unlocked! I barely have a moment to react: my instincts throw me away from the wall and into the bathtub. The feline inside me still has some life in her. I draw the translucent shower curtain closed just as the bathroom door rattles open.

Through the translucent curtain, an amorphous silhouette rushes into the bathroom as I crouch in an attempt to make my own outline as small as possible. I lean against the edge of the bathtub as the girl huddles over the toilet bowl. Her grotesque retches fill the bathroom, sending shivers of shame up my body. She flushes the toilet, jumps up and rams her shoulder against the bathroom door, then locks herself in with a decisive click. It's just the two of us now in the bathroom, while the other girl is already at the other side of the door, rapping and mumbling with rising concern.

The silhouette then moves to the sink and leans against it. I slide along the bathtub and peer from behind the edge of the shower curtain. She hangs her head above the sink, and I watch as a few strands of silky black hair escape through her scarf, obscuring her face. My sneakers remain on the tiled floor along the outer edge of the bathtub. Should the girl turn slightly to the right, they'd be in plain view and then in an instant so would I.

Another knock at the door, now sharper, is followed by, "Are

380

you alright in there? Please just let me in."

The girl at the sink straightens. "Just give me a minute, okay?" she says, then opens the faucet and splashes several handfuls of water on her face. She looks into her mirror and from behind a veneer of water, tears, and sweat, she studies her face intently. And so do I. Even in her disheveled state she possesses a beauty that fills me with pride to be a woman. A wave of pleasure fills my heart, and my knees buckle under my weight. The soft curve of her cheek defines an angular profile culminating in a prim nose and an eye as black as onyx, lined with charcoal mascara. Along her neck, ripples of nausea shoot up and down like celestial showers, but then the face in the mirror relaxes into the perfect symmetry of a full moon, an ancient moon of a million years ago, unmarred by man or craters. All color has drained from it, which only accentuates its porcelain perfection, but her eyes twinkle with the decisiveness of a supernova. Perhaps just a play of the light, perhaps an expression of resolve, but in that instant the faintest trace of a smile kisses the edges of her lips.

As the knocking on the other side subsides, she wipes her face with a towel and I hold my breath. She replaces the towel on its rack and a moment later opens the door and hooks her arm into Nadine's. I peer further from behind the curtain and watch the two of them follow the doctor down the corridor. They exchange a few words at the secretary's desk—too distant to make out what they're saying—and then with another ding dong, they walk out of the clinic. I slide back behind the curtain as the doctor makes his way back down the corridor and steps into the examining room, closing the door behind him.

Out of the bathtub and back into my sneakers, I head down the corridor to the secretary. "Alright Miss," she says. "The doctor will see you right after Mrs.—" She points her pencil at the red-haired woman behind me, who interrupts her with a wave of her hand.

"Let her go first," says the woman, indicating me. "I'll be a while."

The seat where the cat basket sat is empty and the big box of Kleenex is now in a different position on the desk, at the foot of which now sits a wastebasket and in it a handful of charcoal-stained tissues.

No time to waste, I reply, "Never mind. I feel much better now." And before any of them have the chance to engage me in polite Lebanese insistence, I ding dong out of the clinic.

I'm done roleplaying for the day. No more Anastasia, no more make-believe duchesses, no more fluffy female fantasies and fairy tales. This is a hard reality, one where fluffy girls end up in abortion clinics. I'm Nancy, and that name will mean whatever I want it to.

In the hallway, I kneel down on the cheap carpet and my phone falls out of my shirt pocket with a thump. Its display lights up with a message marked an hour ago, "Crossed the border."

I tie my shoelaces (who says I never learn from my mistakes, huh Professor?) and pick up the phone. "I just crossed one too," I type back, inhale deeply, and run down the stairs.

◆

The morning is well underway by the time the taxi's tires crackle against the gravel of the lot. I step outside, glad to stretch my limbs, if not entirely pleased with where I get to do it. I don't press Nancy for more details since I'd rather not admit how little progress of my own I've made so far. A fleet of about twenty white taxi cabs extends before me.

In the distance a dark boy of about fourteen waxes the hood of one to a mirror-like sheen. Besides that, there's nothing else but highway as far as my eyes can see. Motels, airports, and taxi lots are nowheres between one place and another. Behind the closer end of the fleet sits a single-story building of one or two rooms. It's topped with a sign that reads, "Phoenicia Taxis" in English and Arabic, with an encircled logo of a man wearing a Turkish fez tarboush and a similar mustache to my driver's. How the image and logo go together I'm not sure, maybe a vague reference to Greater Syria, which traditionally comprised both Lebanon and Syria. Or maybe it's a reference to the earlier Ottoman Empire, or perhaps even to Phoenicia itself, before borders between the two countries even existed. I drape my jacket on my arm as Babooshka says "*Itfaddal*," and leads me through the doorway.

The dispatch office is clean and well kept, with maps over three walls and a desk and open doorway along the fourth. Capped with a rusty nail, a perfectly rectangular spot marks the wall, perhaps where a framed photograph of the president once hung. At the desk in front of it slouches a man who looks exactly like my driver Babooshka, but scaled up by a factor of one-point-five. Babooshka shakes Big Babooshka's hand warmly and they exchange good-mornings. I'm not sure how uncanny the resemblance really is, but through my bifocals the identical white mustaches make them twins.

"Number 72 is missing a jack," he says, pointing out our vehicle through the window with a stubby thumb.

Big Babooshka grimaces. "What, no jack? Sonofa—" he says, then turning to the window he bellows, "*Ya* Raed! *Raed Fada!*"

I'm sure "Astronaut" is not the boy's real name, nevertheless he ducks frightfully behind a car outside, leaving only his hand and wax cloth visible on its hood.

"I'll deal with this later," says Big Babooshka from the other end of the desk, where I now notice another man nodding silently to both Babooshkas. This third man has the same thick white mustache, though he's too skinny to resemble the other two. Still, I believe this facial accessory might be a staple of this taxi company, making the three specimens look like they belong to the same set of Babooshka dolls. When I was a kid my Aunt Jamila gave one to my father as a souvenir from Russia, where she went with her husband to get reconstructive surgery for her injuries.

So there I stand, as Big Babooshka (behind the desk), Babooshka (my driver) and Little Babooshka (the skinny one) exchange pleasantries. I think I'm still drunk. When they're done, Big Babooshka heaves a thick "*Ahlein*, welcome," through his mustache and throws another glance at Babooshka. I nod my hellos and wait to see what comes next as Little Babooshka mutters through his mustache.

Babooshka slips through the door along the desk wall and I hear the clanging of metal as he beckons me over. He reaches into an open locker and hands me a towel and a bar of soap. "Here," he says and points into the room at a tiled *bac-à-douche* on the far wall. "That's the shower. Careful, it's slippery."

He reaches into his locker again and pulls out a folded shirt. "It's mine—I mean, if you don't mind. I think we're about the same size." I look down at his belly, not sure if he's quite correct on that one. Nancy's teased me about my waistline lately, but I'm sure it can't be that bad. Taking that as courteous hesitation, Babooshka adds, "You can just return it to the office in Beirut." I take the shirt and thank him.

With the exception of the Arabic-style hole-in-the-ground toilet behind a flimsy door, the shower space feels quite homey. The head pressure and water temperature are just right and I feel my tiredness drain away.

I get dressed—sadly, the shirt is a perfect fit—and put my jacket back on. As I comb my hair in the foggy mirror—one two three and part—I catch a whiff of thick Turkish coffee, and sure enough, back into the office a pot brews on a single-eye portable stove on the desk.

"*Naiman*," says Big Babooshka, as Little Babooshka mutters and my Babooshka pours three cups of coffee. I've always loved that untranslatable world of congratulations mothers say to their children after they've stepped out of a bath.

"Alright," he says handing me a cup of coffee with the tips of his fingers. "Where did you wanna go?"

"It's a Sunni Mosque," I say taking a sip. "They say it's the biggest one in town." The coffee kicks through my hangover, now a much milder throb along the back of my neck. I find myself feeling at home in this office, among these mustachioed drivers doing all they can to help me out. Nancy was right, somewhere that feels like home can't be nowhere.

"We have a thousand mosques in Damascus," says Big Babooshka with unconcealed pride. "Eight hundred of them Sunni and at least half of those claim to be the biggest."

Little Babooshka mumbles something in agreement.

"Biggest, you mean by size?" my Babooshka asks. "Biggest building? Widest grounds? Biggest congregation? Oldest? Most important?" With senses heightened by the cold shower, I realize his annoying meticulousness is merely his way of being helpful. He adds, "I mean, you have to be more specific unless you want to spend the entire day driving around."

"True," I say, unsure what else I could add to narrow down our search.

"Here," says Big Babooshka, as he slides his chair back and gets up. I was wrong, he's closer to twice the size of my

Babooshka, in height and in girth. As he walks past me to the far wall, I feel like I'm caught in an eclipse. He stabs a stubby finger into the map on the wall showing the city of Damascus.

"We're here," he says indicating a red pinhead. "Now the nearest mosque is," he pulls out a mechanical pencil from his shirt pocket and draws a circle around a brown rectangle, "this one. That's Alzahra, but no that's mainly Shia. Let's see."

Little Babooshka says something from his perch on the chair as my Babooshka walks over to the map. "You're right," he says, tapping his finger to it. "There's Al-Omari here. That's a big Sunni Mosque. Hmmm."

Twenty minutes, twenty circles from Big Babooshka, twenty more suggestions from my Babooshka, and about the same number of mutterings from Little Babooshka later, we've covered the entire map. "You're right," I say. "That's a lot."

I scan the map, a patchwork of brown indicating religious structures, gray for building mass, orange for taxi routes, blue for water and green for, well, greenery. Then I remember. "Olive trees," I say. Nadine said she played there as a child.

"What about them?" asks my Babooshka.

"The mosque is surrounded by a grove of olive trees," I squeeze between the two men, and slide my hand down the left side of the map. "This here's a plateau, right? That's where olive trees grow. The rest we can exclude."

"Ah, good," says Big Babooshka. "One, two, three, four, five," he says marking thicker circles around the mosques speckled along the flat stretch of land. "See the green around these? Those are forests of course, but the map won't tell us what kind."

"That's progress," says my Babooshka, "but it's still a good day's worth of driving, not counting traffic if you wanna hit all of them. Cost you a fortune in gas, but I don't mind if you don't."

I think for a minute then say, "The olive is technically a fruit, but it has very little in common with, say, the apple or orange. A lot of it goes bad if not harvested and used on the spot." I turn to Big Babooshka. "Try and remember. Which one of those mosques has lots of local shops next to it? You know, grandmothers, *tetas*, selling jars of oil, soap, candles, that kind of thing?"

"Al-Moqbil!" exclaims my Babooshka.

"And you know where that is?"

"Let's go," he says with a triumphant jiggle of his keys. We step out as Little Babooshka mutters under his mustache.

◆

When I step onto the ground floor of the blue building, the girls are already getting into a dusty brown taxi. With no time to catch my breath and with complete abandon, I sprint after it. Please let there be another one, I pray as I watch it make its way up the hill then cut to the right. I step onto the street and watch a yellow Honda approach. Not a taxi, but I have no choice. They're getting away.

I stretch out my hand in the universal Stop sign and the Honda comes to screeching halt, the man behind the wheel gawking at me like I were a blowup doll in the middle of the street. No time for courtesies, I hop in.

"See that brown car?" I say indicating the taxi an instant before it disappears around the bend. "Follow it."

A woman in distress? A hijacker? A raving lunatic? I can't be sure what impression strikes the young man, who, perhaps driven by a lustful curiosity of his own, nods wordlessly and hits the gas.

No explanation is demanded, and I offer none as we remain hot on the tail of the brown taxi. This time I'm not in a car Nadine would recognize, so there's no need to maintain a distance. "Bumper to bumper, alright?" I say. "I don't want to lose them."

"Where are we going?" the young man finally asks. I now realize he's barely a boy out of high school, all pimply and testosterony.

"Wherever they are," I say.

We drive through Aisha Bakkar then make a right at the Sanayeh Gardens, then left across Hamra and down to Ain Mraise. At every cross street, the boy glances left, then right, then steals a quick glance at my boobs. He then quickly brings his eyes back to the car ahead. It's fun watching him fight his baser instincts as he fancies himself, what? A rescuer? A good Samaritan? A hostage? Whichever it is, he remains doggedly focused on the brown car like his life depends on it, or like he thought mine did.

We now drive through the wide boulevard separating the west side of Beirut from the renovated downtown area. The brown taxi makes a right but instead of entering Downtown proper, it takes another left and continues north toward Dbaye.

"*Matmozeil*, where are you taking us?" the boy finally asks. Again a vague question. Is he scared or aroused? Then he adds hesitantly, "Listen, you're pretty and all, but I have no money."

A whore! Of all the things I could be! Would I be dressed like a tomboy if I were out to sell sex? I pull the pashmina down around my shoulders and wrap it around my chest. But no, I can't be indignant under the circumstances. I'd probably have assumed that too, if I were in the boy's place. Claiming the contrary would be blatant chauvinism. What, a woman can't be a chauvinist? After all, it is I who hopped into the poor guy's car without a shred of pretext.

So he thinks I'm a whore. And I think I'm a stalker. Yes, if only inwardly, I must admit it's what I've become, plain and simple. I've been tailing these girls since last night, and have no intention of stopping until I find out everything I want to know.

"This isn't about you or me," I finally say to the boy. "It's about them. I must find out where they're going."

"Who are they? Did they steal something?"

"No," I say. Then, "Maybe… I don't know. But one of them played me for a fool, and now it's my turn to play her."

He nods, apparently satisfied with my answer. The "hell hath no fury" argument—men just eat it up. Good.

The taxi ahead comes to a stop outside Charles Helou station, and the boy keeps us at a safe distance as the two girls exit the dirty brown vehicle. They pay the driver and sidle into the gargantuan structure.

"I'll get off here," I say, open the door, and step out.

The boy says nothing; he just looks at me dejectedly as I hold the door open. But an unspoken question plays on his lips: is that it?

Turning around, I slide back into the vehicle, while my legs and behind remain outside. As I lean toward him and kiss his cheek, his soft, perfumed stubble tickles my nose. "You rock," I say and he smiles.

The yellow Honda shrinks to the size of a dot on the highway, and I step into Charles Helou Station.

◆

The taxi skirts along the lower ridges of the Anti-Lebanon mountain range, a name I've always found amusing, as the dry breeze beats against my face. This is called the rain-shadow effect, because these mountains prevent the humid air from reaching the plateau on which this part of the city sits.

The Syrian capital takes its original name Damascus Al-

Sham from the pre-Semitic language of Aramaic, (the language of Jesus, Nancy might say, though I think she knows that from the movies, as I do) and it means "the land north of Syria." The reason for that, of course, is that the entire region, including my own country, was known as Greater Syria, up to and during the age of the Ottoman Empire. But say that to a Lebanese nationalist, and you'll get a dirty look at best, and today maybe even a black eye.

The taxi makes a sharp right at the southern bank of the Barada River and follows the waterfront for a couple of kilometers along the main city thoroughfare. To my left, a string of high-rise banks and minarets cuts through the modest skyline, and to my right sprawls the ancient part of the city. Straight ahead, a line of trees converges to a vanishing point, but soon the driver makes another sharp right into the heart of the old city. The fragrance of olive trees fills the air and I know we've arrived.

The car comes to a stop and I step out. Leaning through the front window, I say, "You must've missed your morning prayer. Wanna come in too?"

"I'm Shia. I'll drive over to my own mosque, it's not too far from here," he says. "Unless you need me."

"No, I'm okay from here. I'll be a few hours," I say, passing him my cell phone. "Here, save your number and I'll call you when I'm done."

He dials it in then hands me back the phone. I read his name above the saved number.

"Thanks, Bashar," I say, and with an *"Ahlein!"* he drives off, leaving me alone on the side of the road. So it's not Babooshka, but close enough.

The olive grove stretches far and wide, ripe olives perfuming the air. It's the tail end of harvest season, when the scent is the strongest and only a few branches of ripe fruit remain. Soon these trees will be all leaves, which remain green all year round. This is an excellent choice of foliage to plant around a mosque, and I make a mental note to commend whoever made the decision if I get the chance. The Olive Tree carries a great amount of symbolic connotations, too numerous to list for a non-historian like myself.

At the other side of the grove sits the mosque, and I'm thankful for Bashar's choice to drop me off at the far side for the refreshing walk I now enjoy. I need it to clear my mind through the fog of distractions and deceptions, the first of which is Nadine's description of the mosque itself.

It grows as I draw closer, minaret catching the morning sunlight and bouncing it back onto its blue dome. Nadine said she played here as a child, a time when everything appears larger than life. She said it was the largest in the city, but even during the brief taxi ride through Damascus, I passed at least three much larger structures. Perhaps through the eyes of a child, which, all things considered, Nadine really still is, this structure is grandiose. That may not be a lie, just an exaggeration. It's all relative, yes, but then there are her other claims, chief amongst them the one that her relationship with Tariq Jaber is platonic, impossible to reconcile with the image in the Polaroid.

She's as slick as pure virgin oil. I can't suppress a laugh. But no, she's worse than slick. She's sick. Incestuous. Surely she had no idea that she and Tariq Jaber are half-siblings? Or are they really? If they are, and she doesn't know it, the fact that they ever crossed paths would be a coincidence of astronomical proportions.

Astronomical. I laugh as I remember the telescope, then look around hoping no one spotted me guffawing to myself. I'm losing my focus. I wonder what I'm even doing here when

I should be back at my desk with my Acacia, grinding away at the paper that will make or break my career. Anyone with half a brain knows that being passed over for a promotion is tantamount to a demotion.

Or has it gotten to the point that I care more about Tariq Jaber?

A breeze teases my hair and I stop to enjoy it caressing my face. Standing in the morning sun, I take a few deep breaths. The throbbing in my neck has all but subsided, leaving behind it the sweet lull of a morning hangover. Reaching into my messenger bag, I pull out the tape recorder and pop it open, replacing the tape with the one marked in red, and hit Play.

My voice keeps me company as I walk ahead, thinking back on the experiments I conducted two nights ago at LUST. "An Acacia tree can survive on as little as a quarter liter of water a year. It builds itself from carbon in the air. However, minerals are crucial, and often scarce in the arid soil of urban districts. The *Acacia tortilis* enters into a *quid pro quo* relationship with bacteria that provide it with a nitrogen fix, so to speak, but then it requires the soil to provide it with the rest."

The mosque continues to grow, though much slower than I anticipated. I didn't realize from the other side how immense it really is. Nadine was right—perhaps her words weren't merely the memories of an over-imaginative child after all.

I must keep these notes on this tape, and this tape alone. Remember not to write them down anywhere; if they fall into someone else's hands at the Botany Department, well, that would be the end of this research. Why? Does anyone else on the faculty care about a relatively minor area of study as the *Acacia tortilis* is in this part of the world? The answer is no, they don't. They don't care about my research. And they decidedly don't care for me either. Not one bit. Alright, I'll say it. They flat out dislike me, and they'd jump at a chance to anonymously drop my notes into the pigeonhole of some rival researcher at another university if only for the sheer pleasure of watching me lose my chance at tenure once and for all. That's what hangs on my paper. Move forward or die.

I flip back through this memoir and read, "Taxonomist this, taxonomist that." Maybe by this cabal of unnamed taxonomists, it is those petty little academics around me whom I actually mean, those small people who'd prefer to remain exactly where they are for the rest of their lives, and who'd do all they can to keep everyone else there with them. It's as if the only way they can progress is for everyone else to regress. Left to its own devices, this is the natural state of equilibrium this field often forces upon the timid. Quite simply, things could remain as they are for years on end. And those "taxonomists" are happy to ride that wave of inertia. But this has been a big week for the Acacia. And I believe—What? Me? Sure, why not?—Yes, I *believe* the most important thing is yet to come. Listen well, Professor. Listen well.

The entrance to the mosque is marked by a five-story archway, which I step under as I press Stop, replacing the recorder in my messenger bag and zipping it up. A wall of mosaic tiles covers the interior wall along several layers of *muqarnas* ornaments, each reflecting and refracting the light as if with a mind of its own. Up the stairway toward a wooden rack in the corner, I slip out of my shoes and lay them there, then wipe my feet on the straw mat surface and walk in.

The mosque interior is at least ten degrees cooler than the outside, and as I cross the hallway I find myself engulfed by the cubic space of the mosque proper. The belly of the dome above fills me with awe, as it must have thousands of people before me and undoubtedly will thousands more to come, long after I'm

393

dead and gone. I'm glad I washed up before coming, because regardless of one's otherworldly beliefs, this space is a humbling miracle of physics. How a structure so voluminous could rise so high, with such grace, and with such minimal support, boggles the mind. It feels like the entire cosmos was pulled inside it, and closed shut with the dome cap above. A huge space that does not fill me with anxiety and dread is a novel experience for me, and already makes my journey here worthwhile.

The space is quite empty, though it's hard to tell for sure because when I do see people they're much smaller than I expect. Some walk toward the mihrab on the back wall, others return along the sides, and a few sit cross-legged in circles of four or five. Some wear turbans and dishdashas, but most are dressed casually and wouldn't be out of place anywhere else in the city. I walk to a larger group of about seven, careful not to startle them. "Excuse me, I was wondering if you could point me to the Imam in charge?"

One of them, a bearded man of about thirty looks up, perhaps amused by my reference to the head sheikh like he were the boss of some commercial establishment, and says, "Yes, you'll find him over there by the mihrab. But I believe he's conducting a *katb kitab* marriage ceremony at the moment."

Thanking him, I make my way toward the mihrab, taking my time to admire the elaborate walls. Horror vacui. Fear of empty spaces. How different from the pool where I last saw Nancy, I think, as I continue forward and sit down against the wall at a spot within viewing distance of the mihrab.

Katb kitab ceremonies are quite brief, unlike the marriages that follow them. I smile. Not a great joke, but I try to keep myself entertained. I rest against a pillar and the heat dissipates from my back into the cool marble. It shouldn't be long now.

And indeed what may be seconds later, I wake up to the

swish of a neatly pressed black and gray dishdasha, its hem sewn with a thread of white cotton. Next to it, a white dress flows with hundreds of silver sequins. And around them shuffle shiny black shoes, six or seven pairs. I look up at the handsome middle-aged man in the dishdasha, dark pink skin and short white beard, a dignified smile on his face.

"*Mabrouk*," says the Imam. "*Baraka Allah Feekum*. God bless your union."

The bride and groom both blush. He shakes hands with each member of the group individually, and then extends both hands to the tuxedoed young man, who grips them eagerly and gushes, "And God bless you too, Imam."

The Imam holds a hand to his chest and turns his smile to the bride, whose face, barely visible under her white veil, streams with tears. The group exchanges congratulations and hugs, men with men, women with women.

Wobbling to my feet as the group disperses, I wait until the Imam waves his last goodbye. I take a deep breath and prepare to walk over to him, but he turns around and approaches me instead. "*Asalam alaykum*," he says, extending his hand.

"*Wa alaykum asalam*," I say as I grip his hand.

"You wanted to speak to me?" he asks, and I look over his shoulder and notice that the circle of people with the bearded man has disbanded as I slept.

"Yes, please." I nod. "Come then," the Imam says.

I follow him, but instead of leading me to an office, as I would've thought, he simply chooses a spot in the hall where the sun shines through an archway along the wall, and he gestures to me with a polite "*Itfaddal*." We both sit down cross-legged like the other people around us. He adjusts his white turban, whispers a "*Bismillah irhaman iraheem*," and studies me with sharp gray eyes. "How can I be of service?"

"I'm trying to find someone," I say. "I only know his first name. Maurice." I choose not to mention Nadine unless I absolutely have to. "I think he lives nearby and is a member of this congregation," I continue. "I believe his family comes to this mosque." I'm careful not to say "wife," thinking it might be too direct.

"And may I ask why you seek this man?" says the Imam.

Never lie more than you have to, certainly not in a house of worship. "I arrived this morning from Lebanon, where I've been following a trail of circumstances leading to him." What? That doesn't make sense, even to me. The Imam clearly agrees, because he says nothing, his unwavering gaze piercing right through me.

"Imam, I don't understand how these things work. To be honest, I've never been a mosque-goer. I suppose there must be a vow of confidentiality between you and your... congregation." (The word feels heavy, foreign, too Christian perhaps. But I have no equivalent.) "But the fact is," I continue. "I must speak to this man."

"How important is this?" asks the Imam. "Is it a matter of life and death?"

"In a manner of speaking, yes."

"Yours or his?"

"Maybe both. It involves someone he cares about deeply." I inhale and add, "And that person is dead."

"I see," says the Imam, his silver eyes exploring mine. "A family member?"

"Perhaps."

He pinches the hem of his dishdasha with the tips of his fingers and stands up, inviting me to follow. Hands clasped neatly behind him, he leads me along the mosaic wall and follows the colonnade toward the entrance. I'm worried he's simply showing me the way out, but I find no more words to convince him not to.

We stand in silence under the entrance archway as the Imam scans the olive grove from atop the stairs, hands still tucked firmly into the small of his back. I curl my toes against the straw mat and wait quietly.

"Yes, I know Maurice Akkad," he says. "His wife and daughters come regularly. He does too, once a year."

Akkad. That's it, Nadine's family. Maurice Akkad.

I venture a guess. "Ramadan?"

"No. He comes every July, at the height of the olive harvest. He helps with the picking, then spends a day in prayer." I nod and he continues, "His elder brother died one summer, many years ago of a sudden illness. It was back in his town Tartous. So when you come to me with a request, one that could save him the same kind of suffering, all I can do is oblige."

"Thank you," I say, breathing a sigh of relief.

"Come with me," he says as he unclasps his hands. "I'm heading in that direction for another ceremony."

We each pull our shoes off the rack, slip into them, and walk down the stairs. We walk around the mosque to a back street lined with olive trees on both sides. I enjoy the silence of the path and the white noise of the city beyond, glad that the Imam is not one for small talk either. In the middle of the road, we make a right onto a dirt path and follow another line of smaller olive trees before we arrive at a white stone house.

"This is it," he says. "Good luck." I'm surprised by the sudden secularity of his wish, so I laugh. He laughs too, clearly aware of the incongruity.

"I'm grateful," I say. Then I remember Babooshka's advice. "Imam? I'd like to make a donation to the mosque. Something symbolic."

"Offer your *kaffara* to the Akkads. They're a good family."
Then by way of goodbye he adds, "My condolences to Lebanon."

He clasps his hands behind him, and I can swear I hear the Imam hum as he continues down the road until his white turban disappears among the trees.

◆

Charles Helou Station is pandemonium. The five-day hiatus has caused a bottleneck, and anyone with no other means to commute back to Damascus is here to catch the first bus. Everyone. To one side, a group of twenty blue-collars, still in their work clothes, huddle around an attendant, patches of sweat soaking into the armpits and back of his white shirt as he is pelleted with angry insults. To another side, a family of five with suitcases that could fill a caravan wait patiently, as the mother, clearly the head of the family, chops through the air, muttering curses through a plump red face as the father nods silently.

The only oasis of relief is an improvised living room at the rear of the station structure, on a stretch of dirt lit by an opening between two limbs of the highway above. The room is wall-less, defined simply by a pair of discarded ornate sofas bridged by a makeshift countertop in between and a coffee table in the center. On it lounge two drivers, one smoking a cigarette and another reclined, hand forming a visor along his brow, sleeping like the dead.

I half-wish the two girls were sitting in that tranquil living room, because everywhere else is turmoil. It's impossible to spot them here amidst the carnival of colors and symphony of noise, and what makes it worse is that the more I try to look, the more I risk being seen. I shouldn't let Nadine spot me, but when I can't see the person I'm hiding from, there's nowhere to hide.

Further into the station, I spot a larger, more varied group of people, a more textured, diverse crowd. These must be individuals traveling alone, I think as I worm my way into the morass. This group is the most riled up, each member armed with their own unique—and deafeningly loud—opinion.

"I booked my ticket two weeks ago!" says a young woman in Woody Allen glasses.

"My father is sick!" says a man who himself is so old that his father should be lucky to be alive.

"*Kiss ikhta shu ma fi dawle*? Is there no fucking government?" says a third. With that, the entire crowd jeers in agreement. Throw in a curse word with a municipal word, and you're guaranteed instant consensus. This proves a good choice: colorful and noisy, a great spot to hide. I slide the pashmina off my shoulders and wrap it around my head in a scarf. Angry mob plus headgear equals the perfect Lebanese camouflage.

"*Wlik eh, eh!*" I say, joining in. "*Wein el zoama*? Where are the leaders! Let them come see this!" This riles them up even more—but then I realize it may have been in bad taste. The last time a leader used public transportation, he was gunned down.

I'm invisible here; even if the girls spot me they won't recognize me. I throw a sideways glance in the direction of my group and at the protesters and passengers clustered around the buses. The one marked "Damascus" draws the largest group, among it men and women of all ages, children, infants too. The little ones are the quietest; most seem to enjoy that it's the adults making all the rumpus today.

Fleets of buses line the space, but only a few seem to be running. The rest are there, functionless, like carcasses in an elephant graveyard. Upon closer inspection though, I find that quite a few have their baggage compartments open, and in them one or two reclining drivers, barefoot, shirtless, smoking cigarettes or sleeping or both. Safely tucked into my group, I can now scan the area without the fear of being seen, casting my eyes on one bus and the next, trying hard to make out the individuals in each crowd.

And there they are: the two of them stand among the Damascus crowd, their bodies forming a single outline against the bus as they hug each other tightly. I slip out of my group, shielding myself behind the broad shoulders of a porter carrying a suitcase on his shoulder, I inch closer to the girls. They remain tightly wound together, faces buried in one another's cheeks. When they pull apart I lean behind the front of the bus and watch as Nadine wipes her forehead with the sleeve of her dress. The other girl touches her face, and I realize her hand is wrapped in a bandage. She then taps the cat basket in the other hand, and boards the bus.

From behind me, a man in an official uniform waves as he herds the remaining passengers onboard. "*Yalla, yalla,*" he yells. "Only those with IDs and tickets. This bus is full." The remainder of the crowd disperses as the last few board; the others step back and watch helplessly. One even spits on the ground in vain. When all else fails, expectoration is the final form of dissent.

Filled to bursting, the bus wheezes out a heavy cloud of smoke and eases out of its lot and onto the road. Nadine watches the girl in the window, blind to me and everyone else as the bus grinds into gear and drives off. She wipes her face and turns.

In spite of everything, I find myself walking toward her. And a moment later, in an instant, we lock eyes.

Behind the tears, she looks no older than twelve. I remember how as a child I used to cry when my mother would go out, not knowing if she'd ever come back. Even when she died, I didn't shed as many tears at fourteen as I would when at six she'd stand in the doorway, assuring me it was just to the grocery store, pleading with me to let go of her dress for just a few minutes, promising she'd buy me something sweet. But for a child every goodbye is a farewell.

A curious melancholy fills me as I watch Nadine's delicate face, unmarred by the sins I've attributed to her over the past few days, empty of lust and anger and pride. Instead, all I find is loneliness.

As I approach her, I reach into my pocket. "This pack has two cigarettes left," I say. "One each?"

♦

The house of Maurice Akkad stands before me, a single story of corbeled rock that should have been rough and beautiful, except it's been systematically defaced year after year with layer upon layer of sloppy white paint. This was clearly a decision that prioritizes convenience over aesthetics, and I can see why. The late midday sun beats down on its surface, which responds by bouncing it right back out into the forest beyond. This culture considers black the most discreet of all colors, but I think it's white. It lets nothing in, not even the light. Perfectly opaque. The most impenetrable veil from the outside world. And now, somehow, I have to go inside.

My shoes totter on the side of the dirt road, on a short cobblestone path leading to a painted brown door. On either side of me is a grass lawn, and on either side of the door a single green window of painted wood panels, lined with vents. Shut.

My body rocks on the heel of each foot, first to the left and then to the right, but the windows reveal nothing more through the thin slits between their panels. Beyond the walls of the house is nothing but trees, growing wild in this spot, which means if I choose to go around the back, I would achieve nothing, except getting apprehended as a trespasser, or worse, as a voyeur. A man like me would be guilty until proven otherwise. After all, this is a household with two women: Nadine's mother and her sister—three if I count Nadine herself, but I will not. I arrived here before she could. The tortoise has beaten the hare.

There's no way around it. As Nancy insists, the only way to the other side of this place is through it.

◆

Nadine pulls out the last two Lucky Strikes and hands one to me. The off-duty driver leans toward us and lights mine first, then brings the same flame to hers as she dips her face into its golden glow until her cigarette tip catches fire. I've literally never seen her in this light, which tints her pallid cheeks with a warm hue. She's still leaning forward as the driver pulls back and turns to the makeshift counter. Splayed along the sofa facing ours, another driver remains asleep, as dead to the world as ever.

After the departure of the bus bound for Damascus a few minutes ago, the hubbub at Charles Helou Station has quieted down significantly. The concrete world-unto-itself, lit by incandescent lamps along its center and natural light from the sides, now feels eerie and desolate. And at the very edge of that world, in our rough-and-ready living room, open to the sky and the highway above, Nadine and I start to speak.

Her scarf hangs loosely on her head, revealing more of her face, features soft, even malleable, not quite fully-formed. Except for the cigarette, which she puffs at with an expertise that belies her years, she could pass for a girl of sixteen. Her

402

eyes sparkle with undefiled youth, looking like fragile jewels unblemished by time and experience. Could this really be all there is to this girl?

"So Nadine, it's quite clear," I say. "I'm not crazy about you."

"I don't mind you as much," she replies quietly.

Our tones are hushed, but the driver at the counter doesn't seem to be listening anyway as he sways a *rakwe*, a pot of Turkish coffee, over an electric burner.

I twist my leg onto the couch and rub my sore knee as I continue. "In the beginning I didn't mind you either," I say, now close to her ear. "When we first became friends at LUST you were someone I could trust, someone I could bring into our home. God knows Professor needs someone around the house, and I can't always be there for him. But when you started working there... I don't know—I suppose I started thinking. Maybe over-thinking. But something about you changed too."

"I'm still the same person," she says. "You just got to know me more." She exhales a waft of smoke, hitting me right in the face. Perhaps the person before me truly is a child. Only someone who hasn't yet grown an ego would recognize, as she does, that we're not engaged in a battle of wills, that at this moment I'm in fact extending her an olive branch.

As the smoke disperses between us, her face reemerges. Washed by the tears, completely devoid of makeup, a new clarity defines the edges of her eyes, distinct and lucid.

Our exchange is what writers might call "on the nose." Her face is only visible to me in profile, allowing me to say things as they come to my mind, without thinking, without wrapping them in etiquette or euphemism. I've always been direct with Nadine anyway, perhaps because she works for my boyfriend, so I give myself the right to be both blunt and sharp, neither of which, I imagine, are very pleasant for her.

"You see, Nadine," I say. "When someone enters your home, you need to know who they are."

"What you don't know about me, I don't know about myself," she says, looking straight ahead. "Being away from home… in a way, it orphaned me."

"Tell me about that."

The driver brings the *rakwe* of boiling Turkish coffee and lays it discreetly on the table, avoiding eye contact as he places two cups, before us. He nods to himself then steps away to the inside of the station.

"I never admit it, but when I'm alone here I'm always terrified. Damascus is a big city too, but I grew up in a family of four and had very few friends. My parents and my sister are all I've ever known. That was my world, small and cozy. I'd stretch out my arms and I could touch its edges."

Cigarette clamped tight, she extends her arms and wiggles her fingers, "But here, my fingers just touch air. It's a big, scary place. I'm a stranger in a strange world, lonely and alone."

"Then you met Tony," I say, watching a sliver of smoke dance out of the coffee *rakwe* on the table. "And you fell in love with him."

"Yes," she says, bringing her hands down to her chest. "God, did I love him. I felt we were destined to meet, like the stars aligned that day and brought us together. But never, for a single moment, did I love him like a girl loves a boy. He was several years older, yet we were two kids on a merry-go-round. Except we didn't spin, the world did."

"But do you know who Tony really was?"

"Now I do," she says. "But somehow I've always known. He was the man from the South who fled his hometown. But God knows somehow inside me I felt, that we were… related. Still I

404

just wanted him to hold me. Warm and snug and safe."

She puts out the cigarette in a glass ashtray on the table, then leans back, picks some ashes off of her finger, and continues. "That passenger on the bus, the young man whose name was revealed much later than the others, I felt it was him." She gazes at the underside of the highway and the afternoon traffic above us. "The moment his life was snuffed out, I felt a knot in my heart. It's still here. And then I found his apartment empty, and I knew he was gone. Your revealing it to me that night just confirmed it."

"But how did you know you were related?"

"From a moment in my past, many years ago. A boy named Tariq Jaber came to visit my father in Damascus. Nissrine and I never knew who he was, but we've spoken about him since. He was supposed to stay with us for weeks, but there was an accident and my father sent him back a day later."

"How old were you back then?"

"Old enough to remember, not old enough to understand," she says, looking at me. "But then after you and I had that big fight, it all came back to me. So we called my father, and he told me everything... about his wife, abut my half-brother Tariq, and I understood. Tony and he were one and the same person, just as you said. It's like the merry-go-round suddenly stopped and I could see."

"We?"

"Huh?"

"You said 'we' called your father."

"Yes, my sister and I," she says. "Nissrine has been here for a month. She wants to be a nurse, but back in Damascus she could only finish the first year before our savings ran out. She insisted the rest of it go to my own education—that's how I'm here today. I'm helping her to apply for a scholarship, without her knowing.

Kind of my 'thank you' to her."

"So the papers from the yellow folder you left at our place the other day, those were hers?"

"I secretly filled out the application, and that was her personal statement. I wrote it for her and submitted it. She doesn't know a thing. My sister isn't well; she's been sick for weeks now."

From my pursuit earlier today, I know what she means by "sick." But of all Nadine's secrets, I know this is the one I shouldn't trespass upon. I squeeze her hand and a thin veneer of tears forms in her eyes, but she holds them back.

"Nadine, I also have a secret to tell you," I say, choosing my words. "We know about Tariq. Professor was on Damascus Road when the bus was gunned down. He was the last person to see your half-brother alive."

Nadine grips my hand tighter and lowers her head. She sniffles, and when she raises her face again her nose is moist. The tears cling precipitously to her lower eyelids.

"Did Tariq say anything?" she says.

"He asked, 'Where is she'?" I answer. "Nadine, that 'she' was you. And he said something else. He made a curious request. He said 'Feed the cat.'"

Nadine pulls her hand away and brings it to her lips.

"Oh my God," she says. "That cat meant everything to him. It was his—our—father's. When I spoke to Dad last night that was the one thing he asked for. The cat."

"It's more than that," I say. "Professor honored his last request. That day when we all watched the news at his place, he had just returned from Tariq's apartment. He went there for the cat, and among its food he found Tariq's journal. Tariq was relentless. After he found you, he made every effort to find your father too. That entire journal is about him."

"He never said anything to me. All this time, nothing."

"And he wouldn't," I say. "He kept secrets to protect you from a family back in Nabatieh that would stop at nothing to find him, or anyone he cared about. Tariq lived in constant fear for the people he loved."

Nadine's pupils dilute in terror, and the tears finally escape her eyes. "I shot him," she says finally. A car horn from above sends a jolt down my spine.

"What? What do you mean?" I ask, burying my back into the sofa.

"Not that day on Damascus Road. But I did shoot him. Many years ago, before I knew who he was. I almost killed him."

"You mean that accident back in Damascus."

"The Wicked Toe incident," says Nadine. "That's what Nissrine and I call it."

18

Wicked Toe

A shot rang across the plateau and a moment later, a scatter of gray dots filled the sky. The sun cut through the shaking branches of the olive tree, and Nadine could see the sandy hills through gaps left by the fleeing plumage. An instant later another shot rang and one of the gray dots careened toward them. She closed her eyes again.

"*Allahu Akbar*! Nadine, come see!"

She'd never seen her father as excited as he was today. He didn't allow her to come on these hunting trips—"Wait until you're Nissrine's age," he'd say. "But Daddy, how can I be Nissrine's age? She'll always be four years older," she'd say and he'd laugh. She never understood why. But today her father had made an exception. Today was special.

"What're you girls waiting for?" he yelled again. "Nissrine, bring your sister! We got a big one!"

Nissrine's hand wrapped around hers and they ran across the woods into the clearing where their father stood, rifle propped on his foot, broad smile across his face. "Wait until you see this," he said as they breathlessly made their way to him. "Tariq! More to the left, where that clump of trees is! Yes, yes over there!" he yelled. A moment later the boy ran toward him, cradling the bird in his arms. The three of them huddled around him and watched as blood squirted from a hole singed into the quail's chest, tingeing its gray feathers a violent red.

"Does it hurt, Baba Maurice?" she said.

"No, it's over. Tariq got it clean through the heart."

The boy looked up at him then placed the first kill of the day in the sash bag on the grass by Maurice's feet. "Your turn, Nissrine," said Maurice. "The flock perched back over there." He pointed at the treetop under which they stood a moment earlier, where she had closed her eyes. She was only allowed to watch, but her sister, who had been her father's only hunting companion, had recently earned her own rifle. Nadine admired her sister's handling of the heavy weapon with the precision of a sharpshooter, much more becoming than the air gun Nissrine had until just last week.

Nissrine released Nadine's hand and lifted the weapon to her eye. Both girls wore red veils today. The color of blood, of Little Red Riding Hood, the complement of green, easiest to spot amidst the foliage, her mother Zeinab had insisted. Her sister squinted, her nose cocked to one side, her incisors piercing through her lips. Nadine watched, trying hard not to close her eyes as her sister's shoulder recoiled and the bullet hit its mark in the midst of the upper branches of the tree. The birds flew out then Nissrine fired again, clipping one of the birds in the wing. Its flight trajectory faltered then it free-fell onto the earth with a thud.

The boy ran after it, but then it hopped up again and landed a few meters away from him. The girls watched as he chased after the bird, and finally dove on top of it, his outstretched arms trapping it in a makeshift cage. He lifted the prey above his head like a trophy, and then ran back toward them.

The bird was only injured, still very much alive in the boy's hands. Maurice took it from the boy and stroked its tiny head, then handed it to Nadine. The bird's body felt warm against her skin, its bones jutting through the broken wing.

"Just hold it," said the boy. "Don't let it fly away."

"It can't fly," said Nissrine. "Its wing's shattered." Her sister took the bird from her and squeezed it against her chest in a tender embrace. Nissrine squeezed the bird tighter, coiling her hand against its neck. Tighter, tighter she hugged the bird, tighter until Nadine heard its neck snap and watched the wings flop against its body. Nissrine walked over to the bag and tossed the lifeless bird in with the other. "Your turn, Father," she said.

"Alright," he said. "Tariq, you go over to that corner and I'll focus on that other tree over there. Nissrine, look after your sister. Remember to always shoot away from us, alright?"

Maurice and Tariq each ran off in opposite directions while the girls watched from the middle of the clearing. Nissrine propped her rifle against her foot and rubbed the small of her shoulder where she had rested the rifle butt.

"Nissrine, does it hurt?" asked Nadine.

"It's got a bigger kick than my air-gun, but I'll get used to it."

Her sister looked just like a wizard with her long abaya and the rifle like a wizard's wand. She wished she could be like her someday. So strong, so fearless. She leaned against Nissrine and hugged her waist, her hand falling against the neck of the rifle.

On either side of them, across the clearing, her father and the boy each inspected their areas, looking for new prey. The birds had been alerted to their presence here, her sister explained, so now they had to spread out into a wider circle.

"Why is it so hot?" said Nadine, indicating the muzzle of the rifle.

Nissrine released herself, cocked the rifle open, and pulled out the spent cartridges. A burning smell filled Nadine's nostrils as her sister held out the pair of cartridges and plopped them in her hand.

"See these?" she said. "Inside are pellets of gunpowder. Explosive stuff, like dynamite. This little piece of metal is called a lever. It hits the cartridge here on that little gold circle, and the powder goes boom! Shoots the bullet at the speed of sound. Very, very fast."

Nissrine reached into the pouch at their feet and pulled out two fresh cartridges. "You just load them here, two by two into these openings, then crack!" She swung the rifle shut. "The rifle is loaded and ready to shoot."

"Tariq! Anything on your end?" yelled Maurice from a distance.

"Nothing here! I'll check that tree over there," echoed the boy from the other side.

"Where is Noblatee?" asked Nadine. "Dad said that boy lives there."

Nissrine laughed. "Nabatieh, Nadine. It's called Na-ba-ti-eh. It's a town in Lebanon, the country next door. Tariq's visiting us from there."

"How long will he stay?"

"Father says many weeks."

"Is he Dad's friend? But he's just a kid like us."

"He's fourteen, I think, one year younger than me," said her sister as she watched the boy tap another tree with a stick. "He's the son of Dad's friend from when he worked there. It was before you were born."

"He's strong, like you."

"You think so?" her sister said, then she pulled Nadine against her, kissing the top of her head. The rifle jutted into Nadine's chest and she recoiled.

"Don't be afraid," said Nissrene. "I have the safety on, see?" She brought it up and aimed at a spot ahead of them. She pressed the trigger but it just clicked lifelessly. "As long as you have the

412

safety latch on, nothing will happen."

Nissrine ran her hand up and down the length of the barrel. It was beautiful. Safe now, a harmless toy. Like a friend. Nadine loved that and it made her feel safe. But one flip of the latch and it would become a deadly weapon.

"Can I try touching it?" she whispered. Her father would never let her, but maybe Nissrine would. Just a touch.

To her surprise, her sister clicked the safety lever again, off then on, made sure it was secure and passed the rifle to her. Nadine's outstretched hands dipped under the weight, but it was lighter than she thought. Wow. She felt powerful, like the world was hers, like nothing or no one could harm her.

"Okay," said her sister. "This notch is your sight." Then she pointed to a clump of rocks a few meters away. "Point it there. That's right." Nissrine slid behind her and adjusted her shoulders until she could see the notch line up along the length of the barrel with the rocks. "Perfect. Now if that were a bird, you'd get it with a single shot."

Wow, a single shot. Aiming at rocks didn't feel as bad. Rocks don't bleed.

"Can I try?" asked Nadine. "Can I shoot the rocks?"

Nissrine released her shoulders and swung in front of her. "No," she said but then added, "Aim for something farther. These are too easy." Nadine put the rifle to her eye again and focused. She felt the heft of the weapon bore into her bones with a dull ache. The butt quivered in her hand as she felt her palms grow sweaty.

Bang!

Startled, she dropped the rifle to her thigh.

Nissrine laughed. "Don't worry! It's not you!" she said, and sure enough she heard her father's voice come through the distance to her left.

"I missed," he shouted. "No birds here, Tariq!"

The boy had disappeared into the growth of trees to their right, deeper into his own search.

"When you hear it," said Nissrine, "that means it's not your rifle. Like thunder. The bang means it's far away. Here, try again. It's safe."

Nadine brought the rifle back to her eye and scanned the horizon across the clearing. The hillside, then the trees, then more trees, thicker now, scrolled through her sights. Nissrine gripped her shoulders again and gently swiveled her around, guiding the rifle as it swept across. "Aim for that tree over there," she said pointing the rifle in the direction of the growth to their right. Nadine felt at one with the weapon, and her entire body rotated under her sister's guidance.

Nadine's right hand slid down the length of the rifle and her finger fell naturally into the loop of the trigger, coming to a rest within its curve. "There," said Nissrine. "The tree is in your sights. Now just close your eyes and imagine releasing the trigger."

Nadine squeezed her eyes shut, and in the blackness felt her sister's grasp tighten around her shoulders. In her mind, she saw the tree bark lined up with the neck of the rifle, dead center within her sights.

This time, she didn't hear a bang. She just felt the violent recoil burst through her shoulder as she flew back and landed on the grass. An instant later, the shot echoed back to her ears. Again the burning smell, now intense, punched through her nose as she opened her eyes, burning with the sting of gunpowder. Then came the sound from a distance, first just a whimper, then a groan, then a scream. She dropped the rifle as Nissrine screeched "Oh my God! Oh my God! Oh my God!"

"Oh my God!" echoed Maurice from the other side. An

414

instant later he was behind her, the rifle in his grip. "What have you done? Oh my God! No, no!" Rifle in tow, he sprinted toward the clump of trees to their right, where she had aimed and disappeared into the foliage. Nissrine ran after him.

The bloodied bird tore back into Nadine's mind as she ran ahead, several meters behind her sister. Its bloodstained wings, its twitching body, the hole in its chest flooded her senses.

She squeezed through the branches into the outgrowth and found her sister and father crouched above the boy. He hugged his knee, leg folded toward him and cried. Blood spurted out of the tip of his shoe, soaking into a red puddle on the grass under it, and his wooden stick lay by his side, drenched in red muck. The boy cried with pain as Maurice knelt above him and touched the bleeding foot. She looked at Nissrine, but her sister just gazed back at her emptily.

Maurice's words sounded like nonsense to her. Meaningless. "My boy!" he said. "My poor, poor boy. *Habibi, habibi. Ya Allah*, what have you—my God!"

Whatever he did mean that day, Nadine couldn't fathom. But many years later, the gunpowder would sear through her memories, scorching them with her father's choked cries.

"What have you done, Nadine? Oh God, what did you do to my son?"

19

Antithesis

I take a timid step toward the house of Maurice Akkad and tap at the door.

Nothing.

Once more, harder this time. Knock, knock, knock. Again, nothing.

I lay my cheek against the wood. Nothing. I pace back. The wall outside is bare. No name. No doorbell. Nothing, nothing, nothing. An opaque white surface.

I retreat and stare at it until my eyes ache. I squint through the vent slits along the right window. Careful to stay on the path, trying not to fall onto the lawn or brush my forehead against the shutters. The light changes through some of them. A shadow perhaps?

I take a breath and step toward the entrance, raising my hand to knock a third time. But instead, the door creaks open.

Through a gap in the doorway, a pair of hooded dark eyes peeks out from a sea of black. Framed by a dark abaya like an epic letter-boxed movie (I instantly imagine Peter O'Toole on camelback crossing a strip of desert and sky), it's a startled stare marked by fifty-odd years.

"Yes," says a voice muffled behind the veil.

"Madame Akkad," I say. "Good morning. I was wondering if

I could have a word with your husband."

"Who are you?"

Good question. Where do I start? "I'm a college professor. A dendrologist." Even I think, *So*?

"No," she says and the gap separating us narrows to a sliver. The crowfeet around her eyes cut deeper into her skin with a familiar edge, and I find it hard to imagine that one day Nadine's eyes will age into the hardened stare that leers back at me.

I try a different approach. "I spoke to the Imam from Al-Moqbil," I say, fighting the urge to hold the door open. "He led me here," I add, my hands gripping my pockets tightly.

The crack widens, but just enough to poke her hooded head through it to look around. "Well then, he should've come with you." She pulls the door toward her adding, "I'm sorry sir, my husband's not seeing anyone today."

That's it, I hold the door and blurt out the word I've been avoiding, "Nadine."

"Huh?" Her grip loosens, but I don't push.

"It's about Nadine," I add softly.

She holds her palm to her chest, and for the first time I catch a glimpse of her upper body, all covered in black. "*Auzu billah. Oh my God. Is my daughter okay?*"

Her daughter, she says. So I'm definitely in the right place. The door is loose now, but I take a step back to avoid scaring her. "Yes, of course. She's fine." Never lie more than you need to. "I teach at her school in Beirut."

The door finally creaks all the way open and the woman slides inside. I suppose if custom didn't prevent it, she'd drag me right in. Her eyes smile and she says, "*Mashallah. Mashallah.* Yes, that's my daughter. She studies in Beirut."

Her parental pride gushes through as the door swings wide open, and I step into Maurice Akkad's home.

◆

We stand in the *dar*, the main living space of the house. It's furnished with years upon years of objects, all antiquated, some perhaps a decade old, most much more ancient. A tapestry scripted with the *Kursi* verse from the Koran covers the main wall, and on each of the tables sit brass, wood, and copper trinkets from all over Greater Syria. Busy, but tasteful, in stark contrast to the pale exterior. This was once a rich family, now living in sentimental poverty amidst years of relics. ("…And sometimes she does them in iron that goes around like a swirl…" continues the mother's rattle about her daughter's metallurgical work.)

Blatantly missing from this visual cacophony, however, are photographs. This is a conspicuously private family that recognizes the *dar* as a somewhat public space. ("…I didn't want to send her to Beirut, but the things she brings back with her. Those rings, those bracelets, you should see them. But what am I saying? Her professor would know!") Or maybe there's more to it. Maybe this is not such a loving family, as Nadine painted it. Either way, the only human feature in the room besides my own is the sliver of eyes beaming back at me through a veil fluttering with excited proclamations about the wonders of Nadine's jewelry. It soon turns into white noise, but I allow it to play its course as we stand there.

("…Those on the table over there: she made them during her first week. Can you believe it? I can't. She didn't even do jewelry back then, and…") I notice a glass door leading to the exterior. Every house should have a garden. But from where I stand, only an olive branch is visible, but then as I inch closer I spot another species: a single Acacia branch peeks through the open doorway, and under it, a pair of seated legs.

Maurice.

("...And sometimes she just makes things for fun. I don't know how in God's name she makes all those things.")

"Can I see him now?" I ask. Those five words are all I manage during a brief pause in her outpouring.

"Oh yes... of course," she says. "But he hasn't spoken for days. That's the honest-to-God truth." She gestures toward the open glass door and I make my way toward it as she trails behind me.

The garden is modest, fenced in from the olive trees, taking out a good chunk of the land. I understand that it's Maurice's only recluse from the world, maybe even from the house itself. He leans back in a wooden chair under the Acacia tree, a different species from the one I've worked with. It's more mature, its needles softer, more pronounced, a darker shade of brown. And Maurice himself is a different type of man than Tariq, not just older, but more... grounded. He's about fifty-five, yet he could be forty from the thickness of his hair and his undisturbed skin, or a hundred from the grave silence with which he occupies that corner of his world.

He seems like a fixture in the garden amidst the earthy tones of the tree behind him: his khaki suit and tie, white shirt and black leather shoes are as much a part of the landscape as they are of his own body. I take a few steps toward him and he continues to look blankly in my general direction. Unsure if he even sees me, I stop as the woman behind me leans over my shoulder. "The *Istez* here is a university teacher from Beirut," she says awkwardly, but it's as good an introduction as any I could have mustered. "He's come to talk about Nadine."

Maurice lifts a firm finger and points right at me. I'm startled, but then he wags it in the direction of a pair of chairs. They're metal and rickety, which confirms that the man neither expects nor appreciates visitors. I make my way toward the one farthest from him as his wife nods and turns back into the *dar*.

A moment later, I hear a distant click, and as I sit down the woman's words come from inside the house, "Ah, she's back." Then in a shrill voice, which registers as distinct annoyance on the man's face, she yells "*Ya* Nissrine!"

Maurice's blank stare doesn't change, yet I can tell now that my presence does register with him because his jaw tightens. I should be the one to speak first, but I should arm myself with tact. Beating around the bush isn't always a bad thing when I'm the beater, so I give it my best whack. "Sir, I've come from Beirut," I say. "I'm here to speak to you about your daughter Nadine. I've wanted to speak to you for days now, but didn't know how to find you. I—"

He raises his hand and I stop. I look up as a younger woman walks in carrying a tray of tea. She too is wearing a full abaya, but the sway of her hips and the slender motion of her limbs hint at a less hardened body beneath the black surface. She moves past me and places the tray on the table between us. Then she leans forward, picks up a glass, and places it in front of me without looking up. The top of her head remains far from her body, but I notice her delicate ivory fingers. The nails on the left shine with red manicure, while the others remain bare, their pink cuticles glistening with cream—except for the index finger, which is wrapped in a fresh Band-Aid just like mine.

She turns to Maurice and slides his tea in front of him, then plops in a sugar cube and stirs it. I watch it break down and dissolve. Force of habit. She then slides behind Maurice as I watch her silently and props her chin onto the top of his head, her hooded veil obscuring most of her upper face.

"*Habibi Baba*," she says gripping his temples with her asymmetrical hands and laying a kiss on his forehead. "I'm back. You'll be fine now."

Maurice taps her hand with his own and says, "*Yislamo*

421

dayyetik. God bless those hands." She releases him and soundlessly takes her leave.

Maurice takes a sip of tea, and when he lowers his glass I continue, "Well sir, as I was—"

Maurice raises his hand again. I look up expecting someone else to have walked in, but it's just us, Maurice and me.

He sets his glass down and says, "Enough."

"Mr. Akkad, I—"

"My wife Zeinab believes anything. School nonsense isn't why you're here."

I was wrong. This man is like me. Enough small talk. "You're right," I say. "School nonsense isn't why I'm here. But the matter does concern Nadine."

Maurice leans forward, his patience running out. "Who are you and what do you want?" he says.

My back stiffens and I bring my eyes level with his. "I'm from Nabatieh," I say. "My name is Mohamad Taha."

◆

I'm not sure how long the silence lasts. An eternity or an instant. The sun breaks through the clouds across Maurice's face. In it I see Tariq Jaber again, a young man of twenty-one.

"What I want, sir, is to learn about your son," I say.

Maurice straightens, gazing at a point above my head. His lips have lost their firmness, but his eyes remain dark and distant. "Tariq is dead," he says.

I rest my elbows on my knees and hunch toward him, my hands clasped together like a saint in prayer. "I was there."

Maurice's body tightens. His eyes are fixed on me, but behind them his mind's eye seems cast into another place and time. Now every word I say matters. "I was on the side of the road when it happened. I got to the bus just a few seconds later. He was on his last breath. But he said something, just a few words, which led me to you."

Maurice looks down and says, "He was on his way here."

"And I believe Doreid Fattal was too. They were traveling together, did you know that?"

His teeth clench, but then he breaths in and bellows. "Zeinab! Come here."

It's over. He's throwing me out, I'm sure of it. All for nothing.

Maurice's wife hurries out, the veil swaying to reveal a small stretch of skin along her arm, white as a blanket. "Close the door and sit down," Maurice says. I'm not sure what to expect; I just watch her sheepishly as she clicks the door shut and takes the other empty chair between Maurice and me. He leans into the triangle between us and speaks in a hushed tone.

"Zeinab, this man is from Nabatieh," he says, nodding blankly in my direction.

I turn to her and choose my words carefully. "On November sixteenth, a bus bound from Beirut to Damascus was ambushed. A Lebanese politician was on board."

Zeinab glances at Maurice, whose face remains empty of all emotion. "Yes," she says, catching on. "The man worked with my husband, many years ago in a mining company."

"That job in Nabatieh went terribly wrong," I say.

Maurice stares ahead absently, beyond our geometry. Now it's just two, Zeinab and I. She glances at Maurice, but he ignores her.

"Back then, Fattal wasn't yet a politician, just a man, a kind man," she says. "They were friends and coworkers, Maurice and he. Engineers. After the mine exploded, Maurice escaped with only the skin on his back. Doreid offered to help keep us afloat. Again and again, over the years, he sent us money from

Lebanon, but my husband refused it every time, and he never looked back."

"Except Maurice did look back," I say. "He left a wife and son behind."

After a silence, Zeinab turns to Maurice. "Is this true?" she asks, but he says nothing.

"Yes, it is," I answer in his stead. "After the accident, he married Balkees, the widow of the man who died in the mine."

"How do you know all this?" asks Zeinab, her voice wavering between anger and confusion, her face barely visible behind the veil.

"I learned a lot over the past few days," I say. "Your husband had to keep his second wife and son a secret to preserve the peace between your families."

Zeinab submits to my apparent omniscience. I'm the shadowy professor from Nabatieh and Beirut who knows the ins and outs of their lives. She refrains from questioning this strange reality further, so I continue. "I'm here today because the boy, your husband's son, died on that bus with Fattal."

Zeinab palms the veil to her face, but her eyes remain focused, a testament to her solemnity. Instead of the gushing woman from just a few moments ago, now sits a stoic matriarch who, against all odds, has wound herself tightly around this family, securing it like a bundle of sticks.

"When my first husband Mahdi, God rest his soul, passed away," she says, "Doreid Fattal paid us a visit. It was a very difficult time, you see. The Akkads and my parents were the most bitter enemies. We only had a daughter, but no son to keep the peace."

"So, Nissrine there. That's Mahdi's and your daughter."

"Yes, but Maurice raised her as his own. He loved his brother, and he loves her. We got married and moved here to Damascus.

Then little Nadine was born to both of us. She's the jewel of our lives, but one more girl made matters impossible between our two families. We lost everything, and with Maurice out of a job, we had no money."

"But there was someone else," I press on. "You called your wife out here. Tell her."

"It's true," he says. "The Jabers." His voice is now so hushed that I have to lean onto the edge of my chair to hear him. "Fattal was head of the excavation project. Mahmoud Jaber had hired our company to dig deeper into the mines. And there in Nabatieh, one day, I met his wife Balkees. But then the tragedy struck."

"Was it a tragedy? Or a blessing?"

"Both. The mine explosion was both. Doreid made a mistake and it took the life of Mahmoud Jaber. Many other people were injured too. It was a problem for the company, but the insurance people buried it fast. Still, someone had to take the fall. And it was me."

"Why did you do that?" she asks.

"I had to. I lived in constant fear for my family, if the Jabers ever knew the truth about Balkees and me, and about our son Tariq."

"Maurice, what did Doreid Fattal have on you?" asks Zeinab. I watch both their faces as the interrogation takes its course.

"That's not how things worked back then. We had worked together for many years and after my brother Mahdi passed away, Fattal helped me get by. We became close friends. We were friends. We did each other favors. We each had our priorities in life, and mine led me elsewhere."

Zeinab falls silent.

"Doreid Fattal threatened you," I say. "You were with Balkees when the mine exploded. She was your alibi. That's what Fattal had on you. And she was already pregnant with your son."

I look up at Zeinab, but her eyes are fixed on her husband. And in them I see a love born not from the folly of youth but from years of companionship. Pick your battles, they say. Choose when to fight and when to hold back. No one knows that more than a mother. In a storm, a tree leans away from the wind, to shelter its newborn buds. Zeinab must know that too; I can see it in her now. She does not recoil, but instead rises from her chair and takes her place a few steps behind her husband, pressing her palms into his shoulders.

"I saw the tree crashing down the hillside," he says. "Somehow Mahmoud Jaber found out about Balkees and me and chopped it down. I feared she was next, so I went to her."

"And he went after you, to the mine rigged with explosives," I say.

"Yes, but I had already gone to her. And forty days after he died, Balkees and I were married," he says. "Only a handful of people knew. The Sheikh and two witnesses, our friends. One was a farmer who used to come here to sell his crop."

"Ibrahim," I say.

"He was our go-between for the remainder of Balkees' life. And then there was—"

"Fattal," I say. "He was no friend of yours. The day he died he was on his way here to make you an offer. What was it?"

"I had only seen my son four times," says Maurice bitterly. "That's it. One day when the boy was fourteen I brought him back here. I thought I'd tell Zeinab and the girls back then, maybe even have him stay with us. For his own good. 'I'll be fine with Tarboush,' Balkees said."

"The cat," I say, and smile in spite of myself.

"But we had an accident," continues Maurice. "We went hunting and his foot damn near got shot off. An Armenian

426

doctor worked a miracle to save it, leaving him with a second toe that bent crookedly onto the first," continues Maurice. "Not crooked. 'Wicked,' he said. It was a sign from God that even if his mother had wished it, the boy shouldn't stay here with us. Not for a week, not for a day. So I took him back to her. And when Fattal called me last week after many years, he said he had my son, that he would bring him to me. He came to sell me my own son."

"In return for what? What did you have in exchange?"

"The Mahmoud Jaber fortune. Tariq didn't know, but Fattal had a copy of the marriage certificate in his briefcase. He held onto it for years, as a bargaining chip. In return for my Tariq, he demanded I sign a statement declaring him my son. The two documents combined would entitle the Jabers to their inheritance. Fattal was a politician. He was hungry for power, but I just wanted my son."

"Do the girls know about this?" asks Zeinab.

"Only Nadine does," says Maurice. "She called me yesterday with questions, so I told her. And you know what our sweet daughter said? 'Don't worry, Father. I'll make it better. We'll get you Tarboush.'"

He wipes his hand across his mouth and adds, "So she sent me the cat. He's all that's left of Balkees and Tariq."

"No, he's not," I say. "There's something I should give you." "What's that?" asks Maurice.

I glance toward Zeinab, who nods in support. Reaching into my pocket I pull out the photograph of Tariq and Balkees and place it into his hand. "A *kaffara*," I say.

Maurice's lips tremble into a smile.

◆

427

As the door to the Akkad house closes behind me, I step down the stone path. I'm tired but relieved. In the end, perhaps I found what I came for: Tariq Jaber's true birthright. As for his death, maybe we'll never learn what happened—no matter what those people on TV say.

The olive grove stretches between me and the mosque, its dome now a darker shade of blue. The sun has fallen behind the house and I find myself in its shadow. I wrap my jacket between my chest and the cold wind.

"Professor," says a soft voice.

Nadine? Where is she? Only the empty lawn stretches to my right and behind me stands the closed door of the house.

On my left, behind the white stone wall, a black hemline drapes the grass. From under it two big white sneakers, very much at odds with the rest of the attire, poke out. I step onto the lawn, careful not to disturb it, and there in the shadow, on a bench, sits the young woman. Next to her, a pouch of makeup lies open, with a compact mirror and a bottle of red nail polish.

"Nissrine," I say to the top of her veiled head.

"Don't come back to this house," she says, looking up at me with a pair of onyx eyes. "Ever."

She must have pulled her veil down to do her makeup. It hangs carelessly across the back of her head. Her creamy hands, all ten nails now painted red, glisten starkly against the black of her abaya. The Band-Aid remains, the only blemish on her translucent skin.

"What happened to your finger?" I ask.

"Nothing."

"I cut mine on some glass, see?" I say, raising my palm as I approach her.

"*Salamtak*," she says. She folds her arms in her lap, hiding her finger in the crease of her elbow.

428

Something brushes against my feet, and when I look down, Tarboush the cat coos and purrs. As Nissrine recoils from me, her abaya sleeve hitches up her wrist, pockmarked with tens of small red dots. I sit down next to her anyway, shoulder to shoulder, with only the makeup bag between us. She slides her pelvis along the bench until she's at its very edge.

"Show it to me," I say looking straight at her.

"No."

"It might be infected."

"*Haram*, it's forbidden. You're not a doctor."

"I'm the son of a doctor," I say.

"The son of a doctor is no doctor."

"I'm a PhD."

"That's just letters."

"Okay, I won't touch you," I say, lifting my hand toward hers. "But you're a nurse, so you can touch me. That's allowed, right?"

Much to my disbelief, that logic somehow agrees with her. She picks up my hand, first hesitantly, then more firmly, and lays it on hers. As I inch my fingers down the fabric of her abaya sleeve, she brushes her wrist against my fingertips, allowing them to curl around it as her pulse beats against my thumb. With my hand now gently clasping her wrist, she lifts it onto her lap. She then turns her palm and curls her fingers upwards. Finally, she rotates her hips, bringing our hands closer to my knee, and moving the rest of her body further away.

I study my face in her eyes. "Nissrine, I'm peeling off the Band-Aid."

She nods silently, and I tug at its tip. It sticks stubbornly, but she slowly tugs her hand away until the Band-Aid unfurls around her finger. I roll it between my fingers, and place it into the makeup pouch. It has left two grimy lines around her swollen fingertip, and between them, from the center of the dark pink skin, is a small, green, protruding dot.

"Got a safety pin in that pouch?"

"Yes," she says timidly.

I fumble through her pouch with my loose hand, and pull out a safety pin and a pack of cotton pads. I take one out and lay it on her knee, then take another and lay it on my own.

"Don't worry," I say. "I pull out splinters every day."

I pop the safety pin open, take out Nancy's lighter from my pocket, flip it to High, and burn the tip of the needle until it turns a bright orange.

"This will hurt."

"Go ahead," she says, her breath tickling the top of my ear.

Keeping her hand supported on her knee, I prick the pink mound of her fingertip. She winces against my ear, but doesn't move as I maneuver the needle and squeeze. The splinter head pokes out, and I extract the rest of it with the edges of my thumbnails. A fresh drop of blood rolls off Nissrine's finger and lands on the cotton pad on her knee.

"Wrap that around the wound," I say.

She does, gripping her finger tightly with her other hand as the crimson spreads through the white cotton. I lay the red-tipped splinter onto another cotton pad and take out a small bottle of alcohol from the pouch. She pulls the veil off her chin and raises her finger to her lips.

"No," I say. "Use this." I hand her the alcohol, and as she cleans her wound I look down at the splinter resting on the bed of cotton on my knee.

It's a thorn. An Acacia thorn. My Acacia's sibling's thorn, from that same patch. I've found the needle in the haystack, but unlike my own sickly specimens, this one is green and healthy. It's very much alive, like it continued to grow into Nissrine's finger, feeding on her blood.

As she nurses her finger, I wrap the thorn in the cotton and slip it in my messenger bag. Inside, I feel for my machine and blindly hit the Record button. This will tape over my research notes, but in this moment, I have to pick my battles.

I look at Nissrine's full face for the first time. She's wearing no makeup besides some mascara along the roots of her lashes. Her slanted gaze follows my tiniest movements, like the woman behind it can't quite make up her mind about something. For my part, I struggle with the question of why such a creation must remain hidden behind an opaque veil. Eyes still fixed on me, her lips purse into a pout as she twists the alcohol shut.

It's now I who feels the weight of *haram*, of the forbidden. I drop my eyes to the grass; her white sneakers are so out of place with the rest, three sizes too large.

Her face has turned as blank as the wall behind it. Her lips part, the very lips I now realize I've seen somewhere before, painted with gloss, just a few hours ago.

"It's you," I say, snapping back up. "It was you, at the jazz club with Tariq. Your face in the photograph. Your ring. Your sister's first ring. She gave it to you."

"And it was you, by the bus."

"Two nights ago, someone was watching me at the university," I say. "That was you too."

"Yes."

"Why did you run?"

"Because you followed me."

"But Nissrine, Tariq was your brother."

"My cousin," she says. "Or my stepbrother. Whichever way you look at it, we're from different parents. Growing up, I put it together on my own, from bits and pieces I overheard from *Baba* Maurice. As a child, I despised the idea of Tariq, but circumstance brought us together as adults. And everything changed."

431

"How could you know it was him? How could you be so sure that you bet his life on it?"

"A hunting injury," she says. "Years ago *Baba* Maurice brought him here. There was an accident. Nadine pulled the trigger. Maybe the safety latch was on, maybe it wasn't. When Baba Maurice kneeled over Tariq that day, I saw it in his face and heard it in his words. That boy was his son. Then Tariq found my sister in Beirut, and I found him through her. He was Tony, a man, much changed from the child we almost killed. But when we were alone, I saw his Wicked Toe twisted against the others; I knew he was the same person."

"So all the trips to Beirut," I say. "Nadine mentioned something about you applying to nursing school. That was all a lie."

"Nadine never lies," she says. "And neither do I."

"Did Tariq know who you are? *What* you are?"

"He hid from me, so I hid from him. He was Tony, and I became another woman, with another name. If he'd ever asked who I was, I would have told him. But he didn't until the very end, on that bus, when Fattal recognized me. If the bus had ever gotten to Damascus, it would've spelled the death of my family."

"Other people died that day."

"There were eight people on that bus," says Nissrine. "One of them an unborn child."

"And they mean nothing?"

"They're my burden to bear. Mine alone, for the rest of my life. But it was either them or my family. I was only after Tariq. He should never have gotten on that bus, but he was pigheaded and selfish. He wanted to meet his father. He was blind to everything else. To all of us. His very being on this earth would've torn my parents' tribes apart. Forever. We still have a chance at peace, at a better future for Nadine, but Tariq's arrival here would've killed it. And then he would've led his nasty uncles from Nabatieh straight to our doorstep, with their thirst for revenge and money. I couldn't let my mother's house, the family she gave her life to build, be destroyed in one day."

"You were with him that morning, weren't you? His apartment was spotless, except for a carton of milk, which he'd never have left out because it makes his cat sick. You cleaned up after he left, hiding every trace of yourself. But the fact that you left no trace behind was itself a trace. You failed to mention that if Tariq had come to this house, he would've found out about you. What really made you get on that bus, Nissrine?"

"Love did," she says, her hand clenched around her knee.

I remember my father's favorite words, "First do no harm," says the Hippocratic oath taken by doctors. They also govern the profession of Nursing. Not a spiritual promise, but a purely pragmatic one. Those who require care must receive it. Nissrine must know that too.

"That's not love," I say. "Love is good. What you did was—"

"Evil?" says Nissrine. "'I've never killed anyone.' People say that every day, like that's what it takes to be decent. They don't see that decency isn't measured by what we do, but what we don't do."

I look away.

"I know you more than you think," she says. "When Nadine stepped into your house, it was as if I walked in behind her. And when Tariq watched you, my eyes were on you too. Tell me, Professor, when did you last call up your best friend from high school just to say hello? Or return things you've borrowed before their owner asks for them? Or clean the trash out of your car before selling it? Or, instead of empty words like 'please' and 'thank you' do something for someone in return? And what about not cutting people out of your life when you have no more use for them? Or realizing that when a person asks you for a favor it's not the first thing they thought of doing but the very last choice they had? Or realizing that when someone says 'it was no problem' it doesn't mean you can ask them again and again and again without giving anything back? Or knowing that, besides your parents, no one will ever care about you more than you and that the last thing you should do is bash people over the head with what you think life owes you? And how about believing the only truth is the one you feel in your heart? Instead you choose a life of platitudes. While you busy yourself with not doing evil, you do no good."

A heavy calm descends upon us as the olive trees stand still. "Do no harm" hangs in the back of my mind like a withered leaf, and another oath creeps into place, "Do good."

"Your mother knows about Tariq. Maurice just told her. The secret is out, and somehow the two families will have to live with it."

She searches my face for traces of a lie, but finds none. "It doesn't matter anymore," she says. "That secret is worth nothing with Tariq dead. Not to his family and not to mine. But it's worth something to me."

Nissrine brings her hands to her belly and breaks the silence. "After Tariq died, I couldn't get the taste of iron out of my mouth. He left something of himself inside me. In Beirut I wanted to pluck it out like you did that thorn, but I couldn't take another life. I have the last piece of my dead father and of Tartous. Far from this place, I'll bear the son my mother never had. And both families will take him into their arms. Maybe not tomorrow, but soon. That day will come."

"Nissrine, are you innocent or guilty?"

"It's all relative, Professor."

Nissrine pulls the veil over her forehead, casts her black eyes upon me for the last time and cradles the cat back into the house.

◆

On the drive back to Beirut, I dream of the nurse in black and of her underground well of desire. I've known that longing, and I know that it doesn't last. When its subject dies, it dies with it. Not instantly, but soon enough, it withers into nothing. Maurice knew it, and soon Nissrine will discover it too. What remains is regret, the one emotion that multiplies with time, immune to the patience that ran through the Akkad bloodline from father to daughter. That's her future, an ocean of regret.

The taxi takes me deeper into the dream. She enters Beirut with one wish: to keep her stepfather safe in his ignorance. She's driven by a hypothetical love she never received. But what she finds is Tariq Jaber, reborn as Tony, masquerading as her sister's platonic friend. How does she know it's him? She doesn't. Not yet. Just a subterranean hunch.

She tries to set the hunch aside, but again and again it returns to her with increasing force. First a tickle, then a flutter of the heart, then a dull pain in her head, then the full force of a sharp desire. She must find out. This man is in her sister's life, which means he's *in* her life. Now he's still in Beirut, but soon he'll find Damascus. He must be stopped.

But first, she must know it's him.

She could just ask him. No scheming, just flat out ask him, "Are you perchance Tariq, my lost half-brother, apple of my stepfather's eye, usurper of all his love, of everything he should've been to me?"

No, that wouldn't work.

She must get into his house. She must search through the drawers of his life, who he is and who he was. She must become his friend and gain access to his home and play his video games.

But he never leaves her alone. If he does have anything, any secrets, then they're all safely tucked into his drawers and closets, or perhaps in the one room she's not yet seen: the bedroom.

Nadine's key. Her sister is out with him right now. She pulls it from its hiding place. She's inside the apartment again, but this time she's alone. In the living room, in the kitchen, anything that's closed she opens and looks inside. Closets, cupboards, drawers. She finds nothing but more video games and notebooks. Then she remembers the bedroom.

She steps inside, goes through the wardrobe first (sneakers, many, many pairs of sneakers), and she finds the photograph on the nightstand. She kneels for a closer look. Tariq and Balkees. It must be him. But she has to be sure. Then she sees something else: a metal case under his bed. She pulls it out, opens it. A beautiful, brand new Kalashnikov lies inside.

Across the living room behind her, the apartment door clicks, keys jangle. She must get out. She wishes she were in a movie where the camera would cut to a shot of the door opening and then back to the empty bedroom with her gone. But she only has time to crawl halfway across the living room before Tariq is there, standing right above her. She's on her knees, hair falling out of her veil, bedroom door wide open behind her, afternoon light streaming through the living room window, casting her culpable face in his shadow.

But guilt is not what she feels. Nor shame or fear. His ankles are a few inches from her face and she cannot look up. And then she recognizes the feeling: it's exhilaration. This is an utterly new sensation, but she knows what must happen now.

She holds up the key. "I had to get in," she says, eyes fixed on his shoes. "I had to see you."

Tariq leans down and takes her hand, tucks his arm under

her shoulder, and cradles her into the bedroom.

As he lies naked on top of her, the weight of his pelvis almost crushing hers, she tilts her head up for a view of his right foot. The Wicked Toe. It's him.

But by then the body on top of hers quivers as Nissrine and her step-brother climax violently.

I wake up as the taxi cuts through the moonlit Geitawi street and my apartment building looms into view. I cast my heavy eyes through its windshield at my lit window three floors above.

The taxi comes to a gentle stop outside the entrance and I step out. Babooshka (though I should probably call him Bashar, after all we've been through) leans out of his window and I pay him the rest of his fare. We exchange thanks as I slip my hands into my jacket pockets against the brisk night air and watch the taxi disappear up the road.

On the third floor, I reach for my key and before I insert it in the door, it opens to Nancy in the dim doorway. She rises to the tips of her toes and falls into my embrace. Keys in one hand and tape recorder in the other, I wrap my arms tightly around her waist and rest my face against her breast.

"It's gone," I say. "I taped over all my work. It's all gone." All weariness drains from my eyes. Nancy's chest moistens as she runs her fingers through my hair.

20
Possibly Definite

On the morning of November 16th, Nissrine awoke from a bad dream.

The man she had spent the night with wasn't beside her, but she could hear his voice from the next room. Over her shoulder she saw his shirt next to her on the bed, and through the doorway his naked back as he paced in and out of view.

She was already too late.

◆

She lifted her head and was instantly hit with a dull pain. Last night she had thought she had handled her drink quite well for a beginner. But now she barely caught snippets of the voice in the other room. She twirled her ring around her finger as she cocked her ear upwards. "Thanks *Ammo*..." he said. "Yes I understand... I'll see you on board... Delete, yes of course..."

The iron aftertaste of red wine sliced through her head like a crown of thorns, and the murmur of running water filtered into the dusky bedroom as she sat up and slipped into his shirt. She wondered what could have set his day in motion as early as—she glanced at the alarm clock—ten-to-five in the morning.

By the clock, the faded picture stood in its golden frame. She always hated that frame, since that first night in his bedroom six weeks ago. Back in Tartous, her next-door neighbor always bragged about her first experience, how it felt like her insides were being ripped apart. But that night she had felt none of that as she lay under him. That had been something much worse: the pain of scorn, the agony of that woman's stare, that woman in the wheelchair, her eyes stabbing straight into her soul.

She reached for the photo and turned it toward the doorway until she could only see the wedge propping it up. She picked her panties off the floor and slipped them on under the long shirt. Its silk felt good against her, his scent of man and cigarettes still lingering onto the fabric.

But then he walked in, and before she looked up at his face she knew the dreaded day was upon her. He adjusted his pants with one hand and tapped at his cell phone with another. "Delete," he said as it beeped its confirmation. She watched him circle around the bed and pull out a freshly pressed shirt from his closet.

"I have to go somewhere," he said as he put it on and slipped the phone into his pocket. She had a hunch where that somewhere was, but she had to be sure. The cell phone couldn't tell her, even if she found a way to get to it. She had to know from him.

"Where?" she asked.

"I'll be back tonight," he mumbled. She knelt on the bed, and watched him tuck in his shirt. He checked himself in the mirror, quickly but intently. This man was meticulous and messy in equal measures. His bedroom was in shambles, but like his life, somehow everything had its place. She had to know what hers was.

He leaned onto the bed and kissed her, but as he pulled back she gripped his hand and studied his face. She saw nothing.

Perhaps it was the dim light, or perhaps there wasn't anything for her to see. As he pulled away, she gripped tighter and said, "Stay here. Please." He wiggled loose and straightened up. She watched him helplessly as he strode out of the room and tossed the towel on the sofa. "Tarboush! Tarboush!" she heard him singsong the cat's name and wondered if she ever heard him utter her name that way. Not "Nissrine" of course, she could never tell him that. But even her false name would've been good enough if it meant she was the first person he thought of instead of that cat or the other person she feared was the reason he woke up this morning.

She jumped out of bed and walked through the doorway, watching him "Psst, psst, psst," but the feline was nowhere to be found. She couldn't stand that sound, so she picked up the remote and flipped on the TV. A brisk gazelle mutely tried to escape a pack of lions. She fidgeted for the volume button but was distracted by him walking out from the kitchen again.

He brushed past her and put his eye to the white telescope, jotting down a few notes in his notebook. He carried it over to the stack of shelves and lay it there neatly.

He brushed past her again into the bedroom, sat on the edge of the bed, and leaned over his sneakers. As he tied his laces she climbed back on and kneeled behind him, sliding her hands down his chest. "Stay with me today," she said into his ear.

No answer.

As he got up, she pressed her entire weight into her arms. She pressed down on his shoulders so hard his pelvis sank back onto the bed. "Don't go," she said.

"What's wrong with you?" he yelled, twisting toward her. Then he glanced past her to the frame on the side table.

"Did you move this?"

"Yes," she said. "It was staring right at me."

Before she even finished speaking, he had already turned the frame back toward him. Nissrine straddled him. "Come on," she purred. "Stay with me."

"What's gotten into you?" he yelled and as he struggled to get her off of him, he knocked over the alarm clock and both it and the frame crashed to the floor.

He flung her off of him and knelt down. "Goddamn it," he said as he set the frame back in its place, wiping its surface with his thumb. "I told you never to touch it."

Sliding into his blazer, he popped open a drawer and pulled out his keys and passport. He pressed them both into his pocket, and over his shoulder he said, "Please feed the cat before you go." He flashed her a smile, and walked out.

A few seconds later, she heard the main door close behind him.

◆

She sprang off the bed, landing a few inches away from the glass on the carpet and the alarm clock lying on it side. It was frozen at 4:58 a.m. She had to hurry.

She pulled off the shirt without loosening the buttons and tossed it in the open closet. She picked up her bag from the other side and crossed through the living room into the bathroom. On TV, a pack of lions ripped mercilessly into a gazelle, its hind legs twitching under their weight.

A toilet flush and a few seconds later she emerged from the bathroom, a paler mascara-drenched version of herself from the previous night. Her black mini-dress stretched to and fro as she strode across the room. She paced back again, and again, and again, twirling her ring around her finger. The static room dashed past her—the windows, the sofa, the wild animals raced at the speed of a thousand thoughts.

She had no choice.

She tossed her purse on the sofa and slid back into the room. She picked up her stiletto heels by their straps like a pair of kittens and sat down on the edge of the bed where he had just been a minute ago. But she put her shoes on the floor, and crawled across to the closet. She rummaged through it and pulled out a pair of white sneakers. She sat down on the carpet and put those on instead. She then pulled out a long gym bag and crawled over to the other side of the bed. Finally she slid the pile of clothes into the closet and shut it.

Next, the bed. She straightened the pillows, whacked the mattress until all the contours disappeared, and slid the covers on top, tucking in the corners. She pulled the vacuum cleaner from behind the door and flicked it on. She ran it all over the floor, and finally on the bed itself. When Nissrine was sure that it had sucked in all traces of her, every stray strand of hair, she switched it off and tucked it back behind the door.

Then she reached under the bed and pulled out the long metal case. When she was a kid that was her favorite hiding place, under her parents' bed. She didn't recall which house she used to hide her stuff in—it was one of many—but the bed was a distinct memory she held on to for years. She remembered how a few weeks before, when she had first come across this case, she had thought, almost amused, how this habit of hiding things under the bed ran in the family.

She wasn't amused now.

She unclasped the box and popped it open. The beautiful Kalashnikov lay before her, a full magazine tucked into the felt lining next to it. She had shot rifles before, many times during hunting expeditions with *Baba* Maurice. This couldn't be much different, she thought as she snapped the magazine into the rifle.

She rested it on the bed then closed the case and slid it back under the bed. She leapt up and slid the weapon into the gym bag—a perfect fit—and tossed her heels in there. On her way out she pulled a hooded sweater off of the hanger on the door and wore it over her dress.

Back in the living room, she placed the gym bag on the couch. She pulled off her ring and put it into the inner pocket of her purse. She then squeezed her purse into the gym bag, but it wouldn't close. She pressed and squeezed, but the purse was too big, so she unzipped it, rummaged inside it, and pulled out her pack of tampons. It was useless now anyway, she thought, as she flung it into the closet and it landed neatly on a pile of toiletries in the bottom.

She slipped her purse into her gym bag and made her way to the door.

But then she doubled back into the kitchen and opened the fridge. The thermostat stuttered and she had to tap it a few times to get it to work. She pulled out a carton of milk and closed the fridge, then filled a saucer and set it down in the living room. She threw one more glance toward the bedroom, but all she saw was the framed faces smiling back at her.

She opened the door and slid out.

◆

Nissrine raced down the stairs, gym bag on her shoulder, lifting her feet clear off the treads so the sneakers wouldn't squeak. At the ground floor she noticed his bicycle was gone—a good sign. He didn't take a taxi; that should buy her some time.

She looked left and there he was on his bicycle outside the grocery store several meters away.

"Tariq Jaber! Tariq Jaber!" The shrill croak of the grocer's parrot made her heart jump. She had to be careful not to be seen—both he and the grocer had their backs to her, but the parrot had seen her. "*Sharmouta!*" he squawked as she turned right and traipsed up the hill.

She cut across the hillside, the gym bag now digging through the sweater and into her shoulder. She got to the main road and waited for a few seconds as three girls in miniskirts and heavy makeup cut past her. She wondered if that was how she looked too as a tumbledown Mercedes came to an abrupt stop in front of her.

The driver leaned eagerly through the passenger-side window. "Service?" he said and she got in. "*Lawein?* Where to?"

She got in. "*Dighre.* Drive straight," she said, happy to finally rest the gym bag in her lap. The car made its way past the American diner "There goes my heart!," past the church, the restaurants, the mosque.

"Go left here," she gestured, noticing her nail polish start to peel off. "And keep your eyes on the road *iza bitreed*. If you don't mind."

She zipped the sweater up with a shiver as the car made its way to the Sodeco crossing. Before living in the LUST dorms, her sister Nadine had stayed just a few blocks from here. She remembered visiting her for the first time, how content her sister had seemed, even as she struggled to adjust to this hedonistic city. The second visit went well too, until Nadine mentioned her friend: the man she knew as Tony, the man Nissrine was on her way to intercept now. Even then, Nissrine had instinctively known who he was.

The driver stretched his arms in a loud yawn, but Nissrine remained focused on the road ahead. She remembered reading somewhere that not yawning with other people indicates a lack of empathy, like a sociopath. In her case, it was surely just a quirk.

445

The car continued through the crossing as the bus station materialized before her. And parked outside was his green bicycle. He had arrived there before her after all. But the buses were still there, revving up their engines.

Good, she had time.

The taxi got onto Damascus Road, where a billboard on the left read, "Beirut Night. LIFE!" Not funny.

"Here," she said. "At the traffic light."

She reached into her dress pocket and tossed a large bill at the driver. He looked like he was about to complain but when he saw how much it was, he just smiled.

◆

What was she doing at the side of Damascus Road at five-thirty in the morning? She didn't have to think about that long, nor could she ponder, hesitate, mull over its consequences. The bus was approaching steadily. In her mind it was already done.

Now she just had to do it.

The bus heaved to a stop at the traffic light. The driver, puffing at a cigarette, looked down at her through the tantalizingly open hydraulic door. This wasn't an official stop, so it must have been open the whole way. One less thing to worry about. One less obstacle. And one less chance to turn back.

She climbed on, gym bag clanking against the sides of the door. Through a cloud of cigarette smoke, the driver raised his hand. "Stop," he said. "This is bound for Damascus."

"I won't be going that far," she said, pressing a crumpled bill in his hand. He looked down at it as she made her way inside and the bus resumed its motion.

Too many passengers, five, six, maybe seven. How did it fill up so early? Not what she wanted. But there's no turning back, for there he was, at the very end, in the back seat, his face turned, talking to a hefty mustachioed man next to him.

She stumbled through the aisle, gripping one empty seat then the other for support, first past a middle-aged man, then past a rotund thirty-something woman breathing heavily in a half-sleep, her hands wrapped around her belly.

One by one she passed the passengers, none of them paying much attention to her, until she was just a row away from him. She plopped the bag onto an empty seat to her right.

The hefty man noticed her first, and an instant later her prey turned to her in mid-sentence. There she stood, face to face with Tariq Jaber.

"What?" he said breathlessly. "What're you doing here?"

"You're panting," she said, not sure why.

"I ran to get on," he said. "But—"

"I wish you hadn't," she said, then turned to the bag and opened the zipper. She pulled out the Kalashnikov in one quick motion, pulled the clutch, and aimed it at Tariq's chest.

The bus shook as it hit a bump, but none of the other lazy passengers seemed to notice her. Only the two men before her, staring in silence.

To her surprise, it was the hefty man who spoke next. "Wait!" he said, holding up his hand. Through his fingers she recognized a face from her past, mustache streaked with gray but otherwise unchanged.

"Wait... You're Nissrine," he said.

"Nissrine?" echoed Tariq Jaber, his eyes narrowing.

She wasn't sure how long she closed her eyes. An eternity or an instant. But when she opened them the first thing that struck her was the sadness that now shrouded his face.

"I'm so sorry," she said, and squeezed the trigger. It gave way, letting out three loud bangs. Behind her the shrieks of commotion filled the bus, which now shook and swayed. She fell onto the seat, onto her gym bag, with another loud bang. When she looked up, the hefty man's blank eyes stared back at her, a splotch of red on his forehead. Both men slumped over each other, red all over their bodies.

The shrieking was louder now and she swiveled around and fell forward into the aisle. The weapon kicked back into her chest as several rounds went off. Her finger stayed on the trigger as its roar mixed with the break of thunder outside. The screams of a hundred women filled her ears. No it was more. A thousand… Hundreds of thousands… All the women in the world. Her sister's. Her mother's. The crippled woman's. Her own. A loud screech mixed with that sound, like the death throes of a wounded animal, and then it fell silent as the bus came to an abrupt halt.

She swung the gym bag onto her shoulder, balanced herself against the back of the seats, and waded through the sticky red muck on the floor to the front of the bus. The driver turned to her, cigarette stuck to his bottom lip, and with the same gesture, raised his palm toward her. "Please, I have a family."

She stared at him blankly, Kalashnikov raised waist high. She had no time to think. The driver, perhaps realizing she was just a young woman, charged forward and impaled himself on the bayonet. His eyes bulged as she instinctively withdrew her weapon, ripping his stomach open. He dropped back into his seat then coiled around the steering wheel in agony. A few seconds later, he was dead.

"I have a family," he had said. The same thoughts ran through her mind as she lowered her eyes and breathed out.

◆

The rain fell hard and fast on the side of Damascus Road. The bus had tipped onto three wheels, its front bumper mangled against the foot of the billboard. The gym bag felt much lighter now as she wiped the rain off her face and slicked back her hair.

To her right was an open mud-field. It was empty—except for... a man.

He just stood there, palms to his face. Is that luck? Divine intervention? She slipped the weapon into the gym bag and slung it over her shoulder, then slid behind the bus and walked along the side to the back. From behind the rear bumper she peeked again into the open field. The man there now stared straight in her direction, but not quite at her. He was looking at the bus. He started walking over slowly then picked up his pace, now a skip, then a trot, then a run, and then a dash.

When he was just a few meters away, she made a run for the open field. She sloshed through the mud as quickly as the sneakers would take her, fast, fast, fast.

Following a low ridge, she cut across the field and along a line of trees, her feet splashing through the puddles. When she got through to the lowest point she looked back over her shoulder at the bus. The man was gone. As she turned back she tripped and crashed into a short tree, her entire right forearm taking the weight of her fall.

She picked herself up and continued to run until she could see the street on the other side. Light traffic swooshed past, its sound drowned by the rain. She set her palms on her knees, and caught her breath, then spotted a group of steel garbage barrels. Green, blue, red. She stumbled toward them and took off the sweater, its right side caked with mud, the entire front sprinkled with red stains. She pulled out her purse from the gym bag, kept her heels inside, then rolled up the sweater and shoved it in too. She zipped up the gym bag and crumpled it, then peered into the barrels. One of them was almost filled with garbage. Shuffling through the refuse, she squeezed the crumpled gym bag deep into it.

Tariq's sneakers protruded from her ankles like elephant feet. She stomped into a puddle until their white faux-leather surface was clean, and made her way to the side of the road. Within seconds a taxi had come to a stop and she had gotten in. Before the driver could say anything, she waved a crisp bill in front of his face and he plucked it from her wet grip. "Take me to Damascus," she said.

She leaned back, pulled out a black veil from her purse, and laid it in her lap, warming her legs. She ran her hand through her wet hair. Droplets of water fell onto her shoulders. "And keep your eyes on the road *iza bitreed*," she added.

Nissrine wrapped her veil around her head as the car shifted into gear.

21

Interdependence

It must be disconcerting to have eyes looking over your shoulder, watching you from above, where you cannot see them, not knowing when those eyes are singling you out from the twenty-nine other people in the room, or when they're on someone else entirely, someone whose own eyes squint onto your answer sheet and perhaps catch a mistake or two, or perhaps behold it with envy, noting your elegant reasoning and astute problem-solving.

This breathless thought would cripple me if I were in any of those students' seats right now, as they work through the second half of their Dendrology final. Yet what an odious, unbearable pleasure that must be, when the consequence of failure is but an abstract letter of the alphabet or perhaps a cumulative number that is merely a measure of performance rather than a concrete result with real-world impact.

I wish I could exchange places with any of these students today, not just Janette or the good ones in the front row of the classroom, but even one of the slackers closer to me here in the back. They all write with the enviable knowledge that at the 120 minute mark they can just set down their pencils and walk out of here unscathed by the experience.

Instead I find myself at the workbench watching them

through the rack of test tubes, now completely filled. Tugging at the Band-Aid on my finger, much like Nissrine allowed me to yesterday, I unfurl it and rub off the black gluey residue. The cut has formed a pocket of brown coagulated blood.

Pushing the rack of test tubes aside, I pull out a fresh one from its plastic wrapper and set it into a metal clamp by its lonesome.

Pulling out the napkin from my messenger bag, I unfold it on the workbench. The single thorn I pulled out of Nissrine's finger yesterday can only be used once, can only be dipped into one solution before it either reacts or simply atrophies beyond use. One chance, that's it, to do what must be done. If there is an answer to the conundrum of the unhealthy Acacia, then this must be it. The leaves of the tree itself are all gone now, and it sits bare as a bone on the workbench. Leafless, lifeless.

If I do find a mineral reactive with this one Nissrine sample, then I only have to feed the solution to my own Acacia to confirm the result. This is it. With a pair of fine tweezers, I drop the thorn into the empty test tube, and with a pipette add a few drops of distilled water as a solvent.

Now for the main ingredient. I pull out my shaving kit and unzip it. Inside waits a single safety pin, prepared just for this occasion. A quick glance at the students ahead confirms that they're focused on their exams. Then I place my wounded finger a few centimeters above the test tube, take a deep breath, and prick its tip near the cut.

I squeeze it until I've worked up a perfect bead of fresh blood, which I allow to drop into the test tube. It swirls into a red ribbon around the Acacia thorn. I bring my eyes level with the tube, and wait.

No more than a few seconds later, I have my answer. I jot down a note into my logbook and look up at the clock. "Pencils down everyone," I say. "The test is over."

◆

Cradling the Acacia, which I now have covered in a thin protective veil, I make my way down the hallway and into the administration office as Garo ducks behind an overgrown computer. As I step into Chairman Ramala's empty office, I set the Acacia on her empty desk. I walk into the conference room.

Ramala's been waiting. She nods primly from the head of the table, past the dozen or so people assembled around her. From my messenger bag I pull out my folder and slide it across the table. It only makes it halfway.

"Have a seat, Professor," she says. She eyes the folder, but no one else seems willing to touch it, as if it may contain radioactive material. Ramala ceremoniously rises from her seat and makes her way toward it, her eyes fixed on me.

"We'll take half an hour to review it," she says as she weighs it in her manicured hand. It must be lighter than she expected because she scowls at me and adds, "Then we'll call you in."

Back in Ramala's office, a strange calm falls upon me as I step behind her empty desk. A picture window overlooks the Corniche Boulevard, empty swimming pool, and rocky beach beyond. With the conclusion of the final exam period, Dendrology being the last one, the school grounds are empty. With utmost efficiency, students have performed a mass exodus into the fall vacation, no doubt as far from this campus as they can go.

In thirty minutes, I too will be done. This wait is but a formality, which will no doubt culminate in one side rubbing the other side's nose into its outcome. I know how this will turn out and I don't look forward to it. Formalities, diplomacy, bureaucracy were never my thing, least of all today, on this sunny November morning. Years of working the lab have taught me how to align my own internal clock with real time. I don't need to consult my watch to know that Ramala will reemerge through the connecting door in five, four, three, two, one second.

The door opens.

"Professor," she says. "We're ready for you." She disappears inside.

Acacia in tow, I push the door open and slip back in. Ramala takes her place at the head of the conference table, but I now notice the other faces: on each side of Ramala sit five senior taxonomists, all close to her end of the table. They are the number crunchers of my discipline, and I loathe them with the magnitude of a very, very big number. On my end are five empty seats, and in the middle is a chair pulled out for me. I set the veiled Acacia on the table and sit down behind it. All eyes are on us.

Ramala speaks in a deliberate, rehearsed tone. "Your conclusions are shocking," she says. Ten heads bob up and down in agreement. Good, a consensus. "Professor. I know that just last week, your work was on a dying species."

"Chairman Ramala, you know nothing," I say. She raises a defensive hand, but before she can intervene I continue. "And when it comes to the trees with which we share our land, neither do I. Dendrologists may not have the answers, but we ask the right questions. Taxonomists are blind to the truth in our questions. You hold us accountable for your own conclusions. You're the fact-checkers and accountants of our discipline, but fail to see what your facts and figures mean. You get bogged down by form and forget the substance, and as long as you draw a line from one label on a chart to another, you're happy. We're the artists and you're the art critics. We practice our craft while you just sit back and talk about it. I've not achieved wider recognition in this field because I refuse to pander to financiers or peddle my wares. I don't care about your pats on the back here, your nods there, and your underhanded trading of opportunities. All I want is for you to leave me alone to do my work."

"I understand that your experience here hasn't been ideal," says Ramala. "But allow us one question. How on earth did you build from a failing research paper into... into... this?"

I study her face across the table, and then clear my throat. "The initial findings, as you say, were indeed a failure," I say. "But no amount of building would've fixed that. What I did, Chairman, was not build, but destroy the walls of the classroom, the line separating what you value as fact and what you dismiss as experience. When you begin your questioning with 'What did you do to build?' you've made a foregone conclusion relevant only within the limits of the question itself, trapped in a circle. And then who else should care about your findings but yourself? We have much to learn from historians and archaeologists, artists and musicians, and from the neighbors, and grocers, and housemaids, and taxi drivers."

The files of taxonomists on either side of the conference table are now my students, and I'm their teacher. "Listen with your eyes and look with your ears," I say. "Feel with your breath and breathe through your skin."

I lift the Acacia and approach Ramala, as the ten suits adjust their positions asymmetrically to face me. "The difference between a building and a tree is that the builder must scaffold his structure at every phase of construction, and only remove the external support when the building can stand on its own."

I set the Acacia pot in the center of the table.

"This tree is structurally sound at every stage of its growth.

It needs no scaffold and no outside help to carry itself. My experiment is like that. I didn't build on previous findings, as you say, since every stage of the process was independent, needing no support from the outside. Once I understood that, I realized that what I needed wasn't more experiments, but a complete paradigm shift. I didn't alter the variables; I altered the way I looked at them. I didn't play better, I changed the game."

I pull the veil off the Acacia. Ramala leans against her elbows, and the ten taxonomists echo her motions. All eyes are on its bare branches, the intricate structure that, even in this dilapidated state, is perfectly upright. And along it, the tiniest hints of new leaves show their delicate heads.

"On the final limb of the experiment," I say, "my line of thought took me away from the previous stage, and closer to the truth. The answer wasn't to look further, beyond my initial findings, but deeper at the very first stage. I found this Acacia on the side of Damascus Road six days ago, the day a bus crashed and everyone on board was killed."

An uncomfortable shuffling accompanies my declaration, but I continue. "I have no problem admitting this to you now. I saw nothing pertaining to the murder. But what I did see made a difference to me. Over the following days, the trees near the bus flourished. Yet the others continued to wither and die. A single thorn sample grew the healthiest. It was the direct result of receiving a saturated helping of blood iron."

The eleven people in the room break rank and mumble discordantly. Suddenly they're no longer clones of one another, but a gaggle of individuals, each with a distinct voice and personality. Some argue, some exclaim, some just sit in a stupor.

As I speak again, the voices around me quiet down. "I'm sure the symbolism of a tree feeding on blood to remain evergreen isn't lost on anyone in this room, but as scientists we can see past that: the Acacia needs iron to grow. Feed it iron, and it will become the most abundant tree in the country. That's the simple answer to the question of the dying Acacias.

◆

The city rumbles with the growl of the distant parade. It comes muffled through the windows of the Volvo: a trumpet flourish here, a cymbal crash there, the percussion undercut by the steady stomp of boots.

Instead of making a right into the traffic, we turn left onto Damascus Road, but as if by force of inertia Nancy leans over her seat and looks through the back window. In the rearview mirror, Nadine and Rony do the same behind us. Barely a sliver of the Downtown festivities is visible through the gap between Achrafieh Bridge and the street. Over the radio, an announcer narrates the events we drive away from.

"We can go if you like," I say into the mirror.

"Today let's all be children," says Nadine. "Independence Day will come again next year."

"A quarter of a day later," says Rony. "It's a leap year."

"A lot can happen in three-sixty-five days and a quarter," says Nancy. "Maybe by then this Independence will be real." She turns to the front and adjusts her seatbelt.

I drive ahead then flip the left signal and make a U-turn onto the other side of the street, bringing the Volvo to a stop a few meters ahead of the billboard. The three of us get out, and Nancy walks over to my side, handing me my bag. Nadine cradles the Acacia pot and trails behind us. "I can't believe how it's grown!" she says.

Since the night I was here last, the "Beirut Night. LIFE!" billboard has been torn down, replaced by a sheet of solid black, perhaps awaiting the next ad, or perhaps to commemorate the site where Nancy and I now stand. Rony catches up with us.

We step off of the gravel and follow the dip of the field to its lowest spot. Nadine overtakes us through the line of Acacia shrubs until she gets to the empty spot. She turns back to us yelling, "Is this it?" Her face is barely visible behind the green needles of the baby tree between her arms.

"Go down a bit further to the lowest spot," I say, gesturing with my bandaged finger. Nancy and I continue as she slips her fingers between mine.

"Does it hurt?" she asks.

"Nah, it's fine."

"That thing's a bloodsucker," she says melodramatically. "Who'd have thought the Christ Thorn fed on His blood?"

"And the blood that washed from the bus onto the soil here," I say brushing my shoe against the ground. "For the tree, it's all just iron."

"You're mad, Professor!" she says as she circles in front of me, then turns and, tugging at my collar, adds, "I mean, Associate Professor."

She presses her lips to mine for the briefest moment then skips ahead, catching up with Nadine and Rony. I walk slower now, watching the two girls kneel as they set down the tree. The two of them shovel soil with their hands as Nancy instructs Nadine. A few minutes later, Nadine lifts the Acacia from the pot and plants it in the ground. They cover its roots as I look on proudly. Next to me, Rony gazes straight up, counting midday stars.

They straighten and beat the dust off their jeans. I watch them intently as they look down at the tree. We stand there in silence as time passes, ticking away the distant beat.

Nancy draws the sign of the cross on her chest and kisses

her fingertips. I run my hand through her hair as she leans her head on my shoulder and brings her hands to my chest. "Oops, sorry," she says to the dusty handprint she leaves there.

I reach into my bag and hold my tape recorder between my chin and shoulder, then pull out a wet wipe for her. As she cleans her hands, I hand her the tape recorder. "Here, hold this for a second," I say. "I have something for you." I pull it out. As I give it to her, she looks up at me and says, "Your diary."

"My memoir, yes. Take it, and fill in the gaps."

I take the tape recorder from her as she opens the memoir to the front page. "Good title," she smiles, looking into my eyes. I examine her face then glance past her at Nadine. She stands by the Acacia, hands angled in front of her in the shape of an open book as if in prayer. "She told me Nissrine got a scholarship to a nursing school in Romania," I say.

"Those tears weren't for the research you taped over, were they?" says Nancy. "Admit it, Professor."

"Yeah, yeah," I say, and look back at the recorder, then up at Nancy as I pop it open and take out the cassette. I tug at the brown tape with the tips of my fingers as I look at her. I arch my arm back until my jacket scrunches under my shoulder blade. Nancy nods, and I toss the cassette along the road with all my force. A brown ribbon of tape spirals upwards then unspools through the field as the cassette clatters and crunches against the gravel, plastic shrapnel flying everywhere.

Back in the car, the radio continues indifferently

"...and during these dark times," the Minister's familiar monotony continues through the speakers, "...on this day... we stand tall... heads raised high... united... Fellow Lebanese, I stand before you today, and tell you once again: the Truth shall be—"

I switch it off.

"I have a chess rematch down south," I say.

"Are we all in?" asks Nancy over her shoulder. Through the rearview mirror, Nadine and Rony are too far into an elbowing game over the armrest between them to answer. Today let's all be children. I shift into first gear and the Volvo climbs onto the highway.

Behind us on the side of Damascus Road, the Acacia receives the sunlight of a new morning.

Acknowledgments

This book is a love letter to the people in it. You appear under different names, but you know who you are. The rest is exactly as it happened.

◆

One day not long ago, these pages arrived to me marked "From Nancy." Whether you took them as truth or fiction, thank you Rana, Yasmina, Souraya, Souly, Shibly, Loryne, Noura, Mira, Outi, Nadine, Werner, Samar, Lynn, Dima, Souha, Salma, Mona, Hind, Donna, Ana, Hisham, Zoe, Susu, Yasue, Nathan, and Karen. For the space to grow, thank you Nadime, Cheri, Karl, James, Saeromi, and Bill.

I also thank Marilyn for promising that a burden lightens when shared (despite the Professor's "better" judgment), and the fine people at Tamyras and Interlink for making this my unburdening. Tania, Cyril, Dima, Muneira, Kanzi, Patricia, Vanessa, Nasri, Whitney, Michel, this one's for you. For making science an art, thank you Lisa.

Today these pages have found their way into your hands, dear reader. With each word, my child takes one step closer to home.

So I save my final thanks for you. Yes, you.

— Nissrine